BROOKLYN CROSS

BAD BOY

XIII

UNHINGED
CAIN

BUCHANAN BROTHER'S DUET BOOK 1

UNHINGED CAIN

BROOKLYN CROSS

✾ Created with Vellum

Also by BROOKLYN CROSS

The Righteous Series

(Vigilante/Ex Military Romance - Dark 3-4 Spice 3-4)

Dark Side of the Cloth

Ravaged by the Dark

Sleeping with the Dark

Hiding in the Dark

Redemption in the Dark

Crucified by the Dark (Coming Soon)

Dark Reunion (Coming Soon)

The Consumed Trilogy

(Suspense/Thriller/Anti-Hero Romance - Dark 4-5 Spice 3-4)

Burn for Me

Burn with Me (Coming 2022)

Burn me Down (Coming 2023)

The Buchanan Brother's Duet

(Serial Killer/Captive Romance - Dark 4-5 Spice 3-5)

Unhinged Cain by Brooklyn

Twisted Abel by T.L Hodel

The Battered Souls World

(Standalone Books Shared World Romance/Dramatic/Women's Fiction/All The Feels- Dark 2-3 Spice 2-3)

The Girl That Would Be Lost

The Boy That Learned To Swim (Coming Soon)

The Girl That Would Not Break (Coming Soon)

The Brothers of Shadow and Death Series

(Dystopian/Cult/Occult/Poly MMF Romance - Dark 3-4 Spice 3-4)

Anywhere (Coming Soon)

Seven Sin Series

(Multi Author/PNR/Angel and Demons/Redemption - Dark 2-5 Spice 3-5)

Greed by Brooklyn Cross

Lust by Drethi Anis

Envy by Dylan Page

Gluttony by Marissa Honeycutt

Wrath by Billie Blue

Sloth by Talli Wyndham

Pride by T.L. Hodel

Playlist

YOU ARE MY SUNSHINE — CHRISTINA PERRI
EDELWEISS — CONNIE FISHER
DON'T WORRY, BE HAPPY — INNER CIRCLE
READY OR NOT — FUGEES
LOST CAUSE — BILLIE EILISH
FEED MY FRANKENSTEIN — ALICE COOPER
PSYCHO KILLER — TALKING HEADS
ANOTHER ON BITES THE DUST — QUEEN
HAPPY — PHARRELL WILLIAMS
RING OF FIRE — JOHNNY CASH
JIGGLE JIGGLE — DUKE & JONES & LOUIS
THEROUX
EVERY BREATH YOU TAKE — THE POLICE
POCKETFUL OF SUNSHINE — NATASHA
BEDINGFIELD
SWEET DREAMS — MARILYN MANSON
BUTTERFLY — CRAZY TOWN
FOLLOW ME — UNCLE KRACKER
LIGHTS OUT — VIRGINIA TO VEGAS
SURVIVOR — NATHANIEL RATELIFF
LET'S FALL IN LOVE — MOTHER MOTHER
DOLLS — BELLA POARCH

T.L. Hodel
You My Friend
Make Me Smile On A Cloudy Day

Hello Sunshine

PROLOGUE

The other night dear, as I lay sleeping
I dreamed I held you in my arms
But when I awoke, dear, I was mistaken
So I hung my head, and I cried.
You are my sunshine, my only sunshine
You make me happy when skies are gray
You'll never know, dear, how much I love you
Please don't take my sunshine away.
I'll always love you and make you happy,
If you will only say the same.
But if you leave me and love another,
You'll regret it all someday.
You are my sunshine, my only sunshine

You make me happy when skies are gray
You'll never know, dear, how much I love you
Please don't take my sunshine away.
You told me once, dear, you really loved me
And no one else could come between.
But now you've left me and love another;
You have shattered all of my dreams:
You are my sunshine, my only sunshine
You make me happy when skies are gray
You'll never know, dear, how much I love you
Please don't take my sunshine away.
In all my dreams, dear, you seem to leave me
When I awake, my poor heart pains.
So when you come back and make me happy
I'll forgive you, dear. I'll take all the blame.
You are my sunshine, my only sunshine
You make me happy when skies are gray
You'll never know, dear, how much I love you
Please don't take my sunshine away.
By: Jimmie Davis / Charles Mitchell

Hello
Sunshine

CHAPTER 1

CAIN

I lay in a bed that was too small for me, but my parents refused to get new beds for my brother or me. I had no idea why. Their answers never made sense when I asked them questions. Looking over at my nightstand, I let my eyes follow the globs of red lava and sparkles ever so slowly as they floated around inside the glass container of the nightlight. It was supposed to look like a spaceship, but it reminded me more of the thing that vibrated in my mother's drawer, just fatter. My eyes drifted from the slowly moving gloop that was meant to relax me into sleep to my small angel statue and my leather-bound bible. Sitting up, I pushed the little angel in the middle of her face, and the miniature statue fell back with a tiny thud.

"Stupid statue."

I grabbed the bible that was not much bigger than my hand. My eyes traced over the gold cross, and the words 'Holy Bible' splashed across the front of the book. Like, I wouldn't know what this boring book was as soon as I opened the cover? My thumb bent the book and let the pages flutter, the tiny words nothing more than a blur. That was the other stupid thing about this book. Why did they make the words so small that everyone interested in the crap the pages held would need glasses to read it? I couldn't explain why, but I found that strange little fact funny.

Being born as intelligent as I was was a blessing and a curse. I was far more intelligent than even the smartest adult I knew, although they'd argue that fact. Adults didn't like being told they were wrong about anything, and their favorite answer was 'because.' That word was not an answer to a question. Even a kindergartener could tell you that.

Sighing, I was bored, and the air in the room was hot and sticky. Glancing at my window, I took in the curtains that were hanging perfectly still and decided to fan my face with the book since it was the only thing it was good for—well, maybe except for burning it. I'd lit one or two on fire, and they burned hot and fast, the gold pages sizzling as they turned to ash.

Church was interesting, not because I cared what the priest said, but because it gave me the perfect place to watch those that came and sat among the pews. They were never the wiser that I envisioned how I wanted to kill each and every one of those stupid people. They were lemmings in my game, and just like the little floppy-haired animation, they would follow along one after the other. Sure as shit, if one went over the cliff, they all would. I could picture them yelling, 'praise Jesus,' on the way down.

I stopped fanning myself long enough to stare at the words again and wondered why adults tried to say the words inside were from God's lips to our hands. This statement was filled with major issues that they all liked to ignore. If this book was so perfect, why was it missing major portions that no one wanted to discuss? Or why did they say that boys shouldn't have sex with one another and that God would be angry when that wasn't referenced until the King James version in 1946? Did God come down again and whisper in some old man's ear that he didn't like it? I highly doubted it.

Last Sunday, I was marched out of church because I stood up and told the priest that the Noah's Ark story was actually a retelling of Gilgamesh. When we got home, my father smacked my ass until I couldn't sit without wincing for speaking out in church and making the priest look bad. You'd think that the man would know if he's teaching the crap. Seemed logical to me. Then my father made me stand in the corner like I should be wearing a dunce cap, but really it should be on his head. Should be on all their heads.

Sitting the book down on the nightstand, I slowly shook my head. I didn't like the sheep in the barn, they were noisy and stupid, and the human versions that lived in this house were no better. Someone needed to cull them from the herd, and as far as I was concerned, they'd get whatever they had coming to them.

A memory of hunting season drifted through my mind. It was this past season when dad had gotten lucky. He'd shot two deer, and their dead carcasses were hung in the shed, and with the memory came the rich metallic scent of fresh blood. There was something about the scent of blood that stirred desires in my young body, desires I didn't fully understand, but I knew I wanted more.

My tongue ran along my teeth as I felt every rough ridge and sharp point. What would it be like to have fangs and be able to tear the flesh right off the bones of my prey?

My parents were my prey.

I mean, they named me Cain and my brother Abel. What did they expect to happen? I always thought it was funny that my parents were the smiling and faithful parishioners that prayed to a fake god while I was the devil planning their deaths. I suspected that my brother had the same urges. He seemed to enjoy the little games I'd ask him to play as a test. 'Pull the wings from the little bug' was the first game. Abel was so enthusiastic that I turned the game into 'pin the kitty to the board.' He excelled at that, but my brother was erratic. That was what my parents called it. I saw it, too. He needed to be guided, but if he had someone to point him in the right direction...

I smiled at the thought.

It was too hot to sleep. Untangling myself from the white sheet, I padded my way down the hall and stairs to the kitchen for a glass of water. The fridge light was bright as I opened the door, and I blinked as I grabbed the clear thing with water that mom liked to keep in the fridge. She said it made the water healthier to drink. I just liked that it was really cold. Pulling over the stool, I climbed on top and opened the cupboard for a glass. I didn't like using the kiddy plastic ones with farm animals all over them and instead reached for the clear adult glass. If mom saw me, she'd freak out and squawk like a chicken about to have its head cut off.

Sitting on the counter, I let my feet swing and poured the water into the glass before chugging the cool liquid down. As I was pouring myself a second glass, I noticed the block of knives that was pushed to the back of the counter. The deer memory came to mind again, and I wondered what my father would look like hanging upside down with his throat cut. Pulling the largest knife out, I stared at the metal blade that looked like a sword in my small hand. As I turned it from side to side, the metal glinted in the moonlight streaming through the window.

I took a deep breath as I remembered clearly the first night the dark thoughts of blood and pain entered my dreams. I hadn't been out of diapers, and every time she changed my smelly white diaper, she'd make these weird noises and smile down at me. When you get bigger, I'll show you how to do this or that. She'd ramble on as if I cared, but all I wanted to do was to rip her pretty blue eyes out of her head. The sound of her screaming was loud in my mind as I imagined my mother's fear while she cowered in a corner as I cut her over and over again.

Hopping off the counter, I walked out of the kitchen and up the stairs toward the bedrooms. I noticed Abel looking at me from the crack of his doorway. I didn't look his way or acknowledge that he wasn't hiding as well as he thought. Even at seven, I knew that if Abel wanted to be like me, he needed to come to me, not the other way around, and if not...

Well, then he'd have to be taken care of at some point, but of all the humans I'd met, the boy that occupied the same woman's womb with me for nine months was the only person I had any connection with on this planet.

My feet were no louder than a mouse. The kids at school would say dark basements and hallways had monsters hiding. I didn't know what lies they were being fed, but there were no monsters in this house, except maybe for me.

Stopping at my parent's door, I stared up at the gold-colored knob of the handle. New energy I'd never experienced before was going through my body and excited me as I reached for the handle. I liked this new feeling. I turned the knob so slowly. It never made its normal squeak sound as I quietly pushed open the door.

I stood in the doorway for a long time. It felt like I was there the whole night watching my parents sleep. I found myself mimicking their sleep, the way their chests rose and fell. My father was snoring loudly, an arm laying over his eyes as his mouth hung open. My mother had a strange mask on her face and her hair up in curlers as she, too, made strange little noises in her sleep.

One light step after the other, I finally reached my father's side of the bed and watched his chest move with each loud and annoying breath. My hand tightened on the wooden handle of the knife as I imagined slitting their throats and shutting him up for good. Would their snoring turn into strangled screams? Would they scream at all or just look at me? Would they be scared or die in seconds like the animals did when we slaughtered them? My eyes took in the white sheet lying on their bodies, and my lip curled up with the thought of it turning red.

As if sensing my presence, my father startled awake and opened his eyes. He turned his head, looked at me, and then down to my hand. He sat up quickly, and I noticed the change in his breathing. He was breathing fast, his eyes wide. He was scared as he stared at my hand holding the knife. I liked that.

"What are you doing, son," my father stupidly asked.

I wasn't much for lying, so I simply answered, "I'm thinking of killing you."

Hello Sunshine

CHAPTER 2

CAIN

I stood over Heather's body and stared at her mere inches away from her uninteresting face as the light slowly faded from her eyes. It was always the same. Even when they were silent and didn't scream, there was this moment of complete fear as their body clung to life. Then as they finally died, you could see the shift. I wanted to understand this moment of acceptance and peace. The muscles in her face relaxed as the fight in her body disappeared and the eyes that seconds ago had stared at me in horror and fear now stared up to the ceiling at nothing.

Moving closer to her head, I got low to her body, so our cheeks almost touched. Turning my head to stare at the metal ceiling, I could only see the rafters, chains, and the plastic I used to protect from splatter. There was no bright light or hell-bound demon—everything was exactly as it had been before.

"What did you see," I asked, my tone soft as I brushed her bloodied hair away from her face. "I want to know what you saw." Her skin was damp, and yet I could still feel the softness under my touch. "I have to say that you were very unhelpful. Completely useless, just like all the others." Sighing, I shook my head. "Just once, can one of you fucking people say what you see before you die? Is that too much to ask?"

Straightening, I stared down at the woman. I needed to find a way to bring them right to that moment of death but force them to hang on just long enough to tell me what they saw. I brushed the few stubborn strands still clinging to her forehead out of the way so I could continue to work. The warmth in her skin would remain for some time yet. I stared at her exposed body, taking a moment to marvel at my work.

The carved lines that created the intricate pattern on her pale skin were stunning. It was some of my finest art to date, and I appreciated this moment. I didn't fully understand what it meant to be happy or experience happiness, but I was able to comprehend that these moments with my prey were the closest that I'd get to that feeling. I'd heard all the clinical reasons why I was the way I was, but it didn't matter to me why I took pleasure in killing others. I was simply myself, which meant I was at the top of the food chain.

My father insisted they put me in therapy after finding me in their bedroom with the knife. It was the only smart decision I'd ever seen them try to make, but what they failed to understand was that I didn't need help. Their smart decision turned into stupidity when they continued to throw good money at a non-issue. They truly thought the help would fix me, but I didn't want to be fixed.

I lasted two sessions before swapping places with Abel, who enjoyed the game of becoming me. I scoffed at the memory of the psychiatrist's stuffy office and the idiot doctor who thought he was treating me the entire time. Or worse yet, my parents drove us both there but didn't notice which son went into the room. On the other hand, I should thank them if they weren't already dead. The doctor's ignorance and my parent's idiocy gave me the idea to make sure that from that moment on, Abel and I remained one hundred percent identical. If he cut himself and it turned into a scar, I'd purposely cut myself in the same spot. When I broke my left arm falling from my bike, Abel followed suit and fell the exact same way I did, so our breaks would be as close as possible to matching.

We may have been two people, but we slowly became one person to the rest of the world.

I picked up the expensive professional camera and took pictures of the woman from every angle. I wanted to capture this moment. The last image I took was of her eyes, and I made sure to get close enough to see all the detail.

Setting the camera aside, I softly whistled Edelweiss, the lullaby that my mother used to sing. My lip curled as I remembered exactly what it felt like to cut her tongue out and how her voice was no longer soft and beautiful as she choked around the blood pooling in her mouth. Sadly, she'd already been close to death by the time I got to have any fun. It had been important to me that she understood who and what I was as she reached for me, silently begging for help. Abel had lost his cool and decided to kill her. Not surprising with my brother, and that was when I put my rules in place that he needed to follow.

I quickly adjusted my cock in my jeans as the image sent a shot of adrenaline through my body. This woman hadn't screamed as sweetly as my mother had. No one had since, and it was always disappointing to think that the best kill I'd ever experienced was already behind me. Then again, like plucking a virgin's cherry from her pussy, maybe it was always the first time that was the best.

I designed all my tools. Each one was specifically crafted to fit my hand and be used for a specific purpose. My favorite tool had a curved end to the blade, like a subtle scoop. Picking it up, I held it in the light, admiring my invention.

"Well, Heather, our time together has almost come to an end," I said, and I leaned over the woman to peel her eyelid back. Grabbing the small suction cup tool, I placed it over the colored portion of her eye and gave it a gentle tug so it was forced away from the rest of her face. My other hand worked quickly with the blade that could cut silk as easily as any ninja sword. With two small swipes, the pretty hazel eye that held golden specs in its iris was cut free. I held up the eyeball and smirked at yet another flawless job. A soft sucking sound was created as my little device released the eye into the collection jar I'd created for her eye color.

A little of the formaldehyde jumped out of the jar as the eye landed in the clear liquid with an audible plop. I quickly cleaned up the smattering of liquid and then turned my attention to cleaning up the room. I had many laws, but when in came to my work, there were only two rules that I lived or died by—Don't get caught, and be smart, precise, and clean with my work.

I sighed as the outer door's alarm announced a new arrival. The large television I used as a monitor in the corner showed Abel swaying his way inside the house.

Lovely.

I loved my brother, at least what I thought was love, but I didn't know for sure. I genuinely enjoyed his company and didn't dream of killing him or dismembering his still-breathing corpse. For me, those understandings were the closest I came to the feeling that many described as love. Unfortunately, my brother reminded me of a cartoon character of a peacock with its dick out, wanting to fuck every hole it could find. He was a show-off, loud, messy, overbearing, unpredictable, and tended to be a pest like a cockroach trapped inside your boxers.

I actually knew what that looked like—I'd created an inescapable pair of metal shorts designed after the chastity belt. It was amusing to take notes of the man's reaction as I released the cockroaches through a small trap door in the armor-looking shorts and then locked the hole back up. A smile spread across my face, remembering how that man screamed.

Bang!

The door slammed open, but I was used to Abel's dramatic entrances and didn't jump as the sound of the heavy metal door echoed through my work area.

"Blame it on the rain," my brother sang out, the sound grating on the ears.

I was sure that only cats in heat would be interested in the caterwauling he tried to claim was "singing." The ridiculous walk he was performing made him look like a monkey who needed to take a shit while trying to be a circus clown. I lifted a brow at the latest ass wiggle he called a walk. The chain he kept on his jeans jingled as he continued to bop oddly forward.

During moments like this, I had to wonder how we could be identical twins. How could the DNA of the same people create such opposite personalities? Abel stopped when he saw Heather on the table, his face shifting from shocked to annoyed and then angry within the span of a heartbeat.

"What the fuck, man?" Abel said as he held his hands out toward the body.

I closed the lid on my bobbing eyes before they got knocked over. When Abel was around, I made sure that nothing was left out and that I didn't mind getting messy or broken. Anything within arms reach was fair game for Abel. I turned my back on my brother to return the treasure to my special storage.

"What has you all annoyed now, Abel?"

"You're supposed to wait for me. You know I like to kill them together, and you never include me anymore." I rolled my eyes as I turned around to take in his theatrics. "I mean, look at her. She has hot tits even without her nipples and a fuckable face. You could've killed her while I fucked her. Why are you no fun?" He held his hand out to me, clutching a brown paper bag in his fist. "I even got you your favorite cookies, man, and you do this to me. No chocolatey chip for you." He snatched his arm back.

I shook my head at him.

"First, I never make it a habit always to include you. Besides, you have kills that you do without me." I held up my finger to stop his objection. "Don't fucking lie to me. I know exactly what holes you stick your cock in and when."

Abel snapped his mouth shut and crossed his arms over his chest.

"Second, I don't mind sharing, but there are times I prefer my way of doing things, and that doesn't include you," I said and closed the massive refrigerator before pulling the panel back to cover my hiding spot. The large metal shelves were next, and they slid soundlessly into place.

My brother could pout like a petulant child better than anyone else I'd ever seen, just as he was doing now. His face morphed into an innocent person, his eyes going to the floor and his lip jutting out. It was an act. It was always an act when it came to Abel. He'd become a master at emotional manipulation.

"When I talked to you earlier, you said you had a girl, and I said I was in the mood to fuck her shit up. Then you said you were working on her already, but there would be some left if I hurried. I thought that meant we were going to share. You know, you'd take one end, and I'd take the other." He thrust his hips forward while he made grunting noises.

"Oh, is that what you meant," I said and smirked. "You do know that it sounded to me like you wanted to physically fuck her shit? I did save you what came out of her ass if you're interested in that." I pointed to the container holding large quantities of Heather's feces. "But, I never said I was going to wait for you. Why do you always continue to see if you can manipulate me? You do understand what a hyperthymesia memory means, right?"

Abel waved his hand in the air dismissing the argument, then screwed up his face as he glared at the plastic container.

"What the fuck is wrong with you? I don't want to fuck her shit. That's just crazy."

I stared at my brother and wondered if he recognized the irony of his statement, but he didn't seem to, so I let it go. Abel shrugged as he stuffed his hands in his pockets, which pulled his jeans further down his body. There was nothing like looking like 'you've crapped your pants' as a style choice.

"I just like to see if you're on your game," he said.

"Right. How about you be clearer next time? She's still warm if you want to fuck her. She was good at begging, but she didn't have much talent. I doubt you'll get much engagement now, though," I teased and smirked as Abel rolled his eyes.

"If you hadn't taken her eye, I woulda, you selfish prick. She looks like a cyclops now. It's creepy." Abel walked around Heather, whose legs were splayed open on my work table, and I knew that Abel was still considering the idea.

I preferred blood, whereas my brother only required a hole. Where that hole was didn't really matter to him.

"Fuck it, why not," Abel suddenly said and whipped his T-shirt off over his head.

My lips curled up in amusement and then fell again as I stared at his chest. Marching a few strides toward my brother, I poked him in the chest with enough force to make him step back.

"What the fuck is that," I growled as I pointed to the tattoo across his chest. "Scrub the P? Are you fucking serious?"

Abel smiled wide, running his tongue along his teeth. "It's fucking sexy right?"

"No, not right. I should slit your fucking throat. Now I have to get the same fucking thing."

"Only if you promise to fuck my throat after." Abel waggled his tongue at me as my body shook with the barely contained rage.

These were the moments when I needed to remind myself he was my brother and was purposely trying to get under my skin. He took it as a personal challenge to enrage me since I was ninety-nine percent of the time unflappable. Being a clinically diagnosed psychopath had many advantages, but as my hand curled into a fist, I had to remind myself that I didn't want to kill him. The urge was strong, but it was the look in his eyes daring me to attack him that ultimately made me step back.

"No more, I mean it. I already have this fucking Joker clown on my neck from you and an angel riding the devil on my ass that I didn't want. You'd think that if you were going to get tattoos, you'd at least get something half decent." I marched away from Abel before I reconsidered slitting his throat.

"Aw, come on, that one is hot. The girl has big titties, and I even got him to put blood dripping from her pussy. What more could you want?"

I cleaned my blade, keeping my back to Abel as I waited out the impulse to kill him. "You get another one without passing it by me, and I will return the favor." The rag dangled from my fingers as I turned around, pleased with my threat.

Abel sucked his teeth, and I almost grabbed the scalpel and threw it at his head. "Don't be an ignorant fuck. You know I don't tolerate it."

He rolled his eyes. "What kind of tattoo?"

"I'll think on it, but it will be something you hate, something that would make you want to cut off your fucking dick, and that's exactly where I'll put it."

"Nothing could make me want to do that," he said.

"Oh, I wouldn't dare me, Abel. I'm thinking little pieces of black

21

licorice or a Care Bear...no, I got it, a cobra, and every time you stare at your fucking cock, it will look like a cobra hissing at you." I smiled at my brother's horrified face. "That way, if you don't cut it off, you'll have to see that image expand every fucking time you get hard, and it will stare at you whenever you stroke Abel Junior."

Abel froze mid-motion as he climbed onto the table with the woman, or what used to be a breathing woman. "You wouldn't?"

"Test me, brother, and see what happens. Also, since you seem intent on having fun, you can clean the body and scrub the room down. I'm heading out."

"You're not staying? I came over to hang."

"Bullshit, you came over to worm your way in on my kill and get your dick wet." I looked at the dead woman and thought for a moment. "I guess she won't be wet now, but I have lube in the drawer if you like."

Abel smirked. "You're just as much of a sick fuck as I am, Cain, but it's why I love your crazy ass."

"Mmhmm, I'm sure. Look on the bright side. Now you can sing your stupid pussy song the entire time without me punching you in the face."

"Yee-fucking-ha, gladly." Abel wiggled his hips, his cock bouncing around and making me shake my head.

I hated the annoying song and yet always found myself joining in —stupid addictive thing, just like that damn purple dinosaur my parents forced us to watch as children.

I made my way out of my special workspace into the underbelly of my home and locked the door in place as the singing and grunting started.

It was the end of summer break, which meant more than normal college kids were traveling in cars on roads they had no business driving down. Parents did a crap job teaching their kids to be safe, but I wasn't one to complain. Their crap parenting meant more prey for me.

I started my large truck and gave her dash a caressing pat. "Let's go, Petunia. We have some piglets to catch."

CHAPTER 3

K IRBY

Pulling my long braid over my shoulder, I avoided glancing out the car windows and played with the end of my hair. I didn't want to think about where I was heading. It was supposed to be a coveted experience to be a student of Quantico, but it was nothing more than a fancy jail to me.

The stuffy dorm was too small and smelled like old cheese and dirty socks, no matter how much air freshener I stuck on the walls. It was enough to make even the most trained stomach want to turn inside out. I had no idea what the hell people did in those rooms to make them smell that bad, and I honestly didn't want to know.

My room was fine in that concrete-block-boring kind of way, and my roommate, although quirky, was not much better. The first twelve weeks of basic training were enough to make me want to poke my eye out with a pencil.

Well, I guess there were a few interesting parts. The criminal psychology class was fun. Serial killers fascinated me, particularly how and why they killed. Forensic science class wasn't bad, either. They let us play with bones and insects at different stages of flesh decay, which was interesting.

I was also getting into the physical training courses the school required. Hand-to-hand combat and running were great stress relievers, but I wasn't a gun person and preferred my paintbrushes over gun violence.

The idea of having to start another sixteen weeks felt more like wearing concrete shoes in a dark lake rather than water wings in a shallow pool like my mother seemed to think it was. I thought when I finished basic training and told her that this wasn't the place for me, she'd let it go. Instead, she threatened to cut me off completely and not help me pay for another program. I wouldn't even ask her to pay for another program if I had any options. However, since I'd never been allowed to work because she wanted me to focus on school, I had no extra money saved. Now I was wondering if she'd done that by design.

"Shit," Peter said in the middle of his fiftieth time going through the same story.

How many times could one person repeat how they got to meet the owner of some corporation while golfing? We were supposed to be on a camping trip. Who goes golfing at a private golf course in the middle of a camping vacation with their girlfriend? Of course, Peter insisted he quickly go to the country club that happened to be a short drive away since his dad was a member. He said it would look good to drop in and rub elbows with all the people his dad was trying to kiss ass with and elevate his status. Pretty convenient coincidence considering he booked and planned the trip. I, of course, ended up sitting alone in a tent, waiting for him to return. Angry didn't even begin to describe what I felt while he was high on pure jubilation.

Peter stopped rambling.

"What is it," I asked and turned my head to look at Peter.

It was rare to see anything about him out of place, but his hair was a mess, and his shirt had wrinkles and a stain on it—god forbid. I thought he was going to combust when he realized that all the other clothes we'd brought with us were dirty, and he'd have to continue wearing a shirt with a spot of ketchup on it.

Peter held out his hand toward the dark road. "Don't you see? One of my headlights just went out."

"Okay, we still have one," I said and placed my elbow on the window edge and my head on my hand.

"Kirby, this is a Mercedes Benz," he said.

Like that was supposed to enlighten me as to why he was acting like this was a life-and-death scenario.

"I swear you never listen to me, Kirby. I've told you like a hundred times that a headlight can cost a fortune. It probably cracked when that stone hit us from that dump truck."

He smacked his hand off the top of the steering wheel, making me jump in my seat.

"Now I'll have to put it in the shop to be fixed, which you know I hate." He sighed heavily, like the weight of the world was squarely on his shoulders. "It always comes back from that garage with a scratch on the paint, and I swear the speedometer has more miles on it. I think they take the cars for joy rides," he continued complaining.

"Then why did you insist on bringing this thing on the camping trip? The entire trip, all I've heard about is how you hope it doesn't get scratched and how a splotch of bird poop would ruin the paint and how dirt was going to get into places you couldn't get out. And that is all before you made us sleep in it for four very uncomfortable nights since you thought you heard a bear." I crossed my arms over my chest and glared at my boyfriend, who had effectively ruined my last week of freedom. "We don't even have bears in this part of the country."

He glared back at me, his jaw twitching as he clenched his teeth together. I had no idea why I thought this guy was hot. Well, that's not true. On the surface, he was a golden-haired god of a specimen that only ran skin deep. Underneath, he was a narcissistic, arrogant prick that thought the sun shone out of his ass.

"I brought it because this vehicle is much nicer than your little shit box. I'm sorry that the luxury of a Mercedes wasn't to your liking."

I rubbed my eyes, unable to take the self-centered bullshit right now. I kept asking myself why I didn't just dump good old Peter. The answer was easy. It kept my mother happy. Dating Peter was the one thing I'd done in my life that my mother approved of other than going to Quantico, and because of that, it kept her off my case.

The only issue was that I'd simply traded my mother, a pain in my side, for Peter, who'd turned into a pain in my ass. I crossed my arms and stared out the window. I didn't want to return to my life, but I also didn't want to stay a second longer in the woods or this car with Peter. An unsolvable challenge to be sure.

"You're right. I'm sorry that I'm being a pill. I just wanted our time away to be special, but you didn't seem to enjoy anything I'd set up for us to do," Peter reached out and tugged on my arm until I uncrossed it and let him hold my hand.

I stared at the side of his perfectly tanned face and white, blonde hair and wondered if I ever actually liked him or if my hormones had simply seen an opportunity to ride a hot cock. The jury was still out on the subject.

"I'm sorry too," I lied. "I'm tired and hungry, and you know how I get when I'm hungry." I gave him my best make-your-dick-stand-at-attention look and bit my lip for added effect.

It worked. Peter had a one-track mind and looked down at the lump in his pants. Some people often referred to a person as having a one-track mind and meant it as a joke, but with Peter, it was a fact. It was like all he thought about was how big his office was going to be and how big his cock was. One time I'd caught him taking pictures of it in the full-length mirror as he flexed, and another time. I caught him filming himself doing the helicopter. He had more photos of his cock on his phone than I did.

Playing the part, I reached over with my free hand, squeezed his leg, and instantly saw the bulge thicken in his khakis.

"We better get you something to eat then," Peter said and squirmed in his seat. "Don't you think?" He looked at me and then at his pants like I couldn't put together the sexual innuendo on my own.

Peter let go of my hand and spread his legs a little wider so I could get at his belt and zipper.

"Fuck," Peter yelled and swerved hard, forcing my hand to smash into his crotch. He yelled again as my fist collided with his precious dick, his eyes bulging out of his head at the impact.

I screamed even though I had no idea what we were avoiding. At the last moment, I spotted a large, old tow truck with one dirty light flashing and a car up on the hoist.

Everything stood still as I stared out the window at the guy by the front of the truck. My heart jumped in my chest, and my body flushed hot when the man locked eyes with me. It was only a moment, just a second, really, and yet it felt like a lifetime. All my muscles clenched in places that had nothing to do with the swerving vehicle I was in and everything to do with the look in the man's eyes. One word flashed in my mind, dangerous, but I still looked back for as long as possible until we could no longer see each other.

"What the fuck? What is a tow truck doing out here without all the bright lights and shit?" Peter used one hand and rubbed at his deflated cock. "That hurt. Did you have to punch me?"

Even though I knew it would piss Peter off, I couldn't resist as I crossed my arms once more and stated the obvious. "You're the one that swerved with my hand an inch from your crotch. Besides, maybe his lights just burned out too."

CAIN

I backed the tow truck into the front of the garage and flicked off the engine. I sat and drummed my finger on the top of the steering wheel as I waited for the door to finish closing and was plunged into the complete black of the windowless space.

Eyes so unique and delectably different played through my mind. They very easily could be contacts or just a reflection from the dull lighting, but I didn't think so. I couldn't say why, but an unusual surge raced through my body as I locked eyes with those violet beauties. I didn't have that color in my collection. They were like a rare gem and worth my time hunting down.

On the plus side, the elderly man I'd stopped to help actually got what he paid for and then proceeded to thank me enough to make a broken record seem less annoying. Thanks to my parents' early demise and insurance policies, I didn't need the money. But tax returns looked much better when you actually showed income from a business.

Getting out of the truck, I flicked the door closed on Petunia and made my way toward the interior house door. I didn't need the light to find the handle. I'd memorized every room and noticed immediately when something had been moved. I'd spent an entire year with my eyes closed, pretending to be blind. My parents were aghast that I'd do such a thing, and the doctor called it a phase when they asked. In reality, I was training myself. The darkness was where I knew I was going to live, and now here I was with a talent that made it extremely easy to stalk my prey even when they thought they couldn't be found.

The television was on as I pushed open the door. The unusual combination of a modern comedy mixed with screams was loud. Grabbing a pair of beers, I wandered into the rec room to find Abel laughing at a random sitcom on one television while jerking off to a video of one of our kills on a second television.

"Interesting combo," I said dryly and handed over the beer.

"Couldn't make up my mind." He shrugged as he continued to work his cock. "In the end, I decided, why limit myself?"

I flopped down into my identical recliner beside him, my eyes flicking back and forth from one image to the other and hated to admit it, but the dual visuals were entertaining.

"Don't make a mess on my floor. If you do, you can lick it up," I said and leaned back to relax. "Didn't Heather give you enough release for one night?"

"Meh, she was a cunt and just laid there. I only dribbled. You were right. She has no talent."

I glanced at my brother's face to see if he was joking, but he was fixated on the video, and I couldn't tell.

"You gonna join? I can hold off until you're ready," Abel smiled wide as he let go of his prick and squeezed the armrests tight. "Oh yeah, get back down in those balls." He made a sucking sound like he was reversing his come with his vacuum impression.

"You can continue. I'm not in the mood," I said, even though that wasn't entirely true. The pair of violet eyes were still bright in my mind, and the thought of them made my cock come alive and twitch in my pants.

Abel turned in his chair to look at me. One naked leg flung over the side of the armrest as he grabbed his cock and continued. "What's the problem?"

My eyes danced from the screaming girl on one screen who was deliciously covered in blood to the colorful and smiling faces on the other screen and finally fell on my brother's hand as it traveled the length of his shaft. His had a slight bend at the end, whereas mine was perfectly straight. Other than that, our cocks were identical to the rest of our bodies. They have the same length, same girth, and the same ability to fuck for a really long ass time.

"There is no problem," I stated.

"You're fuckin' lyin', man." I tore my gaze away from my brother's hand only to find the screaming girl, which continued to harden my shaft and make my jeans uncomfortable.

"I'm not lying, and I don't have a problem."

"Oh yeah, then prove it. Where's your next piece of art at," Abel asked and then sucked in a deep breath, his head falling back and his mouth opening. The girl on the screen now had my cock in her mouth. Abel had filmed this part, and the visual of me pinching her nose closed while tears and black makeup ran down her face was becoming more than I could handle.

"I didn't find anything that would be suitable. One old man paid a ton to have his car towed, but that was it. I have higher standards than you do." The girl on the screen gagged, a gurgling sound mixing in time with my cock sliding down her throat and then completely choking off her air supply.

"That's not true...okay yeah, it is. Oh, fuck, that's good. I love it when you make them do that, and I get to watch. So delicious is their gagging that I could close my eyes and still see their fear," Abel moaned loudly, and my eyes flicked back to him and his ever-quickening hand.

"Shit, fine, hold up," I bit out.

I should have been annoyed that my brother was playing me. However, I couldn't stop the rising need making my cock ache. I'd never been one to hold back on taking what I wanted.

"Yeah, now that's what I'm talkin' about," Abel chuckled as I unzipped my fly and pulled my throbbing cock out.

"You're a fucking prick."

"Ooh, come on, you know you wanted to. Now tell me, what's wrong? Tell your baby brother what's wrong so he can make it all better," Abel teased, his lower lip protruding out like an annoying child, but his hand never slowed.

I could tell he was gripping himself hard as his cock began to turn a wicked shade of angry purple. We both enjoyed our sex rough, but Abel liked it painful. Not only for his prey but also for himself. The more you smacked his cock, the harder he got. More than a few people found out the hard way that trying to hurt Abel only excited him more.

I glared at him as I got comfortable. My brother was much like the kid in a store who wanted a new toy and begged while stomping their little foot and pulling on his mommy's jacket, not knowing when to shut the fuck up. I'd seen a few of those hideous little brats and wondered why their parents didn't suffocate them in the night and why I hadn't suffocated Abel.

"I met someone," I said, slowing the jackrabbiting of my brother's hand.

My strokes were controlled, but Abel always looked like he had a pogo stick for a cock that his hand was bouncing on while he was being electrocuted.

"You met someone? What the fuck does that mean? You meet people every fucking day. You drive a tow truck and own a garage. People literally walk in all the time."

"I didn't actually meet her, but she had the prettiest violet eyes," I said, my voice wispy with the thought of her dark hair in my hand as I fucked her mouth like the girl on the screen. Those eyes staring up at me from beneath thick lashes was a whole new interest I didn't know I had. I groaned as the image sent a surge of pleasure through my body until it tingled the tip of my cock.

Interesting.

"Ah, that explains it. You always did get a little obsessive when you found a new shade of eyes to pluck." I glared at Abel as he dismissed me and my distress. "Don't look at me like that, man. It's creepy."

"Whatever," I bit out and fixed my stare on the girl that was now blubbering that she didn't want to die, so she'd do anything we asked.

She crawled toward the camera dragging her bloodied leg and cut body across the floor and leaving a trail of red behind her. The sounds of her begging were loud in my ears, but my eyes didn't see her blonde hair and hazel eyes.

No, my mind had found another to fixate on, and it was the delicate features of someone else that filled my fantasies as my hand moved faster along my shaft. It was harder than normal, and I actually felt a building of excitement for the coming release. It was rare that I got truly excited about anything. Even the kills only mildly stirred an interest, but at least it was more than the meager amount of feelings I had the rest of the time.

"Fine, if it's bothering you that much... oh shit, here it comes," Abel blurted as a white jet of come flew across the room and almost hit the television. "Fuckin' yes, kill that bitch."

He stood and fired the next one at my screen, the glob finding the girl's face and sliding down her cheek like she was in the room. I ignored Abel as he continued to rant.

My release was close, and as the knife smoothly slid across the girl's neck on the screen and the gurgling started, I came harder than I'd ever come. Slumping back into the chair, I felt my chest heave, yet I still couldn't get the girl from the car out of my mind. No one intrigued me. I'd seen millions of faces with eyes of all colors, and none came close to the level of fascination I was experiencing.

"That's better, woohoo!" Abel shook his body like a dog after a bath before flopping back into the chair and reaching for his pack of smokes. "As I was saying, then find her. Make her your next project. You're like the best at fucking hunting people down. I'm sure you can find one girl," Abel said as he grabbed the remote and switched the television from the girl to a different night. This one was a pair of girls Abel had found drunk and needing a cab. Worst mistake they ever made.

It was Abel's thing to break people. He loved nothing better than having those who swore how much they loved one another turn on each other. He was right, though. They always broke in the end. Every relationship had its breaking point. I looked my brother up and down, wondering what it would take for me to kill him finally. Shrugging off the thought, I stood and stuffed my dick back into my jeans.

"You not staying for round two?"

"Not tonight. Make sure you clean up. I don't want to have to scrape your come off my television."

"What the fuck? Why am I on clean-up duty again?" Abel slouched over in the chair like a child sulking.

"Because you're still planning on stroking, and I'm not. Because you're in my house making a fucking mess and, most importantly, because I said so." I grabbed a handful of cookies from the table and wandered into the kitchen in search of a glass of milk.

My brother had a decent idea. Finding her and collecting what I wanted seemed like a mighty fine idea. One I was looking forward to starting first thing in the morning.

CHAPTER 4

MARGARET

I grabbed the blue blazer off the coat hook, stuffed my arms in the sleeves, snagged my leather briefcase, and made my way out the door. This case that had fallen on my desk was troubling for so many reasons. The number of dead and missing people was enough to make even the most hardened agents squeamish, and they thought this whole case was attributed to one person.

Closing my office door, I strode down the long hallway toward the larger offices. I'd been summoned for a meeting with my boss, the director of my field office, who was supposed to be an all-around good guy. At least, that was what everyone said when they arrived. Agent Mulligan certainly had his way with people, I just didn't happen to be his favorite person, and the feeling was mutual. Mulligan's door was closed, and I checked myself in the glass before straightening my spine. Raising my hand, I knocked to announce my arrival.

"Come in," Mulligan's deep voice called out, and I pushed open the door and closed it again.

This office was huge, with plain beige walls lined with navy trim. My goal was to sit in his chair one day. Granted, he did not need the space to be so big other than to gloat about its size. I was pretty sure many said he had to be compensating for something at least once or twice. Mulligan had turned the space into a personal shrine of his accomplishments, and there wasn't a wall that didn't hold some form of an award.

My eyes roamed over the second man in the room. He was someone that I was pretty sure I'd seen on television, and my sixth sense told me I wasn't going to like how this meeting went.

"Agent Lawson, this is Agent Hanson," Mulligan said.

"Nice to meet you, Agent Lawson." Hanson nodded.

I took in his deadpan stare and the salt and pepper short haircut that had become standard issue with men in the FBI. His suit was a deep shade of navy, and his long coat was still firmly in place, which told me he had about as much interest in being in the office as I did.

"Same," I replied. I offered my hand for Hanson to shake and was surprised when he moved to take my hand.

Mulligan leaned back in the large leather chair and gave the impression he was someone of grand importance. "Agent Hanson is from the San Diego office and has agreed to help with the Chameleon case."

"I don't understand why you're bringing in another agent. I've only had this case for a few months?" I clenched the handle on my briefcase a little harder.

It was difficult enough to get the men that ran the old boy's club to let me in the door, and the last thing I needed was to be seen as the female agent that couldn't close the deal on an assigned case.

"Hanson here has worked many serial killer cases, and although you are a fantastic teacher to your students, this will only be your third official case as the lead. If our initial speculation is correct, then it is a massive case and needs an experienced outlook."

The fact that there seemed to be so many bodies attributed to this killer was what intrigued me when everyone else backed away from the task. Now I was going to have to share my hard work and all my findings with some agent that would steal my glory simply because he had a dick. Anger simmered in my gut as I kept my face void of all emotion. If this Hanson thought he was going to come into my city and take my case, he had another thing coming.

"The two of you will work together on this case. Hanson will take the lead since he has the most experience, and you will get to learn from one of the best."

My gaze flicked over to the other agent, and it was obvious that he didn't look any more comfortable than when I first walked in. The tense body position screamed that there was more to his sudden appearance than my boss was saying.

"I don't understand. You're acting like I've already failed, but it was only because of my research that I found the connection between the inconsistent MO."

Mulligan sighed like he was dealing with a child, and I seriously wanted to wipe that condescending look off his face. "Agent Lawson, I'm sure you can admit that this case is too large for one person to handle. Besides, I still want you to teach your new classes as no one else is available at the moment, which divides your time."

"So you don't want me to give up my classes?"

"No. Your classes will still be conducted as scheduled."

"I'm sorry, but I have to say that although I understand the importance of having more eyes and hands to help with this case, I don't agree with the person that has the most knowledge to date being demoted."

Mulligan stood from his desk and leaned on it as if that would make his point clearer. "Agent Lawson, are you questioning my authority and decision-making ability?"

This was a trap question. No matter how I answered, I was fucked. I'd learned this the hard way a very long time ago. "No, I'm not, Sir. Just trying to understand the situation better."

"Unfortunately, I have another meeting starting shortly, so I will have to clarify this situation for you another time. That's everything. Oh, and I trust you'll share what you've gathered so far with Agent Hanson."

"Of course," I smiled and turned for the door as if I had a choice in the matter.

Yanking open the door, I walked out and could feel Hanson following me. I rounded on him when we were out of earshot from Mulligan's office. "Just so you know, I don't appreciate someone coming in and stealing my case."

"Trust me. I don't want to be here any more than you do. I'm sorry he pulled you off as the lead. I was told I was coming to assist, and that was all."

I opened my briefcase, pulled out a thick file, and held it out to Hanson. "Here, I have a class to teach. You might as well make yourself familiar with what I've collected so far, but I will warn you the deaths are disturbing, and there are no solid leads."

"Sounds like fun. Those are my favorite kind." Hanson smiled as I hung onto the folder and finally released it with a sigh.

Turning, I marched away toward the other end of the building. "And I like Szechuan chicken with a side of rice, and get me an egg roll," I called over my shoulder. If the man was taking my case, the least he could do was buy me dinner.

It had become something of an obsession to catch this Chameleon, the guy was most certainly unhinged and twisted, and I feared there were more bodies we hadn't found and more yet to come.

The classroom was full when I arrived, and as always, my eyes found my daughter in the middle of the room. I'd pushed Kirby to get into the FBI program and even gave her a glowing endorsement. They needed more women in the FBI, and I was positive that my daughter needed direction in her life. This job filled both needs.

"Alright, class, today we are going to look at Dr. Harold Shipman."

KIRBY

I sat off to the side of the large classroom, and still, my mother found me and smiled at me, making me want to sink down into my seat and hide. Didn't she understand that everyone already thought I didn't deserve to be here? Everyone else had to apply and be vetted. I was granted a free access pass because of my mother's credentials. I had no idea how they knew. It wasn't like I ever said anything about who my mom was, but the boys to my left and the girl to my right glared in my direction as my mother nodded at me.

The class my mother taught was interesting, not that I'd ever admit that to her. It would be all the ammunition she needed to keep me in this place until I made Special, Special rank, or something. As the lights flicked on at the end of the seminar, I tried to escape with the crowd, but that was pointless. My mother spotted me and called out my name loud enough that even the dead would have heard her.

"Kirby, can you come here for a moment, please?"

I groaned internally but slowly moved toward her as she packed up the papers strewn across the teacher's desk. As we waited for the rest of the students to clear, I looked around the room. The space really needed an upgrade. Even a paint job would be a good idea. The problem was if I had the choice, I'd paint the walls something bright and colorful or maybe something that would freak everyone out for fun. I could picture a slew of flowers or maybe crazy-looking clowns. That would fuck with everyone's minds, and I smirked at the thought. Really anything would be better than 70s orange.

The door to the hall closed, and my mother snapped the clasp shut on her briefcase before looking at me.

"We need to talk."

I internally groaned.

Those four little words were the most dreaded in any relationship dynamic. 'We need to talk' was the equivalent of 'I'm punching you in the face with my words before I fuck you up the ass without lube and with something you won't like.'

"We cannot have a repeat of your behavior from the last session. Unlike the first twelve weeks of your training, these next sixteen weeks must be taken seriously. That means no tardiness, and you need to keep your grades up," she said. "Do you have any idea what it took for me to get you in here? What strings I had to pull, and what promises I had to commit to in order to make this a reality for you?"

I crossed my arms over my chest. I'd heard this speech before, and it always ended with whatever my mother wanted for me was right and whatever I wanted or said was wrong. It didn't matter that I had no interest in becoming an FBI agent, nor did I want to live with her and her cheating ass when she and father divorced. Yet, I was forced to do that as well, and now I barely saw my father and was shoved into a career I had zero interest in doing.

"Do you have anything to say for yourself?"

"What do you want me to say, Mom? I didn't want to become some special secret agent in the first place. This is all your idea. I'm only here because you didn't like my choices and forced me to attend."

My mother leaned against the desk and stared at me with the same look I was sure she used in her interrogation of killers.

"Really, Kirby? Okay, then tell me, what did you want to do? You're twenty-three now, and the bachelor of science degree you insisted on completing was doing nothing for you. You had top grades, yet you worked at a Denny's making peanuts. You have thousands of dollars of school debt that your father and I have been paying for, but you seemed perfectly happy to sit back and enjoy the lifestyle we've provided without you contributing a dime."

My Mother pointed around the room.

"This is what is going to give you a career. It will pay the bills, and it may not seem like it yet, but it will be a rewarding job rather than where you were headed."

I looked down at my shoes and sighed. "Nothing about this place feels right for me. I wanted to be an artist. I've always loved to paint."

"Great answer, Kirby. A worthless, dead-end career."

My mother grabbed her briefcase off the desk and paused as she went to walk past. "Here's the deal. You can either start taking classes seriously or drop out, but I will not pay for school anymore, and you'll have to find a real job and start adulting, as you call it. That means you'll pay all your bills, including food and extras like getting your hair done, and you need to move out of the dorm. I'll give you three months to find a place to live other than with me. If you want to be treated like an adult, act like one. If you want to paint, do what other people do and make it a hobby."

There was no point in saying anything back. Most of it was accurate, and shamefully I couldn't deny that my parents still paid for all my expenses since I was forced to quit my waitressing job. I watched my mother leave, but I stayed in the quiet class space enjoying the silence.

For reasons beyond me, all I could picture was the man at the side of the road. How could a single glimpse leave such a lasting impression? My eyes looked over the notes my mother had scribbled on the whiteboard and wondered if the two-hundred-plus victims of Dr. Harold Shipman had known what he was when they met him but ignored the signs.

Sighing, I wandered toward the door and flicked the light off as I went. The halls only had a smattering of people in them, and my low black pumps echoed as I walked. This was the other thing I hated about the idea of becoming an FBI agent. We all looked like a bunch of navy-colored robots swarming the halls. It was drab, it was monotonous, and it was so not me.

It was dark and raining as I got to the doors that led to the parking lot, and as luck would have it, I hadn't brought a jacket with me. I stood under the overhang of the building and stared at my car sitting across the street in the parking lot. I needed to get groceries or, at the very least, hit up a drive-thru since my fridge and cupboards were empty, but as the rain continued to hammer the ground, I was tempted to skip food and head straight to the dorms.

Great, just great.

Sucking it up, I ran down the few steps and across the parking lot only to get my feet soaked and water splashed all over my new pants. I hated to admit that I thought this place was creepy as hell at night, but it had this weird vibe. Maybe it was all the killer talk they played over and over or just the trees that shaded the parking lot from the road, making it feel boxed in. Either way, when I reached the car, it felt like eyes from every direction were trained on me, making me twitchy.

I fumbled with my keys, and the stupid fob fell from my hands in my haste to push the unlock button. Swearing, I bent to pick it up.

A scream ripped from my mouth as I stood and saw someone with a hood standing behind me. Spinning around, I was ready to fight off whoever it was, but the person backed up and put their arms up.

"Jesus Christ, Kirby! You just gave me a heart attack. Why the hell are you screaming like a bloody banshee?" I recognized Peter's voice right away and slumped against my car, the initial fear passing, but the adrenaline was still pumping hard in my veins.

"Me? What the hell were you doing?"

"I came to see if you wanted to come to my place tonight, and I can drop you off in the morning?"

"And you couldn't call? I mean, look around. No one is here, and you snuck up behind me with a hood pulled up. What did you think I was going to think," I asked, angry with his stupidity and his assumption that I was going to his house for the night. The worst part was that was exactly where I most likely would've ended up.

I was so predictable.

Staying in the dorm on a regular basis was not my thing, and my roommate tapped her pen on the desk as she studied. More than once, I'd imagined stealing the pen out of her hand and stabbing her with it. Peter's face looked confused, like he had no idea why I would be upset. How could someone be so smart in school and the rest of the time a complete moron? I looked around and then back up at Peter.

"Where is your car anyway?"

"I didn't want to pay the parking fee, so I left the car out there." Peter pointed to the exit, and I shook my head.

It was only ten dollars. Was he really serious? I shivered, realizing I was officially soaked to the bone from standing in the rain. I didn't want to stay with him tonight, but I didn't want to go to my dorm room and spend the rest of the night with my odd-ass roommate or see my mother again so soon. Besides, Peter always had great food. Was I using him? Why yes, I fucking was. If he could use me for sex, I figured it was fair I could use him for food. Besides, it had been a couple of days since I'd gotten any. Since returning from our camping trip, I'd been ignoring Peter, but I could use a good orgasm. Well, the word 'good' set too high of a bar for Peter's skill in the bedroom, but it was better than using my fingers.

"Alright, let's go," I said and followed him to his parking spot.

I really needed to get rid of this guy. He didn't bother to ask how I was or offer me his jacket, and my blouse was completely see-through. Of course, he proceeded to tell me every aspect of his day in painstaking detail and mentioned just how chilly it was. I looked back at my car, wondering if an orgasm and a hot meal was really worth this hassle.

Hello
Sunshine

CHAPTER 5

CAIN

It had cost me a pretty penny to get a hold of this information. I hadn't much to go on, just a partial plate, make, model, and color of vehicle, so it was more expensive than normal. But I needed to get my hands on the name of the Mercedes owner. The only issue was the information given was still a list of ten vehicles. I was currently sitting outside the home of number four. Stalking my prey wasn't an issue for me. In fact, I enjoyed the process, but I didn't like wasting my time. So far, I'd wasted my time.

The sun was beginning to rise, so I figured I'd get myself some breakfast at the diner around the corner. The couple that owned the one I liked to frequent would be perfect character witnesses if ever the need should arise. I'd been going into the same location and eating the same trucker's breakfast with a side of waffles for seven years, three months, and two days.

It was important to keep track of information like that. At a young age, I learned that information was power, and power yielded what you wanted. I'd also made sure to be nice to the owners and leave a generous tip.

Movement caught my eye, and I sat up a little straighter in the nondescript, black minivan that smelled like cat piss from the previous owner. The garage door slowly opened and the silver vehicle backed out onto the street. Lady Luck was on my side as the vehicle turned in my direction. I held the little remote in my hand for the camera set up in the back seat area, but as the vehicle drove past, I slumped back into my seat and put a line through the name.

The man I was looking for was around my age. The silver-haired businessman that drove past was way too old to be the guy. Based on this list and the general information, he didn't have a son either.

My stomach growled, and I decided I'd eat and then continue my search. Eating was never that high on my priority list unless my body reminded me that it was required or I needed to for my cover. Besides, it was never wise to hunt on an empty stomach. It made me hangry, and hangry led to carelessness. Zipping around the corner, I pulled into the mostly empty parking lot and hopped out.

As soon as my foot touched the pavement, I put my mask in place, the one that everyone fell for, the one I'd learned to show the world. It was the one that proved most people were stupid.

"Welcome. Have you been here before?" The new upbeat woman behind the little wooden stand asked as I stepped through the doors.

I smiled wide and made sure that it reached my eyes. Abel was far better at this, but I'd practiced enough to get by. "Yes, many times. How are Lenny and Alice doing?"

"You must be a regular. That's what I like to hear. Follow me. I will show you to your seat. Do you have a preference for a booth or table," she said as she pulled out a menu.

My eyes slid over her features and listed them off in my head.

Hair: reddish brown, shoulder length with a touch of curl.

Complexion: fair with a dash of freckles.

Height: around five feet.

Eyes: green.

But her eyes were not an unusual color of green. They were a cross between green and hazel. I had many of those already.

"Booth, please, and I'd love a corner looking out the window," I smiled wider and gave her a wink.

"I know just the one," the woman said as she walked away, expecting me to follow.

The coconut scent of her generic brand of cheap shampoo made my nose hairs curl as I stepped into stride behind her. If I'd been hunting, she already would have heard her death bell ringing in her ears as she screamed my name. "Lenny and Alice are great. They just got back from Cuba."

"That's very exotic. I bet they have great tans," I said and smiled as she looked over her shoulder at me. A quick flash in her eye said she was unsure about me following so close, but she didn't step away. I instantly knew she'd grown up in a home where she was told to please those around her. She was the type that would apologize for everything she said or did that possibly could've offended you. She was also the type that would let me push every inappropriate boundary because she hoped to hear 'good girl' and feel a pat on the head.

She giggled as she stopped at the booth in the far corner. "Yes, they do. I'd love to go to someplace like that. Here you go, best seat in the house."

I scooted across the wide, worn bench and smiled again, making sure my dimple showed. A flirtatious smile was proper.

"Thanks, this is perfect," I said. A blush crept across her cheeks, and a little rush of triumph raced through my system. "It's okay. I don't need the menu. I already know what I'd like."

She paused before setting the menu down, but it was long enough for me to catch what she was wearing underneath. She had on a white lace bra hidden behind her work blouse. It would be interesting to know if she'd still smile if I cut her nipples off and turned that pretty bit of lace all red.

"Well, alright then, what can I get ya?"

She didn't pull out a notepad, and I smirked. She didn't think she needed one. But if she screwed up my order, I would find her, and there would be no smiling if that meeting needed to happen.

"Your trucker's special, eggs scrambled, bacon crisp, and a side of your blueberry waffles, lots of whip cream with a coffee, black."

"A man that knows what he likes. Comin' right up."

She turned and walked away, and I watched her pert ass bounce under the simple uniform skirt. If she knew how much that statement resonated with me. Right now, I wanted to carve up her slender back. I had a new design that was begging to be put on a back and ass like hers.

There was a local paper on the table, and I picked it up and began to read about the daily gossip. Knowing which politician was openly lying today, who decided to shoot who, or who was seeking something in the classifieds was great information for me. I loved the classifieds. I'd found more than one unwitting individual through the small squares in the back of a paper. Words like 'must sell' and 'liquidation,' as well as 'estate sale,' always piqued my interest.

"Here you go," the waitress said as she returned with my food and coffee. "If you need anything else, just let me know."

"I love lots of syrup. Would you mind if I got a few more of these little bottles," I asked as the door jingled and I could hear more people arriving, but didn't give them much thought.

"For sure, comin' right up."

I turned my attention back to buttering my waffles when the waitress squealed a little and began laughing as she apologized all over the place. I glanced up and sucked in a sharp breath as the woman I was searching for just collided with the waitress. I only caught a glimpse of her face before she stepped behind the half-wall partition, but it was her. Now, the question became, were those unique eyes real, or were they a lie?

I pulled the collar up on my work shirt and quickly turned away so she didn't see me but kept watch on her reflection in the window. My heart beat a little harder as the predator in me laughed with glee at finding my prey.

"What the hell? Watch where you're going. You almost spilled hot coffee all over my girlfriend. You're a useless excuse for a waitress."

"Peter, it's fine," my girl said to the guy, who was obviously an asshole.

The guy stood with his hands on his hips, accentuating the designer suit he was wearing. This was who she chose to date? This fake husk of a man was nothing more than a whiny, spoiled brat that lived underneath a false bravado. I'd have him screaming like a stuck pig before I even had him on my table. I looked at my hand, wondering why it hurt, and realized that I was holding the knife so hard that the handle was digging into my palm.

"No, it's not fine. I told you this place was shit and cheap. I don't know why you insisted on coming here."

The violet-eyed ray of sunshine stood up straight, and as she did, I could see her eyes over the wall.

"That's enough, Peter. This is a great spot with amazing food, and you're being unnecessarily rude."

I could feel the fire in her words, not the ones she did say, but the ones she left out, and my interest piqued a little more. She had a bright fire inside her, and I couldn't help wondering how much she'd fight with my hand wrapped around her throat. My cock tingled with the same joyous sensation it did when I found a new project to play with, but there was more to this than what was normal for me. The possibilities and images that were playing out in my mind were like an exotic ballet.

The argument continued, but I didn't care about what they said. All I could focus on was the sound of her voice. She had a little bird-like inflection she used at the end of each word in a sentence. She took a step back, and I could see her fully. Her dark hair was a rich shade of black ash that fell in waves around her shoulders. She was dressed in a tidy pantsuit, a white blouse that stood out against her lightly tanned skin, and small heels that said she meant business. The long coat she wore had me raising an eyebrow. It screamed detective or Fed.

The arguing subsided, and the couple headed out of sight to the opposite side of the restaurant. I quickly shifted my food to the other side of the booth and slipped around so I was facing their direction. I counted the heads of the other people in here this early. Only six people sat between me and my prey. I could see the top of her head as they slid into a booth and just make out the ghostly reflection of her face in the window.

Appreciating her beauty, she reminded me of an expensive doll that collectors would sit on their shelves. Hopefully, soon, she would sit on mine. Well, part of her, anyway.

The flustered waitress returned with my extra syrup, and I could see the confusion on her face. She'd noticed that I'd changed sides.

"Sun was in my eyes on that side," I said and took the offering.

I poured the multiple bottles of syrup on my waffles and dug into the breakfast that had a lot more flavor than it would've before my violet-eyed ray of sunshine walked in.

Sunshine?

Huh? I'd never given anyone other than Abel a nickname. Most of his were derogatory slurs. I was transfixed and completely fascinated that someone other than Abel was holding my attention.

Time to stalk a pretty girl, pretty girl, pretty girl.

Time to stalk a pretty girl so early in the morning.

Time to make the girl mine, the girl mine, the girl mine.

Time to make the girl mine so early in the morning.

Time to slit her pretty throat, pretty throat, pretty throat.

Time to slit her pretty throat and keep her as my trophy.

The stupid song that Abel created ran around in my head, and I couldn't help but smile. As I ate my fluffy waffles, I was able to admit that sometimes my brother was quite creative.

CHAPTER 6

KIRBY

The rock music blasted through the headphones as my feet pounded along the sidewalk. I loved running but loved it more when I had anger to vent. The afternoon sun was warm, but the temperatures were supposed to drop, and I wasn't looking forward to the cold weather. Veering off the sidewalk, I ran into the woods surrounding the school. The rest of the class was so far behind that they were out of sight. Being in the lead was a rush and pushed me harder.

Peter and I had argued non-stop yesterday, from breakfast to dinner. He'd been excessively rude to everyone, from the sweet man holding the door open for us at his building to the teenage kid working at the gas station. I didn't know what his problem was, but his entire attitude left a sour taste in my mouth. There simply wasn't a reason to treat people like that. Now, every second I spent in his presence, the more I couldn't overlook the issues with our relationship. It was like every time he opened his mouth, more toxicity would spill out and poison the waters further.

My mind kept swirling around the loud arguments my parents used to have. My mother always talked down to my dad. She loved to point out that he didn't have as fancy of a job, and she would say, 'it made him less of a man.' I hated whenever she'd do that and felt this urge to come to my dad's defense, which would put me in my mother's crosshairs. I'd usually end up grounded, but she didn't have the right to speak to Dad like that when it shouldn't matter how much money you make to determine your worth. Besides, she was the fucking cheater.

Mother was the one that ruined our family, and a small part of me hated her for that. I was fifteen when I found out about the affair, and it happened completely by accident. I volunteered at a blood bank and decided to give blood, a seemingly innocent thing to do, right? But then I discovered my blood type didn't match either of my parents.

Did I feel bad about outing her to my dad? Yes, but only because he moved out and eventually left to live in another country, which was totally selfish. I'd lost count of how many times since I'd asked the question, who was my birth father? I didn't have a clue, and according to my mother, neither did she. I was the product of an oops-pregnancy that my mother never wanted. She had a few one-night stands while she was on an op, and 'oops,' here I was. Just what every kid wanted to hear, 'Hey, you were the accident that I didn't really want but got anyway.' She said she'd never wanted children because it would've stunted her career. It honestly felt like she resented me from the day I was born.

I'd been so angry with her that I cheered when they said they were getting a divorce, but the joy quickly subsided when Dad moved out and told me it was best if I stayed with my mother. He'd never been the breadwinner of the family, and my mother would only make our lives hell if I moved in with him. Then he got a job transfer and moved across the ocean to England with his new fiancé. Now, they were expecting a baby, and I barely heard from him anymore. Not only did I have no clue who my birth father was, but I felt like I'd lost the one I'd loved for years.

The sound of my breath was loud in my ears as I pushed my body harder than I ever had. My arms pumped in time to the song's beat, and my heart thumped, thumped, thumped along. I leaped over a small log and flew around the bend in the trail.

So here I was, unsure of who I was and what I wanted. And I'd left behind my life and all my friends in Cali. My mother decided to move us out here with the new teaching position she'd been offered. So now I was halfway across the country only to be stuck in a city I didn't want to be in, with a woman I couldn't stand and doing a program I was not interested in attending.

I'd rounded the halfway point and had barely broken a sweat. This was the hardest part of the trail, and I pushed hard as my legs climbed the steep incline that sent my heart rate through the roof.

Still fuming from my fight with Peter and the memories of why I was even running this fucking trail spurred me on. I burst from the tree line, ready to dash across the intersection, but some asshole in a black minivan pulled out too far as he came to a sudden stop at the stop sign, and I almost ran into the side of it. Angry, I smacked my hands on the hood.

"Hey, watch where you're going," I yelled as I kept running.

The final hundred meters were in sight, and I pushed my body to move faster, loving the breeze in my face and the pounding of the blood in my ears to lull me into feeling something that wasn't disappointed, annoyed, or trapped.

That's what I was, a rat in a trap, and I wanted out before I suffocated to death. I needed to find a way to get my dad to agree to have me move there with him. I knew I shouldn't have to beg, but at this point, I was desperate and desperate times called for desperate measures.

I ran past the coach, and he clicked the stopwatch. He wrote down the time with a smile on his face.

"Great time Lawson. You almost beat the school record."

Coach was a hot man. My gaze flicked over his muscular frame covered in standard-issue shorts and a white T-shirt. I wondered if I could talk him into a fun fuck-session once I got rid of Peter—maybe we could fulfill a fantasy or two about a dirty coach in his office. I'd read a book or two that started that way, and I had to admit that I was curious to try it.

I shook my head and noticed the minivan I almost collided with drive past. It wasn't doing anything unusual. In fact, it was doing the speed limit and driving in a straight line. I couldn't see the driver because of the darkened windows, but I would swear that the driver was staring at me. It felt like the vehicle was stripping me naked, and I shivered.

I seriously needed a good lay and to stop watching unsolved

murder cases so late at night. My brain was a mess, and Peter was useless.

CAIN

A truck flew past where I was sitting, and the wind shook my tow truck, pulling me out of my thoughts.

"Hope you end up wrapped around a tree," I said and glared at the receding taillights before returning my attention to my notes. I'd spent the majority of the day following Asswipe and Sunshine around. I still didn't know her name, so Sunshine it was. I'd almost changed the nickname to Bunny when she bolted out of the trees like her ass was on fire. I hadn't expected her that soon and was planning to be parked on the bypass street a little further along once I realized where they were going to exit the trail. Technically this was Quantico property, so I had to tread carefully.

It was strange to have such a visceral reaction to someone, but I knew it was technically possible. Just because I was a psychopath didn't mean I couldn't feel more than a shallow range of emotions. But for me, it was like getting sucker punched in the face.

I fidgeted in my seat, my cock stirring as I pictured her running from the forest in her too-short shorts and the tight T-shirt with her long hair bobbing behind her in a ponytail perfect for wrapping around my hand. I rolled out the building tension in my shoulders as the image of her slamming her hands onto the van had me hard instantly. There was no mistaking those eyes as real now, and they were the prettiest I'd ever seen. Using the color amethyst to describe them didn't do them justice, but I planned on harvesting those unique jewels for my own. The question became, why did I find myself wanting to say something like she was fucking hot?

"She is fucking hot," I said out loud in the truck to see how it sounded and shrugged. It felt...good.

Unfortunately, I needed to keep a tight schedule, and as she returned to the building, I had to leave her behind. It was only temporary. I'd be back. I watched more cars speed past my location and nibbled on a bag of chips while waiting for someone to need my assistance.

I had a perfectly mapped-out schedule that ensured we never looked like the killer they searched for, and Abel needed some form of a leash. As long as we continued to be as careful, the cops would never catch us. We were too smart—well, I was too smart. Abel was smart enough not to step outside the boundaries of my hunting rules or my cleaning and disposal practices. If he thought he could get away with it, he'd go on a killing rampage and dance in the blood in the middle of the street before dying in a shootout with cops. My brother was the type that he'd never be taken alive, so I controlled him the way I did for both of our sakes.

I picked up my newspaper and flipped to page three, where there was a write-up about the Chameleon Killer. Catchy title—I thought it was fitting. Above the article was a photograph of a crime scene. It showed a sheet laid over a body while officers and Feds stood around.

This was perfect. It was what I'd been aspiring to accomplish. One day a book would be written about me. I'd make sure of it.

I'd dreamed of the moment when the world would see the quality of my work while they scrambled to figure out who would be next and who I was. This was the ultimate game of chess, where I was the king and had the queen by the throat. I'd played the game for years with those at school and my parents, but they were pathetic players. Nothing more than little pawns for me to pick off one by one. My eyes roamed over the image again. The cops and the Feds were much better opponents.

The idling tow truck and the thought of my parents took me back in time to when my father had underestimated me for the last time.

I wiped my brow with the back of my gloved hand. It was hot, like 'fry an egg on the metal of the tractor hood' hot, with scorching temperatures and a drought that I'd never experienced in my seventeen years. Everything was dry, and fires were starting all over the state, but here I was out slugging bales of hay. Sweat dripped from every inch of my body, and my muscles were already sore from doing the same thing for the last three days. Lugging square bales from early morning until dusk was the chore I hated the most. I liked the privacy of the farm, but being a man of the land was not for me.

"Hurry up, Cain, the bales are piling up," my father yelled from the comfort of the tractor seat.

I turned my glare on my father.

"I'm going as fast as I can," I yelled over the churning noise of the baler and rumble of the old tractor. The sound was bugging my ears.

A small breeze changed direction, causing hay dust to billow in my face and stick to any possible piece of skin on my body. It made me itchy and was irritating as fuck. I had trouble controlling my anger when I was overstimulated and irritated. It was one of the few emotions that didn't elude me.

I grabbed another bale from the small pile created as they were pushed out of the shoot onto the wagon. Turning, I walked to the wall I was creating to toss the next one up and over my head. The tractor lurched as it came to a sudden halt. With a hard crash, I landed on the floor of the wooden wagon.

"Ouch," I hissed and looked at the large sliver that felt like a tree branch sticking out of my palm.

Looking up at the baler and tractor still running, I caught a glimpse of my father's boots as they walked toward the wagon.

"You're too slow. It's going jam up." His face pulled down into a scowl, his eyebrows almost touching and his nostrils flaring like one of the angry bulls. He swung his leg up on the wagon and towered over me. "You drive," he snarled.

"You're supposed to give a warning if you stop. I could've fallen off the wagon," I said as I slowly stood.

My father fixed me with a hard stare. "Maybe that wouldn't have been a bad thing."

It was the first time my father openly voiced concern about me to my face. In fact, I thought he was perfectly oblivious, living in his bubble of denial after all my therapy sessions, but looking into his eyes now, I realized he knew. That meant he had to die sooner than I'd planned.

"I'm not sure what you mean," I lied and cocked my head at him the way Abel had taught me.

Anger was volatile in my system, and it took all my effort to keep my behavioral control issues in line. I was tempted to grab him by the shirt and throw him onto the PTO shaft, but that would likely only break an arm or leg. The probability that it would snap his neck was slim, and the plaid shirt and already torn jeans would rip off his body. Of course, I could hold his face to the shaft, but he was still taller, had more weight on me, and I needed it to look like an accident. My handprint on his face most certainly wouldn't create that illusion.

A moment of stillness and understanding passed between us while the tractor continued to rumble steadily like a spectator. A subtle jerk of the wagon back and forth felt like it was trying to lull us into a calmer place.

"You don't need to play your games with me, Cain. I've seen the dead in your eyes. The good Lord made you wrong, and the devil crawled into your soul and has never left."

I lifted an eyebrow at him and proceeded to pick the large piece of wood from my hand. "You're mistaken. The doctor said that I'm cured." I pulled out the sliver and tossed it into the wind the way I wanted to do with this annoying sack of flesh in front of me.

My father stepped close to me, and my muscles flexed, ready for the fight. I instantly ran through every possible scenario in my head. At that moment, I knew I'd been too relaxed and given away far too much of myself. That was a mistake I'd never make again.

"There's no fixin' what you are, and we both know it," my father said.

He placed his hands on his hips, staring down into my eyes as if daring me to try something. I had to admit I was tempted to follow through on my fantasy. The images were living creatures in my mind begging to be set free.

I smirked at my father and let my mask drop for a moment. I wanted him to see his death in my eyes. It may not be today or tomorrow, but it would happen, and I wanted him never to have a peaceful moment again until then.

"Just remember, it wasn't God that made me. You did." Smiling, I hopped off the wagon and walked to the tractor."

I looked back at my father, who seemed shell-shocked. His mouth was still hanging open, and his eyes were wide. Maybe he hadn't known for sure what I was, but he did now. The pathetic look in his eyes made my day out here all worth it.

Putting my good old country boy mask back in place, I smiled and gave him a thumbs up. When he returned the gesture, I revved the engine and put the tractor in gear.

We didn't speak the rest of the time out in the field as we worked, but every time I looked at his face, I was more certain that he needed to die soon. There was no way I was letting him send me to a stupid psychiatrist again, and I definitely wasn't getting locked up. No one in a white coat was getting near me.

While I drove along the rows of hay, the seconds turned into minutes. As they ticked by, my skin felt like it was on fire as the simmer of anger turned into rage, and it prickled at my skin, urging me to kill. I took a few deep breaths to try and rein in the all-consuming urges that made me want to spill my father's blood. I needed to be smart about this, and shoving him under a moving tractor tire was an entertaining idea, but it wasn't smart.

Four hours later, I'd managed to pull myself together and once more seemed perfectly calm as I drove the tractor into the shade of the old barnyard.

"We should get the market pigs separated and ready for the truck tomorrow morning. The driver said he'd be here early," my father said as I shut the tractor down. All I wanted was a cold shower and a sandwich, and the idea of dealing with the fucking pigs was not on my list.

"Are you serious? We've been out here all day."

'Besides, I have plans that involve the neighbor's dog. The animal keeps wandering onto the property and shitting on the lawn. Plus, I figured that would give me some relief and help me let go of the urge to kill you.' I thought to myself.

"Yes, I'm serious. Go grab us a couple of waters and apples, and I'll go get the gates set up."

This man was pushing his luck. I'd already reined myself in once today. Twice may become a problem. I stomped away from him and aimed for the house. My hands were balled into fists as I pictured grabbing a knife and slitting his throat when I returned to the barn.

My anger turned to my brother with each step I took toward the house. How exactly had Abel managed to get out of working with the hay again? Oh yes, that's right, he was pretending to be stupid and was sitting in summer school. I wished I could be as skilled as he was with emotional manipulation. I didn't have it in me. It took great effort to hold the proper emotional reaction in place for long periods, but Abel could—the fucker. So now he was able to relax and not be here, doing this farm shit. I would have to find a way to pay him back for that.

Mother was in full baking mode when I stepped into the kitchen and was humming to the radio. I made sure that the door didn't make a sound as I closed it behind me and stared at the back of the woman that gave birth to me. I was supposed to feel love and respect, or a bond with her at the very least. I felt none of that. To me, she was nothing more than a husk of annoyance.

The dress she was wearing was standard country wife, summer dress attire for the area. The little yellow flowers and her hair pinned up gave the impression of the perfect little housewife, but I knew better. She'd been fucking my father's best friend for years. They practi-

cally flaunted it under his nose at parties if you paid attention. Paying attention to details was what I did best.

Making sure I stayed out of her visual range, I wandered to the fridge and grabbed a couple of water bottles. I purposely let the door slam back into place and smirked as my mother jumped and screamed. She spun around, and I made the best oops face I could. The I'm sorry face was the hardest for me to pull off, but she seemed to believe the act as she gave a nervous little giggle and then smiled.

"Cain, you scared the bejesus out of me." The woman fanned herself as she sighed. "Where's your father at? Dinner will be done in an hour."

Do you really fucking care? That was what I wanted to ask, but instead, I tried another one of my new emotional skits. I leaned against the fridge, trying to act like an annoyed teenager.

"He wants to sort the market pigs tonight. We will be a few hours yet," I grumbled and rolled my eyes.

My mother wiped her hands on her apron and picked up the very same knife that had landed me in therapy. I watched her wrist movements and how easily the blade slid through the potato. Skin was much easier to slice. My nostrils flared as the image of my mother bleeding out all over that cutting board and then slipping to the floor with her eyes glassy like a rag doll came to mind. My cock stirred, and I had to look away before I became any more aroused.

"Please don't lean up against anything until you've had a shower. You're completely covered in chaff and dirt." She pointed the knife at me, and my cock twinged again.

I sucked in a deep breath as I wondered what it would feel like to lunge forward and force her hands to stab herself. Would she look shocked? Would she scream? Would she beg for me not to kill her?

"Fine. I better go before dad comes looking for me."

I grabbed a pair of apples from the bowl on the table and let the screen door slam on the way out. I smiled wide as my mother yelled at me not to slam the door. Small things were sometimes just as amusing as the killing itself.

At one time, we only had a couple of the stinky pigs, but father wanted to increase that number and make it a larger part of the farm, so we were currently up to a hundred animals, all of them in different stages of growth. Like I didn't have enough chores to do between the chickens, cows, and cash crops. Now I had to deal with more pigs.

As I walked through the outer part of the barn, I could hear the clanging of the metal gates my father was setting up. He arranged them to make the necessary run to herd the two-hundred-pound animals to lead them into the slaughter truck. Reaching the edge of the first set of pens, I spotted my father in with the forty or so market pigs and leaned against the gate.

"I have your water and apple," I called out and held them up.

"Thanks." My father took a step in my direction and paused, his face contorting into a grimace of pain.

His gloved hand grabbed his left arm, and I stood a little straighter. I knew the signs of a heart attack. I'd watched Mr. Baker, a guy who lived down the street, have one. He'd been yelling at me for cutting through his backfield to get to school faster when he made the exact face my father was now. Fascinated, I'd walked over to Mr. Baker to see what was happening. As I'd squatted down near his writhing body, he reached for me and begged me to call for help, but I didn't. I enjoyed watching him die far too much. I stayed in the same position like I was staring at a work of art until he took his last breath. I watched his eyes glass over as his body finally gave in and shut down. I'd never been so turned on in my life.

"Ah," my father groaned and grabbed for the side of the pen. "Son, something's wrong," my father said, stating the obvious like I couldn't see him.

My head cocked to the side as I watched my father struggle. Sweat poured off his forehead like he was in a rain shower, the glistening enhancing the lines of agony on his face. "Help, me son," my father begged as he went to his knees.

I smiled wide. Oh, Abel was going to be pissed he missed this—the thought making my soul smile with evil glee.

"You were right, Dad. There is no fixing what I am."

Wide, terrified eyes locked with mine as he gasped and then collapsed face-first in the pig shit. This was fucking great. I couldn't have planned this any better, and the little bit of residual excitement from watching my mother in the kitchen was increasing steadily with his continued struggles.

The pigs that had been ignoring him now turned to his twitching body and nosed at him with their snouts. If this had happened in the baby pens, I might have been tempted to jump in and pretend to want to help, but these were the market pigs. When in a mass of fifty, the animals could devour a full-size man in a few days. People thought that pigs were cute, but they were actually one of the most dangerous farm animals other than the bull. They had massive teeth and extremely strong jaws that could crush bone. Also, they were very intelligent and happy to eat anything, like a tiger shark swimming in the ocean.

When I heard the ripping and tearing of material, my hand slid off the gate and found the zipper to my jeans. At the first sound of my father's bones being crushed in the powerful jaws, I pulled out my cock. The scent of blood drew in the rest of the pen, and the pigs began to swarm like sharks.

My strokes started slow, but the image of muscle and flesh hanging from the pigs' mouths as they fought for a mouthful of my father was too much, and my speed increased. I gripped the gate hard to keep myself upright as yet another bloody snout lifted in the air to swallow down a gory piece of flesh with hair attached. A groan that verged on a yell escaped my lips as I came the hardest I'd ever come to date.

"Oh, that was good," I mumbled as my heart rate returned to normal, and I stuffed my cock back into my pants. Maybe these pigs were useful after all. I smirked at the thought. Cracking open the lid on the water, I chugged it down and poured the last bit on my face as I prepared to act out the performance of a lifetime.

Oh yes, Abel would be pissed he missed this. I snickered as I sauntered toward the house.

The memory made me smile. I'd spent many a night since that day replaying my father's death and jerked off every time. I sighed and took a sip of my latest coffee while patiently waiting. Abel kept bugging me that I needed to find a way to make cars break down in the area I patrolled, but that seemed too much like a risk that didn't need to be taken.

There were always lots of people that broke down, and besides, part of the fun was the roulette game of not knowing who I was going to get. Someone like good old Peter from this morning would find themselves on my table, but if they seemed decent and didn't piss me off like the old man from the other night, then I'd let them live. Didn't mean I'd let them live if I came across them again, but it was a bit of a sorting system. It was simply not possible or logical to kill everyone whose vehicle I towed. Unlike most killers or even my brother, I didn't really have a type. Well, that wasn't entirely true. I loved to collect unique eyes.

Headlights rounded the curve down the road, and I knew they would break down before they slowly passed my waiting spot. They were driving slowly, and the man was rocking back and forth in the driver's seat like that might help keep the car going. He already had one point on the idiot scale, and I hadn't spoken to him yet.

My bet was that he'd run out of fuel. The next service station was two miles away, but the car wasn't going to make it because it was sputtering to a stop. I watched the vehicle jerk a few more times, and then he pulled over to the shoulder, the brake lights turning on.

The question became, did I get paid, or did this one find an untimely end? So many choices. I sneered as I drove the truck out onto the road and pulled the vehicle up behind him.

Showtime.

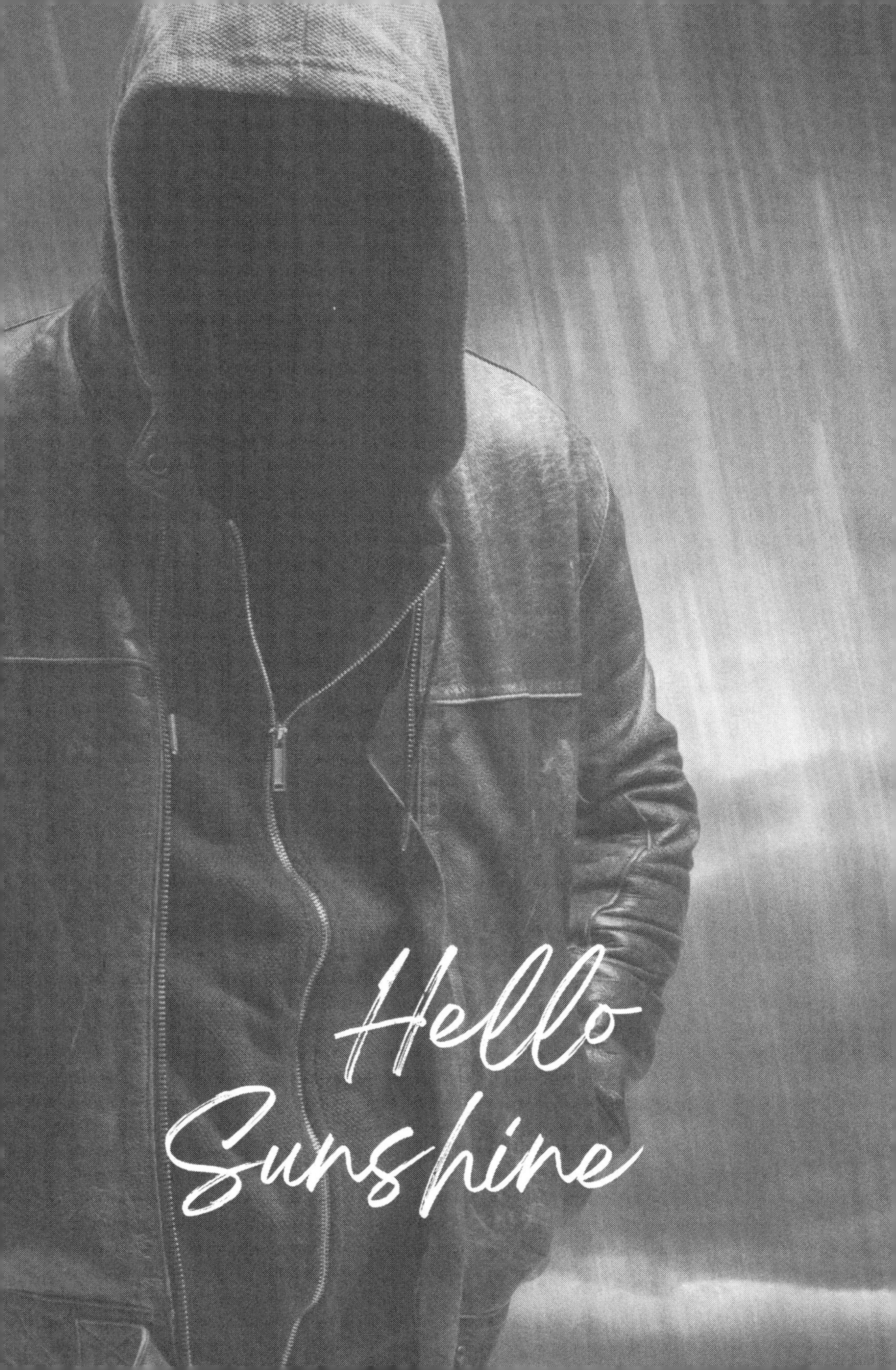
Hello
Sunshine

CHAPTER 7

CAIN

I'd been right about the gas, but as it turned out, the alternator was shot as well. That made for an excellent payday. I quickly hooked the vehicle up and dropped the man off for an extra fee before taking the thing back to the shop.

When Abel pulled in with his taxi, I was wiping car grime off my hands on a rag. Before he stepped out of the car, I knew he had gifts for us.

Time to play.

"Woo-fucking-hoo, brother!" Abel began crowing like a rooster as he shimmied around the front of the bright yellow car. His hips wiggled back and forth, his low-cut jeans and open shirt making him look like he was at a beach dance party. "You just wait 'til you see what I got for us."

"Must be good for you to break out the dancing."

"Right? This new slick style is really drawing the hotties in," he said and ran his hand down his abs while he stuck his tongue between his fingers to wave at me.

I rolled my eyes. "I highly doubt that is the reason they got in your car."

"Ha! What do you know?" At one point in my life, I would've begun spouting off all the facts I did know, but now I realized it was a rhetorical question. He wasn't actually looking for a response. Abel was kind of like a fly. Unless it smelled like shit, or in this case, blood and pussy, he lost interest. "So...what about you? Did you have any luck?"

"I wasn't out hunting," I said.

Abel leaned against the car I was working on and pulled a bag of sunflower seeds out of his pocket. He tossed a handful into his mouth before offering some to me. I didn't like the feeling of the little shells in my mouth and then having to spit them on the ground. It was a disgusting habit.

"I'm working, aren't I?"

"Oh, fuck off," Abel snorted and spat shells on my shop floor.

"You better be planning on sweeping that shit up, or I'll make you lick it up." I made sure my tone was calm, but I knew I couldn't keep the glare out of my stare. He knew it wasn't an empty threat. I'd made him lick up a couple of things a time or two. There came a point in any relationship when someone had to become the alpha. With Abel's unpredictable behavior, I needed to take control, or we would've been caught before we'd even gotten started. Our babysitter had been a great example of his lack of control or long-term game thought process. It was also the first fuck up and mess I'd had to clean up after my brother, but it certainly hadn't been the last.

He sighed like I was the biggest pain in his ass, which I probably was, but he grabbed the broom and swept the little shells out of the open bay door. I liked cleanliness in my workspaces, and every tool had its place, which drove my brother crazy. But there was a sick little sense of satisfaction in that knowledge.

"They're all swept. Now tell me what did you get up to," Abel asked, and all I could do was stare as he stepped over the handle of the broom and began stroking the wood like it was a massive cock between his legs.

"You worry me sometimes, brother." Making my way over to the worktable, I folded the rag and put it in the dirty pile. "I found the girl I mentioned."

"No shit? That was fast."

"It helped that her boyfriend or husband—I don't know what his perceived relationship status with her might be—but he drives an expensive vehicle. Oddly enough, she found me." I turned to face my brother.

Abel stopped his now make-believe cowboy roping routine that he was doing to stare at me. "Say that again?"

"She walked into the diner where I was eating breakfast."

"Damn man, that shit is meant to be, like the cosmos were making it happen," Abel smiled wide. I didn't think he could look any more ridiculous, yet he somehow managed it.

"I don't think the cosmos had anything to do with it, but it was fortuitous, and don't think I don't see you mocking me, you prick." I glanced over at Abel, who laughed. I smirked at him. "I'm in my planning stage, but this is not going to be a fast grab."

"Oh?"

"She's going through Quantico to become an FBI agent." I turned to lean against the workbench and Abel's face transformed from shocked to hysterical laughing until he had tears pouring down his cheeks.

"Now that shit is karma, a Quantico girl," Abel smacked his hand off his knee. "Ooh, dear brother, you're gonna need a good plan, but that is shit for another day. You wanna go play?"

"I'll meet you at your place. I just want to finish cleaning up and have a shower."

Abel spun in a circle and put the broom by the door before meandering with a strange shuffle step toward his car. "Don't be too long, brother or all the fun will be over before you arrive." He opened the car door and stopped before getting in. "See, that is how you properly share," he said, giving me a grin.

I really should've smothered him as a child.

KIRBY

"Ahhhh," the kid screamed from behind me. His voice was so high-pitched I cringed, and I was pretty sure the dogs on the next road over heard him. "I want to go home!"

I glanced back at the mother, who looked like she'd been through a war zone. I tried to help by offering her my best reassuring smile as she tried to calm her son, who was in the middle of a temper tantrum.

I turned my attention back to the store owner behind the counter. Why was finding a simple job so difficult? I'd decided to stay and work hard at my studies, but I needed to make enough money to buy anything I wanted apart from school. One more thing for my mother to bitch about, but it would help me feel less trapped.

"Look, I'm sorry. I'd love to hire you, but I don't have enough work right now," she said. "But I do know that the fancy café down the street, *Mode*, is looking for help, one of their baristas left or something."

I gave her a smile. "Thank you. I'll go check them out."

Pushing my way out of the door of the baby clothes store, I decided it was for the best. I had no idea how people put up with that wailing. I guess it was different when it was your baby, but I'd never had the urge to have kids like other women.

I knew which café she was talking about—it was Peter's favorite. They imported beans from all over the world and ground them in-house, but a single cup of coffee could set you back fifteen dollars. Much to Peter's chagrin, I was happy with a can of instant, so I'd never understood the need to come here. However, I would make an exception if they paid me money to be here.

I pushed open the door, and the smell of coffee and fresh baked goods flowed over me like a warm blanket. I sighed as I took a deep breath of the amazing aroma. Cinnamon, apples, pumpkin, coffee, and chocolate all permeated my senses. Okay, I could admit the place smelled awesome. This might be a bad place to work, after all. My mouth was already drooling over the large selection in the display case, and I had a terrible case of a sweet tooth.

As I waited in line, I stared up at the brightly scribbled boards with what felt like an infinite number of selections and wondered how the workers memorized all of these different concoctions.

"Ooh, fresh blood." The guy behind the counter said as he looked me up and down.

"I'm sorry, what?" My eyes flicked to his name badge that boldly stated his name was Jorge.

He pursed his lips and pointed a finger at me, wiggling it up and down. "You, Babycakes, are a *Mode* virgin. I can tell." Jorge gave me a dramatic wink. "But not to worry, I'm the best at knowing what someone would want."

"Oh no, I...."

"Ah, ah, don't interrupt the creative process. I got you, girl." I lifted a brow at him as a blush crept across my cheeks. This was not how I saw this application process going.

"You're a wildling, but you keep it hidden because you feel repressed by something else in your life...could be a person, maybe a job." Jorge hesitated and then continued. "You like rich, bold flavors, but nothing too fancy and a hint of spice that will curl your toes on a cold winter's night. I know just the thing." His fingers moved quickly along the digital register, and he proceeded to smile. "That will be eleven thirty-five, please," he practically sang.

I dug around in my purse and pulled out a twenty to hand over but held onto the bill as his fingers touched it. "I'm here because I'd like to apply for the position I heard you have available, but I'll also take the coffee because I'm very curious how you guessed all that about me with one look."

A wicked smile spread across his face as he handed over my change.

"I'll never share my secret, but as far as the job goes...." Jorge tapped his beautifully manicured, hot pink nail on the counter. "Let me see to the rest of these customers, and if you're still sitting here when I'm through, we can talk about the job."

"This is your place?"

"Don't look so shocked, Sweetie."

"I'm sorry, it's just this is an awesome spot, and I wouldn't know the first thing about how to get something so successful off the ground, let alone the cost involved. I'm impressed."

Jorge smirked as his eyes traveled over my outfit. I looked down to see what he was seeing.

"Coming from one of our next super agents, I'll take that as a compliment. Your coffee will be at the end." He pointed to the girl that was busy making drinks faster than I could move my arms.

"Thanks," I said as I made my way to the end of the counter and thanked the girl working before I sat down.

This felt a lot more nerve-wracking than I thought it would, and my knee was bouncing under the table to prove it. I took a sip of the mysterious blend I'd been served and moaned softly as it touched my tongue. Okay, Jorge was good. I looked at the cup in wonder as I tried to decipher what was in it.

I played some games on my phone and read the daily news. There was another headline about the killer my mother was chasing down. Not that she talked about it much, but I'd seen the paperwork when she left it out and had taken a peek a time or two. The case was fascinating. I found it interesting that the article about another discarded body was on page three while the latest celebrity news was front page worthy. They certainly didn't want it to be in your face that this person was out killing and dropping off bodies as often as garbage was picked up.

"You stayed," Jorge said, startling me out of my thoughts. "Here, I brought you a refill on the house." He sat a cup of the same coffee down, and I smiled wide.

"Thanks again."

"You can call me Jorge, but some days I prefer Jorgina. You have a problem with that?" He pointed to the name tag that I'd already noticed.

I lifted a shoulder and let it drop. "Not in the slightest, but you may need to tell me which you prefer that day until I get to know you better."

One elegant eyebrow raised as he bit his lip. The lip liner and gloss were so perfect that I had a jealous moment staring at them. "Honey, I like you. Alright, so give me the goods, and please tell me you have prior experience as a barista," Jorge asked.

I shook my head no as I took a sip of the hot drink. I think I was officially addicted. "No, I don't."

"Do you have waitressing experience?"

"A little. I worked at a Denny's for a couple of months."

Jorge sat back in the chair, the metallic silver tips of his stylish haircut shining under the lights. "How about baking experience?"

I sighed and sat the cup down. "I'll be honest, Jorge, I don't have any real experience working anywhere. The closest I've come to a real job was the part-time one I had at Denny's, and then there was a school car wash fundraiser I ran. I managed to make more money with my wet T-shirt than I did cleaning cars, so I'm not sure that counts. I'm also great if you want something painted because I've done a few murals for money."

I picked up one of the tube-styled sugar packs and spun it between my fingers as I continued to speak. "You're right, though. I'm attending Quantico. And it's kind of frowned upon to work while you're attending school, but I'm looking to branch out and do more than school all day and workout and study all night. I'll go insane with only those activities. This must sound ridiculous, but the moral of that really long story is that I sincerely want this job."

"You say you want to branch out. What exactly does that mean, and why my coffee shop?"

I fidgeted in my seat and looked around as if my mother had ears everywhere and might hear me say this. With her, anything was possible. "Attending Quantico has never been what I wanted, and although I'm dedicated to finishing the program, I don't think I'll make it as an agent."

"Hmm, I'm not sure this is the right job for you to cut your teeth on, Darlin'. We are very busy all the time, so training someone that has no experience is a difficult task, and I can't pay anywhere near the wage you'd probably be expecting." Jorge said as he started to stand.

"How about if I work for free for a week as a trial? I learn fast, am efficient, and I'm good with people. Please, all I'm asking for is a shot. If you don't think I can cut it after a week, then let me go, and if you think I can, then you can put me on the books."

Jorge tapped his chin as he thought. "What time are you off school?"

"I made up a schedule," I said and pulled out the paper with my available days and times out of my bag to hand over.

His eyes scanned over the month-long calendar. "Alright, I'll give you a chance. I'll see you at three tomorrow, and wear comfortable footwear and black pants. I'll provide the top."

A squeal was on the tip of my tongue, but I managed to hold it back. This would be the first time I'd have something that was completely mine, and the excitement was bubbling in my chest. "Thank you, Jorge. I promise you won't regret this."

"We'll see about that, Darlin'. Toodles."

I gulped down the rest of the coffee and knew I was going to be up all night between the high-powered octane I'd just drank and my excitement, but I didn't care. If this meant a step toward gaining a bit of real independence from my mom, it was all worth it.

It was times like this I really missed Dad. He would've been happy for me and helped me celebrate. I picked up my phone to call him and stopped as I figured out the time zone difference to London. It was like one in the morning there, and I put my phone back in my jacket pocket. It had been hard when he stopped calling every day, but it became even harder when he remarried and moved halfway around the world. Dad always said he loved me the same and that nothing had changed, but I felt the strain between us. He looked at me and saw another man's child. I was the product of his wife stepping out on him and the constant reminder of her infidelity.

I waved to Jorge as I left and marched down the street with my head held high. Was this a step back from becoming an FBI agent? Maybe, but it wasn't like I'd dropped out. Besides, I wanted to do something I was passionate about and not forced to do. The question was, what was going to make me happy?

Hello
Sunshine

CHAPTER 8

CAIN

Abel's house was on the other side of the property from the original farmhouse that I occupied. Although I could just make out his house through the trees and walk the path we created between the two homes, I chose to drive around and found Abel in the basement of his play area. He called it his 'games room,' which I admit was amusing. The muffled sound of screams and thumping music reached my ears as I placed my hand on the heavy basement door.

Having two houses was a much better fit for us. This way, we weren't tripping over each other, and my annoyance with his slobbish habits and irregular schedule didn't start fights. Unlocking the door, I winced as the song "Blame It On The Rain" blared so loudly that my eardrums wept and wanted to bleed.

I was going to need a stiff drink to deal with that shit. Closing the door again, I went to the kitchen to get a drink. I preferred a strong drink when I helped work over Abel's trophies but liked to remain stone-cold sober for my own.

"Disgusting," I mumbled as I grabbed a garbage bag, swiped all the empty take-out containers into the black plastic, and then tied it shut.

Staring at the mountain of dirty dishes, I had to stop myself from cleaning them and knew that I was going to be seeing that mess in my nightmares. Well, if I had nightmares, I would see that gross pile. In fact, it would probably be the star.

I grabbed the bottle of whiskey and two glasses before returning to the basement door. The door relocked when it closed behind me, so I made my way down. The noisy creaking stairs and the clunk of my boots would've announced my presence, except you couldn't hear anything over the music. Reaching the bottom, I took in the scene and saw that Abel hadn't wasted any time and was well underway in breaking the two girls he'd nabbed.

Abel spotted me standing at the bottom of the stairs and jogged over to greet me like the perfect host. He wrapped an arm around my shoulders and maneuvered me toward his nightly fun. He pulled a remote out of somewhere and turned the music down to a reasonable level.

"Brother, I'm so happy you made it. Look what I got for us," he said like I hadn't seen him less than an hour ago.

My eyes scanned over the set of twin girls that were tied up with thick leather cuffs. As was Abel's way, he liked to start off having his toys face one another, letting them see what they would lose if they followed through or the pain they would feel when they didn't. Their wide, unblinking stares made me feel warm inside.

"What's on the menu tonight," I asked as I poured my brother a glass and handed it over.

"I'm so glad you asked," he said, taking the glass.

I proceeded to take up my usual perch in the corner to watch the show as Abel went to grab something. He came back and held up the power drill. The end had been converted into the biggest dildo I had ever seen. It would certainly make a horse blush, but the green drywall screws attached to it made me grin.

"You really are creative, brother," I said, and he smiled wide at the compliment.

I'd learned from the time we started playing like this together that Abel was much easier to keep focused and contained when he felt I was impressed. I had no desire to earn my brother's praise, but he seemed to thrive off the few words I offered him.

Abel reminded me of one of dad's old high-spirited horses that liked to take off while riding the animal. I could picture Abel with a set of reins and a bit in his mouth but not behaving unless there was the promise of praise and a sweet apple at the end of the ride. I guess most of the time—I was his reins. If I weren't, he'd be wild all the time. His impulse control was somewhere between zero and none, so I became his voice of reason. If I didn't play that role, I would need to kill him, and I preferred not to do the latter. When it came to bonds that didn't break, I knew ours would last through almost anything— but there was the odd exception to the rule. Like Abel doing things that would get us caught was high on that list.

"What do you think, brother? Is their bond as unbreakable as ours," Abel asked. He circled the women, who looked to be in their late twenties.

"Please don't do this."

"Now, now, Jess," Abel scolded. "Didn't we already have a discussion about begging? Didn't I already explain the rules of this game?"

The one named Jess nodded her head, tears a steady stream down her bloodied face. Abel turned his attention to me.

"Brother, I'm sorry I didn't introduce you to our guests. This one is Jess, which is short for Jessica, but she prefers Jess." Abel yanked on the woman's golden hair, and she screamed as he twisted her head at an odd angle to show me her face. "And this is Jacqueline, but she prefers Jackie. You know, I guess that's one thing we can thank our parents for. Can you imagine having to do this fucking stupid same-letter name thing with us?"

I gave him a nod. "So true."

"What do you want from us," Jackie asked, and my lip curled up as her eyes met mine.

"Why do people ask such stupid questions when they already know they're going to die? I've yet to get an answer to this question. Can you enlighten me, Jackie?" Her lower lip trembled as her sky-blue eyes locked with mine, but she didn't say anything. "No answer? I didn't think so. No one can answer that question, but tell me, Jackie, why do *you* think we're doing this?"

She shook her head back and forth, but the answer was there in her eyes. She knew. She knew what we were and why we did what we did. She simply didn't want to say it out loud. Thinking that there is a monster under the bed and saying it aloud made the situation far more real.

A thunderous crack echoed over the next 80s hit on my brother's 'Kill' playlist. Jackie whimpered as Jess's head snapped to the side with the blow.

"Answer my brother, or your sister gets it again," Abel said and raised his hand to emphasize his threat.

Jackie's big blue eyes looked at Abel and then back to me.

"Because you like it," she blurted out and then cried harder as the words she'd spoken sank home.

"Ding, ding, ding, we have a winner! What does Jackie get Cain?" Abel looked over at me and smirked.

"I think she's won the right to earn her freedom back," I said and loved that her eyes lit up with hope. The kill was always so much sweeter when they thought there was hope.

"Well, alright then, who doesn't like a good game?" Abel leaned over and undid the bindings holding Jess securely to the chair. As the last buckle was released, she predictably bolted for the stairs. I watched her run up the stairs, her feet loud on the wood, but I smiled as she collided with the door.

"Run, Jess," Jackie yelled, and I wondered how long her sisterly sacrificing gesture would last once she saw what Abel planned to do.

The door rattled as Jess continuously rammed herself into it, and I could picture just how fast her little rabbit heart was racing in her chest. The fight or flight panic made the decision for her even though she had no more runway to stretch her rabbity legs.

"Don't run away, Little Rabbit," Abel said, putting voice to the words from my own mind.

The sweet sing-song sound to his voice made Jackie shudder in her bindings, her head dropping in defeat. I memorized the way her body shook as she broke down with acceptance as it slowly settled over her. She'd better get used to that feeling. It was only going to get worse from here.

Sipping my drink, I watched Abel like my favorite television episode. The hysterical screaming began as one heavy boot landed on the stairs, shaking it like the T-Rex in the Jurassic Park movie. "Come back, Little Raaaaabit."

Another heavy thump and more hysterical banging began. I almost spit out my drink as Abel ran the rest of the way up the stairs yelling, "Booga, Booga, Booga."

"Awww, come on," Abel whined and marched back down the stairs holding Jess in his arms. "Little twit just passed out. I hadn't even gotten to do my best impressions."

He stomped past me with the limp girl in his arms and made his way to the one-of-a-kind table I'd made for him. I preferred my table over this one, but I had to admit this piece Abel had me create for him had its benefits. The thick steel rings I'd welded to the sides allowed him to attach prey in any position he desired.

I'd watched him more than once turn the rings and those attached to them into a game of Twister. The game never ended well for one of them. Abel dropped the girl down face first with her feet and ass hanging over the edge at the perfect fucking height.

I glanced back at Jackie, who continued to bawl her eyes out. The sobbing would normally be annoying, but the agony on her features was sweet tonight. She had a good, pained look on her face. She was one of those pretty girls that made ugly crying seem cute.

Within moments Jess was secured to the metal surface, and with a few quick flicks of Abel's knife, the stretchy pants she was wearing ripped away. Abel didn't bother to take the time to get lube before he slammed his cock into the unconscious girl. She only stirred awake as Abel sang loudly to the next song that poured through the speakers as he pounded into her unprepared ass. I assumed it would be a hell of a way to wake up.

The louder Jess screamed, the faster Abel fucked her, and I knew by the look on my brother's face he was just getting warmed up. I watched him out of the corner of my eye, my own cock slowly hardening with the visual of the rough play. He'd wrapped his hand in her long hair and pulled her off the table as far as the bindings would allow her to go. He yelled, "ye ha." He had a flare for theatrics that I'd never cared to use or master as he had.

As entertaining as watching Abel fuck the girl was, the look on Jackie's face made my cock stand at attention. She liked the show. She was trying hard to hide it, but the subtle squirm in her body posture and the way her eyes darted to her sister had me unzipping my pants. Jess's original pained-filled wails had shifted. Now, they were a cross between a blubbering that was most likely caused by self-loathing as she grunted and moaned each time Abel sank into her pale ass.

"No, please, I don't want to...ahh," Jess wailed loudly as Abel made her come. Even I could admit that Abel was good with his cock. He was to his dick what a painter was to his brushes.

"Come on, brother, join me," Abel called out as he nodded toward my hand, stroking my cock.

"If you insist." Setting my drink down, I made my way to Jackie, and she whimpered as I squatted in front of her. "What do you think, Jackie? Would you like to join your sister in the fun?"

She shook her head no, but I could smell her arousal, and the wet spot that had formed on her pink yoga pants screamed she was lying. She tensed as I reached between her knees that she could not close and watched her face carefully as my finger brushed along the hardened peak of her clit. She bit her lip and closed her eyes as she looked away, trying to deny what her body obviously wanted.

"It's terrible, isn't it? To want something you shouldn't? To be something that others think is disgusting?" Jackie whimpered and sucked her lower lip into her mouth. "I understand, Jackie. You didn't ask for this any more than I asked to be born the way I am, yet here we are together." My voice was soft and a little rough from the whiskey, but with each word I spoke, her breathing picked up a little more.

Her chest rose and fell quicker as her heart rate spiked. I ran my finger up and down the damp area of her pants, just hard enough that she'd feel it but not hard enough for any real satisfaction.

I'd become a master at watching all the small tells the human body gave off. Very few ever bothered to learn them. It was sad, really, but it was those tells that I watched now. The ones that Jackie didn't want me to see. The ones that embarrassed her and made her feel ashamed as much as they turned her on. Those were the feelings I wanted to tap into like a parasite.

Jess picked that moment to scream. "Oh fuck, I'm coming again, oh fuck me, please don't stop."

Jackie's eyes snapped open. An almost feral look overtook her as her head snapped around to stare at her sister's face, which was in the throws of carnal lust.

That was the look I'd been waiting for from her.

Yes, she would willingly beg me for whatever I did until the end, and that was the real power. I immensely enjoyed all sorts of physical and mental games with my prey, but the ones that begged for me to do what I wanted while they clung to hope were the ones that entertained me the most.

I increased the pressure just enough, making Jackie gasp and her thighs quiver around my hand. Abel didn't care about things like consent. In reality, neither did I, but I craved power more than sex. To watch them slowly break and give up their morals and ethical code that would normally have them running from me...that was better than any release.

The sounds of Abel and Jess as he continued to fuck her were too much for Jackie to ignore, and a sheen of sweat broke out on her forehead and upper lip. The tears that had been traveling down her cheeks were now dry. They had been replaced with just a hint of drool as her body begged her for more while her mind screamed no. All the while, I continued to stimulate her with my hand. She swung her eyes back to mine and bit her lower lip.

"Please don't do this," she said, then gasped and jerked against the restraints.

"You want it too, don't you? You want me to make you scream like your sister while you come all over my cock." She opened her mouth and closed it again. "No one is ever going to know that you let yourself go and enjoyed the sins of your body."

Standing, I leaned over her until I could whisper in her ear. That was when I deliberately stopped playing with her clit. Jackie whimpered and wiggled slightly in her seat as her body betrayed her once more.

"You need to say the words to me, Jackie. Unlike my brother, I don't take what I want. I need you to say that you want me."

The nervous and sexual energy vibrations pouring off her body were a sweet elixir. Her chest rose and fell in time to the rapid beat of her heart. Each time her chest rose, her tits would hit the charms I had hanging around my neck.

"I promise you'll scream just like your sister," my breath fanned her ear. "Say the words. Say you want me to fuck you hard. Fuck you until you come like no one has made you before. Say the words Jackie, say them, or I go back to my seat in the corner."

The final threads of her control slipped as I slid my tongue along her ear and gave her earlobe a nip.

"Oh fuck," Jess wailed. "Not again, I can't come again...oh fuck, yes, yes, I'm coming."

"Man, this bitch is hot, bro. Even her pussy is like a sopping furnace." Abel was in the process of taking turns with each of her holes.

When he got into a good rhythm, he could do one thrust in one hole and one in the next so fast that it was impressive, and the girls would beg him never to stop. I flicked my eyes from Jackie to the action at the table and rolled my eyes as I caught sight of the stupid fucking tattoo. 'Scrub the P,' was staring back at me.

"Alright then, Jackie," I said softly, pulled my hand away from the sopping wet spot between her legs, and stood straight. I made sure that my open zipper showed off my cock right in front of her face and almost laughed as she licked her lips.

"Yes," she said softer than a mouse squeak.

"Yes, what?"

I stepped away to pull the T-shirt off over my head. I wasn't the roid-buff-jock type, but I kept myself in great shape. I needed to work out and stay fit when my prey might run and fight. I smirked and lifted my brow in the way that girls found sexy. The look promised to back up my words as I ran my hands down the tight eight-pack on display. Jackie's mouth fell open, her pupils dilating as her eyes drifted up and down my body.

Her basic animal instinct had fully kicked in, and I reminded myself of a worm wriggling on a cast line as my hips moved in time to the next song. She opened her mouth, and before a word was spoken, I knew what she'd ask for, what she wanted. I could see the moment of weakness in her eyes, and just like that, I held the keys to her personal kingdom.

"Fuck me, please fuck me." She looked over at her sister once more. Her breathing now labored pants as she leaned as far forward as she could in the chair restraints. "Like that, please."

"Are you sure? You don't even know me," I teased and pulled my cock out for her to see. My hand ran up and down the hard length, and she groaned, her face turning as feral as I'd seen any of the prey we caught.

"Yes, I'm sure, please."

"And you're going to be a good girl and get into position on your own, or am I going to have to chase you? I don't feel like chasing you and will not be as nice if I have to."

"I won't run. I'll get into position, I swear."

There was always the chance she'd have a change of heart once the bindings were set free, but I didn't really care one way or the other. For me, it was always a win, win. If she tried to run, I'd torture her until Abel decided to kill her. But she'd have more fun if she didn't run until Abel decided to kill her. I bent over and slipped the thick leather buckles free. She rubbed at her wrists, the skin irritated from her earlier pulling, but as suspected, the prospect of wild sex and the freedom to be a porn star was too much for her hormone-riddled synapses to handle.

I pointed to the metal table that her sister was still grunting wildly on, and she jumped up and practically ran into place. Abel laughed as the girl flopped down, mirroring her sister's position on the other side.

"Take your pants off," I said and then sighed as I waited for Jackie to kick her shoes off and pull the pink fabric and the floss thong before getting back into position.

I took my time walking around her and fastening the new bindings into place. I wanted her to remember that she willingly held herself like this for me to strap into position. There was going to come a moment when she regretted that decision.

I ripped open a condom from the massive collection Abel kept in a fishbowl and glared at the lime green condom with bunny ears on the end. I shook my head at the ridiculous design before sliding it on and lining myself up to her pussy. She reminded me of the mares in heat. They'd walk around with their tail in the air and their pussy winking and squirting scent to attract a stallion. Jackie's hole was doing the same thing, which only confirmed how much she wanted this now that she'd conceded to being a horny slut.

I stuffed myself in with a hard thrust to the chorus of swearing that ended in a shuddering moan. Grabbing Jackie's hips, I closed my eyes and pummeled my cock into her as hard as possible.

I wondered if my mystery violet-eyed beauty would fight back hard or if she would beg for me as this girl had. Sunshine seemed like she would do both, and that thought sent a shudder through my body. I was vaguely aware of Jackie screaming and coming, but her pleasure was of no interest to me.

"You have a loose pussy," I growled and smacked Jackie's ass hard. "Use your muscles and clench harder."

"Smack me again," she wailed, and so I did until her ass was as red as my hand felt, but it was still like rubbing myself against a wet noodle.

Pulling out, I lined myself up with her tight ass and didn't bother to prepare her as I pushed myself in. She screamed now, but they were wails of pain as I shoved my way inside her obviously virgin hole. She'd adjust. They always did.

"That's much better. You need to work on your cock grip," I said.

The pressure was a much better fit, and as the minutes ticked on, I could feel my own release nearing.

"How close," Abel asked through gritted teeth, his muscles straining as he focused on holding off his orgasm until we could come together.

He had some weird kinks I didn't get but went along with because it was easier. You had to pick your battles with Abel. Worrying about him wanting to come at the same time was low on my priority list.

With each thrust, Jackie screamed louder as she found her third orgasm. As I heard her high-pitched scream, another face appeared in my mind. Those violet eyes stared into mine as Sunshine came screaming for me. The image was unexpected, and the response even more unusual, but I didn't question it as my balls strained.

"Now," I said, and as if I'd pushed a button on Abel, we mimicked the same pose as our cocks unloaded into our prospective holes.

I held still as I waited for my dick to soften, pulled out, and disposed of the condom in the bathroom toilet. I wandered over to my original perch, but there was no point doing up the zipper. I'd be hard again soon when Abel turned the girl's pleasure-filled experience into a whole new game filled with horror and agony. Abel let out a whoop of satisfaction, his body shaking like he was a dog before he wandered around to lean on the table. His stare went between Jess and Jackie and back again.

"I was going to give you the chance to win back your freedom Jess, but you had to try and run, so instead, I think I'm going to give your sister here the option." Abel turned his head to look at Jackie. "What do you say, Jackie? Do you want to be fucked again and earn your freedom," he asked.

"Yes," she said without hesitation, which made me smile.

"Very well." Abel un-fastened her bindings, and she smiled wide as she stared up at Abel, thinking she would get to fuck him now.

But the smile slowly slipped away like ice melting in the middle of a heat wave when Abel held out the special dildo drill for her to take. Her hand shook as she took the contraption and stared at the sharp screws that protruded from the entire head of the thick, fake cock.

"What do you want me to do with this?" Her voice was quiet, but luckily the songs were in the midst of switching, so the room was silent except for her innocent question.

"What do you think I want you to do?"

"I...I don't know," she mumbled as Abel took her by the arm and made her stand behind her sister's well-fucked ass.

"You girl are gonna use it on yo sista," he mocked.

"What?" the two girls said in unison. I gulped another large mouthful of whiskey as the show continued. "I can't do that. She's my sister," Jackie whined, the energy in the room shifting from fun and dirty to nervous and terrified in the blink of an eye.

My brother's brand of twisted manic pleasure was dancing in his eyes. The perverse pleasure of breaking the family bond between the two girls was laid bare to the naked eye as Jess's raised ass.

"Jackie, you have a choice, you either use that on your sister and do whatever else I tell you to do, or you'll end up back on the table right now and have this shoved up your ass."

The Michael Jackson song "Beat It" chose that moment to come on, and I had to laugh.

I didn't laugh hard often, the emotion tended to sit on the periphery of my mind, but the moment did strike me as amusing.

"I love her. I can't hurt her," Jackie cried, and Abel yanked her arm hard to drag her to the other side of the table. "No, no, no, no," she begged and pulled on her arm.

Jackie swung the drill at Abel's head, but he stepped back just in time and snatched Jackie's wrist out of the air.

The switch in Abel was instant.

He went from joking and loving the moment into a murderous place, his face darkening as he glared at Jackie.

"You'll pay for trying that," he pulled the drill out of her hands and slammed her down onto the table hard enough that it knocked the fight out of her.

Her hands and legs were quickly and efficiently attached to the table, and I smirked as she fought the restraints with all her strength. She was back to being the wild animal caught in a hunter's trap.

"Okay then, Jess, it's back to you. Do you want to make the deal?"

Jess's eyes found Jackie's, and she shook her head back and forth, but the words that tumbled from her mouth were vastly different. "I love you, sis, but I don't want to die. I'll do it."

"What?" Jackie squealed, her eyes wide as her fighting reached new heights. Abel grinned and unfastened Jess's straps.

"This is a twist I didn't see coming," Abel exclaimed as he handed over the power tool. "Just for that, I'm going to fuck you again."

I noticed how he conveniently left out the part about whether she'd be alive to enjoy it this time, but you never really knew with my brother. Like the girl was walking the plank on a ship, Jess slowly marched up behind her sister, with Abel following close behind.

"No, no, no, don't do this, Jess!"

Jackie thrashed in the leather bindings, and I sat a little closer to the end of my seat. Jackie's face had warped into an interesting combination of disbelief and terror.

Tears streamed down Jess's cheeks, her face now a mask of determination as her hand inched closer to Jackie's backside despite how badly it was shaking.

"Do it. It's the only way," Abel encouraged, his eyes fixated on the spot where the drill was pointed as Jackie continued begging her sister not to do this.

The sound of the drill was loud enough to drone out the music but not loud enough to dull the screams that filled the room. Blood and once tender flesh were flung around the room. Some of the blood hit me in the face, and I picked up the napkin that my drink had been sitting on and wiped it off. The bright red streak was a sharp contrast to the white napkin.

My cock stood again as the screams reached a whole new pitch, and blood pooled on the floor.

Jackie's eyes locked with mine as she screamed, "help me."

I cupped my ear and pretended that I couldn't hear her. She screamed louder, making my lips curl up in a maniacal smile. Tonight had turned out to be quite enjoyable, after all. I sat back in the chair and reveled in the rest of the show with my cock in one hand and drink in the other.

CHAPTER 9

KIRBY

I glanced around at the people passing by that were giving Peter and me a wide birth. It started because he wanted me to come over tonight, and of course, I had to tell him that I couldn't because I had to work.

"I can't believe you took a job at a café," Peter said.

The look of disgust on his face made it obvious what he thought about my decision. I ground my teeth together and kept my face calm, but I couldn't keep the anger out of my voice. "What does it matter to you if I got a job?"

Peter stepped in close, his body language threatening. Instinctively, I took a step back even though he'd never hit me. There was an edge to him that I didn't trust when he got like this. "I don't want a girlfriend that is working at some café even if they do have great coffee. It's a bad image for my family and me, and you should've thought of that before you ran out and made that decision," he said, lowering his voice, but the heat in his tone was still very evident.

My mouth fell open, and I had the sudden urge to claw his eyes out of his head.

"Are you kidding me?" I couldn't even form the sentence I wanted to say.

I hated that about myself. Whenever I wanted to tell someone off, the words simply didn't form until hours later, and then it was too late. I envied those that could come up with amazing comebacks on the fly.

"No, I'm not kidding." Peter glared down at me.

"What's going on here?" I internally groaned as Mother came walking down the hallway, her low flats making a dull thud with each step.

I didn't want to deal with her and Peter right now, but my luck had always been terrible, so why would this situation be any different?

Peter straightened, his demeanor instantly morphing into a more relaxed version of the man he'd just been. "Mrs. Lawson, I was just telling Kirby how disrespectful I thought it was that she got a job at *Mode* down the street."

My mother looked up at Peter and then at me. I'd always loved her dark blue eyes. They were always so commanding, but my eyes were different and attracted attention. I'd been called Devil's Spawn, Witch Girl, and much worse from the time I started school for the color of my eyes. Granted, they were unusual, but people unconsciously stared longer than they should, and the entire time all I could hear were the childish chants of my youth.

"You went and got a job. Why? I thought we talked about this, and you wouldn't get a job while you were here?" My mother held her brown leather briefcase in front of her.

"I wanted to have some spending money, and you were right the other day. I have to ask you or Dad for money all the time for the simplest of things, and I don't like that. *Mode* is close by, they are willing to work around my classes, and it gives me my own money to spend on things like clothes. Before you ask, I'm not quitting Quantico. I intend on finishing my classes," I said, hoping my reasoning would resonate with my mother.

"As long as it doesn't interfere with your grades. If they begin to slip, you'll have to quit, but otherwise, I think it's a very reasonable decision," my mother said, and my mouth fell open. She never agreed with me about anything, and I had the sudden urge to run out and buy a lottery ticket.

"But, Mrs. Lawson, it's a café...." Peter was aghast.

"It is, but she is not slinging garbage, and if this helps Kirby focus on school enough to finish her classes and teaches her responsibility, then it is better for everyone. You wouldn't want her begging for money all of your life together, would you?"

The two talked as if I wasn't in the room. They didn't even look at me. Worse, they spoke to each other as if they'd already planned the wedding and the rest of my life without consulting me. I was pretty fucking positive I'd never marry this ass. Livid, I spun around and marched down its now empty hall toward the exit of the school.

"Where are you going," Peter called out.

"Work, it's my first shift, and I can't be late," I yelled, not bothering to look over my shoulder.

Peter, thankfully didn't chase me down and try to walk with me. I might've been a little too tempted to push him out in front of a moving bus. It was only a ten-minute walk, so there was no point in taking the car, and it was hard to find a parking space around the café.

Finally reaching the entrance to *Mode*, I quickly snuck inside and waved to Jorge, who was making drinks today. Another girl was working the cash register, and another seemed to be assisting him with getting the long line moving. The line was so long it had spilled out of the door.

"Hello, Kirby. I'll show you around. Brandy, can you handle this on your own for a little while," Jorge asked the petite girl with cute glasses and spiky hair in a wide range of colors.

She nodded and took over. Her hands were moving fast as she dumped out one metal thing of coffee grounds and added what looked like a flavor shot into another.

"Come on, girl, we don't have all night," Jorge said and held open a portion of the counter for me to walk through.

Once he was on the move, I had to jog to keep up with him as he gave me the rundown of the inner workings of the café. Stepping into the kitchen, I saw three more people at work. Some were mixing batter. They had to be making delicious-looking treats in the front cases. They smelled divine. The third person was making sandwiches and filling soup bowls.

The three people never even glanced our way as we walked through. I had to admit I was astonished to see the synchronized dance they did to maneuver around each other and remain totally focused on their task.

"Don't worry, dear. I'm not going to have you working in the kitchen other than to do some cleanup." Jorge stopped and pushed open another door. "This is my office. It's off limits unless we have a meeting, or you need to leave money and receipts inside."

Jorge stepped into the moderate-sized space that was as colorful as Jorge was and grabbed the simple black blouse and golf shirt off the desk. He looked me up and down before nodding.

"Yup, these should fit you." He handed them over, and I took the offering as he quickly moved on.

"This is the changing room area for the women. Men's is across the way. I suggest you don't get them mixed up. That always ends up in a few screams." He winked and gave me a warm smile as he joked. "They are not big, but you'll find an empty locker you can use. The employee washroom is inside the changerooms. Hurry up and get changed, and I'll begin showing you the basics of your job."

Jorge marched away before I could thank him. I peered into the dark changeroom and flicked on the light. He hadn't been lying about the size. The first opening was a changing stall, the next was a shower, and the last was a closed-door toilet. There was a pair of sinks, one long bench, and a half dozen lockers, all with the *Mode* logo on the front.

I took a deep breath and smiled as I tried to shake off the nervousness. This was the first real independence I'd ever had in my life. I'd decided that as soon as I could, I was going to move to London and do whatever I needed to stay with my dad and get away from my controlling mother, jerk of a boyfriend who I planned on making ex very soon, and a job I didn't want. Nothing was going to stop me from getting out of here once and for all.

CAIN

I enjoyed this part of the stalking process. I could even argue that I enjoyed it as much as licking the tears from their cheeks. It took a great deal of patience to sit and watch someone for hours and learn all their nuances. I jotted down everything, including the things that no one else would think were worth remembering. It wasn't good enough to memorize their schedule and habits. I liked knowing exactly what they were thinking and feeling at any given moment. How would they react when I wrapped a hand around their throat, would their pulse race? Would they get turned on? Would they try to cry out in fear?

To know one's prey the way I did took more effort than the average person was willing to put into a relationship. It was also why other relationships failed, whereas mine always ended the way I wanted. My brother had no appreciation for the hunt. I, on the other hand, was the breeze against your skin before my blade found your throat.

"I don't just want to pluck the wings from your back, Sunshine. I want to pull the little legs from your body until you can no longer run."

The blue pick-up truck I was using fit in with the other vehicles in the area and didn't look out of place. I tossed a few more of the peanuts I was snacking on into my mouth as I waited for my Sunshine to emerge from the beige building.

There were too many exits in this place, but I'd followed the silver Mercedes here, and it was still parked in the visitor area. It was a pretty good bet that they would come out this door. I grabbed the binoculars as more people filed out the double doors, but none of the people were her or the dink she was dating.

Someone else rushed out the door, and I pulled up the binoculars to inspect the tiny speck from a distance. My adrenaline spiked as I glimpsed her delicate features before she jogged down the stairs. I expected her to get in the silver vehicle. But instead, she marched toward the exit and turned to head along the street with the shops. I waited until I could no longer see her and pulled out of the parking spot. Not too far down the road, I spotted the guy Sunshine had come with, but he emerged with another woman.

They stood closely at his vehicle, and I watched earnestly as the man placed a hand on the woman's shoulder. She smiled at him and then walked away.

Interesting. The action wasn't inappropriate, yet I got a distinct impression that it was. I filed the information away in my brain to use later.

Pulling away from the stop sign, I continued until I spotted Sunshine as she walked into the front door of a café. Like the rest of the stores and shops in this part of the city, it still had this old worldly feel with wide cream trim surrounding the black front door. The sign above announced the place was called *Mode*.

Parking the truck, I hopped out and casually walked down the street, finding a spot to sit at a bus stop that allowed me to stare through the windows of the café. Multiple people came and went, but Sunshine didn't re-emerge. After an hour, I stood and jogged across the street. Taking advantage of the darkening sky, I pulled my hood up on the black sweater and tugged the hat down lower on my face as I slowly walked past the windows and stared inside. I paused at the menu that hung for those interested to read and pretended I was reading as I watched the people move around the space.

It was very busy in the café, and I was growing impatient with those continuously blocking my view. I was on the verge of walking inside when she stepped into my line of sight. A weird unease settled in my gut as I observed her through the window. A man that was either the owner or manager pointed at things as he spoke.

She was here for a job. Very interesting indeed. Why would a Quantico girl want to work with sludge-slinging, raging customers at a shitty-paying job?

I walked on down the street and then circled back to collect the truck. The feeling of little pins and needles started tingling in my hands. The sensation grew and physically itched at the thought of touching her skin.

My phone vibrated, and I picked it up to see a smiley emoji from Abel. I opened the text and swore.

A: Hey, bro, don't forget you still need to get the new tattoo. Oh, and I grabbed pizza for dinner.

My hand clenched on the phone at the reminder of the ridiculous tattoo I'd avoided getting. I knew I had to, though. It was my idea to make it look like we were only one person, not two of us, much to Abel's dismay. If I went back on my word now, I'd only open the door for Abel to press more boundaries, ones that undoubtedly would be a lot more dangerous.

The people who had known us as children had either died, moved, or didn't know our family well enough to speak about us one way or the other. However, I'd taken out the people that happened to be threats over time. Each one had helped fatten up my pigs before they went to slaughter. I always found the idea amusing that someone somewhere was eating a piece of one of my pigs that also happened to be part of those I'd known. If they only knew. Now, no one from our childhood remained that would know Abel and me were twins. My lip twitched up at the thought of those few that found their way to the end of my blade.

Cursing under my breath, I punched in the number for the tattoo artist we used. Mick was the only exception to my rule because I'd seen Mick for what he was. It was easy to spot the dark parts of yourself in others. Mick didn't participate in our games, but he liked to watch, and we had enough dirt on the man to take him down with us if he ever decided to open his mouth.

"Yeah, what's up?" Came the gruff voice on the other end of the line.

"It's me. I need to get the new tattoo my brother did."

"Sure, can you do it tomorrow? Say four o'clock," Mick asked.

I hated the idea that I'd miss something important that Sunshine did, but it was better to get this done before I changed my mind and killed Abel for having the stupid tattoo done in the first place.

"Yeah, I can do that."

"You're booked, man."

I hung up the phone without saying goodbye. There was no point in wasting pleasantries on Mick. My stomach growled, reminding me it had been a long time since breakfast. Sure, I had a few snacks earlier, but I was staying in this truck. Seeing where Sunshine went next was more important than my hunger. The key to what I was doing was creating a timeline and a schedule to follow.

Most people didn't realize how predictable they were, right down to their bowel movements. I picked up my phone again as I had an idea come to me and began searching the endless supply of images for a face with a specific emotional response on it. I paused in my search and made the image larger. There in the background...that was perfect. He was the face I needed to become.

A sadistic chuckle left my lips and had me settling into the large seat as I continued my search. Sometimes social media really was your friend, and right now, I was learning all I could about the unassuming Ricky Rossi.

CHAPTER 10

KIRBY

I'd only ever been this tired a few times in my life, and those times included a club, lots of alcohol, and some hot sex. My legs ached, my feet felt like they had blisters on them, and I'd managed to burn myself badly enough to warrant a bandage on my hand. Not exactly a stellar start to my new job. Jorge had put me through my paces, and when he said that learning to be a barista was an art form, I hadn't believed him until I saw Brandy working up close.

The water and milk had to be at certain temperatures for different drinks. Then there was the consistency of the foam and balance between the rich coffee, flavor shots, and the rest of the mind-bending concoctions. I don't think I'd seen anything this complicated in my science classes.

On the plus side, Jorge didn't kick me out and said goodnight with a smile on his face. I was going to take that as a good sign.

The breeze was cool tonight, and I shivered as I stepped out of the overly warm café. Pulling my coat tighter, I stuffed my hands in my pocket and looked up and down the mostly vacant area. Although this was a busy spot during the day, once it neared ten o'clock, the groups of people disappeared like they were all on a curfew.

My eyes scanned the darkness as an unsettling sensation washed over me. I searched for the cause of my unease, but the street was quiet except for a few cars parked across the road. The vehicles were all dark and looked vacant. I was pretty sure I could kick almost anyone's ass if I needed to—that was one thing I could thank Quantico for, but I wasn't stupid either. I was still a woman alone, and being cocky was a sure way to end up killed.

More than one of the stories in class proved that if you were attacked by surprise, it wouldn't matter if you were a good fighter. Your chances of getting away safely were greatly diminished. I rubbed at my arms as goosebumps rose. Looking over my shoulder, I didn't see anyone. The wind blew my hair around my face, and I had to pull the strands away from my eyes to see properly. I would've sworn someone was watching me, but I couldn't see anyone.

"You're losing it, Kirby." My voice echoed quietly in the night air.

Slipping my hand into my purse, I pulled out my keys, stuffed them in one pocket, and put the small bottle of pepper spray in the other. As I continued on my walk up the street, I slid my fingers between the individual keys to give me a vicious set of knuckles if needed and gripped the pepper spray tight.

The loudest thing on the street was my sneakers on the sidewalk and the sound of my breathing. It seemed to get colder the further I walked, which was ridiculous, but I couldn't shake the cold sensation pressing in on me.

Although I understood and appreciated the wall of bushes that lined the sidewalk surrounding the dorm buildings, they unnerved me whenever some of the leaves blew in the breeze.

A car came in my direction along the road, and my shoulders tensed as the new style of bright purple lights blinded and hurt my sensitive eyes. I was shamefully startled as a blue pickup truck drove past, but neither vehicle stopped nor had someone tried to drag me into their means of transportation. Even though I knew I was being silly, I couldn't stop the jitters.

The bushes suddenly rustled behind me, and I jumped and spun around as I whipped the pepper spray out of my pocket. My heart was pounding hard in my chest as I searched the shadowed street for the attacker.

"Jesus," I swore as a cat darted out of the bushes and bolted across the street. "What kind of agent am I going to be if a freaking cat scares me? Not exactly tough agent status," I mumbled and stuffed the pepper spray back into my pocket.

Turning around, I froze. There was a shadow across the road about a half mile up the street's pavement. It looked like a man in a hoodie, but the hood was pulled up, blocking all facial features. Another car drove up the street, and the shadowy figure was gone when it passed the spot.

"What the fuck? I need to lay off the stalker movies."

My body relaxed once I stepped onto the school property. The massive complex of buildings and parking areas had cameras positioned all around it, and security guards were always watching.

Wait. Who was I trying to fool? I'd met all those guards, and they'd all have their feet up on the desk with a bag of chips in their hand while music blared. They'd never see a damn thing, but no one would know that other than those who worked or went to school here.

I yanked open the door to the dorm area and was assaulted by bright bulbs that felt much stronger after being out in the dark. The next things to reach my senses were laughter and the smell of something burning. When I first arrived here, I used to be concerned when I smelled something smoldering. But I quickly realized that half the people here were lucky if they could boil water, let alone make a meal.

I pushed open the stairwell door and jogged up the stairs to the top floor. I had an aversion to elevators and would avoid them if I could walk. I'd never minded the extra exercise, but the stairwell felt just as terrifying as the street had for whatever reason. I heard a door open and close above me, and I instinctively stopped moving and listened.

Wild images of a serial stalker were racing through my mind until I heard a female voice laugh. I continued up and past the girl as she jogged down the stairs. Yanking open the door to my floor, I marched down the hallway and sighed as I reached my room. My roommate would be there. Although I wouldn't call her good company, she was more like a strange little alien from another planet.

Tina was in her usual place at her desk, headphones on and pen tapping away to whatever song was blaring through her headphones. Within seconds the steady ticking noise of her pen hitting the wooden desk made me want to leap across the room like a crazed animal. The girl's mass of purple and pink curls was piled on top of her head with a pen stuck through the messy knot. I wished I could pull off the look. It was adorable and stylish in its own way, but I just looked like a crazy person that had been dragged from bed if I tried to do the same thing. Her thick glasses were firmly in place as she read whichever textbook she was studying. To make sure she knew I was in the room with her, I stepped into her view and waved, but other than a flick of her gaze up at me, I didn't get any more of a response.

"Good talk," I mumbled as I walked away.

Grabbing some comfy clothes, I made my way into the bathroom and groaned as I saw the mess that was me. I shoved all of Tina's items over to her side of the counter and reorganized my side. I had no idea why she moved my stuff around, but it drove me crazy. The girl was like Pig Pen from *Charlie Brown*. The only difference between her and the cartoon character was instead of a dust cloud following her—it looked like she was practicing Used-Container-Art while trying to recreate the Leaning Tower of Pisa.

I stripped in a way that would make my mother cringe as all my clothes ended up on the floor in a single lump, but I didn't care. I still had a couple of hours of studying to get done before I could go to bed and would be up early for my morning run.

Setting the water on hot, I jumped inside the shower, letting the day's stress ease away as the heat soaked into my skin. I was starting to feel sleepy and decided to get out and make myself a coffee, so I could get some much-needed homework done. I threw my hair up in a towel and pulled on my comfy pants and T-shirt before heading back out into the bedroom area.

As I was making a coffee, my phone began vibrating on my desk. I jogged over to get it and then rolled my eyes when I saw Peter's name.

How had I put up with this guy for so long?

Peter: Are you coming over tonight? It's getting late, and I'm tired.

Me: No, I told you that I wasn't.

Peter: Why not? I thought you'd want to spend the night.

Me: You mean you want to know why I'm not rushing over to have sex with you?

Peter: There is no need to be so crude or rude, Kirby.

I seriously couldn't believe this guy. It was like he never saw a single thing he did as wrong. He never apologized for anything, and texting for a booty call set my rage on edge.

Me: How am I wrong? Was there another reason you wanted me to come over?

Peter: Fine, whatever, if you don't want to come over, then don't.

I could practically feel him sulking through the phone.

Me: Peter, I told you I had work, and then I needed to study before I could get four hours of sleep. Hopefully.

Peter: See, this stupid job is already getting in the way of our relationship, and its only been one night.

I rubbed my eyes. The frustration of this stupid conversation was giving me a headache. Did I break it off with him now and save myself the trouble of having to do it in person? No, that was a shit move, something he would do, and I wanted to be a better person than that.

Me: We can talk tomorrow when I'm done with work. Night Peter.

I waited for a response, but it became obvious he wasn't going to say goodnight in return. Frustrated, I slammed the phone down, making Tina jump.

"When did you get out of the shower," Tina asked, and I stared at her face wondering how much she actually missed when she was zoned into the books.

"Like ten minutes ago."

"Oh, okay. Anyway, while you were in the shower, the lights flickered a few times again, and my computer shut down with the weird outage, so I called maintenance. I had to leave a message, but hopefully, they will be out tomorrow."

I looked at my computer. "Oh, that sucks. I hope it didn't do any damage to my computer. Fingers crossed, they come soon. I don't need another phone to fry because of the crap wiring in this room."

"Yeah, if anything happened to my computer and my projects were lost, I'd have to go jump off a bridge."

I laughed, thinking Tina was being dramatic, but her serious stare made me snap my mouth shut. "I guess we better hope they show up tomorrow, then. I really don't feel like the building burning down around us."

"So what was with the slamming of the phone, guy troubles?" Tina had turned back to her book, but her headphones hung around her neck, which was her sign for 'I'm listening.'

"Just Peter being Peter. I know I have to dump him, but...."

"Sometimes it's easier to stick with the devil you know over the devil you don't?" Tina looked over, and I nodded as I pondered her words.

Was that really why I was staying with him? Was it simply easier than finding someone else? Yes and no. It was easier not to deal with my mother when I would need to explain why I'd broken it off with Peter. But I didn't think that was any better of a reason in the grand scheme of things.

"Yeah, that's exactly what it's like. Thanks for listening." I looked up at Tina, but her headphones were back on. I guess that meant I was dismissed.

I made my way over to the desk and sighed as I opened the textbook on the different forms of psychological behavior issues. Taking a sip of my coffee, I pulled out my trusty highlighter and got to work. I'd only read the first line when I felt eyes on me and lifted my head to peer around the top half of my desk at Tina. She had her back to me with her nose buried in a book. Turning my head, I looked out the window. All was black except for the glow of the lamp light, but I swallowed hard at the feeling gnawing at my gut.

I couldn't stand it any longer and stood quickly to close the drapes. I had no idea what was going on with me tonight, but I'd officially freaked myself out.

CHAPTER 11

MARGARET

I pulled up to the multiple flashing lights and the bright yellow tape that was already set up. No doubt the stupid local cops would've destroyed what little evidence was around the bodies.

I turned to Hanson as we stepped out of the black car. "You don't get more remote than this."

"I'd say," Hanson answered.

I took a moment to look around, and there was very little to distinguish this as a trail. The trees were tall and dense, and the only access to where the bodies were dumped was the well-hidden dirt road they'd driven down to get here. No one would have been able to find it unless someone was pointing and waving with a flare at the entrance. In this case, a police car had been stationed at the tree-lined opening and only allowed emergency vehicles to pass. Even the coroner's van had gotten stuck trying to get in, so once they were done with the scene, the bodies would have to be walked out on gurneys.

Being unnerved wasn't something that happened to me easily. I'd seen a lot of terrible things over the last twenty-nine years, but for some reason, this case felt different. It felt personal, and the fact that I couldn't find a single solid clue made it feel like the killer was mocking us.

The entire area was blindingly bright with floodlights, and I was positive we would get a call that an alien ship had landed in the woods before they were done. Slipping under the yellow tape, I shook my head at the million footprints surrounding the scene. The bodies had been covered, the white material glowing brightly under all the lights. As Hanson and myself got closer, the Sheriff spotted us and made his way over.

"Sherriff Watts," he said and held out his hand to shake mine.

"I'm Agent Lawson, and this is Agent Hanson," I said and nodded toward him. Watts looked at Hanson and smiled. I knew right away that I'd just been booted out of the old boy's club once again.

"Aren't you that famous serial killer hunter? I know I've seen you on television." Watts smiled and put his hands on his hips.

"I'm only assisting on this case," Hanson said. "Agent Lawson here is the lead on the investigation."

I had to give Hanson a point for that one. At least he tried, but it was no use. Watts stuck out his hand to shake Hanson's like he was a red-carpet celebrity. "Well, I'm sure glad we have you on this one. Whoever this killer is, is one sick fuck."

Sheriff Watts turned to walk toward the bodies, and Hanson mouthed, 'sorry' as soon as the Sheriff's back was turned. There was no point listening to the Sheriff gab on like he knew what he was talking about as he tried to show off his investigation skills for Hanson.

Instead, I took in the scene and the two girls who once had been beautiful. Their bodies were mutilated and broken, and the pain and fear were etched into their features even in death. There was no mistaking that the girls were twins and no older than their mid-twenties. Their blonde hair was matted and thick with leaves and dirt, but their bodies were crisp and squeaky clean.

Hanson stepped up beside me and grumbled under his breath. "So, what do you think?"

My eyes traveled over the image of the girls entwined in a hug, their lips sewn together. "Whoever this guy is, he's strong and capable of tossing around the combined weight of, say, two-hundred and fifty pounds."

I squatted down and stared at how the girls were wrapped around one another like they were frozen in a lover's embrace.

"I think our guy has a split personality and definitely has a thing for connections. I mean, look at the random abuse on the girl on the left. She has a breast cut off, and she's missing fingers and toes. I'm not sure what did that to her buttocks and anal cavity, but it looks like the person just did random things to the body. It's all very erratic."

I looked up at Hanson as he scribbled a few notes into a small notepad.

"The other girl is not missing any body parts, and the lines carved into her body took time and precision. This was done by someone that values his work. The lips sewn together makes me wonder if this perp was abused...or maybe had a sibling that passed away or had something similar done to him. Or possibly someone wronged him."

"Like turned him in for a crime?" Hanson's tone was inquisitive. "Do you think our guy just got out of jail?"

I ran my thumb across my lower lip as I thought. "No, I don't think so. These types of dumps have been going on for a few years."

I slowly stood and walked around the girl's forms that practically glowed under the lamps. "We have too many bodies that could be the same serial for him to have only been out of prison for a short time. I'm not sure yet but the lips sewn together is too deliberate not to mean something," I said, pointing to the matted hair. "And why are they pristine except for their hair and faces?"

Looking around, I spotted a forensic team member taking photographs and made my way over. The woman bent over to take a photograph. She stood up straight and scowled before taking in the outfit. I peeked at her name tag before speaking. "Ann, What can you tell me?"

Ann lifted a shoulder and let it drop. "I can't tell you much. The tire tread is a standard ATV mark, and tens of thousands of them are made and used on these trails every year." She pointed to the strange drag pattern. "Now that is more interesting but not very helpful."

"What is it," Hanson asked before I could.

"It's the mark from their hair dragging on the ground." Ann pointed to the marked spot in the mud. "We already followed the trail that way as far as we could, but we lost it once we got to the paved road."

"So, they were on the back of an ATV with their heads dragging on the ground," I asked and looked back to the girls. Once more, the MO for this serial was all over the place.

"No, just their hair. The trail was so heavy at this point because the hair collected mud, leaves, and branches the further the person drove. It was laying behind the four-wheeler like a horse's tail."

Hanson scribbled the notes down and then scratched his chin. "Wouldn't that be an odd position to have two bodies in that you're trying to hide?"

Ann nodded. "For the bodies to arrive the way they have, they must have been wrapped in some sort of protection except their heads. Based on the length of their hair and the average height of an ATV, they would need to be hanging over the back end with their legs straddling the driver." Ann bent over as she tried to demonstrate the position.

"So, let me get this straight. Whoever this killer is, drove with two naked girls' legs wrapped around him as he drove?"

"Essentially, yes," Ann replied.

"What the fuck?" Hanson mumbled. For once, I seconded his sentiment.

I stepped away to once more go and stare at the faces of the two girls that could easily have been Kirby. They were that close in age. "What are you trying to tell me?"

"What?"

I looked over at Hanson and shook my head.

"I was talking to the girls." Crossing my arms, I cocked my head as a thought came to me. "What if it's not one killer with a split personality but two separate killers with two separate MOs?"

Hanson scoffed, the sound coming out like he thought I was ridiculous. "You know as well as I do the likelihood of two serial killers working together is unrealistic. For two killers to be at this for at least eight years without killing one another? Impossible. They're known predators. They would've deteriorated by now."

"I know that is what would normally happen, but what if that is the reason why we can't find a pattern? What if there are two killers at work and then dispose of the kill as one person?"

Hanson shook his head like she was speaking in tongues. "No, I'm sorry, but I've seen many cases where there have been two killers, and for that to work, one has to be a subordinate."

Hanson pointed to the bodies.

"Do either of those bodies look like a subordinate did this? No, this is an alpha personality, a lion at the top of the food chain. Maybe he has different tastes or a split personality like you've been theorizing, but two alphas together for this long is impossible."

Hanson walked away and ended the conversation like I'd been dismissed, and my hand clenched into a fist. My gaze fell on the girls once more. There was a good chance I was wrong. Hanson had made logical points, but weren't the Tsavo Man-Eaters two lions that learned to kill together? A freaking movie had been made of the real-life accounts of those that had horrifically died.

Stepping around the bodies, I made my way toward Hanson and Sheriff Watts, were laughing about something, most likely my idea.

Hanson may have worked many cases, but it was my gut that was telling me I was on to something, so even if I had to do it on my own time, then that was what I'd do.

One way or another, I was going to find and stop this killer or killers, even if that meant I didn't have the FBI's top agent's support. Hanson could go fuck himself. I'd knocked far tougher guys down a few pegs, and I'd do the same to him.

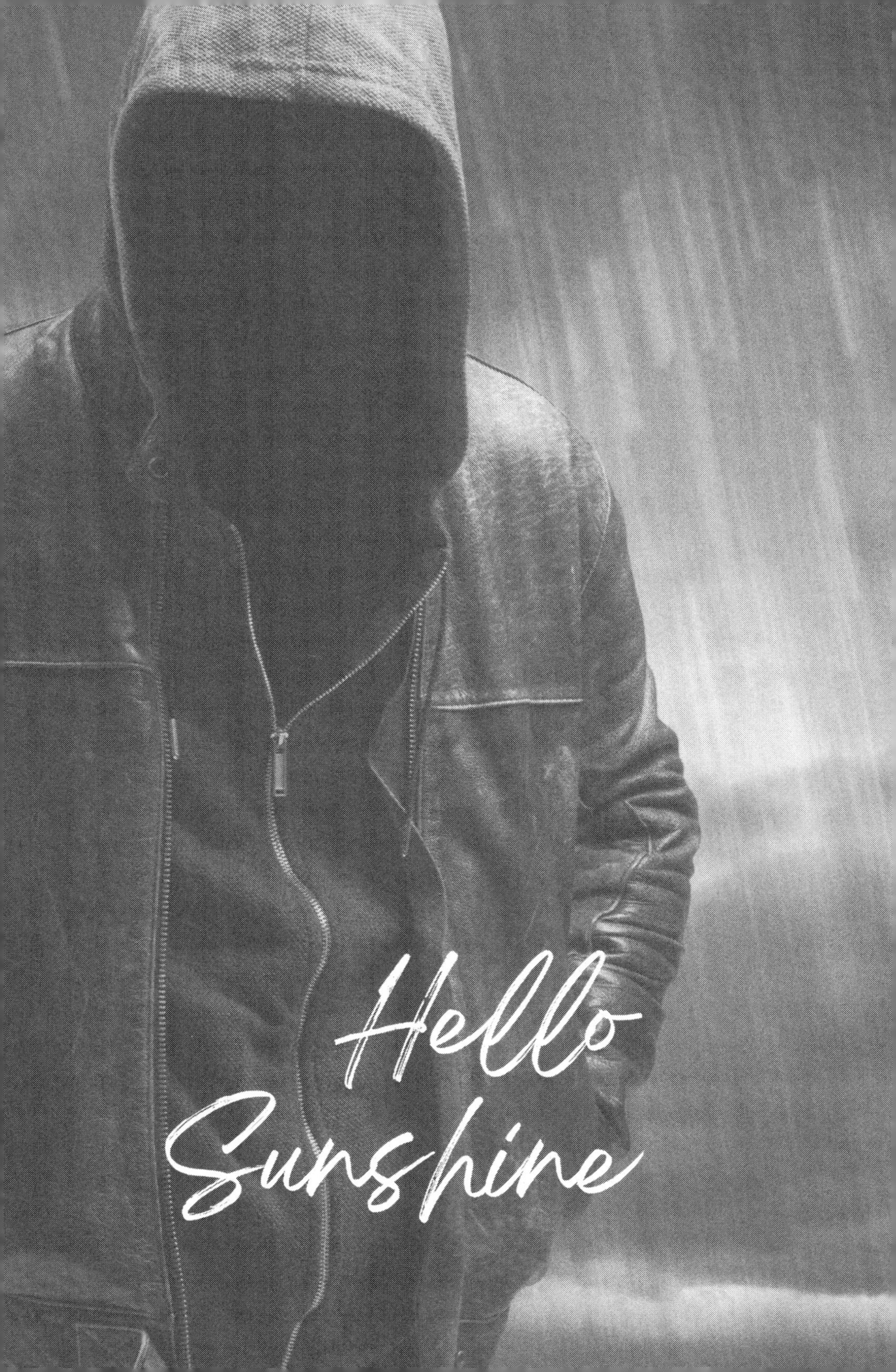
Hello
Sunshine

CHAPTER 12

C AIN

Thanks to Ricky Rossi, I now had a shiny new ID card and maintenance clothes to match. I looked in the rearview mirror and smiled at the baseball cap that said Quantico across the navy-colored material. Picking up the clipboard of work orders, I slipped out of the white truck and closed the door with the school logo on the side.

I'd already done my homework and knew where my Sunshine's room was. I'd also gotten a glimpse of her wearing a thin white tank top, and I could clearly see her perky nipples from my hiding spot in the darkness under the tall oak tree. She looked spooked as her eyes searched the night before she closed the curtain. I liked that. I liked the fact that she was aware of me. On some level, she already felt me coming for her.

The thing I liked best about people was that their behavior was fairly predictable, so I figured it was a pretty good guess that Sunshine would want to have a shower after a long day. She'd been running late to class because her morning run started later than normal, so she wouldn't have had time to shower. Such a naughty girl...staying up so late.

Raising my hand, I knocked on the dorm door. I wasn't sure who would answer, but it didn't really matter. My story would be the same.

As luck would have it, a pixie-like girl with vibrant purple and pink hair answered the door. My eyes flicked from the curly mop on her head to her plain blue eyes and finally to her mouth that was chewing a piece of gum like a cow. I watched the wad move around in her mouth, and I immediately wanted to stuff it down her throat and watch her choke before I ripped her tongue out of her head. What a disgusting display of our next crop of FBI agents...They were really going downhill.

"Yeah," she asked, pulling the large earphones off her head and letting them hang around her neck.

"Maintenance, checking all the rooms on this floor to make sure the phone and internet are working properly."

"Is this about the power flickering all the time?"

I nodded. "That's what the work order says. I need to check all the rooms to see if we can find the cause." I was such a smooth liar. I had no fucking clue what she was talking about, but I was happy about the free information.

"Oh." She looked at her phone.

"I won't be long and won't need to turn the WiFi off if that's what you're worried about." I gave her a smile, the corner of my mouth pulling up the way Abel had made me practice endlessly until I pictured wrapping my hands around his throat. I pictured doing the same thing to the pixie, but then she blushed and held open the door wide for me to enter. I really hated to admit it when Abel did a good job.

I took a deep breath as I entered Sunshine's personal space for the first time.

"Since your roommate is not home, I'll check yours first so you can get back to work," I said and pulled a tool out of my pocket that, in reality, only checked for power, but it looked professional when the little tip lit up.

"Oh, she's in the bathroom," the girl said. "She'll be a minute. You can take your time." She smiled brightly, and I suddenly wondered if I'd done too good of a job in the flirting department. Then again, it might be good if the girl wanted to keep inviting me in. I had no idea yet when I was going to be able to take my prize home. Bending down, I leaned under her desk and made little noises like I was thinking. Standing, I scribbled a curlicue on the note-pad. Giving the girl a good old panty-dropping smile again, I nodded. "She's all good. The problem is not with your side."

"Thanks," she smacked loudly, making my teeth ache and my hand twitch.

I could hear the shower running, and I'd planned a simple mission. Figure out Sunshine's real name and maybe get her class schedule, but there was very little on the desk. I scanned the few items and knew right away that my Sunshine had a bit of OCD. Everything was perfectly symmetrical. There wasn't a single item sitting out that wasn't needed for daily use, and it made me smile. I liked the organization, and I hated clutter—points for Sunshine.

The issue it caused was the increased risk of needing to go through her drawers. I was reaching for one of the desk drawers when I heard the shower shut off.

"Dammit," I whispered under my breath, annoyed at not finding anything useful. I waved to the pixie, who didn't bother to look my way now that she was fully engrossed with whatever was on her screen.

If I'd actually been there to kill her, she would already be choking on her own blood. She was lucky she was not on the menu, at least for tonight. I opened and closed the door and then stood perfectly still to see if she'd notice I had only pretended to leave.

Stupid. Way too many stupid people were walking around, still breathing.

When the girl continued to ignore me, I slipped toward Sunshine's bed and slid underneath. It was stimulating to be this close to her, to smell her in the room. Her feet padded out of the bathroom, and right away, I noticed the bright purple nail polish. The heat from the shower and her body wash was strong in my nose, and I sucked in a slow deep breath savoring the scent. My cock stirred with the combination of mint and lavender. Not scents that would normally turn me on, but an intoxicating aroma on her. I wondered if she'd smell as sweet with the scent of blood rolling off her body.

"I'm going to put on some coffee. Did you want some," I heard her ask, but there was no response. "Tina! Coffee?"

"No."

If I held my head just right, I could make out Sunshine's face from where I lay, and she looked annoyed. I liked her voice. It suited her features. That was important. I fucking hated it when you looked at someone, and they didn't sound anything like they should. If she'd opened her mouth and had sounded like a squeak toy...well, I'd have to kill her sooner.

"Hey did you see where I put my highlighter," she asked, but again there was only silence from the other side of the room. "There it is. Shit."

The yellow highlighter dropped and rolled partially under the bed. She got down on one knee and groped under the bed with her hand. Lifting my arm, I nudged the bright yellow pen with my elbow, and she almost touched my arm as she wrapped her hand around the plastic. The thought of her touching me and freaking out as I grabbed her arm and dragged her under the bed next to me sent a jolt of excitement through my body. My nose flared, and I suddenly wanted to push up my timeline.

I scolded myself and managed to keep my body perfectly still as I waited like the perfect stalker that I was. I loved this cat-and-mouse game, loved the thrill of hiding in someone's home and following them around while they were none the wiser. The minutes ticked by, but I didn't mind getting this time with her. It allowed me to understand her habits better. Like how many times she needed to use the bathroom after a coffee and how she liked to hum softly to the music she was listening to while her toe tapped the floor.

I could hear her yawn and watched as she stood from her desk and the light clicked off. My Sunshine lay above me, the old wood complaining about the sudden weight. I turned to stare up at the bottom of the bed and thought about how she was only mere inches away from being able to wrap my hand around her throat as I fucked her. I could picture her lying on top of me and my body hardened with the thought of having her right now. Reaching up, I softly petted the bottom of the bed like I was stroking her body and smirked. It would happen. I would make sure of it.

I closed my eyes and focused on the steady intake and exhale of her breaths that made my body tingle with the building urge to touch her skin and stare into those violet eyes as I fucked her. My cock was hovering on that delicious edge of pain and desire as it begged to be touched, but I refused.

Waiting for both Sunshine and the roommate to fall asleep was an agonizingly addictive game of wills. I sucked in an uneven breath as she finally drifted off to visit the sandman. I wondered if she'd see my face in her dreams. All too soon, she would. I'd make sure of it.

Like a creature from a horror movie, I silently slid out from under the bed enough that I could sit up, and there she was. She was lying on her back, her face peaceful as she slept. She was like a delectable doll, a collector's piece. I laid my arms and chin on the bed, stared at the side of her face, and memorized every little feature, including the little freckle she had on the right side of her cheek.

I heard the pixie move around in her own bed and decided I better get moving. Sunshine's phone was on the nightstand, and I grabbed it and tapped the screen. It asked for finger recognition, and I swore in my head as I stared at her hands that were thankfully on top of the covers. Choosing to start with the index finger of her right hand, I slowly pushed the phone down into the mattress and slid it under her finger. It didn't unlock, and I moved my gaze to her face, which was still slack with sleep. Leaning over her body but careful not to touch her, I did the same thing with the phone to her left hand and smirked as it unlocked.

Before I could move, Sunshine mumbled something in her sleep and raised her arm above her head, smacking me in the chest.

Oh fuck.

I held perfectly still as I waited for her eyes to snap open.

"Peter, I said no," she mumbled and rolled toward me on her right side.

I didn't like the sound of his name on her tongue. That was the first name she was never allowed to say again. Leaning dangerously close to her ear, I growled softly. "Never say his name again near me unless you want me to remove your tongue."

Convinced that she would remain asleep, I slowly rose to my full height and stared down at the woman stirring unusual sensations in my body. The old behavioral control issues that I'd managed to lock up tight were rekindling in my mind, and before I knew what I was doing, I saw my hand reaching for her face.

For a fleeting moment, I pictured wrapping my hand around her mouth and nose as I suffocated her. I held back a groan as the image of what she would look like as her eyes snapped open, and fear danced in those violet depths. That would be too fast. I wanted to enjoy her and prolong this new feeling for as long as possible. Her lips were the perfect shape, with a slightly larger lower lip that would be perfect for biting.

My finger brushed the side of her cheek, and a tremor of need rippled through my body. I couldn't hold back the gasp as the sensation hit.

"What would you do if I climbed under the blankets and fucked you the way you should be fucked, Sunshine," I whispered in her ear. "I want to see you bleed, but I strangely want to do things I don't normally bother doing. Things that don't normally interest me."

She murmured something in her sleep, and her tongue wet her lips. If I didn't know she was indeed deeply asleep, I'd have thought she was teasing me.

"Do you want me to taste your sweet pussy? I want to decorate your body with your blood and lick it off you while I fuck you hard and fast."

My cock was throbbing in time to my pulse, a steady drum inside my pants, but I still refused to touch myself. I wanted my next load to be on her body, which wasn't happening tonight. I tilted my head and wondered what she'd think happened if she woke up with dried come on her chest and face. Would she blame that guy she was with? Would she think her roommate did something to her? The thought made me smile, but it was too dangerous to try.

I shivered and pushed the idea out of my mind. That was too big of a risk to take right now. Sunshine's little murmur held only one recognizable word, and that was yes. The corners of my mouth curled up even as she rolled over onto her side away from me. My hand flexed over her arm as I restrained myself from touching her again. I was already playing with fire. If I wanted this one, I needed to follow my rules and be smart.

Forcing myself to look away from the creature that was so stimulating, I flicked through her phone and found everything that I was after. Who she was, who her boyfriend was, and I even knew that the woman I'd seen earlier was her mother. Her schedule, room numbers, exam dates, and even her period cycle were all at my fingertips. She had a list of passwords to all her social media accounts, credit cards, bank account, and emails. It was a small purple phone made of gold, and I sent everything to myself and then deleted the evidence before taking a few minutes to clone her phone.

Now I'd know about every text she sent, every call she made, all her passwords, and even what she looked up on her internet. I shook my head as Abel, and his terrible singing came to mind. I could totally picture him singing the song "Every Breath You Take" by the Police.

On a last-minute whim, I changed her background screen saver to a clown and smirked as I turned off the phone.

Leaning over my Sunshine, my Kirby, I rememorized every detail of her face. Each little dip, line, and imperfection were recorded in my memory.

"Sleep well, Kirby." Taking the risk once more, I got low and could feel the heat coming off her skin as it pressed into my own. "Every breath you take, Sunshine. I'll be watching you." She shivered as my whispered words fanned her face, and I loved watching the goosebumps rise on her delicate skin.

I pulled the ball cap back into place as I silently slipped out the door into the quiet hallway and made my way toward the exit like I was a lover doing the walk of shame. I guess, in some ways, I was. She was mine, but she just didn't know it yet.

I smiled wide as I stepped outside. I had some plans to make and a boyfriend to visit. Peter and I needed to get better acquainted.

CHAPTER 13

KIRBY

I'd had the weirdest fucking dream last night and couldn't shake it. When I woke up with a start this morning, I would've sworn someone other than Tina was in the dark bedroom with me, but nope not a soul. All I could hear was Tina's weird whistly snore, and not a thing was out of place. I even checked under my bed, but no one was there. I wasn't sure what the fuck I would've done if someone had been.

When I went for my run, a guy was jogging on the second trail. He had a hood up, and all I could think was that he was there to kill me. I mean, he had track pants on, and it was a cold morning, but no, my mind had to tell me he was a serial killer. So, I ended up tripping over my own damn feet and landing face-first on the trail. Now I was

147

sporting an inch-long gash on my chin that, luckily, didn't need stitches.

Oh, but the fun didn't stop there. My messed-up morning made me late for class, and of course, it had to be my mother's class. She called me out in front of everyone. Why? Because she decided that today of all days, she wanted to prove that I was not above her wrath to the rest of my classmates.

Now here I was at work, and my phone hadn't stopped dinging with fucking Peter's incessant badgering. He kept whining about how I needed to come over after my shift, how I shouldn't be working at the café, and how things needed to stay normal—blah, blah, blah. Not to mention my screen saver had suddenly changed to an image of the Joker from Batman. I had no memory of changing it, which only added to my creeped-out feeling that someone had been in my room.

"What is going on, Sugar? That is the third coffee in a row you got wrong," Jorge asked, and I wanted to cry and didn't even know why. I was off my game and an emotional, nervous wreck.

"I'm not sure. I can't seem to focus. I'm really sorry," I said as he fixed my latest screw-up. The line had finally died down, and I leaned against the counter and crossed my arms. "I guess I'm really making a mess of things."

Jorge smiled at the customer as he handed over the hot drink before looking at me. "In the words of the great Swifty Legend, you need to shake it off. Tell me what you think is going on?"

I sighed, and as if he knew I was thinking about him, my phone dinged again. I was tempted to throw it across the room. "For starters, my boyfriend. I need to dump him, but it's complicated."

"Is he the one that's blowing up your phone?"

I nodded. "He's driving me crazy. I don't know what I ever saw in him."

"I bet he's a pretty boy with a sizeable package." Jorge bit his lip, and I laughed as heat crept up my neck.

"Is it obvious I'm that shallow?"

Jorge made a face and waved his hand in my direction. "Darlin', shallow has nothin' to do with it. You don't think we have all been bamboozled by a sexy bod, a pretty pair of eyes, and a totally delectable sausage." He smiled wide, and I burst out laughing. "But Sugar, let me tell ya' a little somethin' I've learned over the years. Your happiness is worth more than all the complications in the world. If this boy is bringin' your inner diva down, then it's time to send him packin'. You feel me?"

The door jingled, and I pushed away from the counter. "Yeah, I do. Let me get this customer. There has to be at least one order tonight that I don't screw up."

"Have at it."

Still smiling, I made my way over to the customer that was waiting quietly by the register. I really knew it was time to say goodbye to Peter when my first assessment of the stranger was that he was fit and tall, making my heart pound a little harder. The guy was looking down into his wallet as I stepped in front of the keyboard to place the order.

"Welcome to *Mode*. How can I help you this evening?" I said, but my smile slipped as he lifted his head.

The blue eyes I couldn't forget were staring at me. The image of this man standing next to the tow truck raced through my mind like it was yesterday and not the night Peter and I were heading back from spring break. This man's face haunted my dreams. I sucked in a sharp breath and held it as we stared at one another longer than was appropriate.

The corner of his mouth curled up with a half smile, and I wasn't sure if it was meant to be sexy or unnerving, but to me, it was both. My pulse was racing through my body faster than if I'd run a marathon, and my hand shook slightly as it hovered over the cash register. His eyes moved slowly to my hand and then back up to my eyes, and I couldn't decide if I wanted to melt into a puddle of wanton desire or turn and run for the hills and never look back.

"Do I have something on me...." His voice was everything and more than I could've imagined. It was rich with a hint of gravel that was rubbing me in all the right ways. His eyes darted to my name tag, and it was only then I realized how hard my nipples were. I prayed he couldn't see them. "Kirby?"

"Um..." I cleared my throat and braced both hands on the counter to try and stop the subtle tremble that felt like it was also scrambling my brain. "No, of course not. I'm sorry. It's just I think I've seen you before."

"As long as I was memorable," he smirked, his blue eyes were filled with humor, but something else lurked under the gesture. I bit my lip as a sudden and very unexpected surge stormed through my body and ended right between my legs.

What the hell was it about this guy?

"With eyes as nice as yours, I don't think I'd be able to forget," I said and internally groaned. It took all my willpower, but I finally managed to break the stare and look at the numbers and words on the touch screen that barely made sense.

"I could say the same about yours. They're a really unique color."

It wasn't what he said but how he said it that had me shivering with emotion.

I licked my lips and cleared my throat as I tried to make it work, but only a squeak came out, and he smiled wide. He was beyond sexy, there was something about him that was all-consuming and commanding, and it called to me like a fucking beacon in the night. I took a deep and steadying breath.

I can do this, don't make an idiot out of yourself. At least no more of an idiot than you've already made.

Smiling, I looked up and dared to lock eyes with him once more. "Thank you, but they've been more of a curse than a blessing." He furrowed his brow and looked like he was going to say something else, but I figured it was safer to move on from this topic that felt way too intimate and personal. "What can I get for you?"

He didn't look up at the board as those magnetic blue eyes continued to bore holes into me. It felt like he was trying to communicate with me telepathically—like he was trying to will me into understanding something, but the signal wasn't clear enough.

"I'll have a large coffee, one sugar, and a splash of cream, and I'll also have one of your raspberry sour cream muffins."

"Good choice. They just came out of the oven and are my personal favorite. That will be eleven seventy-five, please."

He pulled out a twenty and handed it over, but he spoke again before I could get him his change. "Keep the rest."

"Thank you, that's very generous of you." I put the tip in the colorful jar that Jorge had put rhinestones all over, picked out the largest muffin, and was happy to get it in the bag and not drop it on the floor.

I handed over the bag, and a ripple of excitement soared through my body as his finger gently brushed mine as he took the offering. The touch was so mild that I barely felt it, yet it seemed more intimate than any interaction I'd ever had with Peter in the bedroom.

Swallowing hard, I tried not to notice Jorge staring at me from the sitting room area as he cleaned off tables. "Sorry, I forgot to ask. Would you like to stay or go?"

"I have to get back to work, so I'll take it to go. Thank you."

Nodding, I turned and grabbed the paper cup. "What do you do for work?"

"I have a car shop. I guess you could say I'm a grease monkey." His voice changed subtly and dropped a little lower. "I'm good with my hands and really like to get them up in there."

I was officially a pervert because all I heard was, I want to stick my fingers in your pussy and then fuck you senseless. My cheeks were flaming hot by the time I had his coffee made, and I turned around to face him. As odd and intense as this interaction was, I couldn't deny that I didn't want it to end.

Holding out the cup, I offered him a smile, but just then, the door opened. He looked to the door, which showed off the side of his neck. Gasping as I stared at the Joker clown tattoo on his neck, my hand let go of the coffee, and it hit the counter and burst open. I stupidly reached for it as if I could save it, but the coffee splashed all over my hands and arms.

"Ouch," I yelled and jumped back from the counter.

Jorge came running from the front sitting area, and I was positive he was going to fire me, but instead, he undid the sleeves of my shirt and pulled them up to look at my arms.

"Are you okay?"

"Yeah, I will be. I'm just so embarrassed. I can't believe I did that." I looked up at the man on the other side of the counter. His face was blank of all emotion, but his eyes were hard, holding a look I couldn't decipher. "I'm really sorry, and I seem to be saying that a lot tonight."

He blinked a few times as if coming out of a trance. "I'm just happy you're alright."

"Why don't you go tend to your arms and head on out? We were about to lock up anyway. I can finish making the customer's orders." Jorge laid his hand on my shoulder, and for the second time, he acted like more of a mother than my own mother would have in this scenario.

"Thanks." I locked eyes with the sexy stranger and offered a smile. "Have a good night. It was nice meeting you." Turning, I slipped into the back and made a direct line to the changing rooms.

I ran my arms under the lukewarm water, then plunked myself down on the bench to stare at the red marks that hadn't blistered, thankfully. My phone dinged again. Groaning, I pulled it out of my back pocket. Ignoring the million and one messages from Peter, I tapped the screen and stared at the clown's face.

I was officially losing my mind. I'd been dreaming about this man, and now, I'd subconsciously added a very similar image of his tattoo onto my phone. Pinching the bridge of my nose, I shook my head.

Maybe I could talk my dad into letting me fly out sooner than the end of my semester. I could help with the new baby and figure out my new career path. All I knew was that I needed to get out of this place. It was making me nuts.

Hello
Sunshine

CHAPTER 14

CAIN

"I don't understand what she ever saw in this guy. His name is Peter. I mean, can you imagine being called Peter your whole life? That's just opening yourself up to cock jokes. It's almost as bad as the name Dick."

I sat up and stared at the detailed line I'd just finished and wiped the area with a towel to remove the dripping blood before moving on.

"He does have money, so that could be the attraction, but I don't think so anymore. It may have been at one point." I paused in my conversation to complete the center of the complicated flower I was creating, and Karen's body winced, almost ruining my design. I stood in a rush and glared down at the woman, her eyes wide with fear.

"What did I say about moving?"

She whimpered as tears streamed down her cheeks, making the blue mascara she was wearing run. "Do we need to have another discussion about the rules?"

Karen's head slowly moved back and forth as much as the head strap around her forehead would allow. I sat back down and stared at the flower that now had a tiny imperfection in the middle and ground my teeth together.

"So about Peter. I can admit he'd be classified as hot in that pretty-boy-prep-school way. But the guy is not very nice to anyone, and based on his texts to Kirby, he is extremely controlling with her."

I thought about all the messages I'd read. In fact, they were what spurred me on to step into the café in the first place. Peter was an emotional abuser and very controlling. The fact that Kirby wasn't begging him not to be mad or telling him she'd run right over to his house were the only reasons that had stopped me from driving over to his fancy condo and slitting his throat.

This possessive sensation was new and stirred the darker, more out-of-control side of my personality. It was the side of me that was kin to Abel, and it was the side that I worked hard to keep pushed down. That side of myself was unpredictable and had almost gotten Abel and me caught a time or two. It was completely fascinating that it was Sunshine pulling this out of me.

The next flower was complete perfection, and I gave Karen a moment to prepare for the next cut as a reward.

"What do you think, Karen? Do you think they sound like a good match to you?" I said, not expecting an answer, and one didn't come. "I also learned that she's smart but doesn't apply herself when it comes to her schoolwork, according to her mother. Her mother is already an FBI agent and seems a bit emotionally depraved. You know, the overbearing, in-your-face type? I think I can use their damaged relationship to my advantage."

I wiped away more droplets of blood and began carving the centrepiece, which was going to be an eye. And not just any eye but one of Kirby's. An image from the café and her yelping as the hot coffee spilled all over her arms kept dancing around inside my brain. My cock instantly hardened. Her scream was as unique and beautiful as the rest of her. I rolled out the tense muscles in my neck as I took control of the unusual emotions.

"So tell me, Karen, why do you think I'm drawn to this girl? Other than her obviously unusual eyes, what is this visceral reaction attributed to?"

She lay there perfectly still, staring up at the ceiling. If it weren't for her chest rising and falling, I would have thought she was already dead. I smacked my hand on the table beside her head, and her body jerked as another muffled sob came from behind the ball gag in her mouth.

"It's not nice to ignore people, Karen. Do you not have any manners? I suppose not. That is why you're on my table, after all."

She turned her head as much as the restraint would allow her to look at me, and I stared into the plain, shit-brown eyes that did nothing for me. There wasn't even a fleck of another color—no gold, green, or even hazel. Her eyes were completely and utterly uninteresting, just like the rest of her annoying existence.

"Foook, heee eeels foook."

I rose a brow at the woman and reached forward to undo the ball gag impeding her speech. "You may try that again."

"She feels stuck."

I leaned on the table and was mildly impressed with Karen.

"You may be right. I suppose that he could've already dug his claws into her psyche and made it feel impossible for her to leave. Kind of like you right now." My lip curled up as I tormented her. She looked frozen in place, her eyes wide as they focused on mine.

"What, you have nothing to say?" She reminded me of a wind-up toy.

"Please don't do this. Please don't kill me. I don't want to die, please. I'm begging you," she blubbered like a broken record. "I have a husband and a daughter, and I need to get back to them and...."

"Karen, stop."

I leaned over her body and brought my face closer to hers as I analyzed her with an artist's eye. Her features were nondescript, nothing that stood out as being unique, but I could picture what she looked like in her youth before the years of self-abuse. I poked at her cheekbones that had some promise with the right makeup.

"Why do you think I'm doing this to you?"

"Please," she cried. "I'm begging you."

"I said stop." I smacked the table with the palm of my hand again, and she sucked in her lower lip and closed her eyes. "Now answer the question."

"I...I...I don't know," she blurted out, and I shook my head at her.

"You don't know what? You don't understand the question, or you don't know the answer?"

Tears poured out of her eyes and fell on the table below, the moisture now smearing her blush and the foundation she'd haphazardly caked onto her face was now a rainbow of colorful streaks. I liked the look, an idea coming to me.

"I don't know why you're doing this."

Karen broke down into yet another round of blubbering, which was quite the contrast to her earlier attitude. She had been screaming at an elderly man in the convenience store about 'being in her way.' She used a few racial slurs about him being black and practically shoved him down an aisle. If I hadn't been standing behind him and caught him as he fell, he surely would've broken something or worse. He could've died if he'd cracked his head.

I didn't like people. I found them to be useless and a waste of good air, but I really didn't like those who thought they were at the top of the food chain when in reality, they were nothing more than bullies.

This Karen not only didn't apologize when I righted the man on his feet, but when I calmly suggested she go elsewhere to buy her armful of heart attack items, she rounded on me. Her finger waggled like a worm on a hook in my face while the six-pack of beer cans rattled with the mistreatment of being shaken. Little did she know that prey rarely knew it was prey until it was too late.

I liked this particular convenience store. It was in a low-traffic area, there were no cameras on the property, and the parking lot was around the back of the store. When this Karen poked me in the chest, I knew she was coming home with me. There were many reasons I would take one bag of skin over the next, but usually, it had to do with my mood and the opportunity that was presented.

If I had a scale of respect, 'Karen's' would be at the bottom of my list. They bothered me because they were the most aggressive form of liar, and it angered me when one thought they could speak to me at all, let alone touch me. She was lucky I didn't rip her finger right off her hand in the middle of the store. Pulling myself out of my thoughts, I sighed and laid my finger on Karen's lips. She'd been begging nonstop the last couple of minutes.

"Karen, if you're not careful, I'm going to rip your tongue out while you're still breathing." She clenched her mouth shut tight, her lips trembling under my finger. "I'm going to ask you one more time. Why do you think I'm doing this, Karen," I asked, my voice calm.

"I don't know, and my name's not Karen."

I shook my head and rubbed my eyes at the level of her stupidity. "I know your name isn't Karen, but you are one, and I don't care what your real name is."

A flash of intelligence or maybe just understanding passed over her face. "I promise I won't be such a bitch. I've learned my lesson." She nodded her head like that might help me to agree with her.

I nodded along with her and then shook my head no. "Just answer my original question."

I stepped aside to retrieve the rest of my tools. When she spotted the leather case, she let out a sound that was part word and part incoherent animal noise. Once I unrolled the leather case and all my tools of choice were on display, she lost her mind and began hysterically screaming. I sighed when it became obvious this woman was not going to answer. My eyes roamed over her jiggling, stout body as she thrashed in the restraints.

I took my time to finish wiping down Karen's body, and she involuntarily giggled as I cleaned her feet. It was good that I was used to living on a farm with animals because she smelled like a stuck pig that had been left out in the sun all day for a maggot feast. She made me wonder if bodily hygiene had gone out of style.

I ran my fingers along the metal tools that glistened in the light and decided on the one I'd had specially made. It was like the tip of a scalpel fitted with a foot from a sewing machine, and for the fine detailing I planned for the rest of her body, it was going to be needed.

This tool was best to use on those that were still alive when I did my artwork. The movement that accompanied pain and fear tended to screw up the depths of the small details on my pieces. This way, no matter what, the blade would cut at the same depth. Pretty fucking brilliant, I thought.

I visualized an assortment of screaming faces among crosses on her stomach. I was about to start my first cut when the sensor dinged to let me know someone had just arrived. Looking up at the security screen, I groaned as I saw Abel heading my way. A moment later, the outer door slammed open with a bang. He never just walked in. He always slammed my door open because he knew it angered me. I heard the song he was humming before he moseyed into the sound-proof area I was working.

He stopped in his tracks as his eyes took in the woman who'd shut up long enough to see who the new arrival was, but from the whimper she made, I don't think she was too happy to see the two of us.

"What the fuck, man? Again?"

"You need to be clearer in your questioning Abel."

He rolled his eyes at me and crossed his arms over his chest. "I shared the twins with you, and you don't give me a call about this one?"

"You were at work, and this one wasn't on my schedule. She just happened to piss me off enough to warrant some...entertainment for the evening." Abel crossed his arms over his chest and looked exactly like he was a child as his bottom lip protruded from his mouth. "You do know I'm not mom and dad. That look doesn't work on me?"

"Come on, man, fair is fair, and you don't like being in debt to me. This would even shit up."

He did have a point. The last thing I wanted was to be indebted to my brother. It always led me to do something I really had no interest in doing.

"Fine, you can join in, but I was planning this whole pained scene, so don't go cutting off too much before I'm done."

"Always the party pooper. Has she been scrubbed," Abel asked as he wandered over to the assortment of scrub brushes.

"If you mean, did I clean her pussy, then no. I didn't fuck her, and before you ask, I'm not going to."

I leaned over Karen once more and then decided I didn't want to hear her annoying voice. It sounded like nails on a chalkboard, so I laid down my tool to grab the silver roll of tape. Tearing off a piece, I slapped it over her mouth, and the hysterical screams dulled to a muffled roar.

Abel returned with a brush almost the same size as a toilet brush. He dumped a giant glob of the special cleaner right between her spread legs. The thrashing got worse, and the screams more insistent as she stared at the bristly object.

"You ready, brother?"

"You don't really expect me to sing that stupid song with you again, do you?"

"Awe, come on, it's always better with two people."

"Isn't it bad enough that I'm going to get that stupid tattoo later today?" Abel just stared at me, and I groaned. "Fine, I'll sing it."

"Woohoo! One, two...one, two, three." Abel dipped the brush into the special cleaning solution and then jammed the large scrub brush on the long handle inside Karen's pussy with a single thrust. The scream was still loud behind the tape as her back arched against the straps holding her to the table.

"Scrub da puussy. Scrub da, scrub da puussy. Scrub da puussy. Scrub it all day long." Abel and I paused as he thought about what he wanted the second line to be.

"Ram it in the chubb, chubb, chubb. Ram it in the chubb, chubb, chubb," Abel yelled and then held his finger up as his voice went up a few octaves. "Chubb, chubb, chubb."

He pointed his finger down and lowered his voice until it sounded like a tuba. "Chubb, chubb, chubb."

He continued to work, his arms flexing as he jammed the brush into her so it disappeared and reappeared in time with his singing.

"Oh, scrub da puussy. Scrub da, scrub da puussy. Scrub da pussy. Scrub it all day long." He finished and raised an arm in the air with the crescendo. "That was awesome. Why hadn't I thought of that second verse before?"

"Can I get back to what I was doing now?" I picked up my prized tool.

"Such a bore, but fine, just don't cut up her asshole. I want to fuck it."

"Of course you do," I said under my breath as I turned on the music to some classic rock and focused on my task. I ended up having to knock her out for her to be still enough to complete my art. But in the end, she was a masterpiece. It was a shame that no one would see this one, but not every body could be left for people to find. It was simply too dangerous.

I managed to finish the artwork across her stomach before she woke up, and Abel took advantage of fucking her ass. I cleaned my tools and made sure they were still as sharp as ever while Abel and Karen had fun behind me. It was more like Abel was having fun, and

Karen was wailing, but her screams would only egg my brother on. If only she'd learn to shut up.

"You look splendid, Karen," I said as I took my final pictures. "But, I have to say it's not really a shame that our time has come to an end."

Her eyes pleaded with me, the word please still coming through loud and clear. Unfortunately for her, I didn't care how much she begged. There was no guilt, no pull in my gut that said this was wrong. Nor was there a second thought as I slit her throat like we used to do to the pigs and then removed her dull and depressing eyes.

As I finished my final touches, while Abel was working at stuffing his cock back in his pants. "Where do you want to put her?"

I sighed as I stepped back and stared at her body. "She can feed the pigs."

"Wise choice, brother. I'll go get the wheelbarrow for this sow," Abel mocked like this was a big game.

I killed for far different reasons than Abel, so I had to keep the choke collar on his throat and the leash wrapped firmly around my hand. Abel whistled and returned with the large wheelbarrow through the underground passage of the work area.

Abel picked up Karen's body and tossed it into the wheelbarrow before wheeling it in a circle and heading for the passage once more. I pictured Sunshine in the wheelbarrow, and my hands stilled. The idea didn't sit well, but I couldn't explain why. Shaking my head to clear it, I began scrubbing away Karen's blood.

CHAPTER 15

KIRBY

I could see Tina's confused expression in the mirror, but I ignored it and continued to put on my mascara.

"So, why are you going to this party when you said you're going to break up with him," Tina asked.

It was a logical question. In fact, it was the number one question I should be asking myself, but I didn't have a great or even a good answer.

"I'd agreed to go to this event months ago, and as much as I want to break up with him, I'm just not enough of a bitch to do it right before his family's business fundraiser. They hold it every year. His family and the media attending will be expecting me since this would technically be my third one." I finished applying my lip gloss and took a step back to admire the long evening gown that shimmered a soft purple and gold. "I can break up with him after the family brunch tomorrow."

"So basically, you're doing it to save face, or you're too scared to deal with the fallout of just cutting the cord tonight? Weak move for a next-gen FBI agent, just sayin'."

I turned around to tell Tina off, but she already had her headphones on and was walking over to her desk. Fuming, I grabbed the small matching clutch and marched toward the door. The problem was I didn't have an argument against what she said. I kinda hated myself for doing it this way as well, and it would be a total boss move to dump him before the party.

Stepping out into the hall, I let the door close with a slam and grumbled as I headed outside to wait for Peter.

"Shit," I swore and looked back inside the building.

I'd forgotten my shawl, and it was a cool night. Seeing Peter's car, I decided it was too late to go and get it. A cool breeze picked up, and my hair blew around my face. The long dress's slit flapped like a flag around my legs. Wrapping my arms around my body, I looked to the right. Lights turned on, revealing the property, but I still felt like I was being watched.

"Not this again," I mumbled as I mentally scolded myself for being ridiculous. The only thing I could see was a white maintenance truck, and no one was inside.

Peter pulled up, and even though I was standing on the step beside the car, he blew his horn. I was tempted to change my mind, dump him, and go back inside. The window opened as my feet started to move down the stairs.

"Come on, Babe, let's go. We're already pushing it to be on time."

The window went back up, and I rolled my eyes at the stupid comment. I literally couldn't move any faster in the strappy heels, and he wasn't even gentlemanly enough to open my door for me. He used to be, and I could clearly remember our first year together. I genuinely liked how he'd jog around and smile as he opened the door for me like I was his Princess.

As I opened the door, a shiver raced down my spine, and my eyes flicked over the roof of Peter's car, but nothing moved. Shaking it off, I slipped into the warm car and almost gagged on the cloud of cologne that permeated the air.

"Nice dress, but didn't you wear that last year?"

I looked down at the dress I'd spent hours looking for specifically for this event and then fixed my glare on Peter. "No, I didn't, and if this is how you're going to be all night, then stop the car right now. You can go alone."

As we sped away from the school property, Peter made his usual annoying sound, which was a cross between a snort and a scoff.

"Don't be so dramatic. I said it's nice. It just looks familiar. Why are you in such a mood all the time lately? It's like everything I say annoys the shit out of you."

That was an understatement. I think his breathing annoyed me. "I've just got a lot on my mind," I said, dancing around the question.

"I keep telling you that adding that shit job onto your schedule was a bad idea, but you never listen to me."

My hand clenched around the clutch, and I was tempted to beat him with it. I wanted to see the headline for that one: 'Man Dies In Beating After Girlfriend Bludgeons Him To Death With A Clutch.'

"What did I say about mentioning my job again."

Peter sighed and shook his head. "Fine, whatever. My mom is

excited to see you. She asked if you were coming and said she was looking forward to catching up," he said, and I wanted to laugh out loud.

I highly doubted that. Peter's mother could pass for the Ice Queen. She was that cold and calculating. She had no interest in me being with her son the moment he took me home to meet them and had been vocal in her passive-aggressive way about it ever since. Peter didn't see it. He didn't see anything she did as wrong. That was the first red flag I should've noticed. It would have warned me how our relationship would turn out.

I kept my eyes out the window and ignored Peter as he began telling a story about what happened at his work and how great he made himself look to the board members. His number one goal was to take over for his father when he decided to retire, and there was nothing wrong with that, but he talked about it like it was a life-or-death situation. Meaning if he didn't get to be the next CEO, then the world would crumble around him. His voice droned on as we reached the city and the bright lights from the tall buildings.

My eyes flicked to the side view mirror and stared at the head-lights of the truck that was behind them. Staring directly at the bright lights, it felt like the vehicle was coming for me and would run me over, and maybe I wanted them too.

As usual, whenever one of these events was being held at the sleek silver tower of Peter's family business, a red carpet was lined up out the door and down the few stairs. Limousines and an array of other fancy cars were lining up to pull up to the VIP section. This was where the media were waiting to take pictures. Mr. and Mrs. Cunningham were standing outside, acting as gracious hosts. We pulled into the line behind another silver car and waited for our turn.

"Now remember what I told you, don't mention anything about the Fisher debacle," Peter said, and I turned to look at him for the first time since getting in the car. I had no idea what he was talking about, so he didn't have to worry about me saying anything.

We pulled up to the front of the building, and I plastered a smile on my face. Guess this was show time.

CAIN

The moment that Kirby stepped outside her dorm building dressed in the unbelievably sexy dress meant to please another man, I knew she would need to be taught a lesson. She needed to know who she belonged to, and it wasn't Peter. My cock hardened, staring at her, and once more, I was confronted with a primal reaction that I couldn't wrap my brain around.

I shifted in my seat as I waited for them to reappear across the street from the lavish event. With every hour that passed, the anger that had always been the one consistent emotion in my body burned a little brighter. My hands clenched the steering wheel of the truck as my gaze never left the front doors or the VIP section. The attendants were bringing cars up to those heading out for the night.

I couldn't help wondering what my Sunshine was doing inside that building. Was she eating fancy little finger foods and making meaningless conversation, or was she pressed against some dirty bathroom wall and being fucked like the bad girl she was?

A limo pulled up to the front, and the driver got out and held open the door. I didn't pay too much attention until the flash of violet caught my eye. Kirby had obviously had too much to drink. She was holding the dainty heels in one hand and was swaying as she tried to make it down the stairs. Peter was close to the same, his shirt was partially undone, and the tie he'd been wearing was now hanging from a pocket.

The idea that this worthless piece of pond scum had actually fucked what was mine inside that building turned my anger into something dangerous in my gut. This was the part of me that I kept a lid on. It was the part of me that had a nasty habit of making mistakes. It was the part of me that was irrational, more animal than man, and harder to control.

As the limo pulled out onto the street, so did I, and I followed at a safe distance until we reached an expensive condo building. Sitting across the road, I watched as the two practically crawled out of the back of the car. Halfway to the door, Kirby stumbled and fell onto her hands and knees. I shook my head as Peter laughed. He reached down to help her up but missed her hands, so she fell onto her knees again.

Chivalry was not a word in my vocabulary, but even I had to give this pathetic display an eye roll. I waited until the limo drove off, pulled my hood up, and ran for the front of the condo. Luckily, if the building had a security guard, he wasn't at the desk, so I ran to the elevator and watched the numbers climb. The elevator stopped on the twenty-third floor, and I looked around for the sign that pointed toward the maintenance room.

Two things I never went anywhere without were my travel pack of tools and my leather gloves. A quick scan of the hallway showed there were no cameras, and I was inside the maintenance room, opening my tools within moments. I could pick the lock on Peter's door, but this was simply a better option. Wandering over to the metal cabinet marked keys, I opened it and smiled as I spotted the one labeled 'master.'

Snagging the key, I took off for the stairwell and jogged to the twenty-third floor. Fucker needed an extra special death for making me run up all those stairs. I'd already memorized the floor plan and knew that his room number unit was 2313 from the information I'd gathered. The key slipped into the lock like butter, and I was inside the quiet space with a quick turn of the handle. I stood with the shadows, melting into darkness until it was like we'd become one.

The large condo was very quiet. I took a deep breath when there were no wild sex sounds or bed squeaking noises, which calmed my turbulent rage. As I slipped around the condo, my hand palmed the knife from the sheath on my belt. I took in every piece of artwork and trinket in the place. All of it spoke to this man's extravagant taste and how very opposite it seemed to Sunshine. Taking a moment, I analyzed the one wall of framed photos, and not one of them had Kirby in them, which I found very interesting.

My footfalls were like a choir mouse as it scurried across the floor, no one the wiser. Poking my head in the first open door, I found a bedroom, but it was unoccupied and sparse of any furnishings other than a bed and nightstand. The next was the bathroom, but the last was what I sought. I stepped just inside the doorway of the main bedroom, and my eyes locked on the two bodies asleep on the bed. The moment reminded me of the night I'd visited my father with the knife in my hand, and my palm squeezed the handle of the knife as I pictured slitting Peter's throat.

I could see his death as clearly as their bodies moving in time to their breathing. Peter had made it under the covers, but Kirby was still in her shimmery dress, lying on top of the grey sheets. I decided the color suited her as I stepped around to Peter's side of the bed. Kneeling down, I brought my face so close that our noses almost touched. I willed him to wake up. I wanted him to open his eyes and see my face before I rammed the knife into his neck. My mind pictured Kirby waking up to find this useless waste of space dead beside her and smirking.

It would teach them both a lesson about who I was and what I could do, but that moment never came. Peter was doing a drunk snore, and I knew the likelihood of him opening his eyes was slim to none. Standing, I counted his breaths, wondering how many more he'd take until I took what I wanted.

Kirby moaned something in her sleep, and her right leg pulled up into a position that resembled the number four and, in the process, pulled her dress up around her ass.

"Well, now, I can at least teach one of you a lesson," I whispered, making my way around her side of the bed. "Is that what you're wanting, Sunshine," I asked, my voice soft.

The zipper sliding down on my pants was loud in the quiet room, and a wave of excitement went straight to the base of my cock. This was breaking a major rule. My brain screamed not to do it, but I knew I was going to, no matter what. Sunshine was mine.

I normally liked my prey begging at my feet for a taste of my cock. I'd taken my turn with the odd blubbering person to appease Abel in his games, ultimately to shut him up. The difference was that they'd always been awake and very aware of what was happening. There was something new and thrilling about taking control of Kirby now.

Seeping into her mind and impregnating her with thoughts of only me while I pushed myself inside of her to claim her body.

Crawling on the bed behind her, I lifted the shimmering fabric and smirked at the little purple thong. I would've pulled it off, but there was no need as they'd moved to the side of her body to expose her pussy to my eyes. Lowering myself down, I ran my tongue up the inside of her thigh until I could bury my nose between her pussy lips. She moaned and wiggled against my face as her body encouraged me to continue. Flicking my tongue between her folds, I tasted her for the first time, and she tasted as good as she smelled. Oh, there was definitely something strange about her, something that piqued my curiosity.

My tongue swirled around her sensitive clit, and she moaned again and spread her legs further apart. I licked my way up the side of her ass cheek until I could take a bite. I was careful not to bite too hard and force her out of the drunken stupor, but it was hard enough that I could hear the sharp intake of air as my teeth pressed deeper into her skin.

"You taste like addiction on my tongue." I slowly moved up her body until I was hovering over Kirby, my body so close I could feel the fabric of her dress against my shirt.

"Is that what you're trying to do to me, Sunshine? Are you trying to make me addicted to you," I whispered softer than a butterflies wings into her ear, and she murmured something undecipherable, but her ass pushing up into my cock told me what she wanted. "I don't get addicted, Sunshine, but you are mine. You need to learn that."

Like a snake wrapping itself around its prey, I slid my hand around her throat as the head of my cock edged into her tight little hole. She gasped but didn't open her eyes, and with a single smooth stroke, I sank into her hot pussy until I couldn't go any further.

"Oh..." she said, and I tightened my grip on her throat.

I knew how to toe the lines. I'd squeezed the life out of many throats to know how much pressure to apply to keep her in a state of erotic asphyxiation. Her drunken state would only heighten the experience for her, while the thought that I could kill her at any moment had my cock wanting to explode already.

Sucking in a steadying breath, I began to move, and as I did, my naughty Sunshine began to moan louder and hump her ass up into me.

"Were you craving my cock, Sunshine?" I said as I drew wet lines up the side of her neck.

I thrust into her harder, and her body shuddered underneath me.

"Peter..."

That one word sent a jab of fury through my body, and I slammed my cock into her hard as I tightened my hold enough that she'd struggle to breathe.

"Don't say his name. Never say his name again. You're mine now. Do you understand me?" I practically growled into her ear, and goosebumps rose on her body.

I loosened my grip just enough not to kill her, but my hand was shaking with the urge to teach her the ultimate lesson. "Say you understand? Say you're mine, Sunshine."

She moaned loudly as I thrust harder and faster into her pussy. Despite being unbelievably wet, she was like a fucking vise on my cock.

"Say it," I ordered into her ear as the bed began to shake back and forth hard.

I wanted Peter to wake up and see this, see me taking what was mine and giving me the opening to kill him, but it didn't matter how hard the bed shook. He never blinked.

"I'mmm...yours," she slurred out.

Hearing her say that calmed the anger enough that the urge to end her subsided. "Fuck, you feel good, Sunshine. You have a nice tight hole."

My teeth latched onto the sensitive edge of her ear as I stopped holding back and pummeled her pussy as hard as I could.

"Oh. Oh. Oh," she moaned with each thrust. With a deep moan, her body jerked beneath mine a moment before her pussy clamped down hard around my cock. What felt like a flood of warm wetness coated my cock as her body came all over me.

"That's right, Sunshine, you only come for me now," I groaned and then had to push up out of her fast as I felt my own orgasm begin. Kneeling behind Kirby, I grabbed my cock and stroked it so fast and hard that the sound of slapping was still loud.

"Uhhh," I groaned out as my come shot from my cock and landed all over her ass.

Each stroke brought out more of my orgasm. It was like I'd never had sex before.

"Fuck yes," I said as the last of my release landed on her leg.

Using the tip of my cock I spanked her bare ass and loved that she continued to moan and wiggle like she was starved for more. I looked over at Peter, who was still obliviously passed out.

"Can't satisfy her, can you? Well, you don't have to worry anymore. I'm going to be fucking her from now on. At least until I'm tired of her and end her."

Kirby mumbled something, and then her breathing deepened as

she fully passed out once more. Standing, I was tempted to wait around until I could go for a second time, but with the orgasm came a little clarity, which meant I was already pushing more limits than I should have. I had to admit it was worth it, though. Settled with my decision, I stuffed my cock back into my pants and zipped up.

My lip curled up as a thought occurred to me. Marching into the bathroom, I searched all the drawers until I found what I was after and pulled out the tube of lube. The next stop was the kitchen, and I hunted around in the fridge until I found what I needed. Making my way back to the bedroom, I found the pair in the exact same positions I'd left them. Holding my treasure up, I squeezed a large dose of lube on the end of the thick cucumber.

I gripped the top of Peter's boxers and smirked as I pulled them down enough to expose his asshole. This was a win, win. If he woke up, I'd get to kill him, and if he remained asleep...I'd get to laugh for days to come. Holding back the snicker, I took a bite out of the end of the cucumber and put the piece in my pocket. Positioning my green weapon into the proper spot, I jammed it in a solid foot without any prep and prayed that the fucker woke up. Instead, he groaned loudly and then shuddered, his body spasming as he came.

"Unbelievable," I muttered as Peter's body bounced around on the bed as his hips continued to flex and release around the large cucumber. "You like it that much you get to wake up like that."

I stuffed it in a little further and then let go. Not what I'd planned, but I was sure it would be one interesting conversation in the morning. I swiped Peter's phone off the nightstand and used his finger to unlock it, but I was surprised he hadn't used his dick when I saw his photo history. I liked my cock just fine, but I didn't have a thousand pictures of it on my phone.

"You're an interesting kind of asshole, Peter," I mumbled as I searched his contacts, texts, and emails. "Well, isn't this curious," I said and made sure to take screenshots of all that was usable or important.

Done. I snapped a shot of the cucumber in his ass and saved it as the home screen on his phone, and then to add salt to the wound, I spent a few extra minutes changing every person in his contacts to the same image. No matter who called him next, that photo was going to come up. The thought made me grin, something that I don't often do. Tossing the phone on the bed, I quietly scooted around the bed.

"I guess this is it for now, Sunshine," I said. "I hope that every time you move when you wake up, you still feel my cock inside you."

I took the piece of cucumber out of my pocket and nipped the end off so it matched the size of Kirby's mouth before placing it on the pillow beside her head. This may actually have worked out better than I could've planned.

Heading to the door, I paused when I reached the opening and drummed my fingers on the knife. It felt comforting as I touched it.

"Remember, Kirby, you're mine now, and you better not forget it." I smiled as I backed out into the hallway. "Or the next lesson won't be as much fun for you.

CHAPTER 16

KIRBY

There are some things in life you wish you could unsee and others you wish you could remember, but to the best of my knowledge, I'd never experienced both conundrums in the same breath. That managed to happen this morning. My head felt like it was going to split into two, I had a wildly erotic dream about the guy with the Joker tattoo, and I still had no words for the fucked-up argument that ensued when Peter woke up screaming, 'get it out of my ass.' Words I can honestly say I never thought I'd wake up to, let alone hear from him.

"Are you not enjoying the cucumber salad, Peter?" Mrs. Cunningham said.

I choked on the mouthful of salad I was swallowing, and Peter glared at me. His sister-in-law, Michelle, patted my back until I dislodged the stuck piece of vegetable. Thanks for helping Peter.

"I'm just not that hungry this morning, is all," Peter said to his mother and winced as he leaned forward to grab his mimosa.

My coughing became worse as I tried not to laugh and covered my mouth. I could feel my face turning red as everyone stared at me.

"Is she going to be alright," his mother asked Peter, ignoring me like I was not a few seats away and not supposed to be part of the family. Not that it mattered.

I was ending things. The more I thought about it, the better I felt.

And if I had any second thoughts, they'd been wiped away after the strange dream I had last night. I crossed my legs under the table as the searing memory of the best sex I'd ever experienced flashed through my mind. The sad part was that the sex came from a dream or fantasy or something, but it certainly wasn't Peter. The dried come all over my back was his, but nothing else was. He'd never made me feel a fraction of what the dream had. Not even when putting forth his best effort. Adding insult to injury, after Peter screamed at me to take the cucumber out of his ass, he said I was a bitch for putting it there. His accusation most certainly had sealed the deal.

"I'm fine, thanks for asking," I said, but I couldn't quite remove the sarcastic tone from my words and earned another glare from Peter.

"I warned you about drinking too much of that champagne," his mother said, pointing her fork at Peter. "You always did like to indulge a little too much at the company party, but at least this year, you didn't do anything embarrassing."

She always reminded me of a bird. She had sharp features and then accentuated the look with her makeup. She had the same blue eye color as her son, but Peter received his handsome looks from his father. Mr. Cunningham had always been the nicer of the two, and he treated me like I was a person, but he couldn't make it to brunch, leaving me alone with the wolves of the family.

"I'm not sure it was the champagne," I said before I could stop myself.

Maybe I didn't want to, and just maybe, it was great to see his smug face humiliated for a change, even if I was the only one that knew why.

Peter stood in a rush, his chair scraping along the tiled floor. He was trying hard to mask the pain he was in, but it genuinely looked like he had a pickle shoved up his ass, which wasn't far off the mark.

"Kirby, can I speak to you in the hall, please?"

I dabbed at my mouth and stood from the overly extravagant table. The food, drinks, and place settings had been lined up like it was a king's welcome-home meal. I followed Peter out of the arched dining room door and into the foyer. I had the urge not to walk under the hanging chandelier that was so large it looked like it could crush me and most certainly cost more than everything I owned.

"What the hell do you think you're doing," Peter asked as he turned to face me. His voice was a harsh whisper, but it still echoed in the cathedral-styled entrance.

"None of them knew what I was talking about. You could've easily made anything up." I crossed my arms over my chest.

"This isn't funny. As if it wasn't bad enough that you sodomized me with a fucking vegetable, then you have to try and humiliate me in front of my family?"

I was losing my cool quickly. We'd already been over this. I told him I didn't do it, but he didn't believe me. I had no explanation for what happened, but I knew I didn't get up in the middle of the night to go to the fridge.

"For the last time, I didn't do it," I said.

"Come off it, Kirby, stop lying. If you didn't, then who did? Of course, it was you." Peter's eyes narrowed in anger. He was so enraged his body was practically shaking, and when he clenched his fist like he was going to hit me, I lost my cool.

"I don't know! Probably you did it yourself, but I didn't fucking stick the cucumber up your ass," I screamed, and his eyes went wide as he took a step back. Peter hated to be embarrassed. His entire life rotated around his image including in front of his family. I wasn't letting him get away with him making me out to be the asshole this time, and I took a step toward him. Lifting my hand, I gave Peter a hard poke in the chest.

"It's physically impossible for me to stick a foot and-a-half-long vegetable up your asshole while you come all over my back. You need to own up to the fact that you did it to yourself, and then you fucking came on me while I was asleep when you did it. Even worse, you let me sleep like that! I was the one that woke up with the dried crust of your orgasm all over my naked ass, not the other way around. Who's the one with the kink fetish in this scenario. Because it certainly isn't me." I again poked him hard in the chest. "But let me tell you, I really fucking wish I had been the one to do it because I would have made sure it didn't feel so good for you."

I glanced down the hall, and every member of his family was standing there with their mouth hanging open. Peter looked like he was going to faint as he followed my lead and looked down the hall. I rolled out my shoulders and straightened my spine as I marched passed the shocked group of people. Peter could try and spin that story any way he wanted to, but in the end, there was no other explanation, and I was done with him bitching at me. I mean, technically, it could've been someone else entirely, but it was ridiculous to think someone broke in only to mess with Peter and me like that. Then not steal anything, and not leave a trace or sign of a forced entry.

Grabbing my purse, I pushed past the group Peter was trying to explain the strange night to in as few words as possible.

"Where are you going?" Mrs. Cunningham said.

Her face was as angry as Peter's had been a moment ago. I had no idea why everyone was mad at me. Did his mother really think I'd do something like this? If so, it certainly explained why I never connected with her.

"I'm going home. I have work tonight, school tomorrow, and frankly, I'm tired and annoyed with...." I waved my hand in Peter's direction. "All of this. I'm done. We're through."

His mother stuttered, but I didn't stick around to see what she was going to say and made my way out the door. Pulling the phone out of my pocket, I opened the app to hire an Uber. The last thing I wanted to do today was deal with my mother.

Once the car was ordered, I tapped my finger on the cell number to call my dad. I was getting out of here, and I needed to stop fearing he was going to say no.

"Kirbs," my dad answered cheerfully, and as always, I relaxed at the sound of his voice.

"Hey, Dad, we need to talk, and please don't respond until I'm done," I said as the Uber pulled up. This conversation was another one that had been a long time coming.

CAIN

The cleaning cart's wheels rattled as I pushed the large plastic thing down the hall. It always amazed me how, when given the right outfit and circumstance, a person could blend in just about anywhere and not raise suspicion. I had to admit, though, that even for me, this was the biggest risk I'd ever taken, and the thrill was a little intoxicating.

I finished changing out the full garbage bag in the hall across from Kirby's class. It was about to start, and I saw her out of the corner of my eye as she made her way inside. More students filed in, and leaving the cart where it was, I walked into the darkened classroom almost the same time that Kirby's mother, Margaret Lawson, did. The alleged super agent didn't know she was only a few feet away from the man she was hunting, and I smirked at the thought. I'd seen her photo in the news, and her name was always mentioned when they found mine or Abel's bodies. I looked the woman over. Kirby looked nothing like her mother.

Kirby had a ton of helpful information on her phone, like her conversation with her mother about how her investigation was going with the Chameleon Killer case. It really was a catchy name. Margaret didn't reveal much other than the name of her new partner, an agent Hanson, but it didn't matter. It just made this entire situation that much sweeter. I was going to take Kirby, and I could only imagine the frantic outcry from her mother when her daughter disappeared into thin air. Or would she? They didn't seem to have a good relationship. All the texts I read were cold as if they'd been sent between two strangers rather than a mother and daughter.

"Welcome, everyone," Margaret started as I moved toward the silver can at the back of the room.

I made sure to keep my head down, and as the lights went out, I stood among the shadows to see this super agent at work. Kirby was sitting off to the side and halfway down the steep auditorium seating, but she was perfectly positioned for me to watch her. I needed to keep a close eye on my slippery little bunny.

Her mother didn't know it yet, but Kirby was trying to run off to another country, and that was something I simply couldn't allow. My cloned version of her phone showed that she called her dad in England, and she tried to purchase a plane ticket after the call. Unfortunately, as soon as Kirby finished placing the order for the flight, I immediately clicked on the confirmed purchase link and canceled the reservation. I was highly entertained by envisioning the look on her face as she continued to receive canceled notifications. I'd been even more amused when the credit card company froze her card. But I couldn't stop her father from buying her a ticket, so I needed to get my Sunshine in a cage before that happened.

Sorry Sunshine, but you're not sprinting off that easily. I have big plans for you.

"Today, I'm going to put up images on an unsolved case, and I want you to tell me what you see," Margaret said to the class as the first image appeared on the massive screen.

I turned my gaze from Kirby to the screen and sucked in a deep breath as my cock stirred in my pants. The image on the screen was mine. Well, it wasn't one of my photos, I took much better photos than the flat and unimaginative one on the screen, but it was one of my kills.

The image was of a woman I'd left leaning up against a tree with her arms pinned above her head. The artwork I'd carved into her body was that of a ballet dancer with flower petals falling around her. I'd taken the time to sew her eyes shut, so it looked like she was sleeping, but you could tell by the slightly concave look of her eyelids that she was missing her eyeballs. I remembered this kill clearly, but I remembered them all in HD-like detail.

"What do you see," Margaret asked and pointed to a random guy in the front row.

"The body looks clean, so I'd say they are methodical, and they have a large ego, or they wouldn't display the body for everyone to see," he said, and my lip twitched at the pathetic response. I should put the FBI out of their misery and permanently remove him from the class.

"What about the image on the body?"

"I'm not sure. Maybe it's someone that wanted to be an artist and feels scorned and takes out their frustration on their victim."

Margaret tapped her finger on the wooden podium. "Interesting, but I don't think that is what our killer is saying."

Margaret pointed to someone else, and I leaned back against the wall and crossed my arms as each one of the students she pointed to tried to come up with their own hypothesis for what and why I did certain things with my art.

"Kirby, what do you think?"

I perked up and fixed my stare on her face. She looked like she'd rather be anywhere else as she squirmed in her seat. Everything she did was intriguing to me. The way she took a deep breath and straightened in her seat spoke much more about being called out by her mother rather than participating in the class itself. I wondered if this was why she was not applying herself, and I rubbed my chin as I contemplated the possibility and best way to use the knowledge.

"I would say that you're looking for a male. Someone that is skilled with a knife."

"Is that all?" Margaret prompted.

Kirby bit her lip as she stared at the image.

"No, the killer is someone that is highly focused and kills without remorse." She pointed to the soft bruising. "It's also someone that didn't just take this person for sexual pleasure, yet I'm sure the killer was aroused or even assaulted the victim. This individual sees themself as an artist and has a natural talent in expressionism. There is a dark beauty with the dancer."

Kirby pointed at the screen.

"Her movements are elegant, but her face is drawn like she may have been an ugly personality or wearing a mask. So I would think that this person had secrets, maybe wasn't a good person, but all those around her thought she was wonderful and perfect."

My lip curled up as Kirby continued to speak.

"The body was left in a well-trafficked area. That building in the background is near a park downtown, but I'm assuming no one saw anything?"

"That's correct."

"Then he is someone that is local and probably has been local his whole life. He knows how to blend in and most likely works a job we see him doing daily. He also knows where the cameras are and is aware of the time of day that would be optimal to leave a body without being discovered. Whoever did this is highly intelligent and someone that is taking pride in the fact that we, as the FBI, haven't found him yet when he is right under our nose. Maybe he has even shaken our hands."

A smile pulled at the corners of my mouth as she finished speaking. I heard a student close to me snort. Finding him, I became irritated when he crossed his arms over his chest.

"Easy to get the gold star when your mother is the agent in charge," he mumbled to the student beside him. "Maybe, if I started fucking her or her mother, I'd get a gold star too. I'm not picky. I'd take either, Lawson."

The two guys laughed quietly while I memorized their faces. No one insulted Kirby without it also insulting me. She may only be mine for a day, a week, or a month, but it didn't matter the length of time until I released her, and she became the photograph on the screen. Kirby was mine. People didn't mess with what was mine.

"Very good. Does anyone else have anything to add," Margaret prompted, and I went back to barely paying attention to what was being said and focused my energy on Kirby's body language in her natural environment. She didn't lean toward or speak to any student near her. Kirby's eyes would glaze over as she stared at my art on the screen, and even how she shifted uncomfortably in her chair told me about of who she was, what she liked, and what she was trying to hide.

She was a threat.

She was probably the only real threat in the room aside from her mother, and yet all I could think about was how she tasted like a sweet plum on my lips and how I planned on claiming that pussy of hers again.

Maybe even tonight.

CHAPTER 17

KIRBY

I couldn't believe how nervous I was to have a conversation with my mother. My palms were sweating as I stood in her office, waiting for her. My dad loved the idea of me coming to visit him, but he said I needed to finish school first or take what I could from the classes to bring with me before leaving.

By some small miracle, I'd managed to get a sit-down meeting with a counselor to find out my best options for taking classes online. Mind you, it took a whole lot of 'tap dancing' to get it done. I hadn't realized I was such a good liar until the tears began pouring down my cheeks as I blurted out the sob story of my dad being sick and needing my help and my mother being too proud to ask for yet another favor for me. Apparently, it was good enough to grant me a three-week leave as long as I kept up with all my studies online.

"Sorry to keep you. Did you want to get some dinner?" My mother said as she stepped into her office. "I still have work to do tonight, but maybe you can tell me what is going on with Peter? He keeps texting me, asking me to ask you to get in touch with him."

I rolled my eyes as I peeled them away from a picture of my mother and the Director of the FBI shaking hands as she received an award.

"Of course, he texted you."

"He wouldn't have to if you bothered to answer his calls," my mother scolded as she sat down at her desk.

My jaw began to hurt as I clenched my teeth together to keep from swearing. Having a complete meltdown in her office was not a good idea. Did she even realize how controlling she was or how insulting she was about everything?

"It's only been a day. I just saw him yesterday, and I had school today, and now here I am. Not that it should be any of your business. I don't get why he's always running to you anyway." I put my hands on my hips. "I didn't realize that there were three people in my relationship." I conveniently left out the part where I told him we were done. That would've ended up in a massive argument, and I could only handle one fight with my mother at a time.

"Kirby, why do you always have to make everything so dramatic? He reached out because he was concerned and couldn't get in touch with you. It's called being a good boyfriend," she said as she picked up her pen and flipped open a folder. So much for going to dinner.

"Trust me, Peter plays the part well, but he's not as great as he seems."

She cocked a perfectly manicured brow at me, and I waved my hand in the air, trying to stop the crazy train that was this conversation before we ended up in an argument.

"Whatever. Talk to him, don't talk to him. I don't care."

"Well, now that is mighty big of you, Kirby," she said sarcastically and then looked up at me. "Considering we're all adults, and I know Peter is hoping to marry you, that would mean we'd see and speak on a regular basis."

She laid her hands on the desk as if questioning someone in an interrogation. It was a major pet peeve of mine when she did this to me. It was like no emotion was allowed to exist between us unless it was the emotion she thought was appropriate. She was the ultimate Ice Queen, and I was the spawn she got pregnant with by accident. I'd never lived up to her expectations since.

"You do know that marrying him would be what's best, don't you? I mean, he comes from a very influential family with enough money to ensure that if you decided to do your painting, you could. You should be happy that someone of his pedigree even looks your way."

My mouth fell open. "Who the hell do you think you are giving me advice on my relationship when you don't even know who my father is?"

"Excuse me?"

This was not why I was here. I had to remind myself before an entire volcano erupted in the office.

"Look, you can forget about marriage. I highly doubt that is going to happen," I said and crossed my arms over my chest before I leaped across the desk. "I didn't come here to talk to you about Peter. I was coming to tell you that I'm going to go and visit Dad for three weeks, and I've already made arrangements to keep up with classes virtually until I get back."

It was like all the air was sucked out of the room. My mother's eyes bugged out of her head while she turned an angry shade of tomato red. Leaning back in her chair, she gripped the edge of the desk with her hands until her knuckles turned white.

"What did you just say," she asked, her voice low as her eyes narrowed into thin slits.

"Now, who's the one being dramatic? It's not like I'm going forever. As you are already are aware, all my grades are ninety-five and higher. Regardless if you think I'm applying myself or not, I am a top student."

My mother shot out of her chair so fast that I took a step back in shock. "No, I'm not allowing it. I'll speak to someone tomorrow and get this straightened out."

I stepped toward her desk, my hands dropping to my sides.

"No, you will not. I'm not a child, and I'm not your prisoner, no matter how much you enjoy treating me like one. I'm leaving, and if you try to stop me, I'll never come back after I leave." I leaned on the desk, going toe to toe with my mother as the tension built in the room. "I never wanted to come here. I never wanted to be an agent, but I'll finish the course as promised. I need a break, and it's been almost two years since I've seen Dad."

"What the hell would you need a break from? You have more than most people could ever want?" She held her arms open, and I realized she was talking about material things: clothes, food, money, and whatever else she put on that list.

"It has nothing to do with material things. I...I don't know how to explain it to you, but I just need some space to breathe. Away from here, away from Peter, and away from you." I pinched the bridge of my nose and sighed. "You're smothering me, and I can't take it."

My mother laughed, but the sound was not jovial in any way.

"You were always a daddy's girl. I shouldn't be surprised that you'd run to him when things got a little uncomfortable or too real for you. It's what you've always done, and he always allows you to get away with it. You're never going to grow up, and I'm sick of seeing you throw your life away. So, if you decide to do this, then I'm not funding the rest of your school."

I shook my head at the blatant stupidity. "Do you even hear yourself when you speak? Because that was the stupidest thing I have ever heard you say."

"Don't you dare talk to me like that. I'm still your mother. Show some respect."

She pressed the knuckles of her fist into the table, and I stared at her hand, which used to have a wedding ring on it. There used to be a lot of things that were different, but she ruined all of them. She chose her ambition and career over her family time and again. She chose to have an affair rather than be faithful to her husband. She chose to treat me like an annoying parasite rather than her child. I needed to stop thinking that this was somehow my fault when I told dad about her affair.

"Respect is not given just because you're my mother, it must be earned, and you lost all my respect the day you couldn't tell me who my father was," I snarled.

It was as if I'd smacked a dragon. Her nostrils flared, and she sucked in a deep breath like she was going to blow fire at me. She probably would've if it weren't for a man I didn't recognize walking into the room.

"Is everything alright in here," the man asked as he stared between my mother and me.

"Yeah, I was just leaving."

"We're not done talking about this," my mother called after me as I made my way out the door.

I didn't bother to say anything. There was no point when she was like this. I'd learned that the hard way far too many times. I'd get further by banging my head off a wall. Storming down the hall, I felt my coat flutter around me. The few people in the hallway gave me a wide birth, so I must have looked like I wanted to kill someone. My phone rang in my pocket, and I immediately groaned as I stared at Peter's name.

Might as well get this done and over with, rip the bandage off in one go, so I hit the answer.

"Hi Peter," I said after I pressed answer on the screen.

"Hi there, Babe," he said, his voice cheerful, and I pulled the phone away from my ear and stared at it as if he'd just spoken another language. "You still there?"

I stopped just inside the doors and stared out at the dark sky. That was the thing I hated about winter. It wasn't the cold, snow, or even the slush on the roads that made it a slow white-knuckle drive. No, it was how early it got dark.

"Yeah, I'm still here. I'm just trying to figure out why you're suddenly in such a good mood. When I left your mother's house yesterday, I didn't think we'd ever speak again. I mean, I did tell you we were through, or did you not hear that part?"

"Things got out of hand, but I wanted to make it up to you. I know we haven't been getting along much lately, but I miss how we used to be. Can I take you to dinner, and we can talk about us? I really don't want yesterday to be the way we end things."

Just end the torture. Just say, 'nope, I'm sorry, but it's not working for me. Don't agree to dinner.'

"I guess I could do that. When did you want to meet?" Swallowing hard, I closed my eyes as I mentally punched myself in the face.

"I'm just around the corner. I was hoping you'd say yes. I'll be there in five to pick you up," he said. I looked down at the white blouse, navy pants, and plain pumps I was wearing.

"I'd need to get changed first...."

From the door I was standing next to, I could see his lights pull into the parking lot. "Don't worry about it. We will go somewhere relaxed and casual. I'll see you at the door. Talk in a minute, Babe." The phone connection went dead, and every single one of my what-the-fuck synapses were firing on all cylinders.

Pulling up to the curb, he got out and waved as he smiled. Once more, I wondered if I'd somehow stepped into an alternate reality. As I stepped outside from the warmth of the building and walked down the stairs, I shivered as the cool fall air swirled around my neck. An image of walking the plank with a shark swirling below in the water popped into my head.

"Hey Babe, you look great," Peter said as I slipped into the car's passenger side door. He leaned over to kiss me, and I pulled back and stared at him.

"What's going on? Why are you being so sweet? This is not like you at all." I looked him over and even sniffed the air to see if maybe he'd been drinking.

"Nothing is wrong, I swear. It's just that I realized what a jerk I'd been lately, and it's all because of the stress at work. I shouldn't have taken it out on you or let it interfere with our relationship. Work shouldn't come between us, and I've been so stressed and embarrassed to say anything." He smiled and pulled away from the curb. "You know I want to marry you, Kirbs."

He used the pet name that he'd given me when we first started dating. I hated it. This one-eighty felt as if it were too much for me. You don't go from thinking that everything your partner does was annoying to being sorry and acting like Mary Fucking Poppins the next. I watched him closely as he began talking about his day and the new deal he'd negotiated all on his own. Being so focused on him, I didn't pay attention to where we were going, but my red flag soared higher as we pulled into the parking lot of a bar on the outskirts of civilization. This place was a known motorcycle hangout for those passing through and was a complete biker's haven with strippers and spicy wings. It was also a place you never wanted to step foot in as law enforcement of any kind. I was a damn glowing beacon for the FBI in my outfit.

Peter hated everything about this place, from the pub food to those that hung out there and even the entertainment. If Peter liked strippers, he only ever went in secret because he voiced how dirty and disgusting those places were. He said he wouldn't be caught dead at a place where low-life scum came to hang out.

"What are we doing here," I asked as I stared up at the glowing red sign that was mostly burnt out, leaving the sign to read 'Red Ass' instead of *The Red Assailant*. Both were kind of fitting, really.

"What do you mean?"

"I mean, we both know you hate going to places like this, so what gives?" I leaned back against the door and crossed my arms over my chest as I analyzed his face. "I'm the one that likes pub food and doesn't mind watching the strippers, so why are we here, Peter?"

"I thought we'd try something different, maybe have a few drinks and have a little fun."

My brow cocked at his explanation. "Yeah, I'm not buying it. Do you think I'm stupid? I'm not going in there until you tell me exactly what is going on."

A bit of his overly happy mask slipped as it became clear I wasn't going to get out and go into this place with him. I had no idea at this point if he planned on having me become the entertainment or if he thought it would be fun to watch the shit get beat out of me for being a fed.

"What do you think I'm trying to do? Humiliate you, maybe? Kind of like you humiliated me in front of my family?"

I shook my head. "Are you kidding me right now?"

Peter picked up his cell phone and held it up to face me. "Call me. Go ahead and see what happens."

Confused, I reached into my pocket, pulled out my phone, and hit redial beside his name. The song "Ring of Fire" by Johnny Cash began to play, but the picture that showed up had me laughing so hard tears rolled down my cheeks. There, front and center on the screen, was a close-up of Peter's bare ass with the cucumber shoved in until only a few inches were visible.

"You think this is funny?" Peter hit the end button on the screen. I tried to stop laughing, but every time I attempted to get the words out, I started all over again. "This isn't funny! When I was in my meeting today, the phone rang, and that is what showed up. Luckily, I played it off as a prank from the boys at the golf club, but it could've sunk my entire deal. I was mortified."

Wiping the tears away, I managed to get control enough of myself to speak.

"Peter, I didn't do it, and even if I did take the picture, I was in no shape to upload it to your phone. I couldn't even get out of my dress."

"Well, I certainly didn't take this photo. You know I knew all along you were lying, and this proves it." He shook his head, his eyes flaring with anger that made me uncomfortable and sobered the rest of the laughter out of my system.

"I don't know what you want me to say, Peter. Obviously, you don't believe me, yet I can't tell you I did something that I didn't."

Remnants of the dream returned to me as I remembered how hot and sexy it was and how hard I'd come. There was one more weird thing that I couldn't explain—there was a small bruise on the side of my neck. I'd assumed I'd done something stupid at the party, or it had happened when I fell a few times, but now I wasn't so sure.

Peter suddenly grabbed my arm and squeezed hard. "Don't you fucking ignore me when I'm talking to you."

"Let go of me," I said and punched Peter in the face without even thinking about it.

His hands immediately went for his nose as blood trickled down his lips. "You bitch! That's it. We're definitely through."

"Good, I already broke up with you, you narcissistic asshole," I yelled. I grabbed for the handle to get out, but Peter jammed his foot on the gas. The car's sudden lurch slammed me back into the seat as the door locked into place.

"Let me out, Peter. I don't want to go anywhere with you."

I grabbed the 'oh shit' handle as the car flew out of the parking lot. The car revved as it sped up to dangerous speeds.

"What the fuck?" I screamed as we streaked around a bend in the road.

Peter gripped the steering wheel like he was a race car driver, and his face was the epitome of rage. His brows were furrowed, and his lips pulled up like he was snarling. I'd never seen him like this before, and I scrambled with the seatbelt trying to get it back on, but it was locked in place. I jerked on it hard as Peter veered off the main road onto a back road with no lights. I swallowed hard. This wasn't good, and my mind immediately began to go through all my training on how to get out of this.

"Fuck this shit!" The car squealed as he slammed on the brakes.

I hit the windshield with enough force that I must have looked like a cartoon character. A small scream ripped from my throat as Peter slammed on the gas again and then turned the car onto a gravel road I didn't know. He floored it again, and I slammed back into the seat. This time rocks from the dirt road sprayed the underside of the car with little pings, and the vehicle fishtailed all over the road. The fact that Peter was so enraged he didn't notice rocks hitting his car terrified me more than just about anything else.

"Are you fucking crazy? Have you lost your damn mind," I yelled and was tempted to grab the steering wheel.

There was a vehicle coming toward us in the opposite direction. We flew past the tow truck at speeds that made it look like it was standing still. The trees were nothing but a blur, and I thought I was going to be sick. He was going to kill us both. All I could picture was the car wrapped around one of the large trees. I screamed again as we blew through a stop sign, and he didn't even tap the breaks.

"Me, crazy? That's funny." Once more, he slammed on the brakes and yanked the car to the right-hand side of the road, sending gravel flying. "Get out," he snarled again like he was more animal than human.

"Here? Just take me back to the dorm, and you never have to see me again."

"I said get out! Now!" His body was shaking.

Deciding it was better to be left at the side of the road in the middle of nowhere rather than in the car with him, I opened the door to hop out. Before I could move, a harsh fist gripped my hair, and I was yanked away from the door. He practically dragged me into his lap with force as I screamed at the top of my lungs.

"Peter, let go. You're hurting me." I clawed at whatever bare skin I could get my hands on as he roughly stuck his hand down my shirt. "Peter, stop," I cried out as he palmed my boob like he was trying to twist the thing off my body.

I suddenly wished I had more than the meager twelve weeks of combat training. Stupidly, this was not a situation I ever thought I'd be in, and the urge to freak out grew as adrenaline pumped through my body. It was a big thing to learn how to control your nerves at Quantico, but I can honestly say that for all my bravado, it was a fuck load harder than I thought it would be.

I punched up at Peter's face and tried to drive my elbow down into his leg or anywhere soft as I struggled against his much larger size. My nails dug into his chest and twisted hard, making him yell out.

"Stupid fucking slut, you're a sick bitch. My mother was right about you." He lifted my head hard and slammed it into the steering wheel. "No one humiliates me. No one humiliates my family," Peter snarled like a rabid animal as he brought my head down into his lap and once more pushed my face into the bottom part of the leather wheel.

I struck out again, and he smacked my hands away as he ripped open my blouse. The buttons tinged against the dash as they flew off the shirt in all directions. I managed to get my hand on the horn, the sound blaring loud, but even I knew there wasn't anyone around for miles to hear. I screamed again as his hand tightened in my hair and pulled my head further into his lap, forcing me to stare up at his face. At the odd angle, the console and the gear shift were pressing painfully into my back.

"I'm going to make you choke on my cock."

"Spare me. You're a fucking useless prick that couldn't fuck for shit," I spat up at him and lunged for his stomach with my teeth, narrowly missing my target.

"Fucking whore, I'm going to...."

"To what? Hurt me? Rape me? Make me pay," I raged. "You're not man enough to do any of those things."

I could feel the anger coming off him as his body shook with the crazed rage coursing through him. I wanted him to be so angry that he would make mistake after mistake. One thing Peter wasn't very good at was being smart when he was emotional. I planned on using that deficit to my advantage.

Peter grabbed the front of my bra and pulled it up until my breasts popped out the bottom. As I thrashed harder, my foot slammed into the expensive upholstery of the dash and ceiling of the car. I was purposely trying to puncture holes and leave scraps.

"Stop kicking my car!"

"Then let go of me, you idiot! When my mother finds out what you've done, she's going to hate you," I yelled, and he paused in his movement.

It was just a moment, but it was enough for me to catch him off guard and punch up as hard as I could. I caught him in the bottom of his jaw, and his mouth slammed shut with an audible snap.

I had no idea what Peter would've done next because bright lights pulled up behind the vehicle, the headlights illuminating the inside of the car like the sun suddenly rose. Peter released me like a hot potato, and not caring if my shirt was in place, I leaped for the open door and pulled my coat tightly around me.

"Is everything alright here," asked a male voice, but I couldn't see who it was. The voice was familiar, though.

The glare of the headlights on the large truck blinded my eyes, but I heard the engine still rumbling. Peter, the chicken shit, stomped on the gas. The car's wheels squealed as he pulled away from the edge of the road. The door slammed into place, but something flew out the window as he took off as fast as my heart was hammering. The shock of what almost happened was just settling in as my shaking hand covered my mouth.

"Are you alright, Miss..." The voice that sounded was the same rich, gravelly tone that washed through me at the coffee shop.

He took a step forward, and as he did, he stepped into the light's beam. I sucked in a sharp breath as soon as I saw who it was. My eyes glanced at the simple white tow truck and then back to the man.

"You," I managed to spit out. "I know you." He cocked his head and stared at me, his eyes calm. "From the coffee shop, I spilled coffee on myself."

His eyes lit up. "I didn't recognize you out here. You're having a string of bad luck lately."

"You could say that." I shook my head. "Thanks for coming along when you did."

He looked around the pitch-black road. For the first time since my mad escape from Peter's car, I realized that we really were out in the middle of nowhere, and it was very cold outside. I shivered and put my hand in my pocket to pull out my phone. There was no signal.

Great.

"There's no service out here. This entire area never gets service. It's partly the reason I like to work this road. I don't want someone to get stuck out here. No one would be able to find them."

"That's really nice of you. I hate to ask this, but would you be able to drive me to Quantico?"

His eyebrows rose as he stuffed his hands in his pockets, and as shaken up as I was, I couldn't deny that something about him had my blood heating up, which was all sorts of wrong. He rubbed the back of his neck, and I clasped my hands in front of my body.

"Please, I'll pay for your gas, or if you miss out on a call, I will pay for what it will cost you to lose the tow."

He sighed and nodded. "Alright, but I need to go to my shop first. It's down the road a ways, but that is where I was heading when I saw your car. I own a garage and was working on a friend's car that needs parts."

"That's completely fine, thank you." I padded my other pocket, didn't find my purse, and swore as I spun in a circle.

"If you're looking for your purse, it's over there," the guy said and pointed. "Whoever you were with tossed it."

"Oh, thank god." I marched over and bent to pick up the small black purse. "What's your name," I asked as I turned toward him.

He gave me a smirk as he stood in front of the truck. I gripped my purse tighter as I stepped closer once more. His eyes were intense, like they were swallowing me whole even though he hadn't moved.

"Cain," he held out his hand.

"Kirby," I said and reached for his hand. As our hands met, I sucked in a deep breath as the sexy dreams I'd been having of this man rushed to the surface of my mind. His hand was firm and warm, and I had to force myself to release it. "You have really nice hands," I said. Clearing my throat, I felt compelled to explain. "I was expecting rougher hands with the type of work you do."

Awkward much?

Turning, I practically sprinted to the passenger side of the truck. I had no idea where that random comment came from, but he didn't acknowledge my strange outburst as he got in beside me. If an award could be handed out for the worst day ever, I think I may have won.

It couldn't get any worse than almost being raped by my ex.

Hello Sunshine

CHAPTER 18

CAIN

There are just sometimes in this life that I had to wonder if there really was a God, and if there was, did he hate his creations as much as I did? I had a whole plan on how to kidnap Kirby. I'd spent all last night mapping it out to the letter, and then Peter, oh so generously, helped me out. He made my plan so easy that I couldn't even believe it. The man was still going to meet the end of my blade, and as Kirby sat quietly beside me, I deemed it was going to be a far sweeter kill with her watching.

My cock had been rock hard the moment she touched my hand, but the scent of her skin filling the cab of my truck made it hard to think about anything other than getting her under me. Even though the truck was warm, she pulled the coat around her body tighter and stared out the window. I figured that this was one of those moments I should be feeling bad that her night was going to take another turn, and yet that wasn't me. Why should I feel bad that the fly flew into the center of the web I was already making?

I stopped at the metal gate to put the code into the keypad entrance. The little box beeped as I entered in the nine-digit code. You could never be too safe.

"Seems like a pretty remote area to need a large metal gate," she said as I leaned out the window.

"All the more reason to have security. My shop always has many client vehicles parked around it, and people see a remote area as a good spot to steal from. I wouldn't want an upset client because their vehicle was broken into," I said as the metal slowly began to swing open and grant us entry. "Bad for business."

I could almost hear the quickening of her heart as we pulled through the gates and the headlights of the truck showed the long driveway with the overgrown grass and old trees that fanned out on either side. During the day, it was quite a pretty drive if you were into that sort of thing, but it had an unsettling ambiance at night. Also made it very difficult to get through and sneak up to the house without setting off one of the cameras or motion detectors.

Sunshine swallowed hard, and I could feel her sigh as the bouncing truck rounded the last corner to reveal the shop I kept as neat as a pin and our sweet-looking old farmhouse. I'd already closed the gardens up, but there were a few of the perennials that liked the cooler weather flourishing. They swayed next to the little solar lights that were glowing brightly.

"Wow, this is a really pretty spot," she said and looked around.

"Thank you. It was my parents' place but I took the property over when they passed away. I just really thought this place suited me more than moving. Lots of memories here," I said and hopped out of the truck, but Kirby remained in the passenger seat. "Are you not getting out?"

"Oh, I didn't think we were going to be long. I was going to see if I could call—"

She looked down at her phone, and I knew she didn't have anyone to call. Not really. Her mother, maybe, but the only other person on her saved list of people from this state was the man that just assaulted her.

"No, I won't be too long, but I need to take care of a couple of things." I gave a half-hearted shrug and made sure that my body didn't give off any vibes that she was in danger. But she was most certainly in danger. She had been the moment I saw her for the first time. "You can call whoever you need to in here if you want."

Kirby didn't say anything, but she reached for the handle. The old truck door squeaked as she pushed it open and got out. I made sure to walk slowly and with purpose toward the shop as I pulled out the keys to unlock the door. Flicking on the light, I began milling around and patiently waited for Kirby to step inside. This game of seeing just how far I could get her to go on her own was highly entertaining. Maybe I could get her to climb into her cage too. It wasn't really a cage per se, but the idea was the same.

I wandered around the front of the car I was currently fixing and over to the small bar fridge. Smirking as I heard her footsteps on the concrete floor, I bent over to open it. I pulled out two beers and made my way around to the door. She was rigid, her body on alert as her eyes searched every corner for the boogeyman that was right in front of her.

Holding out the beer, I asked, "Would you like a drink?"

"I didn't think we were staying long? You said you needed to pick something up," she said as she stared between the beer in my hand and my face.

"You're right. I did say that." I cracked open one of the cans and took a sip.

Leaning against the edge of the workbench, I allowed myself to take her in up close without having to be quiet or sneak around. As much fun as all that had been, it had led to this moment. Her nostrils flared as she took a deep breath. It was her body's way of expressing that she was suddenly very aware that things were not going her way...again. I took another sip of the beer and continued to stare at her eyes. They were such a prize. Fuck I wanted them so much. So rare, so fucking rare, and they were mine. She was mine.

"I don't understand," she finally said. Her arms pulled tighter around her body, but her legs were set to fight.

Smart girl. I loved the fact that she wasn't a weak mark. It made the chase so much more exhilarating.

"I thought we'd get to know one another better." She narrowed her eyes at me. "I mean, I would love to hear more about what you think of my work."

Her brow furrowed, and I could almost see the wheels turning in her mind as she tried to think about when she would've spoken about my work. She was most likely going over our coffee shop interaction, and she was going to come up short. She shook her head back and forth, and I decided to help her out.

I so enjoyed having a hyperthymesia memory.

"How did you put it again? He is someone that is local and probably has been local his whole life. He knows how to blend in and most likely works a job that we see him doing every single day. He also knows where the cameras are and is aware of the time of day that would be optimal to leave a body without being discovered. Whoever did this is highly intelligent and someone that is taking pride in the fact that we, as the FBI, haven't found him yet when he is right under our nose. Maybe he has even shaken our hands."

I smiled as her eyes went wide. I could see the pulse jump in her throat as the pieces clicked into place.

"I have to say you were quite eloquent and the only one that was correct in everything you said. And I love that you think my work is beautiful." I smiled wide. "I take immense pride in what I do, and I know that you'll be the most beautiful addition yet to my collection."

Her mouth dropped open but quickly snapped into action as she spun on her heels, poised to run, or so I thought. Instead, Sunshine made to grab for my crowbar hanging on the wall, and I gripped her arm tight before she could touch it. I also wasn't expecting the hard elbow that connected with the side of my face. It hit me with enough force to make me stagger back a step, but I kept a firm hold of her arm, forcing her to come with me. She turned in my hold, and I managed to tighten my abs just before she kicked out and caught me in the gut.

She spun in the long jacket pulling it from her body and began to strike me as quick as a cobra. She landed a left jab, a right jab, and then a left one again. Stumbling back, I stopped as my ass came into contact with the car parked in the garage. I saw the kick coming and managed to move just enough so she caught me above the knee rather than it being the debilitating blow it would've been.

Each hit she landed was getting me riled up, but not angry. I was getting turned on. My cock was rock hard inside my jeans, and I had to suck in a deep breath to steady the surge of strange desire that slammed through me.

Her eyes glanced down for just a second, but I knew she noticed how excited I was.

"That's it Sunshine. Keep hitting me, I like it." I licked the blood from my lip and then laughed as her fist came again with a yell, but this time I caught her wrist.

She surprised me further by breaking my hold with a strange move as she attempted to knee me in the gut, which I blocked. She was laboring, and her movements were slowing just enough for me to know she was going to weaken before I did. Grabbing her arm again, she flipped us onto the floor before jumping to her feet and sprinting like a bunny for the crowbar once more.

I snatched her pant leg, and she fell with a hard crash. She made a little noise as all the air was driven from her lungs with the fall.

"Oh, I do like you," I said, licking my lips.

Kirby scrambled on the concrete floor, legs kicking at me until I let go of her ankle. Releasing her on purpose, I smiled.

"Run," I whispered, and run she did. Kirby leaped out the door like her ass was set on fire and took off into the night.

"You can run, but you won't get far," I called out the door and smiled as I pulled myself to my feet. I rolled out my shoulders, cracked my neck, and counted to ten as the excited energy built in my body.

It had been a long time since someone had surprised me like that. I tossed the coat that had ended up draped on me onto the workbench.

"Ten," I said as I bolted out the door after my prey.

"Shit, she is quick," I mumbled as I watched her race along the driveway. That path took her deeper onto the property when she veered off into the trees.

I knew she was quick. I'd been running in the mornings with her, even though she didn't know it, to test her endurance and speed. I knew she'd be tough to catch, but the thought of the chase had made me giddy with anticipation, and I hoped she'd try and run. She just continued to check off all my boxes.

I'd never felt this kind of exhilaration at any time in my life, and with each pump of my arms and legs that brought me a little closer, I knew that no one other than her would make me feel the same way again. She burst from the cover of the trees and ran right past Abel's house, but I almost stopped and laughed as she slowed to see my brother sitting in a rocking chair on the front porch. How confusing that moment must have been for her. I could almost see the expression on her face as she ran under the tall yard light.

"Run, little rabbit, run," Abel cheered her on as another bug zapped itself on one of the twenty zappers he had hanging around his porch like fucking decoration. She sped up again and hopped over his pink fence like she was running hurdles and stopped to try the doors of Abel's taxi.

She smacked the roof when she couldn't open the door and took off again.

"Woohoo! You get 'er, bro! This is the best fucking night of my life," Abel called after me as I flew past, my strides eating up the ground as the gravel crunched and took the same fence Kirby had without slowing down.

"Get your car and come to Devil's Ditch," I called back. I could hear him let out a wild whoop and knew without looking that he would be right on my heels.

Kirby tripped on the rough ground, the little heeled shoes not providing the same traction or support as her normal running shoes. She stumbled again as her ankle buckled, but I was impressed as she managed to stay upright and keep going.

Gaining on her, I could hear her breaths as they labored. I wondered what was running through her mind. Was it the same as when she ran the trail at school? I doubted that. She looked over her shoulder and our eyes locked. Even in almost complete darkness, I could see the fear in her eyes.

I had to give her credit. She managed to push on a lot longer and faster than I thought she'd be able to, and it was taking much longer than I thought it would to catch my Sunshine. I could see lights in the distance and knew she would also see the car. Obviously not hearing me yell at Abel, she angled herself toward the lights like a moth to a flame. Didn't she just see what happens to bugs when they head toward the pretty lights?

I narrated her thoughts in my own mind as she realized that it was the taxi she'd passed that she was running toward, and she understood her error. She shouldn't have run. She should've stayed and fought. Her pace slowed as her mind tried to decide what to do next. Abel stepped out of the car and draped himself over the car door.

"Come on, girly, get in! I'll take good care of you," Abel called out, and her stride faltered.

As she turned to try and go in another direction, my arm snaked around her waist. Sunshine screamed as I took her to the ground with our momentum. The gravel bit painfully as we skidded, but I tightened my arms around her. She managed to crack me in the nose with the back of her head, and I could feel the blood drip as my vision blurred for a moment.

"Keep it up, Sunshine. I'm fucking loving the feel of you struggle."

My cock kicked hard in my jeans as the pain registered, and my teeth latched onto her earlobe. She screamed and kicked out as she struggled to free herself, but her thrashing lessened as my teeth tightened on the delicate skin. The maneuver reminded me of the twitch that our veterinarian would use on my father's old horse. That old nag would kick you in the head whenever it was time to have his feet trimmed unless you twitched his nose. My teeth had just become Sunshine's twitch.

"Ah, shit," I yelled, releasing her ear as gravel and dirt landed in my face. Somehow Kirby had managed to get a handful and toss it up at me. I quickly tightened my hold and wrapped my legs around hers. She was delightfully thrashing and rubbing herself against my trapped cock. I let out a groan against the side of her neck.

"I like your spunk, Kirby. Fuck, it really turns me on."

I gave the side of her neck a nip and then licked the blood from my nose off her pale skin. She became hysterical, but my grip was like two pythons slowly choking out the fight in their prey. Her left leg broke the hold I had with my own leg, and we ended up kicking at one another as I tried to subdue her again.

"Grab her legs," I said to Abel.

"Do I have to? This is the best fucking entertainment I've had in a long time. I don't even know who to put money on, but damn, my cock is getting hard watching this." Abel laughed as I managed to find him and glare at him. "Alright, alright, hang onto her panties."

Abel shimmied over, his feet dancing around our legs as they continued to flail.

"Oh, oh, we have a live one here! Where is my rod? I need to reel this fish in. Better yet, where is my damn cattle prod when I need it?" Abel's rambling was normally annoying, but it was exceptionally so at this moment. "I can't get a good grip, Captain. She's a slippery wee buggar," Abel said in a British accent.

I was really fucking tempted to let Kirby go so I could kick my brother's ass and then chase her down again.

"Just get her to stop kicking," I growled out through clenched teeth.

Her ass once more pushed hard into my sensitive cock. Pain sliced through me, and my cock was tempted to blow its load in my jeans.

"You're always such a pill, man. No fun at all. Fine, you want her to stop kicking, you got it."

Both Kirby and I yelled out as Abel landed crossbody over our waist and legs like he was doing a Superman dive.

"What the fuck?" I called out as his added weight pushed her lush ass impossibly harder into my trapped cock that was now screaming to flip her over and fuck her hard.

"Let me go, you crazy fucks," Kirby screamed, but her fight was slowly waning as she panted.

I couldn't see what Abel was doing, but suddenly, Kirby's writhing body was lifted off of me by her legs. I clamped my jaw down tight, the muscles twitching as much as my aching cock. The thought of pushing her over the taxi crossed my mind. I was so fucking tempted, but Abel would want in on the fun, and this was one prize I had no intention of sharing.

Going with the momentum, I stood. She wiggled back and forth like a worm, only to splay open her ripped blouse and show off the sexy lace-clad breasts. Fuck, her nipples were nice and pert.

"Damn man, she be fine! No wonder you wanted this one. We're gonna have some kind of fun with her! Whoohoo! Giddy up, girly. I mean, look at those milk jugs. I'm gonna motorboat those bitches," Abel licked his lips as he stared at Kirby's chest, and a fury crawled up and gripped me by the throat. I stopped walking, and it jerked Abel to a halt.

"Don't fucking touch her," I snarled over the top of Kirby, who'd gone quiet and momentarily stopped her struggling to look between the two of us.

"Wow, who crawled up your ass and died?"

"Just get her in the car," I said.

"Fine, whatever," Abel complained as he opened the back door with one hand.

Kirby instantly started screaming again, her struggles stronger from the few seconds of rest. I was enjoying the feral look on her face, and I loved the idea of taming her even more. I'd never kept anyone longer than a night or two, but the idea of keeping her around for multiple days or weeks held an appeal that felt foreign.

Capturing victims that we set loose just to chase down had become a bit of a pastime. In perfect synchronicity, we turned so Abel could draw her legs into the backseat. He opened the other door, stepped out the far side, and closed the door.

Kirby looked me in the eyes for the first time since her mad dash, and her stunning eyes were pleading with me. "Please don't do this. I don't want to die."

"I'm sorry, Sunshine, but you sealed your fate to this moment the first time I laid eyes on you." She yelled for help and struck out at me as I laid my lips against her forehead. "Don't worry. I'll break you in slowly...maybe."

Giving her a hard shove, she fell onto the seat and bounced off onto the cab's floor as the door was locked into place. Her hands beat against the door as her feet thumped on the other side. I had to give it to my Sunshine. She was a fighter, making the thought of breaking her much more fun.

"Sleepy by time," Abel sang as he released the sleeping gas he used to knock out the passengers he wanted to keep.

The pounding of her fists on the glass slowed and then stopped as she flopped over onto the seat.

"Thank you for your help, brother."

"To see your runnin' like Forest Gump as you chased your tail down the driveway? Are you kidding? I'm itching to take her up to the house and release her just so I can watch that shit again. Best fucking night ever!"

"Do it and find out what I'll do to you." Abel laughed, but there was no guarantee I wouldn't kill him if he tried something that stupid with my top prize. "Come on, let's go. I need to get cleaned up. I have a very important date."

Smirking, I wandered to the car's passenger side and peered through the glass that separated the front from the back. "I bet you thought to yourself that your night couldn't get any worse."

CHAPTER 19

KIRBY

My fingertips ran through the flowers of the field, the pretty blues, pinks, and whites mixing with the golden rays of the warm sun. Giggling like a young girl again, I twirled in a circle and let the dress flow out around me. A group of butterflies lifted into the air surrounding my body. Some landed on my arms as I held them out to the side. They were beautiful, with multicolored wings glimmering brighter than the flowers below them. One of the butterflies walked up my arm, and I smiled in wonder until it reached my shoulder. The closer it got, the more I focused on it. Finally, I realized I was staring into the eyes of a man and not a butterfly's.

"What? No," I screeched as I realized it was the man with the bright blue eyes. "No, go away."

I swatted at the insect, and all those that had landed on parts of my body swarmed around me. Each one of their faces morphed into the face that made a person want to lock their doors at night and never travel alone. They were eyes parents warned their children about and a smile that could freeze you in place as surely as Medusa could.

Running through the tall grass and flowers to escape the little beasts, I made my way toward the nearby trees. Darting into the shade and cover of the canopy, I turned and looked behind me but didn't see any of the strange insects. Being underneath the trees was far darker than it had looked from the field. Tilting my head back, I could only see a little fragment of light. Shivering, I wrapped my arms around myself and stepped gingerly over the rougher ground until my feet found a wide path. This spot was lovely. The way it opened up and allowed the sunshine to filter through in pockets gave the appearance of spotlights.

Feeling lighthearted once more, I picked up the pace, and my footfalls barely made a sound on the packed dirt. Humming a song that was stuck in my head, my feet shuffled a little faster to the beat as I began singing.

"Take me away," I sang. "A secret place."

Allowing my eyes to close, I felt my body move to the song that was on a constant loop in my head. It was only then that I realized I didn't know where I was going. As beautiful as the path was, it was familiar. I tried to recall where I'd seen this trail before, but the harder my brain worked to remember, the more uncertain I became. The song died on my lips, and my pace slowed as the gentle breeze that had been rustling the leaves disappeared and left an eerie silence in its wake.

The sensation of being watched made the hair stand up on the back of my neck. Spinning in a circle, I searched the shadowed forest for the cause of my unease but didn't see anything move. The sweet smell in the air was replaced with the scent of something strong that I couldn't place, but it was making my nose curl.

"I've got a pocket full of sunshine."

"Who said that?" Still, nothing moved, but the forest seemed darker as the bright spots dulled, the sun disappearing. "Answer me, who said that?"

"A sweet escape...take me away."

"Stop it! Show yourself," I screamed, and a few birds nearby took off, making me jump.

There was a subtle movement in the distance, and then just like that, there he was. He was far away, but it didn't matter. I knew who he was. I could feel his stare boring a hole into me. He was the man with the eyes that wanted to tear my heart from my chest and eat it in front of me.

He stood on the path with his feet apart and his hands in fists at his side, and I couldn't stop the shaking that started in my legs and traveled up my body. He didn't say anything as we stared at one another, but he didn't have to—I knew what he wanted, and my blood was at the top of his list.

Turning on my heel, I bolted along the path away from him, fear and adrenaline pumping through my system. The hard dirt shifted and became sand, and my feet started to slip. The sand quickly got deeper, and the forest moved further away from the trail. Even though I tried to reach for the edge and the firmer ground, the shifting sand kept pulling me further away. Every stride hurt as my lungs and legs worked harder than they'd ever had before.

A scream ripped from my throat as the man casually strolled beside me until he stood in my way. In every direction I turned to run, *he was there. It was like he'd divided himself into hundreds of versions of his image, and they had surrounded me.*

"No, please don't hurt me. I don't want to die."

The man reached out and grabbed my face in his hand. He got up close, and I hated the fact that even with the wild fear racing through my screaming body, I couldn't help being attracted to him. There was something hypnotic about his presence. He was like a snake tamer, and I was caught in his flute's call.

"Hello, Sunshine."

Music was blaring so loud that I could feel the vibration in my cheek as it lay on something soft...my eyes fluttered open, unable to remember where I was or what had happened. I couldn't wait to tell Jorge about my strange dream. He was the type to appreciate my crazy, wild adventure. We'd laugh over his special coffee that I couldn't get enough of as I stuffed my face with a raspberry yogurt muffin.

"Good, you're finally starting to come around. I'll have to let my brother know that he needs to tone down the sleeping agent he's using."

That voice...

The fog slowly cleared with each passing second, and as it did, I wished to go back to sleep and try to wake up again in a different reality. My eyes cleared a little more and what started out as a fuzzy blur began to take shape, and there he was...Cain.

Cain, if that was his real name, was squatting in front of me and gripping my chin in his hand. His fingers dug painfully into my skin as he forced me to sit up. It felt like his fingers had the ability to burn the skin he was touching. I couldn't believe this was the serial killer my mother and the entire FBI were chasing. So far, they had no leads on this man, but here he was, inches away from my face. He was so close, and this might be my only chance to get free. Letting my head lull heavily in his hand, I tested my fingers and wiggled my toes. Everything was still functioning. It was now or never. Giving it my all, I lunged for him with a yell but was jerked to a stop.

"Whoa, I do like your fire, you have such a wild beast in you, Sunshine, and it's just begging to be let out," he said and then laughed. It wasn't a nice laugh, though. No, it was the kind of laugh you'd expect to hear at an abandoned carnival as you wandered the house of mirrors.

I whipped my head around and stared at the leather shackles tightly bound on my ankles and wrists. Shooting to my feet, I instantly fell against the wall and slid down like I'd been out for an all-night bender. The remainder of whatever I'd been dosed with slammed into my system, making the room spin violently.

The song, You Are My Sunshine, ended. Moments later, it began again. I gripped my temples as my head pounded in time to the song's beat. At least he hadn't chosen rave music. The scent from my strange dream was stronger now, and I realized it was a combination of bleach and something else that made my skin crawl.

"Here you go, Sunshine," Cain said, and I lifted my head enough to stare at the cup of what looked like water that was held out toward me.

With a roar of frustration, I smacked the cup out of his hand. The clear liquid splattered everywhere as the plastic cup harmlessly bounced off the floor.

Whack!

My whole head whipped to the side. The strike was fast. I never saw his hand move, but I certainly felt the sharp crack across my cheek as the back of his hand connected. The force of the strike rocked me sideways, but I caught myself just before my face hit the floor.

"That wasn't very nice, Kirby, not very nice at all. You're in my home, and you don't treat your host like that. Do I need to teach you manners?"

"Go fuck yourself," I growled out and dabbed at the corner of my mouth to see if there was blood.

I bit back a scream as Cain gripped a handful of my hair and yanked my head around so I was forced to stare into his unnerving gaze. His blue eyes were like a prism catching the sun's rays. They seemed unearthly, and maybe they were. Maybe that was why the FBI couldn't catch him. Maybe they'd been looking for a man when they should've been looking for the devil.

"I'd prefer to fuck you," he whispered as his grip tightened on my long hair.

I was helpless as he pulled me close to his face. Goosebumps rose all over my skin as he ran what felt like the tip of his tongue up the side of my neck. I despised my body's reaction to this man and had to bite my lip hard as he nuzzled the sensitive skin by my ear.

"I like your vulgar mouth, Sunshine, but be careful how you use it."

He pulled back enough that his face hovered in front of mine. There was no humor, only a raw hunger that terrified me to my core and was mingling with the churning heat in the pit of my stomach. There was something wrong with me and my head because no one should have any kind of sexual reaction in this situation, let alone while they were chained up.

"I can see the conflicted emotions in your eyes. Has anyone ever told you that your eyes hold no secrets?" I quickly looked away, my pulse pounding harder. "Don't worry, Kirby. I won't fuck you...right now. I'd prefer to have you begging me for it, and I promise you that you will." His other hand gripped my face and tilted my head up at an odd angle. It hurt, yet the pain subsided the moment his lips brushed mine. "Mmm, you're so tempting, Sunshine. So very tempting."

"I'll beg when Hell freezes over," I mumbled through the tight grip.

Cain smirked and then chuckled. The sound went straight down my spine and made me shiver in a way that wasn't unpleasing.

"Oh, Kirby, you can't fool me." Releasing the grip on my hair, he sat back on his heels and looked way too casual with his arms draped on his knees. "That's certainly not what you said the other night."

Confusion knitted my brow as I glared at the man who had no business being this sexy. I was starting to think that all men needed to come with a warning label, but one like this needed a billboard sign or someone to sky-write, 'stay the fuck away,' above his head.

"Let me refresh your memory. You couldn't be bothered getting out of your dress." The jump in my pulse was instantaneous as the night of the party came back to me. "Ah, you're starting to suspect now, aren't you? You whimpered when I touched you, and you moaned and spread your legs wider as I licked at your pussy. You were so wet and sweet."

A quaking began in my body, and I sat frozen like a terrified animal in his grip. It was slowly sinking in how much danger I was really in. I was trapped with this crazy man, this murderer, a serial killer with an unknown number of kills and who may have already been in bed with me.

"You have a sweet moan Sunshine. Just thinking about it is making me hard."

Cain closed his eyes and began to moan, and the trembling got worse as he sounded exactly like me. His eyes snapped open, and my reflexes had me jerking back. The chains attached to the cuffs let me know I could jerk all I wanted, but I had nowhere to go.

"The thing is, it's not your moans I want, Sunshine. It's your screams."

The song began to play again in the background, but it felt like a deafening silence surrounded me as his words sunk into the deep recesses of my brain.

"You know what you did next? You thrust your ass up in the air begging to be fucked. 'Mmm, oh yeah, yes, please take me.' That's what you whimpered. That's what your body wanted from me as you spread your legs even wider for me to fuck you. Do you remember the orgasm, Sunshine? Do you remember how your sweet juices tried to drown my cock as you came? You wanted me to do it again. You would've let me fuck you in any position I wanted and begged for more because I know you've never come like that before."

"You're lying. I wouldn't...." The rest of my denial died on my tongue as Cain slowly stood. He'd seemed tall while I'd been standing but sitting on the ground like this in front of him made it feel like he was a giant sent to crush me.

"Am I, though?" His head tilted slightly, the look daring me to argue. "I marked you as mine." He walked away as the song started over again, and I wanted to scream at him to turn it off. "I must admit that my come looked fabulous all over your ass."

I sucked in a sharp breath as more memories surfaced. The fantastic fantasy dream I had and how satisfied I felt...

Those two signs were only the beginning evidence. The strange bruise on my neck was like a fingerprint, and the dried come all over my ass was the next piece of evidence. It hadn't been a dream, and it hadn't been Peter jerking off on me. He'd denied it over and over again, and I didn't believe him any more than he believed me about the cucumber.

"Aw...see? Now you're remembering." Cain walked over with a new glass of water and squatted in front of me once more. This time though, he sat the glass beside the thick foam thing I was sitting on. "Sunshine, you understand me better than the rest of your classmates, so let's see how well you actually know me. Let's play a game."

"I don't want to play your stupid game," I snarled.

He raised his hand to hit me again, and I didn't back away, so I gave myself a tiny pat on the back. This time the strike didn't come. His hand was raised in the air, but instead, he slowly reached out like a snake coming for my neck and wrapped his hand around my throat.

I tried to jerk away, but the subtle pressure increased until I stopped. The look in his blue eyes was terrifying. There was no doubt he could close his fist and end my life right now, and he wouldn't lose a single night's sleep over it. As I swallowed, I could feel his fingers press in a little more as if he wanted to feel my throat working or maybe no longer working. At this point, I wasn't sure.

"You don't want to play? That's fine. We don't need to. I already know what I need to know."

He pulled me forward by my neck as far as the bindings would allow. No amount of training would've ever prepared me for the moment the tip of his nose touched mine. We sat there staring into each other's eyes, and with each passing second, my need to blink and look away increased.

"You should know, Sunshine, that I know you better than anyone. No one else has taken the time to study you and understand you as I have. I know what makes you tick, what dreams you have, what fills your soul with desire, what makes you wet at night, and what lines you're willing to cross. I know it all because, unlike your mother or that poor excuse of a boyfriend you had, I've taken the time to learn the secrets you hold tight to your chest."

"No one knows the real me," I said.

Cain pressed his thumb into the soft tissue under my jaw until I was forced to look at him once more. "I do, Sunshine. You'll see."

He released my neck, and I had to fight every urge in my body not to rub where the feel of his fingers had been.

"What kind of gift basket do you think Peter would want? I really should send him something...oh, I know. I'll get him a basket of cucumbers to play with. He seemed to really enjoy them last time."

"It was you that did that to Peter."

Cain laughed, and the sound chilled me to my core. Was that the sound he'd make when he finally took my life? Tears welled in my eyes. Crying was something I hadn't done for a long time. I didn't think I even knew how to cry anymore, but the tears spilled over now. My three months of Quantico training never could've prepared me for this.

"You ruined my relationship, humiliated me, and then capped it off by raping me."

Cain's face contorted as he snorted. "First, I may have been the final straw in the old proverbial cap, but we both know I didn't ruin your relationship. You were kicking that useless wad of flesh to the curb, and I might add, Peter protested a bit too much, considering he came with a shuddering groan and proceeded to hump the bed looking for more. I thought your mental prowess was better than this, Kirby. I'm truly disappointed."

The way he said the word 'disappointed' sat like acid in my stomach. There was no logical reason for my reaction, but I didn't like the idea that he was disappointed in me. That couldn't be normal. My mouth fell open, but I kept the list of questions to myself.

"Lastly, it wasn't rape. Did what I described to you sound like rape? Dubious consent, maybe, but trust me, you wanted every inch I could stuff into that tight pussy of yours. It was begging to be fucked by a man that could give you what you wanted." Pressing my lips into a firm line, I refused to say anything in response to his obvious gloating. "Go on, say what you want."

I hated that he was able to read me so easily. It was a contradiction considering I used to complain that Peter didn't know me at all, but this was different. I meant what kind of foods I like or vacations I'd want to go on, but Cain had an unnerving way of reading my thoughts. It was like he could actually get into my head with some superpower.

"No, you don't want to ask? Okay, I'll leave you alone, but only because you're going to need your rest." My heart fluttered harder. "The chains are attached to a rail system." Cain pointed to the thick iron rods that lined the wall behind me, then disappeared around the corner. "You can move around as far as the rails will let you. The bathroom is around that corner, and there is a set of towels and a tube of toothpaste in there for you. I've also left something comfortable for you to wear, and I expect you to wear it. If you don't, you'll be punished, and just so you know, sometimes you'll like the punishment, and sometimes you won't."

"Do I get to shower?" I asked, not even sure why I cared if I was clean.

The menacing yet sexy look was back on his face as the corner of his mouth lifted. "Already wanting to get wet?" His eyes slowly looked me up and down, and it was as intimate as if his hands were gliding along my skin. "Yes, you can shower."

Without another word, he turned and walked away and out a large metal door that clanged with finality as it closed. The room was suddenly plunged into darkness, and as crazy as it was, I'd rather have him in the room with me than be on my own in this space where death seemed to breathe from every corner.

A single red light flicked on, and my body flinched. The chains jingled as I looked in the direction of the strange light. I watched the slow-moving red gloop inside the spaceship looking light and found it oddly hypnotic. I glanced around the room and took in the corner that I could see, and it was neat, clean, and shined, which would not normally be menacing, but my mind knew what kind of killer he was.

I'd suspected he was a psychopath from the images and the notes my mother had in her folder but looking into his eyes and seeing his space confirmed the suspicion. No amount of begging or pleading with his human nature would change the outcome of what was to come. There was no making the monster in him feel guilty because he didn't have empathy or sympathy. They were words to him, the emotions non-existent.

The chances of getting out of this alive were slim, but if I had any chance, I needed to devise a different plan. There had to be a way to make him not want to turn my body into his next art project and dump it off in some random spot for the world to see.

Wrapping my arms around my legs, I pulled them in tight to my chest and let the question go as I allowed myself to cry. You were only supposed to see your life pass before your eyes when you died. Something dramatic like you fell from a bridge or were in a car crash. They never talked about how the same thing happened when you were captured by a serial killer and kept hostage like an animal.

Now I had way too much time to think about all the things I would've done differently over the past twenty-three years. Was there a fork in the road that would've brought me to a beach in the Cayman Islands instead of being locked in this room? If there was, what I wanted to know was how the fuck did I get back there and veer off this road? What I really wanted to know more than anything else was, who in the universe did I piss off to end up here? Why did it seem like no one really wanted me but this one sick man, and what did that say about me?

Hello
Sunshine

CHAPTER 20

CAIN

"Shit," I muttered.

The scent of frying meat hit me in the face as I opened the door to my home, announcing Abel's presence. It meant Abel hadn't gone home as I'd told him to do. I didn't want to deal with my brother this evening. He was like cheap cologne. A dab here and there could be tolerable, maybe even enjoyable, but too much, and you wanted to throw up, toss the bottle in the garbage, and cut off the body part that now reeked worse than dog shit.

"What are you still doing here," I asked, walking into the kitchen.

Abel turned to look at me, his face twisted in confusion. "Is this a trick question? I know how you like your fucking mind games."

Abel turned back to whatever he had in the pan, and even though there was no music playing, he wiggled slightly back and forth like he had bugs in his boxers. He hadn't changed much since we were kids. Abel didn't know the meaning of 'sit still.'

"No, it's not a trick question. I told you to go home." Crossing the kitchen, I yanked open the refrigerator door, and all the bottles rattled.

"Yeah, but you never mean it," Abel said as I cracked the cap off a beer and chugged half of it down.

"No, I always mean it. You just have a nasty habit of not listening. This seems to be a recurring argument between us."

Peering over my brother's shoulder, I determined that he was making some sort of meat and macaroni dish. Grudgingly, I had to admit that it smelled decent. Leaning against the counter, I stared at my brother's profile, which was identical to mine. I wondered, and not for the first time, if that's why I had chosen not to kill him.

"You need to lighten up, man. You're always so..." Abel waved the spatula around, and I watched the little droplets of sauce and meat drip onto the floor. "That, right there, that look on your face. You're uptight, bro. It's a little bit of sauce on your floor. It's not the end of the world."

"That's a matter of opinion. Do you see me going over to your house and messing with the things you like?" Unable to stop myself, I grabbed a piece of paper towel and wiped up the red speckles from the white tile.

"Whatever. So when are we going to play with the new girl? I really wanna make that bitch gag on my cock. Ahhhh! What the fuck?" Abel yelled as I snatched my brother by the throat. Pushing him up against the counter, I held him firm and snagged the knife from the counter, pressing it against his cheek. "Have you gone fuckin crazy?"

"I know you don't normally listen to me." I pressed the flat cold edge of the blade harder into his skin. Abel's eyes flicked between the sharp point of the knife near his eye and my face. "So, I'm going to say this really slow, so you have time to process it. If you touch my prize, if you so much as breathe the wrong way near her—I'm going to gut you, and then I'm going to desecrate your corpse. She is my prize, and I'm not sharing her with you. If you have a problem with that, you know where the door is, but don't fucking test me, brother."

I pressed the sharp edge into his cheek until a single droplet of blood formed on the tip of the blade.

"Even our bond has limitations."

His eyes went wide, and I held still as I watched the words swim around his thick skull. Once I was certain he wouldn't push this subject anymore, I stepped back and went to the sink to wash the blood off.

"Fuck man, what has gotten into you?" Abel dabbed at the dot of blood, smearing it down his cheek before looking at his fingers. In true Abel fashion, he licked it off his fingers as he glared at me.

"What's gotten into me is the fact that you don't listen, and you repeatedly push my boundaries. Normally, I'd play along and let you do what you want." I placed the knife back in the same spot I'd picked it up from before relaxing against the counter again. "But, dear brother, this is one topic I'm not budging on, and I thought you should know the line that you are dancing precariously close to—Kirby is my prize. My. Top. Prize. I decide what I want to be done with her and when. You may never get a taste if that's what I decide, so get used to it, or get out."

Abel grumbled as he turned to face the stove and the pan. "I swear, every year you get older, the less fun you become." His movements were jerky as he stirred dinner again before dividing it into two bowls. "Fine, I won't touch her."

"You promise?"

"What are we, fucking two?" Abel said and then laughed. "Okay, sometimes I act like I'm two. Yeah, I fucking promise."

"Great, then let's eat," I said, scooping the bowl off the counter and heading to the table. What just happened between us was what I liked to call an Abel training moment. When we were younger, these moments where Abel needed to be tuned in were much more frequent. I liked to use the 'elephant and the string' analogy when it came to Abel's training. He always had to think he was chained and couldn't escape my rules, similar to the situation Sunshine was in right now in my playroom. As Abel had aged and his erratic and spontaneousness had lessened, so had my training. The majority of the time now, I only had to use a string to remind him to behave. The issue was that every now and then, my brother tested the string, and he would need to be reminded he actually had a chain around his throat, and I controlled whether he breathed the next day again.

I took a bite of my food and watched the disaster that was my brother shovel the meal into his mouth like it was the last time he'd see food and shook my head. Usually, I didn't mean the things I threatened. My brother was a pain in my ass, but I never really thought about killing him. Not that I ever let Abel know that, but tonight I'd meant every word. If he stole this prize from me...stole the one thing that had managed to spark a semblance of interest other than blood in my mind and body, I would kill him and mount his eyes on my mantle.

"Did you want to do something tonight? We could try something new and go hunting together."

I cocked a brow at my brother.

"You're taking people too often, Abel. You're going to draw attention. What's sparked this change in your behavior," I asked as I chewed on another mouthful of food.

"Fuck man, why are you always on my case?"

I flicked the fork around in my hand, and Abel watched it closely, knowing he was nearing my limits. "Stop avoiding and answer the question."

"I'm bored, man. We never go out together to do anything," Abel said and leaned back, crossing his arms over his chest.

"You know why we don't go out together."

"Yeah, I know, but bro, all we do is work and kill people, and my work helps me kill people."

"Are you saying you'd prefer not to kill people?" My hand relaxed on the fork I'd been preparing to use.

"No, of course not. I'd just like for us to do more. We're in a rut, always doing the same thing. Work, eat, sleep, fuck, kill. Not necessarily in that order. Don't you want to travel? We could go to Egypt and see the pyramids, or go to Greece, or...."

"The answer is no. I have no interest in getting on a plane. I have no interest in changing my habits. I have no interest in seeing the world or anything else. I like my life just the way it is." Abel slumped in his chair, his face very close to the same pout as when we were children. "If you want to travel, let me know what weeks, and I will make sure to hunt while you're away. It will help solidify our alibi."

"I meant for us to do something together."

Pushing the chair away from the table, I stood and put my plate in the dishwasher. "I know what you meant, and I also know that it's not possible. Maybe take up a new hobby, or how about you join a dating app?"

"A dating app? Do you really think they have dating apps for serial killers?" Abel tapped his chin as he thought. "You know that's not a bad idea...anyway, I don't want to date. That shit's way too much work. Like this girl you got downstairs, too much work."

"I'm not dating her. She is...an experiment, and her eyes are special," I said as I began cleaning the kitchen.

Abel may cook a meal, but he'd rarely cleaned up after himself. I'm surprised his house didn't have mice lined up to sit at a special small table with small plates of food and belching as they sat on his lap.

"Right. Sure. Like I believe that crap."

"Believe what you want." I finished wiping the grease off the stove that Abel had managed to get everywhere and tossed the cloth into the garbage. "You can see yourself out."

"What? You mean we're not going to jerkoff to our homemade videos?"

"Not tonight, and if you're going to do that, go home." I walked out of the kitchen to a litany of swearing. The restlessness that was coming off Abel lately was palpable, and it was making me edgy.

I was halfway to my bedroom when the front door slammed. Changing my mind, I wandered down to the living room and flicked on the television before going to pour myself a drink. Getting comfortable in my chair, I decided to watch the show that starred my Sunshine. Flicking on the television, I sat back and studied her in her new surroundings.

My Sunshine was highly entertaining, and I had to give her a point for enthusiasm. She certainly wasn't cowering in a ball and praying to god, which was refreshing from what I normally brought home to kill.

I took a sip of my scotch on the rocks as my eyes focused on every little move she made. She was currently exploring the extent of her bindings, and I laughed as she threw a tantrum that I found cute. I didn't find things cute, yet it was the only word that made sense to describe the meltdown.

Her fists beat against the wall as she yanked on the chains. She looked wild, primal even, and my cock stirred at the thought of taming her. There was very little I found beautiful. The morning rays of sunshine, the sight of my artwork, and now I could add Kirby to that list. I enjoyed having my own personal Sunshine. Her hair was in a wild mess of waves, and her eyes flashed with frustration and anger. She had spirit.

Sitting back, I contemplated what my next move should be as she continued to explore her boundary. It really came down to when I wanted to kill her. Right now, I didn't have an exact date, but that could change tomorrow or the next day. Leaving her death date open was breaking my rule, but it was worth seeing how long it took to...to what exactly?

That was the question.

Did I want to turn her into a pet to play with or a lover for physical needs? Did I want to mold her into something more... maybe something close to a partner. My finger tapped the glass, the cubes the only noise in the room. Abel would hate that, no, Abel would fucking hate that. My lips curled up at the thought of annoying my brother and the possibility of gaining a partner who understood my quirks and needs better than Abel. Someone I wouldn't have to keep a choke hold on at all times and could be useful in a multi-faceted way.

She stepped into the bathroom, and I loved how she tried not to touch the soft pajamas I'd left for her, but she couldn't help herself. I saw a woman burning with a desire to rip away the fake exterior that she hated and embrace the darker side of her personality. My Sunshine didn't know it yet, but she'd learn how to hold a blade, crave blood, and kill without remorse. She'd learn to love it or die on my table. Either way was a win.

Like other children, I'd never understood the fascination of having a small pet in a cage. Gerbils, hamsters, bunnies, and fish were all the rage while I was growing up, and I'd see the other children smiling as they stared at their little companions. Was this what they saw? Was this what they felt?

Kirby fought with what was left of the blouse and finally ripped it off her body, leaving her in just the lacy bra. She had great lines like a statue. She fluffed out her hair, which lay on her shoulders and almost covered the entire front of the bra. All I saw was Lady Godiva. I suddenly had the urge to paint her. Lifting my hand, I made the strokes I wanted to do with the brush and my cock when I was through.

Once she was curled up with her back to the wall and the blanket pulled up tight to her chin, I flicked the television off and continued to plot as I headed to bed.

CHAPTER 21

KIRBY

As soon as I had no more tears left to cry, I slowly pushed myself off the thick-foam mattress on the floor. Turning, I stared at the rails that were wide as my forearm. They lined the wall and disappeared around the corner. Reaching out, I wrapped my hands around the bar that held me captive. It was higher than my head and cold to the touch, but it felt solid. I couldn't figure out how he managed to get these in place and not have any support attached to the walls, but at least I could see. To be left like this in complete darkness would've taken the terror to another level.

I gave the binding a slight tug, and the thing didn't move at all, not even a rattle. I'd always thought it would be fun to be tied up, but this was not what I had in mind. In fact, this was the furthest thing from what I'd been thinking. Bracing my foot on the wall, I pulled on the chains again, with more force this time. The thick leather cuffs around my wrists groaned in protest, but the stupid rail didn't shift. It was completely unmoveable. I stared at the locks on my wrist, and they were unique. I'd never seen anything like them.

Changing positions, I tried again, but this time let my arms trail behind me as I pulled until my wrists and shoulders screamed from the leather rubbing at an awkward angle. There was zero give even when I folded my thumbs in and tried to pop them out of the sockets to gain more space, but they wouldn't budge either.

Stupid videos that made it look so easy.

In a world of predators and prey, I'd somehow just ended up on the wrong end of the game and was staring down the throat of a great white shark. Panting hard from screaming like a demon possessed me, I banged the chains off the rails, and did what every rational person would do in this scenario. I yelled profanities as loud as I could.

"Fuck you! I hate you! You don't know me! You monster!"

It shocked me when the guy didn't come running in because I was trying to yell his house down with my screams. Then again, it was a good assumption this spot was soundproof. We were in the middle of fucking nowhere, and the music was so loud that it alone could wake the dead.

Bad pun Kirby, really bad pun. This was great, just fucking great.

Of course, I'd be attracted to a serial killer. That was certainly my luck and in line with my life's trajectory. It didn't seem to matter where I met a guy, how much money he had, or even how good he smelled. Each one got progressively worse instead of better, and just when I didn't think I could find a more abysmal choice than Peter, I ended up in this mess.

"A fucking serial killer! Really?" I wanted to bang my head on the wall. Maybe that would help whatever was wrong with me.

Even though he was a tow truck driver and I'd just had that horrible fight with Peter, I should've known. I should've seen a sign. I mean, I'm an FBI trainee, for fuck's sake. At the coffee shop, something seemed unusual about him, but the look in his eyes set my underwear on fire, and my brain left the building at that point.

I was so fucked. I'd seen his work, and the artwork was always made when the victim was alive. Leaning against the wall, I let my cheek press into the coolness and closed my eyes. I never thought I'd wish for a normal day of classes, but here I was doing just that.

Pushing away from the wall, I let my eyes search the space and drawers closest to me. I stretched as far as the straps would allow and managed to brush my fingertips along one of the handles.

"Come on. You can do this."

I pushed the cuff on my arm as far up as possible and tried again. This time my fingertips were able to make it over the top. Curling my fingers, I pulled back, but the drawer wouldn't budge. I slumped over as I realized it was locked.

"God, fucking dammit! Ahh!"

The sound of my screaming was drowned out by the "Sunshine" song playing on a loop. It was loud enough to rival any concert. I once liked this song, and he was ruining it for me. Giving up on the escape plan, for now, I searched for the clothes he mentioned. My now buttonless blouse was hanging open, and I shivered and wrapped my arms around myself.

Poking my head around the corner toward the bathroom, I stared at the pitch-dark space and swallowed hard. Even though I knew he wasn't down here, the images of what could be waiting for me inside that bathroom felt like shit could still get a whole lot worse. Sucking it up, I took a step around the corner, and an overhead light flicked on, illuminating the simple hallway. I glanced up at the light built into the ceiling before finally focusing on the blinking light in the corner.

Motion sensor and a camera—of course, there would be a camera. There were probably many hidden in here.

Taking a few more steps, I paused when another light came on. I didn't know what was better, the pitch black or the spotlights, but they made everything outside of their glow seem darker. I placed my foot over the threshold of the bathroom doorway like I was in the movie *Escape Room* and expected the floor to drop out or something to try to cut off my head.

Just like the other lights, as soon as the sensor picked up my movement, the light flickered on and showed off a simple bathroom. Soft grey walls with crisp white accents and a few little decorative things gave me pause. A picture hanging on the furthest wall looked like blood splatter had been framed. Given the house I was in, there was the distinct possibility that was exactly what that was—blood. I yelped when the light outside the door turned off and then the next until I understood what it was like to be inside a glowing fishbowl and unable to see what was coming in the darkness.

Stop it, Kirby, you're a bloody FBI agent. Newbie or not, you need to pull your shit together.

Taking a deep breath, I straightened my spine and marched to the sink and the awaiting clothes. Biting my lip, I gave the picture on the wall another look and reached for it and the metal frame, but it was just out of reach. Only my fingertips grazed the surface.

Son of a bitch, he already thought of all of this. He's fucking toying with me.

Swallowing down the anger, I turned back toward the clothes that Cain had left. I had to admit that I wasn't sure what I was expecting, but fuzzy purple pajamas with little skulls on them were certainly not it. I didn't know how the hell he expected me to put these on until I felt the velcro. He was diabolical. Who else got pajamas made with shackles in mind?

It was way too tempting not to put them on and stick my middle finger up at Cain and his ability to crawl into my brain. The material was soft under my hand as I ran it over the top.

What did this guy want with me? I mean, killing me seemed like the obvious answer, but did he always get his victims their favorite sleepwear? Did he always take the time to know what their favorite brand of toothpaste and shampoo were? Did he always turn his victims into glorified pets? The thought was unsettling, and a stab of jealousy sliced through me and was quickly followed by anger that made me want to hit myself.

I needed to find a way to get the upper hand. There had to be a way to make him trust me or let me go. It was just figuring out what the button was. As I turned to investigate the shower, I decided to play his game for now until I could figure a way out of this place and how to get away from Cain. There was no way I was going to end up as his next art piece displayed on the side of the road. Desperate times called for desperate measures, and this definitely qualified as desperate.

"You are my sunshine, my only sunshine."
"You make me happy when skies are gray."
"You'll never know, dear, how much I love you."
"Please don't take my sunshine away."

Would this song never end?

I stopped counting after the hundredth time it played. I was trying to decide how much time had passed, but it was impossible without a window or a clock. Cain somehow snuck in when I was sleeping, which was creepy all on its own, but then he'd leave things as if they were little gifts. He always left food and water for a couple of meals, a fresh set of towels, and sleep clothes. Then he was gone again. I never saw him or heard him. It was like he was a ghost. No matter how hard I tried to keep my eyes open, they would grow heavy, and the last thing I'd see was the red floating goop in the lava lamp as the lyrics continued.

"I'll always love you and make you happy,"
"If you will only say the same."
"But if you leave me and love another,"
"You'll regret it all someday."

How many days had passed now? No idea. He'd left me alone with this song and my thoughts. It felt like every last marble was rolling out of my head and disappearing into an abyss. Maybe it had been five days, or had it been six? I'd always liked time to myself, but now I regret wishing to have more of it. The two questions I had on a continuous loop were: when would he reappear, and when would I take my last breath?

You are my sunshine...."

My eyes fluttered open. Oh, dear god, I was still in this hell. I put my hands over my ears. Please just make it stop. I was sure this was what sensory torture must be like—he was purposely trying to make me insane with this song. I fell asleep singing along and would wake up with it ingrained in my brain. Like the lyrics were the Pied Piper, my lips began to move, and I sang along and shut my eyes tight, not wanting to see anything.

"But if you leave me to love another."

I tried to hum a different song as my body rocked back and forth in an attempt to block it out, but it was impossible. By the next verse, the words were once more tumbling out of my mouth.

"You'll regret it all someday."

The music lowered to a bearable decibel, and I sighed.

"You have quite the nice singing voice, Sunshine," Cain said, and I sat up straight, knowing he was there.

My eyes searched the room, desperate to have contact with a person again but terrified and anxious to find him. It took a moment to zero in on him. It was like he blended in with his surroundings. He was sitting at the far end of the room with a laptop. He glanced over the top of the lime green screen, and a strange feeling whipped through my stomach. It felt like eels were swarming around in there, electrocuting me as they wiggled and moved.

He was lounging in a chair with his feet up, and even though I could only see his eyes, I knew I was already being analyzed. I was in the middle of a metal cage in the ocean, being circled by a shark ready to attack while chum was tossed in water all around me.

"You didn't eat your dinner last night," Cain said, and I glanced at the plate with the peanut butter and jam sandwich and the glass of water.

"I wasn't sure if you were slowly trying to poison me or drug me into accepting whatever you decided to do." I pushed myself back until I could lean against the wall.

Cain chuckled, his eyes looking away, and just like that, I was able to breathe again. If this was what it was like to be paralyzed by a stare, I could now say that I was fully qualified to write a thesis on the subject. He had an aura that filled the room like a hand wrapping around a person's throat.

"If I drugged you or killed you with poison—which I wouldn't do —wouldn't that be a kinder choice than what I normally enjoy doing with my prey?"

He didn't look over the computer, his fingers tapping away, but I could still feel the weight of the question as if he were inches from my face. I swallowed the grapefruit-sized lump in my throat as my brain ran over the question and what would be best to say so I would not end up under his blade.

"Yeah, I guess it would be." I picked up the sandwich, and the bread was dry, but it still tasted fantastic because my stomach was so empty.

That wasn't really the reason I hadn't eaten it. I was attempting a hunger strike, but food was my weakness, so here I was, caving.

"Good girl, Sunshine."

Those words had never sounded so sexy. A heat stirred in my gut to join the buzz of activity and finally settled between my legs. I bit into the sandwich harder and forced myself not to be such an idiot.

He's a serial killer. For fuck's sake, you shouldn't be turned on.

"You're cute when you glower, and I wouldn't berate yourself too much. I planned on making sure you're much more flustered before the day ends."

My voice ceased to work, the rich peanut butter sticking to the roof of my mouth as I stared at the man that seemed to be able to read my mind. It was more than unsettling. There wasn't a word in the dictionary that could describe the creeped-out sensation crawling along my skin.

I needed to get off this topic.

"What are you doing," I asked and instantly regretted it as he put his feet down.

I now had an unobstructed view of his face. The face of a murderer shouldn't be that sexy and alluring. He should look like a hideous beast or have horns as a warning. Instead, he had the most unusual blue eyes I'd ever seen, with a strong jaw and messy sandy-blonde hair that I wanted to run my fingers through. He had tattoos along his fingers and hands that shouldn't be sexy, but they made me pant, but that damn Joker tattoo looked like it was mocking me.

Stop it.

"What I'm doing, Sunshine is schoolwork," he said and leaned forward to set the laptop on the large metal table.

I didn't want to look at the table too closely. The shiny metal piece was large and sturdy looking, but the draining edge and the rings that held thick leather straps made the sandwich I'd just finished want to reappear.

"You're attending school?"

"No."

I lifted a brow at him, and the corner of his mouth curled up, and once more, I felt like I was wearing entirely too many clothes and simultaneously not enough. My eyes traveled from his face to the screen, and my mouth dropped open as I stared at the FBI symbol in the corner.

"My school?"

"Closer. I always did like a good game of hot and cold." He leaned his elbows on his knees to look me directly in the eyes. It took every ounce of willpower I had not to shrink away. "Try again."

Grabbing the water, I chugged the glass down and pushed myself to my feet. I leaned closer to the screen, stepping forward as far as the arm and leg bindings would allow. My eyes grew wide as I stared at the username at the top.

"My schoolwork, you're doing my schoolwork?" My hands balled into fists as a fresh wave of anger flooded my body with adrenaline. "That's my work. Mine. How did you even gain access to my account?"

He didn't answer and simply ran the tip of his tongue along his lips as his blue eyes glanced at my chest. I instantly looked down and noticed two of the buttons were open on the fuzzy pajamas he had me put on. My boobs were practically hanging out of the material, and I quickly wrapped my arms around myself to hold the material in place as the annoying heat traveled throughout my body. Cain stood, and as he did, my eyes shot back to his like a wary animal. He held up a cell phone and waved it back and forth, and my eyes followed it like a metronome.

"I've had access to your whole world for some time now, Kirby. You're an exceptionally smart student, even if you hate the program."

"I don't hate the program," I said, and he immediately tsked at me like I was a bad child.

"What did I say about lying to me," he asked.

Ignoring the question, I pointed at the computer. "What do you get from this? If you want to know how close they are to catching you, then you're not going to find much."

He laughed. As he took a step closer, I forced myself not to retreat.

"I'm not worried about them catching me, Sunshine. No, I just happen to enjoy learning new things and seeing how stupid people are. Besides, you did arrange to do your schoolwork. It wouldn't look very good if you didn't hand in your assignments."

I narrowed my eyes at him as I tried to understand the long game. There had to be one, but what was it? "I don't believe you," I said.

"I don't care if you believe me, but I will tell you that I do have an ulterior motive which I'm going to keep to myself for now." He looked at the phone and walked around the table to a cupboard. My eyes grew wide as Cain pulled out a ball gag.

"I'm not putting that on," I said, backing away as he turned in my direction. He held it up as if it was for me to inspect. The bright purple ball swung from the leather straps from his fingers.

"I got this special for you, Sunshine. I even made sure it was made in your favorite color."

"I don't care what color it is. I'm not putting that on." I pressed my lips tight together. A slight vibration started up in my body as he continued to take one slow step at a time, moving closer to me.

"Oh, I think you will. In fact, I think you're going to turn around for me and open your mouth like a good girl so I can put this on without you causing one single bit of trouble."

My eyes narrowed into slits as I clutched the fabric of the pajamas tighter in my fists. "Why," I asked, but I didn't want the answer.

"You love your father, don't you?" My stomach dropped to the floor. No words could have affected me more. "He lives in London with his new wife and baby on the way. You were trying to go visit him, were you not?"

Warning bells were ringing loud and clear as I distinctly remembered my tickets getting canceled every time I placed the order.

"It was you. You kept canceling my tickets."

"You do catch on quick, Sunshine. I really like that about you. Yes, I couldn't let you fly off to London and not come back." Cain held up his finger as I opened my mouth to speak.

"Don't try to deny it. I know you wouldn't have returned. I told you, Sunshine, I know you better than you even know yourself. Also, just so you know, he's not looking for you or worrying about you. I texted him to say you'd see him after you completed school. You just decided you didn't want to fall behind."

My jaw twitched as I snapped my mouth closed. "Now turn

around and open your mouth, or I'll have to send my brother to visit your father. I must warn you. He's more twisted with his ways than I am. There is no telling what body part he'd cut off first."

"He's the one that leaves them looking mangled, isn't he?"

A cold dread replaced the earlier heat as Cain stepped close to me and stared down into my eyes. He lifted one of his wide shoulders and let it drop, but his eyes held the answer, and the answer was yes. Closing my eyes, I slowly turned around, and goosebumps rose all over my body as he stepped in close enough that I could feel the heat of his body through the material.

"I like this obedient side to you, Sunshine." He grabbed the strands of long hair hanging over my shoulder and pulled them back —his fingers grazing against the side of my neck as he did. "You really are a good girl, Sunshine, and I think you like being a good girl for me," Cain said, his voice no more than a whisper as his breath fanned against my neck and forced another round of shivers from my body. "You want me to touch you, don't you?"

"You're delusional," I said, but my knees shook as his chest brushed my back.

"I'm many things, Sunshine, but delusional is not one of them. Reading people, on the other hand...." He ran his fingers down my arm. "Reading their bodies." Cain groaned beside my ear, and I had to bite my lip hard to keep from moaning. "Knowing what drives them and excites them...it's what I do best. Now open your mouth." His lips skimmed against my ear, and a moan tumbled from my mouth. I expected him to bite it for whatever reason and that sick part of me really wanted him too.

It didn't feel like my body was my own as I gently swayed on my feet. He was intoxicating, and I hated myself for being so easily affected by his presence, but I couldn't deny that there was a charge that stirred in the depths of my body.

Could lack of human contact do this?

Unfortunately, the reality was I'd been thinking and dreaming about him before he took me. His fingers reached around, his hand easily able to wrap around my throat, but instead, he pulled the remaining wisps of hair away from my face as intimately as any lover.

Tears welled in my eyes as the fear and anger, mixed with more emotions that confused me and made me feel out of control, surfaced.

"Open up, Sunshine. Open that pretty mouth of yours, don't make me hurt your dear old dad."

Dutifully, my jaw dropped open, and my nose flared as the hard rubber was inserted into my mouth and the straps tightened behind my head. He placed his hands on my shoulders and slowly turned me around to face him. His eyes immediately went to the tear sliding down my cheek. My eyes snapped shut, and I forced myself to become a statue as he traced the tear with the tip of his tongue.

"Your tears are mine now, Sunshine. Just like everything else in your life."

His finger ran down the side of my face.

"Your mind belongs to me."

His fingers traced down the sides of my body, and sparks erupted under his touch.

"Your body is mine too." Cain gripped my chin and lifted my head. "Look at me."

Swallowing, my eyes fluttered open, and he was mere inches from my face. My pulse, which I'd managed to keep a stranglehold on, went wild, and I could feel it pounding like a drum in the side of my neck.

"And now I own your soul. Do you understand me, Sunshine? Be a good girl and tell me you understand."

I mumbled around the rubber ball. "I understand."

"Very good," he said as he wiped the dribble of drool from the corner of my mouth. "I love this look on you, and I can't wait to fuck you while you're wearing it." His eyes flared with heat, and I could tell he was thinking. "I can't wait to have you drooling like this with my cock stuffed down your throat. Would you like that, Sunshine? Would you like me to fuck your face?"

I was tempted to tell him to try and see what would happen as images of biting it off danced behind my eyes. Cain laughed as if reading my thoughts.

"Take off the pajamas," he said. My eyes went wide as I clutched the material tighter. "Trust me. It's better if you take them off. If I do it...I may become over-eager."

What the hell did that mean?

Hands shaking, I finished undoing the little buttons and then pulled the velcro apart to take the top off. I dropped it on the floor and covered my chest.

"And now the pants."

More tears spilled from my eyes as my thumbs hooked into the waistband of the pants and pulled them off. The tearing sound of the velcro separating echoed in my ears.

"So beautiful," he said as his eyes roamed over my naked body.

The trembling wouldn't stop no matter how many times I told myself not to show fear. Cain walked toward me, holding out a magazine page. I tensed as he stopped closer to me than he needed to, and as if he held a switch, my nipples hardened and ached as the throbbing got worse between my legs. I was pathetic, I was sick, and I needed mental help.

Taking the page from him, I stared at the model standing in a strong yet odd pose, with her body twisted at an unusual angle as she stared at the camera. My eyes flicked up to his.

"I want you to stand like that."

Was he serious?

Cain left the image with me as he crossed the room and moved a large easel into the center of the floor. He smiled at me as he grabbed a massive canvas.

"I'm going to paint you, Sunshine."

Smiling, he walked over to a tin of brushes. A tingling of excitement erupted in my belly. I never hated myself more than at that moment.

CHAPTER 22

MARGARET

I really hated the smell of the autopsy room. As many times as I'd had to come into this room and stare at dead bodies, there was nothing that made the experience better. At least this time, I'd remembered the vapor rub for my nose to cut down the smell.

Pushing through the second set of doors that led to the body, I prepared to face the strange white-haired doctor who seemed way too happy to be staring into the wide-open cavity of the latest corpse. The thick glasses and flip-up optical magnifier clipped to the front made him look like something from a Sci-Fi show.

"I was just about to give you a call," the doctor said, not lifting his eyes from his work. The tweezers he was using pulled a small piece of

267

something shiny from inside the victim's chest before he dropped it into a metal dish.

"Anything I can use," I asked, stepping up beside the table and staring down at the mangled body.

The face had been beaten beyond recognition. The arms and legs had deep lacerations, and fingers and toes were missing, but the arms still had cuts that created strange pictures in the skin. This was the most unusual calling card I'd ever seen, and considering I'd seen my fair share, that was saying something.

"Yes, and no." The doctor lifted his head and stripped his bloodied gloves off before removing the strange glasses. "This kill is the work of a killer and one that knows how to kill, but not your killer."

I looked at the skin again and then back up at the doctor. "I don't understand. This body has the same carvings."

"Carvings, yes. Same kind of carvings, no."

My lips pressed together in a tight line as I tried to decipher what the strange old man that I was positive sniffed one too many jars of formaldehyde over his career was trying to say. "I'm not sure what you mean."

"Look at the carvings closely. What do you see?"

Bending over, I got close to the deep lines that distorted the look of the victim's shoulder. "They don't look quite as smooth."

"Hah. That is an understatement."

I glanced back up at the doctor as he wandered away and pressed the button on the large television screen. Holding up the remote, he flicked through a number of photos and then stopped at one of the bodies I'd collected a few weeks back. The image was zoomed in on the skin and the design that had been created on the woman's chest and stomach.

"Now look at the pictures on the screen and then relook at our current victim."

I wasn't a huge fan of these guessing games, but I'd learned over the years that he loved to do it, and there didn't seem to be any way of breaking his habits now. So nothing to do but go along for the ride.

The lines on the victim on the screen were very thin, almost paper-cut light, and weren't very deep, maybe an eighth of an inch deep. The design wasn't what killed her. It was the blade that had pierced her chest cavity and heart. It was done with a single strike.

Pausing, I thought about what Kirby had mentioned in class: whoever had done this was a true artist.

"Is the Chameleon devolving? Becoming more unstable," I asked and turned around to look at the body and the doctor once more.

"One might think that if they didn't understand art, but no. What you have on your hands is a copycat."

I stared between the two screens. "Give me your reasoning because I have to tell you, the last thing I need is another killer on my hands."

"Unfortunately, that's exactly what you have. Let's start with the face. As gruesome as some of the bodies have come in, the faces were never touched like this. If anything, they were washed and left in pristine condition. Eyes may be missing, etcetera... but the Chameleon Killer doesn't beat them. Whoever killed the woman on the table is angry and most likely hates women."

The doctor walked around the table and pointed at the marks on the shoulder that I could see.

"The lines on this body are rough and jagged, like the killer is inexperienced with a knife or doesn't have the same tool, but that's not what sealed it for me. It's the artwork itself. Do you see how these lines on your victim's shoulder are simplistic in nature? Circles and some sort of a pathetic attempt at tribal art? This artist is not an artist. This killer is mimicking being one to throw you off their trail."

The doctor grabbed the remote once more, and with a couple of clicks, one of the full-body images they'd taken of a previous victim was on display.

"This scene of a mother cradling a child is artwork." I cocked a brow at the way the doctor said the words as if he were envious of whoever had done this. "Every detail, from the strands of hair to the clothing and the facial expressions, is perfection. They show pain and a mother's remorse. Not only is the image of someone who has been trained or is a serious natural talent, but the lines are the same width and depth no matter where the Chameleon Killer cut."

"The exact same depth? How is that possible?"

The doctor gave a little shrug.

"Best guess it is a special tool, but nothing I can name. I mean, it's possible that it is just a scalpel, as that's the right thickness of the blade and sharpness of the tool that would be required. I don't believe that, though. Making these lines perfect while someone is alive is nearly impossible unless they used a strong sedative or paralyzing drug, because no one could hold that still, regardless of the threat. The pain would be far too great."

"We've never had any toxicology come back with drugs," I said.

"That's correct. So, if drugs had been used at some point to subdue them initially, then the Chameleon Killer is keeping the bodies long enough that the drugs are out of their system. The issue is that the bodies show up either the same day or the day after they've been killed, so there would be no time between the initial drug administration, the victim being killed, and when it is left for someone to find."

"Okay, so this killer is methodical and possibly a trained artist and uses a tool to kill, but what about the mutilated bodies we've had? Can you tell if that has been a separate killer as well?"

"That, I'm not sure of. You're aware of the differences you have between the two styles of kills before this one. The notes are already in your file, so you know what I'm talking about. This body doesn't follow any of the other characteristics. In fact, there is not one identical thing. It's all poor attempts to place the blame in another killer's direction."

The doctor held up the young woman's hand and pointed at her dirty fingers that were caked with mud. Then he pointed to her face that didn't even look like a face from the abuse she'd taken, and finally, he pointed to the marks that, at first glance, had seemed the same, but the doctor was right. They were vastly different from the other bodies.

"I believe that your Chameleon Killer is either a split personality, and you get either the artist or the more gruesome and violent kills depending on what personality is doing the killing at the time, or...."

He held up his finger.

"These bodies are from two different killers, but they are a perfectly crafted pair with the same passion for killing, and they have honed their craft over time."

This killer..." The doctor pointed to the table. "Is a cheap copycat, and whoever it is may know how to kill, but they are not very good at making it look like the Chameleon. These bruises all along her body and arms tell me she took a beating over a number of days before she was killed. Some of the bruises are already yellowing and almost healed, while others beside them are brand new."

"Okay, could it be that whoever this killer is didn't mean to kill her and tried to pass it off for the Chameleon because of what has gotten into the media?"

"Also, a possibility, which is no longer my expertise, but I will tell you this much." The doctor looked at the television screen and shook his head. "The Chameleon, whoever that happens to be, has a great deal of pride in their work, and they are not going to stand for a copycat running around town. If I were this copycat, I'd be very scared right about now."

The door opened, and Hanson stuck his head inside. He covered his nose as he coughed. "Sorry, I'm late. Did I miss anything important?"

"I can fill you in," I said. "Thank you, doctor. Have a good day." I followed Hanson out of the door. "I need to make a call. I'll meet you in the car."

Hanson looked like he might argue and demand to know what had been said, but I didn't give him the chance to argue as I turned and walked away. Pulling the phone from my pocket, I tried Kirby's number again. The phone rang five times before it clicked to voicemail.

"Hi there, daughter. I thought you would've had the decency to tell me you arrived safely in London. Considering you took off without another word, it would've been the mature thing to do." I closed my eyes and took a deep breath before I said more of what I thought about this trip and her life choices again. "Give me a call when you get this message. We need to talk. It's important."

Hanging up the phone, I stared at the screen. Kirby had always been a hot-headed child, and now as an adult, I was at the end of my rope with how to keep her from making an ass of herself. On top of this ridiculous trip to London and going before she was done with school, Kirby had broken off her relationship with Peter, and the poor guy was a complete wreck over it. She was setting herself up to head down all the wrong paths once more, and one day her luck would run out. She would find herself in a situation she didn't like. An image of Kirby jobless and sitting at the side of a road begging for money crossed my mind.

Sighing, I stuffed my phone into my pocket, made my way out to the car, and put my stubborn daughter out of my mind. If the Chameleon Killer could blend in so easily, he needed to work a job in the public sector. I'd already marked off the most likely hunting grounds on a map based on the locations where the bodies had been dumped.

We were closing in, I could feel it, and I was going to make sure that it was my name and not Hanson's on the front page of the news.

Hello
Sunshine

CHAPTER 23

C AIN
    I whistled "You Are My Sunshine" as I wandered up
    the sidewalk, leash in hand. The homeless guy a few
blocks back was nice enough to lend me the flea-infested beast for a
twenty. The shaggy dog looked warily up at me as if sensing my true
nature.

"Don't worry, you're not on my list for the evening," I said as I
neared my destination. Thanks to Kirby, I now had a key and the
alarm combination for her mother's home. A quick look at my phone
showed the red dot on the tracker I'd slipped into her purse. It
blinked. Margaret was still at work which gave me time to poke
around her home.

Stepping under the large tree branches that hung over the sidewalk and shadowed me from the streetlights, I enjoyed feeling like I was one with them. Margaret had chosen a very manly look for her home, which spoke volumes about how she wanted to be seen. The woman in charge, one that couldn't be pushed around, and someone aiming for the highest seat in her profession. It was a shame she'd never make it.

The door was dark blue with the lion head brass knocker, and white flowers decorated the front yard, but I was interested in the small camera tucked into the corner of the covered porch.

The fleabag and I continued around the corner of the block, and as I closed in on the backside of Margaret's house, I dropped the leash and braced my hand on the wooden fence. Thankfully, I was able to leap over the five-foot structure in a single graceful movement. Crouching low among the bushes, I listened for neighbors or sounds of anyone on the street, but nothing much stirred at this late hour. Peeking through the shrubs, I opened the home security app on Kirby's phone and looked at the images of the quiet house.

Hitting the stop button, I watched all the cameras go dark, sprinted from my spot, and headed for the back door. With a soft click of the lock, I pushed the door inward and punched in the security code. Now in the laundry room, I knew the other door straight ahead was the access to the garage. I'd already memorized as much as I could see on the cameras, so if one was planning on breaking into a home, then it was a must to research the area. The original neighborhood blueprints were on the builder's website and what seemed like innocent information to promote their business was a treasure trove to me.

Opening the laundry room cupboards, I removed the handful of small bugs from my pocket. I'd managed to get enough for almost every room in the house, so I slipped from one room to the next and installed my little devices. Jogging up the stairs to the second floor, I started the process again and finally made my way to the holy grail spot—Sunshine's room.

The room was painted a soft purple with a dark floral comforter to match. Nothing was out of place, not a book, pen, or even a dirty shirt that didn't belong. Pulling the simple canvas bag from my pocket, I wandered the room and imagined myself in here as if I were Kirby. What spoke to me as her favorites? What did she love above all else?

An art easel was set up by the large window that would look out toward the backyard and the park across the street. Thumbing through the assortment of paintings and sketches, I pulled out one that caught my eye. It was a self-portrait of Kirby sitting among a field of purple flowers, but she wasn't laughing or smiling as you'd think. Instead, her knees were drawn up to her chest, her cheek laying upon her knees, and a loose braid of her hair fell across her shoulder, but her eyes were breathtaking. The tears sliding down her cheeks were very telling.

I set the piece aside and grabbed the small box of paints and the large sketch pad. Rifling through her dresser, I pulled out a few more items, including a lacy purple underwear set and a diary that was tucked in the far corner of the drawer. A stuffed bear was on the dresser with a ribbon around its neck and a simple frame of Kirby in a graduation outfit with the man from her phone contacts. It was her father. Both the bear and the picture got shoved into the bag that was starting to groan.

The lights of a car flashed against the wall, telling me that Margaret was home. Pulling out Kirby's phone, I remotely armed the home and placed the bag and painting inside the closet before making my way to the doorway to listen. As soon as the front door opened, the hallway light upstairs turned on, and I knew Margaret wasn't alone. The sound of a male voice echoed up the stairs, and I smirked. It was Peter.

"Well, well, well, what do we have going on here," I mumbled as I listened to them talk.

The alarm was turned off, and the sounds traveling up the stairs were no longer of them talking. Long shadows of two people kissing could be seen as they moved close to the stairs, and I backed away from the open door and the light as I shrank into the shadows.

Making my way over to the closet, I stepped inside and closed the door with a soft click. The door luckily had wooden slats, making them perfect for watching. The thump against the wall told me they were close to the room, and then the shadow that fell across the threshold gave me the full picture. The two were wrapped around one another like two octopuses going at it. Legs and arms were entangled as they groped at one another. Clothes littered the floor as they stumbled into the room like a pair of horny teens.

Margaret backed up to Kirby's bed and stopped as the couple came up for air.

"Why are we in here?" Peter said as he looked around the room.

The audible swallow he made as he focused on the portrait of Kirby on the wall could be heard from where I was standing. Aw, his manhood just shrank up, and he ran out of the room screaming. The corner of my mouth curled up with the imagery.

"It's just a bedroom, Peter."

"No, this is Kirby's room," Peter said, and I rolled my eyes, wanting to hand him a Captain Obvious sign to wear.

"So what? Does it look like she's around? Besides, she broke up with you and took off without a word to either of us. Wouldn't it be fun to have sex in her bed as a 'fuck you' to her?"

I shook my head in bewilderment, but I wasn't much for turning down a perfect opportunity to get dirt on someone. This moment was what I'd call 'aces.' Pulling up the camera on the phone, I held it up to the open, narrow slat and hit record.

As more clothing was torn off and distributed haphazardly around the room, I had a strong urge to call out pointers. The odd snorting grunts Peter made and the braying-like yells Margaret bellowed out made it feel like I was in some warped version of a petting zoo. The only thing missing was the dispensers of food to toss to them. Thankfully, the sex barely lasted ten minutes before they collapsed on the bed, and after another ten, they passed out, snoring.

Well, that was sad.

If this was the vanilla bullshit Kirby had been subjected to, then the shit I planned on doing was going to blow her mind.

Grabbing the items I'd come for, I cracked the closet door and watched for any sign of movement. When no one stirred, I pushed the door open and stepped out, closing it behind me. Standing near the bed, I stared down at the two faces that had just handed me a powder keg full of information. I was tempted to end the game now by finding a knife and slitting their throats. My hand itched at that delicious thought. It was the same way I'd planned to kill my parents, but I was forced to miss out.

Snapping a few photos, I turned and meandered my way out of the house toward the backyard and the way I'd arrived. Leaping over the fence, I landed softly and strolled along like it was a beautiful Sunday afternoon. The hat I was wearing was pulled low, and the hoodie over it concealed my face from almost everyone or anything. The fleabag mutt hadn't gone far and picked up the leash from the grass a few backyards down from Margaret's.

"Couldn't figure out which way to go?" I said to the dog. Of course, there was no response, but the dog's head twisted while he listened. "Today is your lucky day."

I began to walk, and the dog stood to trot along beside me.

A smile pulled at the corner of my mouth. The world certainly worked in mysterious ways, and if I believed in God, which I didn't, I would say he had one sick sense of humor and was enjoying the drama of the reality television show he'd created.

Hello
Sunshine

CHAPTER 24

CAIN

As one day blended into the next, I realized that Kirby had come to a standstill with her development. She was still giving me heated stares, but she was steadfast in her decision to keep me at arm's length. This annoyed me and fascinated me, which led me to this moment.

Walking into the workroom, Kirby looked up from where she was sitting cross-legged on the foam. There was very little fear when her eyes found me, but I could see the withdrawal in her eyes. She was folding into herself when I wanted her to come out.

"Hi," I said, and Kirby looked from side to side.

"Um...Hi."

"I brought you this." Holding out the hot coffee that was her favorite from *Mode*.

I told the owner Jorge that Kirby was away visiting her sick father and asked me to go in to make her apologies for leaving without saying a word. He then offered up her favorite coffee to me like that would make me feel better. I wasn't sure how that was supposed to make me feel better, but it did spark this situation.

"You got me coffee?"

"Yes, apparently, it's your favorite. Jorge made it specifically for you."

Her eyebrow rose. "You didn't kill him, did you?" she said, her voice worried.

"No, why would I kill him?"

She cocked her head, and I could see the confusion in her eyes as she slowly reached forward for the coffee. "Never mind. Thanks for this. I miss them."

Sitting down across from her, the look she gave me was all I needed to know about where her mind was. She watched me like every move I made might turn into a bite. This was what I always wanted in the past, what I'd thought I wanted from her, but somewhere during our time together—I'd decided I wanted something else entirely. Now her fear felt wrong, and I needed to mold it and reshape it like a piece of clay.

"I want to spend the day together," I said, and Sunshine blinked, her mouth hanging partially open.

"Why?"

"Why not?" I shrugged. "I know you love art, so I brought some things for us to work with." Bringing a large bag around to sit between us.

"I don't understand. What is going on here? You only come in to taunt me, drop stuff off, threaten me, and then leave."

"I want us to get to know one another better. Don't you?"

I pulled out large pads of paper, then bottles of craft glue, followed by a wide range of items to decorate the pages. There were boxes of crystals, stickers, crayons, flowers, and glitter. The glitter slightly terrified me as that stuff was hard to clean up. I'd also grabbed some exotic touches I preferred to work with, but I sat them all out and then grabbed one of the pads.

"You are chained to my wall, and I thought you might like to know more about who has you."

"You want to do kid's arts and crafts with me? That's how we get to know one another?"

"No, of course not. We ask each other questions to get to know one another. This is to give us something to do at the same time. I thought that would be obvious?"

I turned my attention back to the pages, and I was already picturing a blend of how I saw Sunshine and myself. She was the light, and I was the dark, but I wanted to swallow her whole.

The black charcoal I picked up from the pile of choices moved swiftly across the page as

the image began to take form. I waited until Sunshine had given in and picked up the other pad and was in the process of sketching out a woman's face.

"Why don't you have any friends," I asked, and Kirby's head snapped up to stare at me. "I'm not going to use it against you if that's what you're thinking. I'm just curious."

She was slow to answer but eventually sighed. "I don't get along with most people. I do for a period of time, but something always happens. I usually say something inappropriate that offends someone, or my interests don't align, or they don't turn out to be the friends I thought they were."

"So what you're saying is that, in general, you think most people are a waste of time and assholes," I stated and changed out the charcoal for some yellow chalk.

"I hadn't thought about it that way. Most people are fine enough. I just don't tend to get close to people."

I looked up at her.

"Because you can't trust them," I said and sat up straight. "The world is full of sheep, Sunshine, and you can't trust a sheep because they will bolt and run or follow the group if it suits them. That is why you've never felt like you could get close to them. You instinctively know that you can't trust them not to hurt you." I looked down at my artwork. "That's why you trust me even though your mind says you shouldn't. You know that I'm a wolf."

Sunshine opened her mouth, closed it again, and finally returned to her work. "Cain, can I ask you something?"

"Yes, whatever you want," I said and finished flushing out the lighter colors and blending the edges.

"When did you know you liked to...you know, kill people?" Her voice was soft and shy. I reached out and grabbed her hand, and she flinched at the touch.

"You can always ask me anything. If I don't want to or cannot answer, I'll tell you," I said, running my thumb over the back of her hand until she relaxed.

"I've known my whole life." I shrugged. "While other children dreamed of unicorns and being rock stars or what new toy they were going to get, I dreamed of blood, what the inside of the neighbor's cat looked like and what it would be like to watch the light drain from someone's eyes," I said, finishing the shadowing on the soft purple eyes of my drawing.

I glanced up at Sunshine. She was sitting there staring at me, her eyes wide and filled with a mix of fascination and something I couldn't quite place...maybe understanding.

"You do know that's disturbing, right?"

"You wanted the truth. Is there nothing you dream about that others would think is disturbing?" Sunshine gave a half-hearted shrug, which told me she dreamed of many things she wasn't yet ready to share. I would get them out of her, eventually. "And why is it that what I like is disturbing, but someone who likes boxing is normal? Ever wondered where those rules came from and why? Humans have always enjoyed the sport of blood and death. The ancient coliseums are a perfect example. The only difference now is that people hide that they like it or call it a *sport* which is supposed to be more civilized."

"That's different."

I looked at her, and my lip curled up. "Is it?"

She bit her lip as she thought, and I found myself drawn to the action, how it made her mouth look sexier, and how I wanted to lean across the mat and taste her. I could still taste the sweetness of her skin. Laying the mat aside, I leaned forward, and Sunshine leaned back, her eyes going as wide as a new baby deer. Bracing my hand on the wall behind her, I leaned into her body and could feel the heat pouring off her as her cheeks pinked.

"Uh..." I moaned in her ear, and she shivered, her pulse pounding so hard that I could see it thumping in the side of her neck.

Running my cheek against hers, I closed my eyes and savored the feel of her soft skin. "You make me want to do things, Sunshine, things that would make you scream."

She swallowed hard, and I realized how that must have sounded to her. I quickly brushed my lips against hers.

"I don't mean in pain," I added and watched the pupils of her eyes dilate. "I want to taste every inch of your body as you scream my name. That's what you do to me, Sunshine. That's what you make me think about—when I'm near you, I don't think about the pain or death."

Her eyes fluttered closed, and I took the invitation and kissed her softly, waiting for her to kiss me back. When she finally opened, I couldn't stop the groan that made her shiver. Cupping her cheek, I deepened the kiss, and our lips moved in time like a heated dance. Breaking the kiss with a gasp, I pulled back enough to see her eyes. I savored the look of desire that was ready to consume her body.

"I'm not just what you think I am. There's a lot more to me," I whispered and then sat back to finish the artwork.

Sunshine didn't move for a few minutes, and even though I watched her from under my eyelashes, I never pushed her, but a smirk pulled at the corner of my lip as she picked up the pad once more. We worked quietly and discussed a few more questions for hours until I made her dinner and brought fresh fruit and whipped cream for dessert. I was tempted to ask her if I could feed her, but I figured that might be too much.

After our meal, I got Sunshine to play a few hands of cards, and she broke into a smile and a laugh. She'd always catch herself and scold herself for having fun, but it was there, and she couldn't take it back.

Finished with my drawing, I turned my piece around to show her, and Sunshine's eyes lit up as she stared at the decorative piece. Her hands reached out, and she ran them over the softness of the wings.

"What did you use for this? It's stunning."

"I collect butterfly wings." Her fingers stilled, her eyes going wide, but she didn't seem disgusted. "To me, you're as stunning as the most graceful butterfly. I enjoyed today," I said and pushed myself off the floor. "I'll leave the supplies here for you."

Turning, I began to walk away and then glanced back at Kirby.

"The butterflies were already dead. I didn't pick the wings off." I held out the image I'd created of her. My face was shadowed in the darkness behind her while her face glowed in the sunlight.

"Goodnight, Sunshine."

"Goodnight, Cain."

CHAPTER 25

KIRBY
For the last three days, Cain had been oddly... normal, and the pull I'd been fighting was weakened to the point of snapping completely. He truly remembered everything. It didn't matter what I told him. He would remember and do something sweeter than anyone had ever done except maybe my father. I knew that he hadn't changed. He was still a killer, yet I'd seen so many new layers to the man. It was starting to feel odd that everyone thought he was just a mindless heathen.

But, like all cycles in life, I knew that he would cave at some point to the needs that flowed through his body. They called to him like a drug, and today was that day. The door swung open with a bang, and I thought it was Abel until I saw Cain's face. He was carrying a woman like a bag of feed on his shoulder. He didn't look over or even acknowledge that I was still in the room, which was strangely unsettling.

Cain bounced the woman off his shoulder and laid her out as a lover would. My eyebrow shot up, and my nostrils flared as the green-eyed monster rose inside of me.

"Why is she here?" I said, although I knew the answer.

Lowering the volume of the Sunshine song he seemed determined to torture me with—Cain shrugged and continued working. "Why do you think, Sunshine?"

I didn't want to say the words. "Why are you planning on killing her?"

Cain never stopped moving, and his actions were steady and methodical. Although I knew what he was and what he was capable of, seeing his emotionless expression only hammered home the reality of what he was planning on doing to me.

"I kill because I enjoy it. On some level, I need to do it. If you enjoyed shuffleboard, wouldn't you play the game?"

The woman murmured incoherent words as Cain secured both of her legs and drew the dangling, thick leather up to place over her chest. It disgusted me that even with a woman's life hanging in the balance, I could be turned on by seeing him run a slab of leather through his hands.

"Shuffleboard doesn't kill anyone."

"I'm sure it's killed someone with boredom," he said, the corner of his mouth curling up as his eyes flicked to mine. I shivered and crossed my arms over my chest and the newest pair of pajamas he'd brought me. I glanced down at the white bunnies on this pair and was once more confused by the gesture and the choice.

"You're funny, a real comedian. Be straight with me, Cain. Why are you doing this? I mean, why are you doing this in front of me," I pointed to the woman on the table, who was blinking but not yet fully conscious.

"Because Sunshine, you're in here, and I need you to know all of me. Even the parts you don't want to see. If you are looking for a reason why I chose her specifically, there isn't one. She just happened to come upon me, and like a fly in a web, I am the spider looking for a meal."

The last strap pulled snug, and he stalked toward me. Well, that was how it felt whenever he walked in my direction—like I was the next meal on the menu.

"Here is the thing, Sunshine. I want to answer the things you're trying not to ask but still want to know. I like the heady, metallic scent of blood. I like the way it glides through my fingers when I work."

He stopped directly in front of me and held up his fingers, rubbing them together like there was already blood on them. He took another step closer, and I had to tilt my head all the way back to stare into his eyes. Cain was imposing and didn't need fancy gimmicks to act wild like I'd seen his brother do. He was the calm embodiment of death, the reaper that had been pulled from hell to walk the earth and take any soul he saw fit.

Just his nearness caused me to push all thoughts about the woman on the table to the side. She was going to die.

Why didn't it bother me the way it should? My mind screamed because there was no point, but the real answer was much darker than that.

Reaching out, he pulled all my hair over my shoulder. "I've always liked the tightrope walk between life and death. How long can someone walk the line before they finally die? How much pain can someone take before they can take no more? I like to watch the light drain from their eyes and then wonder where they go."

His fingers played with my hair, but I couldn't look away from the blue orbs that held me captive.

"Most of all, I love the power and control I feel and the pride that courses through my veins with the knowledge that I'm the last person they'll see. Those are the answers you wanted, aren't they?"

Cain took another step forward. Mirroring the movement, I stepped back. He kept doing it until my back was pressed tightly against the unyielding, cold wall.

"You want to know something else, Sunshine," he asked, his voice lowering to a gruff growl. It was safer to nod than to try to form words. "Other than killing and reliving my kills through the films I take, there is only one other thing that has ever got my cock hard. Do you know what that is?"

An inferno of heat erupted in my gut as he placed a hand on the wall beside my head. No words would form as my rapidly beating heart made the room swim.

"Do you, Sunshine?" He lowered his head to hover near my ear, and as he did, the heat and energy pressed in on me and made it hard to breathe. "I think you know. You just don't want to say. Are you too shy to say the words, or are you scared to say them?"

Rolling my shoulders back, I straightened my spine and tried to push back the intimidating feeling.

"Me," I said.

I hated that little bit of information made me feel special—just like how the last few days had made me feel on top of the world.

When he was near me, I felt like the rest of the world didn't exist, and I hated that he was the only one that had ever made me feel like that.

"Very good, Sunshine," he said and nipped at my earlobe. I bit my lip as hard as I could to keep from moaning. "I'm hard right now, and not because of what I'm going to do to her, but because of what I dream of doing to you."

"That's not my problem." I flinched as he pushed away from the wall and expected him to hit me for speaking back, but instead, he shocked me by breaking out in a deep laugh.

The sound made me squirm, and I put my hands behind my back and gripped them together to keep from trying to touch him.

"Say, 'dude' in front of that statement," Cain said, his eyes holding the first real emotion other than a predatory one since I'd been here.

"What?"

"Put the word 'dude' in front of that sentence and say it again."

Was this a joke? Maybe a test?

"Dude, that's not my problem," I said and added a dash of dramatic flare as I rolled my eyes.

Cain laughed hard. It was short-lived, but it was a real laugh. My chest warmed with this sensual gooiness I didn't want to analyze. His eyes locked with mine, and his face softened.

"You sound just like Abel," he said and turned away from me.

The image of his twin's sarcastic banter and him doing a superman dive onto us to help contain me flashed through my mind. Suddenly, I wasn't sure if what he'd said was a compliment or an insult.

The woman on the table moaned as she woke up. That could've

been me. Instead of attached to a wall, Cain could've slapped me down on a table and tied me up, and I wasn't sure what was worse.

Cain leaned over the woman, and her eyes grew wide as she tried to move and realized she couldn't. She jerked hard on the bindings, and even though Cain hadn't said a word, the woman began to scream and thrash. I covered my ears and winced away from the sound as the high-pitched octave hurt my sensitive ears.

"Barbara," Cain said, and like a magic trick, the screaming stopped. "You're hurting my...." Cain glanced up at me. "Other guest's ears. So, I'm going to need you to stop, or I'll make you. It's your choice."

Was it wrong to feel the bottom of my stomach fall out as he referred to me so informally? A guest? What the hell did that mean?

Barbara tilted her head back and spotted me, our eyes meeting for a moment before she looked back up at Cain.

"I'll be good. I-I-I will be quiet," she stammered.

In that singular moment, as Cain's face shifted subtly from passive watcher to predator about to strike, I realized Barbara didn't understand. She didn't see him for what he was. If she did, she thought there was a way out, and he might not kill her.

"What do you think we should do to her," Cain asked.

Even though I knew no one else was in the room, I still looked around to see if the question was somehow directed at anyone else but me.

"You want me to decide what happens to her? Okay then, how about you let her go?"

Barbara nodded furiously. Her curly hair bobbed like a fishing line over the end of the table as she moved. "Yes, yes, please let me go."

"You like that idea, Barbara?"

Cain crossed his arms and leaned against the table like he was contemplating the idea, but it was easy to see in his eyes that he was only playing a game. Again Barbara didn't see it or didn't want to—I wasn't sure which, but to me, it was as clear as night and day.

"Yes, please. I'll never tell anyone about this. Just let me go, and I'll disappear."

"No, I don't think so," Cain said and sighed.

Barbara made little whimpering noises. "Are you going to chain me up like her," she asked.

Cain's brow lifted in a sweeping arc that was way too seductive, considering he was teasing about killing someone.

"Like Sunshine? Oh no, I'm sorry, Barbara, but she is..." he paused as he tapped his chin, his eyes finding mine and making my heart rate spike again. "Unique," he finally said.

"Why did you ask me what to do with her if you had no intention of doing what I say?"

Cain's eyes flared with a sexual heat that stole the air right from my lungs. As if we were in the middle of an earthquake, my body trembled from the top of my head to the tips of my toes. It wasn't fair. Why did I have to be attracted to this man?

"I asked you because I was curious what you'd say, Sunshine."

He made his way over to the far wall and a small set of keys I'd never noticed hanging there. I felt like everything in here should have a chalk line around it. Nothing was safe once in his grasp. He wandered over to one of the locked drawers and pulled out a folded leather case.

"I thought you might say you'd like to see her die, maybe run your fingers through her blood or fuck me on her dying corpse."

"What the fuck," Barbara said and started to struggle again.

My mouth dropped open, not sure what the hell to say in response. "Why the hell would you think I'd ever say that?"

Cain unrolled the case and pulled a blade out that even I could tell was sharp from where I stood. It practically sparkled in the light as he spun it in his hand like it was an extension of his arm. A scream bubbled up in my throat but died in place as Cain suddenly had me by the front of the pajamas with the sharp blade pressed into my neck. I didn't even dare swallow, and I had no idea how he'd moved so fast.

"Look at me." His voice was deep and rough with strain.

Even though he didn't say it out loud, he was holding back from slitting my throat. Doing as he asked, my eyes found his. "You see in me what others don't, but more importantly, Sunshine, I see in you what you refuse to acknowledge."

He was wrong. I didn't want people to die. I didn't want to see them in pain or suffering. His firm body felt as hard as the steel blade at my throat as he pushed himself up against me. The flare of unwanted desire that filled my body terrified me. Cain leaned close to my ear, his breath like a hot summer breeze and just as tantalizing as he spoke.

"It's in you, Sunshine. Don't try to deny it to me. I can see the inner demons that knock on your door." The tip of his nose brushed my cheek, and my eyes fluttered closed. "You see the beauty in death, and you're not afraid to die. Do you know how rare it is not to be afraid of death? What's inside you recognizes what's inside me and wants to come out and play. All you need to do is open the door, and I'll teach you the rest." His teeth nipped at my ear, and my hands clenched into fists as a soft moan escaped my lips.

"That's it, Sunshine, let yourself go," he said as his hand slid under the fuzzy top and up my body. The feel of his skin on my own set my blood on fire. "Moan for me again, be a good girl."

Cain's thumb rubbed over the tip of my nipple, and the sensation had me crying out with a whimper.

"You're a one-of-a-kind, a rare gem." His mouth found my own, but instead of kissing me, he bit my bottom lip as his fingers tweaked my nipple, and this time, I did moan.

All I could picture was ripping his clothes off and riding him to the ground. Whether it was hormones or a bad boy attraction, whatever the reason was, my answer was the same.

I wanted him.

I wanted him in a way that I'd never dreamed was possible. As he stepped away from my body and put the knife down at his side, I had this overwhelming urge to leap on him and crash our lips together.

"You're not ready for me, Kirby, but soon you will be. You continue to hang onto the ledge with your fingertips, but you're tired of hanging on to something you never wanted. You will fall, and I'll be here waiting."

We stood still, each staring at one another with carnal lust. I didn't need a mirror to know what my eyes were saying to him. As he turned to walk away, the connection between us broke, and I gasped in a deep lungful of air as my hand grasped my throat. The adrenaline coursed through my veins. I wondered if I was an adrenaline junky, which drove me to want more. As I looked up at him, my heart told me I could keep making excuses. I could try to deny the emotions but I'd already slipped from the cliff. That singular thought horrified me to my core.

I shook my head and cringed away from the loud screaming as my eyes focused on the table with the woman on it. A pang of guilt hit me as I realized I'd completely forgotten about her. I began to wonder if she'd been screaming the whole time. Nothing else existed when Cain was near me, he was the singular focus of every nerve ending in my body. I watched him as he methodically moved around the table and pulled on a pair of surgical gloves.

Ripping a piece of tape off the wide silver roll, he unceremoniously slapped it over Barbara's mouth. "I told you, Barbara, your screaming hurts my Sunshine's ears, and we can't have that."

His eyes flicked up to mine, and I knew I was in deep trouble. It had nothing to do with the blade Cain wielded and solely with the power he had over me. Every second I spent in this place, the more pieces of who I thought I was disappeared, and the reality of that knowledge was more terrifying than a thousand deaths.

As he started to work, I moved around the corner so I didn't have to watch and gripped my head in my hands. It didn't block out the sound, but I didn't want to watch him turn her into one of the bodies I'd seen on my classroom screen.

Rocking back and forth, I pushed the last of the sounds from my mind by humming the song that had become my anthem. Either Cain heard me, or he sensed that I needed to hear the song because Cain turned up the volume of "You Are My Sunshine" once more.

I realized then that the predator had already struck its first blow, but I just hadn't felt the bite.

Hello
Sunshine

CHAPTER 26

CAIN

I wiped the grease off my hands as I stared under the hood of the 1980 Cadillac Coupe Deville. It had a nice candy apple red paint job. I could picture Abel driving this car, his head bopping along to the latest one-hit wonder. I'd never tell my brother this, but there were times I envied his freedom. Not that I didn't have freedom, but I envied his ability to let go and do whatever he wanted, whenever he wanted.

On the other hand, that exact trait was also what I needed to keep under control. I had kept it and Abel in line for so long that it felt like just another breath in my day, but I hated the lack of self-control. Yet, it didn't stop the spark of jealousy from being there.

Sunshine was quickly becoming the one thing I wanted to throw out my rule book for, and I wasn't sure how this would end for her. I'd never kept someone longer than a few days, and that was only to see how long they could handle extreme pain.

The gate buzzed, and I looked up at the camera to see Margaret Lawson and another FBI agent sitting at the end of the driveway. Well, now, today just got a lot more interesting.

Walking to the far corner of the garage, I undid the straps that held my gun, complete with a silencer. I checked the clip and set it in the hidden holster, but I didn't do up the straps. The buzz sounded again, and I walked over to the two-way speaker and pressed the button.

"Hiya, what can I do for you," I asked.

"We are canvassing the area to see if any of the residents have seen anything suspicious." Margaret's voice crackled through the speaker.

"I'm not sure how I can help ya, but you're free to come on in."

I flipped the switch and watched the gates slowly open. Grabbing the remote and pressing a few buttons on my security set up, the channel switched to a restoration show, and the television in my workroom where Kirby was would now be on. She would get to see how close her mother was to help and how it wouldn't matter.

Picking up the torque wrench, I leaned into the Cadillac and pretended to tighten what I'd already worked on as the black car pulled up and stopped. All agents were the same. They thought they looked cool in their crisp suits and blackout sunglasses, and they all had the same arrogance. A thrill traveled through me, knowing I'd gotten to Kirby before all the personality was squeezed out of her body by these lifeless and annoying shells of humanity. They were worse than the sheep. They were the herders.

"Hi there, I don't see too many FBI agents out my way. This must be pretty important," I said as I wiped the grease off my hands for a second time.

"My name is Agent Lawson, and this is my partner Hanson," Margaret said as she pulled out her credentials.

They weren't needed, though, because I could tell who they were easier than a steaming pile of dog shit. Hanson, I hadn't seen around before, but there was something about him that I recognized. Not his face, but his expression. He was different from Margaret. I could feel the emotionless cool of his personality and kept him in the corner of my eye. He was a predator like me. Maybe not exactly like me, but he was a threat that was most certainly a more worthy opponent than Margaret.

"Name's Cain. I'd shake your hand, but...." I held up my hand with the dark grease on it. "So, what can I help you with?"

Hanson stepped further into the garage, and I looked over my shoulder at him.

"Please don't touch the car. I just gave her a good waxing, and the owner is going to be here any minute."

He nodded and obviously didn't like being called out on his snooping as he wandered to the front of the garage. "We won't take up too much of your time, Mister...?"

"Buchanan. You go ahead and fire away. I've been livin' here my whole life and my parents and grandparents before me. If there is anything I can do to help you out, I'm happy to answer."

Margaret and Hanson whipped out little notebooks in tandem and then pulled pens from inside their suit jackets.

Now that was creepy.

"Have you seen anything unusual around the area?" Margaret began.

I gave a small fake laugh, sauntered over to the bar fridge, and pulled out a beer. "I'd offer you one, but you don't seem like the type to drink on the job." Cracking the lid, I leaned against the workbench. "I've got coffee if you like?"

"No, we have coffees in the car," she said.

"Alright, well, as far as your question goes, you'll need to be more specific than unusual."

"Unfortunately, it's an ongoing investigation, and I can't say anything more. Have you seen any unusual vehicles or people in the area? Maybe you saw something that didn't register as strange until later?"

I tapped my chin and looked up as if I were thinking and checking the memory banks of my brain. "Nope, I'm sorry. I see strange cars all the time. It's kind of what I do." I pointed to the Cadillac. "Half the time, I think the entire world has gone mad, so I'm not sure I'm the best person to ask about unusual behavior."

The beauty of a good lie was that it was the truth, just paired down to the bare bones, but you kept the fleshy meat part to yourself.

"Have you seen the news lately?" Hanson said.

"I catch it when I can. Why?"

"Have you seen the reports about the Chameleon Killer," Hanson asked, and Margaret looked like she was going to leap on him and throttle the man.

"You mean the one about the bodies left all carved up?" I forced myself to shiver and chugged the rest of the beer. "Like I said, the news can be depressing, and the world has gone mad."

"So you don't know anyone that lives in the area you'd suspect?"

"Of being a killer? Well, hell, I sure hope not. I mean, that would freak me out if I thought I was living beside a murderer. You'd have gotten a call from me a long time ago," I said, tossed the bottle into the recycling bin under the cupboard, and leaned against the counter again. Both sets of eyes followed my movement as if hoping I'd simply toss it out in the garbage where they could take it for testing.

"That's an interesting tattoo you have on your neck," Margaret said, pointing with her pen.

I turned to show off the clown for them.

"Huge Joker fan. Listen, did you have anything else you wanted to talk about? I should really finish up this car before...." The gate buzzer sounded, and I shrugged. "Too late. She's here." Wandering over to the panel, I pressed the button to speak. "Is that you, Betty," I asked cheerfully.

"You know it is. I'm never late." The older female's voice squawked through the speaker. I flipped the open switch and walked over to Lawson and Hanson.

"I'm sorry, but I better go, or she's never going to speak to me again if her car isn't finished, but feel free to come by anytime with more questions. I'm always happy to help."

Margaret held out a business card. "Give us a call if you think of anything that may help."

"Will do."

"Oh, by the way, are you married?"

"That's a pretty forward question. Are you asking me out?" I lifted the corner of my mouth in what I hoped came off as a flirty grin. Margaret's face flushed, and considering I knew what her extracurriculars entailed, I wasn't sure if it was embarrassment that made her cheeks red or something else. "No, I'm not so lucky, but there's a girl

I'm seeing, and she's like a ray of sunshine. So keep your fingers crossed that things work out for me."

Margaret nodded as the two of them got back into their car and drove past Betty, who was getting a ride from her friend, that was as blind as a bat. I wasn't sure how the woman got anywhere alive.

Dropping the hood of Betty's car, I gave the front a good wipe-off to remove any potential prints as she shuffled up to the open bay door.

"That lot givin' you trouble? They were busy snoopin' around my home earlier. Feds—they always think they can do what they want."

"Agreed, but they're just tryin' to do their job. I don't mind." I held out the keys to the older woman and waved to her friend, who was performing a fifty-point turn to position the car to exit the property.

"You're too nice, I swung at the tall one with my broom and told them to bugger off, or I was havin' them arrested for tresspassin' without cause."

"Maybe I need to hire you to keep them off my property," I said as Betty took the keys from my hand.

"You betcha I would." Betty reached up and patted my cheek. It was something she had done for as long as I'd known her. She moved to the area shortly after Abel killed our mother, and she was the first person I befriended as Cain, the sole owner of the farm. Even someone like Abel and me needed to have character witnesses. It was one of those just-in-case things. "See ya later, handsome."

Stepping out of the way, I waved as both cars disappeared down the driveway, and I could finally let the forced smile on my face fall. It took way too much work pretending. It was just another thing that annoyed me about my brother. Acting always came so easily to him.

Whereas I had to focus hard on every word and twitch my body made. I looked up at the camera in the corner, and my smile was real this time.

Making sure that all the vehicles were indeed gone, I hit the button for the lock on the gate and closed the garage door, locking both the man door and bay door in place before I stripped off the coveralls and washed my hands.

Heading inside, I wandered down to the room that Sunshine was in and unlocked the metal door. Before it was even open an inch, I could hear the cursing and yelling.

KIRBY

It had been the weirdest and quietest twenty-four hours since Barbara had been murdered. I couldn't help but watch a little when Cain was doing what he was...doing. He was oddly kind. I hadn't expected to think that he'd been "kind" after seeing the photos of the bodies, but that was the only word for it. He spoke to her mostly like they were friends, sat quietly as he worked on his art, and then told her, 'it was time,' before he stabbed her through the heart. It was sick and so not right. Yet, the scene was strangely beautiful, like a ballet with death.

To add more confusion to my already muddled brain, Cain had carried Barbara out and then cleaned his work area as if it was a normal job. He then disappeared and returned with my favorite dinner, sketchbook, and paints. Then he handed me an ointment for my wrists. They had begun to rub raw. Once more, the vortex of emotions whipped me around until I was too tired even to understand if I was horrified, angry, felt invaded, or flattered that he was putting this much effort into taking care of me after what I'd seen.

I knew for certain that I would've already been dead if he wanted me to be. I also knew that there was something seriously wrong with me. I felt emotions. I wasn't like him, and yet...there was something in the way he spoke and talked about what I liked and needed that rang so true.

Sitting on the foam bed with the purple blanket wrapped around my waist, I was currently painting a portrait as I sang along to the endless loop of "You Are My Sunshine." Just another thing that was growing on me as time passed. I didn't know what day of the week it was or what time of day it was in this windowless space, but it felt like daytime. It felt like early afternoon, and I missed going for my daily runs and sipping on my favorite coffee. I wondered if Jorge was worried about where I'd gone.

Kind of a sad thought that Jorge, someone I barely knew, may worry more about my sudden disappearance than my own mother. The television screen flashed in the corner, making me jerk.

"Get ready for an Oscar-winning performance, Sunshine," Cain's voice came through a speaker in the wall.

He was standing in the garage and looked like the sexiest mechanic in the world as he wiped off his hands. The sun beamed into the open bay door and smiled at seeing those golden rays. Placing the painting aside, I stood and moved as close to the screen as the chains would allow.

A black vehicle pulled into view. As soon as I spotted it, I knew it was an FBI-issued car. I'd become accustomed to that exact vehicle pulling into my driveway. The driver's side door opened, and a moment later, there she was.

"Mom," I said, the word coming out as a whisper. Was I really seeing this?

"Hi there, I don't see too many FBI agents out my way. This must be pretty important," Cain said as he wiped the grease off his hands.

"My name is detective Lawson, and this is my partner Hanson," my mom said as she pulled out her credentials and flipped them open for Cain to see.

"This is not happening," I mumbled as I watched the screen. Cain glanced up in my direction again, and I wanted to throw something at him. He was taunting me like a bad joke.

"We won't take up too much of your time, Mister...."

"Buchanan. You go ahead and fire away. I've been livin' here my whole life and my parents and grandparents before me. If there is anything I can do to help you out, I'm happy to answer."

"Oh my fucking god," I said as I watched the show.

He could've played the part of the friendly neighbor in any movie and would've convinced the Pope himself that he was a loving country guy, just living a quiet life. My mouth fell to the floor as the exchange continued.

"What the hell am I doing?"

Without wasting another second, I began screaming. I slammed the chains off the rails and hollered at the top of my lungs, but they never flinched. Whatever hole he had me in was unbelievably soundproof. That didn't stop me, though. I continued to scream and swear at the top of my lungs long after the cars disappeared and the television screen went dark. I'd become the girl on the other side of the mirror.

I was no more than a reflection of who I used to be.

The door opened, and as soon as my eyes found Cain, I snatched the sketch pad off the floor and threw it at him.

"Why? Why would you show me that? Why do you want to hurt me? I don't get you! You say I do, but I don't. I'm nothing like you!"

Reaching for the paints, I brought them up to throw as well but stopped as Cain bent over and picked up the pad. He stared at what I'd been working on, and I was humiliated that he had been the model my mind chose to paint. His eyes roamed all over the paper before he looked up at me.

"This is magnificent," he said, and I rolled my eyes, but the stupid butterflies fluttered around in my stomach regardless of what my brain thought.

Painting had always been my escape. It was the one thing I really wanted to do, but I'd always been told it wasn't a career choice. It was a hobby. I should've followed my dreams and lived off the streets until I made it. I envied those that were that brave. Leave home and jet off to wherever to make their dream a reality. I'd always been too scared, but looking back, I could've traveled the world or gone to see my dad, and I hated myself so much that I let my mother control me with her purse strings. I also wouldn't have ended up attached to a wall with a serial killer as my host.

"Don't do that, don't pretend to like it. I can clearly see all you do is an act, and this is no different." He turned the pad around to show me my work, which might have been the best piece I'd ever created.

"I'm not lying. I only lie when needed. I do not need to lie to you about your art. Your work should be on walls in homes or museums," he said, looking down at his image again.

I'd never told anyone other than my mother that painting was what I wanted to do, so he was either doing that thing where he could look inside my mind, or he meant it. My chest constricted, and a warm fuzzy sensation traveled throughout my body. How did he always do that? How did he always say just the right thing?

"Why did you paint my expression like this," he asked as he stepped close.

"What does it matter?" Crossing my arms, I looked away from him and could feel the tears pricking the back of my eyes.

There was no logical reason to want to cry. Was I crying over the life I'd never get back, the one I'd wished I'd lived, or the fact that any feeling I thought he had for me was nothing more than a grand act? Was I crying for all the people that had been in this room before me or those that were yet to come? Or was I crying because, deep down, I had feelings that I shouldn't?

"It matters to me." Cain stopped in front of me.

Sighing, I looked into his eyes. "I painted it because that's how I see you. A man that has demons he wrestles, and the strain that it causes."

"I don't understand." He tapped the image. "I don't have any demons."

"Cain, look at this spot. It's where depression comes to die. You have a desire and need to kill, but I don't think you like everything that you are. If you did, you wouldn't have kept me here this long. I'd already be sightless on that slab, just like the countless others you've brought here before me."

I was fuming. I shouldn't be surprised that he didn't understand. How did you understand sadness or loneliness when emotions were always on the periphery of your vision?

"You think I'm not happy?"

"I think you're looking for something more than what you are. Maybe you were happy or as close to happy as you get, but now you've changed, and part of you has shifted."

The door banged open, and I screamed and jumped at the sudden gunshot-like noise.

"Hello, brother," Cain said, not bothering to look to see who it was.

I didn't think it was possible to be terrified of someone more than Cain, but that wasn't true. There was something severely unstable about Abel. You could tell the difference between them instantly. There was no guessing for me. He looked like a bird on crack as he waltzed in, his shirt hanging open and flapping as he moved into the space.

"Ye ha! I got ourselves a pair of southern girls to have a root 'en toot 'en bloody good time with," Abel said as he swung his arm over his head like a lasso and thrust his hips.

My eyes went back and forth between Cain and Abel, and I wondered why the fuck anyone would tempt the fates by calling their kids those names was beyond me, but I was sure that wherever their parents were, they were kicking themselves in the ass or rolling around in their graves

"I'm busy here, brother," Cain said, his eyes never leaving my face.

"Aw, come on, man! It's been days since you played with me." Abel stopped, his face scrunching up in thought. "I don't mean play with me as in playing with my cock. I mean with other people...oh fuck it, you know what I mean. You have to come and see. They are a pair of the biggest titty girls I've ever seen." He paused and looked off into space like he was thinking exactly about what he wanted to do, making me swallow hard.

As Cain looked over his shoulder at his brother, a pang of jealousy stabbed me in the chest. I didn't want this man, and yet I did. I wanted him all for myself. The thought of him fucking someone else had my jaw clenching shut and my hands balling into fists as an insane possessiveness rose inside me. The other part of my brain screamed that they were planning on killing two girls, and it wasn't normal to feel like this. But once more, there was no rationalizing with the emotions even though my brain attempted to war against them.

"I'm talkin' watermelons, man. There are so many things I want to do to them. Oh, and I bought us a new toy to try out. You have to come. I picked them out specifically with you in mind."

"Oh yeah, and why is that?" Cain took a small step away from me. My body shook as I watched them converse as if they were talking about a dinner menu.

"One of them has two different colored eyes," Abel said as if he'd just found a winning lottery ticket. "You can't resist that. I know you can't."

"I'm going to assume there is nothing I can say to change your mind and not do this?"

Cain turned to look at me, but it was Abel that spoke up.

"Whoa! What the fuck? Who the hell do you think you are, the fun police?" Abel laughed and wrapped his arm around Cain's shoulders, but I wanted to snarl and snap at Abel. "My brother and I have a special bond. You better not be trying to come between that," he said, and his eyes darkened as they looked me up and down.

"Leave her alone, Abel. I'll come see what you got," Cain said.

All I could picture was his dick in some other girl, and the anger I felt flaring inside me was white-hot. The sketch pad dropped to the ground with a slapping noise, and my eyes stared at the painting I'd created. Cain's feet marched away, and I bit my lip to keep from calling him back. If there were an award for the most fucked up emotions, I would've taken first place.

Abel's continuous talking could still be heard when he stepped out into whatever lay beyond the door. Cain stood holding the door, and our eyes locked, but just like that, he turned and left. My body shook with rage and sadness and... I didn't know what else. How could I care more about him leaving me here to fuck someone else over the fact that more people were going to die?

Tears pricked at my eyes, and a soft sob escaped my lips. I didn't even know who to cry for anymore, the girl I'd been or the one I wanted to become.

Hello
Sunshine

CHAPTER 27

CAIN

"Yeah, man," Abel said, clapping me on the back as we made our way outside. "Glad you decided to come. I didn't think you could get stuffier, but since you brought that purple-eyed girl home, you've really turned into a bore. Oh, how did it go with the FBI? On my way home from work, I saw them on the security app and decided to stay in town longer, which is also how I scored these girls. They aren't sisters, but they are best friends."

"The FBI wasn't an issue, they are asking questions of everyone in the area, but it was a good idea to stay away," I said and was impressed that he thought of that on his own and didn't need his hand held to make a good decision for a change.

The stones from our gravel driveway crunched under our feet as we neared his house. "What's the matter with you, man? You look like someone killed your puppy. Oh, wait... I did that. Well, it wasn't ours, but fuck! It's just a saying. Don't look at me like that," Abel laughed hard and smacked his hand off his knee.

I couldn't find it in me to offer even a smirk for his effort. Sunshine had struck a chord, one I hadn't been aware of until I saw myself through her eyes. How ironic that I took her for her unique colored eyes, but they could to see far more than I'd been able to see inside myself. No one had done that before, not my parents, not the therapist, not my school teachers, and not even my brother. I glanced at Abel and understood that his needs were selfish and self-motivated. Our relationship was about him having fun and me making sure we didn't get caught but did he truly understand me? Did he see the things that Sunshine did?

"Abel, how do you see me?"

"Dude, with my eyes." Abel screwed up his face and stared at me like I'd lost my mind. "Is this a trick question?"

"No, I mean, when you look at me, what do you see?"

Abel shook his head. "I don't understand what you're asking. I see my brother, and you have a poor choice of clothing, too boring. What else should I see?"

"Nothing," I answered.

When I took Sunshine, I knew she'd see more of me than anyone other than my brother, but I didn't think she'd see to the depth she'd depicted in her art. It had shocked me, and very little ever shocked me, but my Sunshine had managed to do it a few times.

"Man, what the fuck is wrong?" Abel shoved my shoulder, and I looked over at my brother.

"I have things on my mind, and I'm not interested in sharing them." We walked up the front stairs to Abel's house, and he turned around and shook his head.

"You need to dispose of that girl. Kill her, and feed her to the pigs. If you wanna keep her eyes, cut 'em out and sit them in your display case, but she needs to go. You've been fuckin' weird ever since you laid eyes on her, and it's only getting worse." Abel shrugged, his eyes lighting up. "I'm happy to do it for you if you want? I know how to make her scream."

Anger roared through my body and felt like a million fire ants marching under my skin. I grabbed Abel by the arm before he could walk inside and hauled him back until we were face to face.

"You don't touch her, not ever, or you'll find yourself on the wrong end of my blade, brother. I've tolerated your insubordinate behavior for years, but if you do what I saw in your eyes, it will be your eyes that I mount."

Abel tried to pull his arm away, but my fingers dug into his bicep. "What the fuck, man?"

"Say it." I got up in Abel's face, our noses almost touching. "Fucking say the words, brother."

"Fine, I won't fucking touch her. Are you happy?" For once, I couldn't tell if Abel's promise was legit or if he was playing me, but I let him go, and he crowed like a rooster as we stepped inside his home. "Now come on, I can feel our dicks shriveling up and getting ready to fall off from lack of use."

He already had the girls tied up in what looked like a crazy game of twister on the table. Pouring myself a drink, I took my usual seat in the corner to watch the show. The music blasted through the speakers, and the girls were a mix of moans and screams as Abel got to work. Normally, watching my brother work and knowing that I'd get to join in on the fun would excite me, but my cock lay dormant in my jeans. This show was overrated. I'd watched it a thousand times like a bad television rerun, and it no longer held interest.

Was I the kind of guy that only had eyes for one woman?

How would I even know?

It wasn't exactly like I'd ever dated or had feelings for someone. The idea of anything more than fucking them, making my artwork, and displaying them for the world to see had been the extent of my emotional connection.

The screaming in the room got louder as Abel pulled out a gas-powered tree trimmer. He looked like a mad scientist, pretending to ride the bladed piece of equipment like a horse. I stood, downing the drink in a single swig, and Abel hooted louder until I turned to head upstairs.

"Where the fuck are ya goin', man? I'm just getting warmed up. Tell me a spot you want to try fucking, and I'll cut you a hole." He revved the saw, and the girls screamed and tried to pull away from the noise.

"Not in the mood. Maybe another night," I said.

Abel stomped around the girls, his face livid. "This is what I mean. Look at you. What the fuck is wrong with you? He tossed down the saw and grabbed the knife off the large table.

The girl closest screamed as he grabbed her hair and yanked her head back. Shoving the sharp tip of the blade into her mouth, he forced her to keep it open as he grabbed her tongue and ripped it out of her head with a roar. She flopped forward. She was either dead or passed out as I watched my brother have his child-like temper tantrum. The piece of long flesh sailed through the air, and I stepped out of the way before it could hit me.

He was now completely coated in blood splatter, his eyes wild, and I shook my head at him.

"Sometimes, brother, you really are still just a child." I walked up the stairs while my brother cursed me out, but I wasn't going to let him bait me.

At one point, he'd been able to throw his fits. I'd stay to make sure he didn't make too much of a mess or that he still disposed of the bodies the way he was supposed to, but we were no longer teens, and I had other things on my mind.

Emotions had always been beyond me, so I had no reference for what I was feeling. It would've bothered me at one point but instead, the scientific part of my mind wanted more of what made me feel good.

I wanted to understand this emotion that had me not wanting to fuck Abel's randoms. And why was it that all I could see was the look in my Sunshine's eyes before I left the room? More importantly, why did the hurt look in her eyes interest me at all? The jealousy was there, and a part of me was feeding off that look. It meant, on some level, she wanted me. The words may not have left her mouth, but her eyes had betrayed her inner thoughts.

Abel was right about one thing. Since I'd met Kirby, I had changed, just not how my brother believed.

Making my way into my workshop's outer area, I locked the door so Abel couldn't pay another surprise visit tonight. I wouldn't put it past him to try again. He was annoyingly persistent like that. Opening the heavy metal door to where I was keeping Sunshine, I expected to see her sitting on the mat, but instead, I found her getting undressed in the bathroom with the shower running.

My eyes raked over her body, and I had the urge to paint her all over again. I wanted artwork all over the walls of my Sunshine in different poses, just like the ancient Grecian statues. She still hadn't seen me and bent over to undo the Velcro and step out of the orchid and pink pajamas I found with little paintbrushes all over them.

The bindings around her wrists and ankles were the only thing that interrupted the view as she stood up straight and stretched, which pushed her breasts into the air. I was speechless for the first time since my first kill, and my mind was quiet. The noise that normally plagued me was gone.

As I took a step forward, the light clicked on, and Sunshine jumped, grabbing the top she'd just taken off and holding it to her chest like a flimsy shield. It did no good, though. The image of her perfect skin, as smooth and creamy looking as porcelain, was engrained in my brain.

"What are you doing here? I thought you'd be longer doing whatever it is you do to them," she said. My mouth curved up as jealousy dripped like sweet honey off her every word.

Stepping inside the bathroom, I loved how she stood a little straighter. I knew fear lay beneath the surface of her bravado, but it was time to twist the fear into something else. Holding my hand out, she looked at it and chewed her bottom lip. The wheels were turning in her mind as she stared at my outstretched palm. She would never make a good poker player. With a sigh, Sunshine gave in and held the fuzzy shirt out for me to take, and I tossed it in the small hamper to be cleaned.

"Why do you do that," I asked as I grabbed her wrists and moved them away from covering herself.

"Do what?"

"Cover yourself."

"Sorry, I'm not used to being naked with a killer," she said, but the sharp edge she used to have on her every word was now like a dull plastic knife.

"Clothes or no clothes, I've already memorized every curve of your body and could paint you with my eyes closed. Clothes don't keep you safe. That's simply your mind's fabrication, so does it really matter?"

Those amazing amethyst-like gems flared with a challenge, and I stepped in close to her, crowding her personal space. "Get in the shower."

Her fist flexed, and I knew she was thinking of taking a shot at hitting me. I rubbed my chin where she got me last time and smiled at her.

"You going to hit me again? Where are you going to go, Sunshine? There's the door, but what about after that? Are you going to run back to the home you hate? Maybe the boyfriend that treats you like shit? How about the school that doesn't interest you?"

"I may not run anywhere, but it would feel good to break your nose," she said, and I couldn't stop the laughter that rolled out of me. I'd laughed more in the short time I'd known Kirby than I had my entire life.

"Go on, get in the shower. I promised I'd clean you at some point."

"You really don't...." I put my finger on her lips to stop her from once more trying to deny what she wanted.

The heat in her eyes told me she wanted me, but she needed to say it with words. The power and her submission were hidden behind her words. She needed to hand herself over to me fully, let go of her past and the life she lived, and embrace this new one I was offering her. We hadn't spoken specifics, but she was a smart one and knew what it was that I was offering her.

Sunshine may have been denying everything that her body and heart were telling her, but her resolve was weakening. Like an onion shedding the thin layers that protected the middle, I slowly peeled away the flaky petals to reveal a much stronger and more powerful version that lay beneath. She just didn't realize that yet.

"Get in, Sunshine."

Those big purple eyes blinked a couple of times, and then she turned and stepped into the shower. There was no door, no barriers to hide behind. The chains rattled as she moved them, so they were near the taps under the spray, and I wished that she was ready to take them off and break free of all that held back her potential, but she wasn't ready...soon, but not yet.

I pulled off the T-shirt I was wearing over my head, kicked off my shoes and socks, but left my jeans on and stepped in behind her as she lifted her face to the spray. She turned around in the warm water but didn't open her eyes as she laid her head back and let it run in streams down her body. I recorded this image of her to memory, and it would be the next of my collection I intended to paint.

Picking up the bar of soap, I rubbed it between my hands. Sunshine jumped back with a gasp as my hands gripped her waist. "What are you doing?"

"Come now, Sunshine, don't ask me questions about things you already know the answer to," I said as the bubbles frothed and swirled under my touch. Her nipples stood out in perfect little peaks, and my eyes feasted on her flesh that was unmarred except for a single bruise Peter had made.

It struck me as funny that the one labeled murderer wasn't the one to leave the handprint on her skin. The bruise was a pale yellow now and almost completely gone, but I could still clearly see where he'd grabbed her roughly. Peter would already be dead on my table, but my plans for him were far larger than me simply killing him.

"Why are you back here? You didn't answer the question," she said, her body still rigid even as the passion I was creating in her began to build.

"Why do you care? Are you jealous, Sunshine?"

She looked away from me and crossed her arms again. "No, I don't care who you fuck."

"Your words say one thing, but your eyes are saying another," I whispered and slipped my hand between her thighs.

She tensed her body, reacting to fear first, but then a sweet moan escaped Sunshine's lips. Her muscles twitched as she tried to remain resilient to my touch. I massaged the soft flesh on either side of her pussy lips and then around her sensitive clit. With every quick breath and quiver her body made, I committed the sound and sensation to memory.

Using the bar of soap, I abandoned what she really wanted to run it over and reached for her hardened nipples instead, rolling one of the buds between my fingers. Her eyes fluttered shut, and my hand stopped moving until her eyes opened again.

"Keep them open," I said.

Her eyes filled with desire that could rival that need coursing through my veins. I resumed my soapy assault on her body and ran my fingers down the sides of her waist and back up again. Each time my hands descended toward the apex of her desire, I'd stop just shy and retreat back up her body.

"Tell me what you want."

"I don't want anything from you," she said and raised her chin a little higher.

Giving her nipple a tweak, she moaned and then sucked in her lower lip like that would make a difference. The pleasure was written all over her face, and it told the story her words did not.

"Why do you keep lying to yourself, Sunshine? More importantly, why do you think you can lie to me?" Her arm flinched a moment before her fist came for my face, but the chain stopped her short by an inch. Smiling, I stepped forward so that the knuckles of her fist touched my chin. "Is this what you really want? To break my nose and spray blood all over the shower? You want to take all your frustration out on me?"

She strained against the restraint to get a little further, and I turned my head and latched onto her fist like a shark. My teeth pressed into the skin on her knuckles freezing her in place. I stared into her wide eyes. Biting down hard enough that it would hurt her if she pulled back, I reached out and grabbed her hips and squeezed them in my hands until she gave a small yelp. Releasing her hand, I spun her around and pushed her up against the cool tile.

"Yes, I want to hurt you," she said, her voice laced with a potent combination of anger, passion, and a dash of jealousy.

"Stop lying, Sunshine," I said, holding her hands above her head and laying my lips on the side of her neck. Her body shivered under my touch, and her ass pushed back into my hard cock that was safely trapped inside my soaked jeans.

I knew what that greedy bastard wanted, and even with my exceptional control, I wasn't sure I could hold off on fucking her if I could slide my cock between her pussy lips. "Tell me what you really want to know. Say it. Ask the question that is burning in your gut?"

Unable to resist, I sucked her earlobe into my mouth, and she gasped and pressed her ass back again. Her body knew what it wanted, but it was her mind that I was after. I swirled the soft flesh around in my mouth and sucked and licked it as I planned on doing to her pussy very soon. "Say the words. That's an order."

"Did..." She hesitated, and I could feel the tension in her muscles as her mind fought back.

"Tell me what you want to know."

"Did you...shit, what did you do to them," she blurted out and then sagged a little like it was the hardest thing she'd ever had to ask.

"Do you mean, did I slit their throats or split their pussies open with my cock," I asked and loved that she tensed and her eyes flared wild.

It was just a moment, but it was enough. I knew what she was feeling. Conflicted, maybe, but she didn't like me touching someone else, and I strangely liked that.

"They are people, Cain. You don't have to be so...crass."

"Sunshine, what part of, I see them as any other animal, do you not understand? I am at the top of the food chain, and they are nothing to me."

"So I'm nothing?" she said.

"Don't ask me stupid questions, Sunshine. You're better than that." She licked her lips, her eyes falling to the shower floor, and I knew I was pushing a little too much and needed to reward her before I lost her. "But to answer your question. I didn't do anything to them. I had a drink, and I came home."

Moving one hand down her body, I cupped her ass and massaged it.

"Why?"

"I didn't want to fuck or kill them," I said and slipped my hand between her thighs as a reward for being honest. I loved the guttural moan she made as her body quivered.

"That's it, that's the only reason?"

I smiled even though she couldn't see it and pressed up against her body with mine as my fingers slid between the wet lips of her pussy. She shuddered, her whole body shaking as my finger rubbed a circle over her clit.

"Should I have had another reason," I teased and found myself enjoying this back-and-forth banter more than I ever thought I would. "Is there something you'd prefer I be doing?" I pushed her a little further as I dipped the tip of my finger inside of her.

She moaned louder and tried to drop down and force my finger deeper, but my other hand, still firmly on her wrists, held her in place.

"Is there Sunshine? Is there something else you think I should be doing right now?"

"Oh fuck," she cried out as my finger sank as deep as it could into her pussy before I pulled it out and flicked it over her hard little clit.

"That's not an answer, Sunshine. I need to hear you say it. You need to tell me what you want from me." I ran my tongue up the side of her neck, loving the clean taste mingling with the touch of salt from the beads of sweat. Like a vampire feasting on a meal, I clamped down on the side of her neck hard enough to cause some pain but not hard enough to break her smooth skin.

"Ahh," she cried out but slammed her ass into my cock.

I stood still, taking a few breaths as my tightly wound control slipped a notch. She tempted me in ways that only blood had in the past. My finger slipped back inside of her, and she spread her legs a little wider.

"Say it, Sunshine, you have to tell me, and I'll give you what you want," I encouraged, as my finger moved faster inside her.

I could feel the orgasm building like a volcano brewing and preparing to erupt. She wiggled her ass and pulled down on my hold as she tried to cheat and force my finger in deeper. Most would hate the pain that was building in my balls, but not me. I craved to push myself and Kirby to the brink. I wanted us to toe the line between intense pleasure and the sharp bite of pain that would only enhance the first.

"Say the words Sunshine," I growled into the side of her neck and stopped moving my finger.

Panting, she looked over her shoulder at me. "I don't want anything."

"Yes, you do. I keep telling you that I know you, Sunshine."

"No, you don't."

I should've been disappointed, but instead, my mouth pulled up in a smirk at her tenacity.

"I know that you don't like your mother. On some level, you love her because she is your mother, but you don't like her as a person, and you don't like her or the lies she tells. You also love art and the beauty of life and death. You don't like that I know these things, and you are still fighting urges you don't want to face."

She looked over her shoulder at me.

"I also know your favorite color is purple, and your favorite break-fast food is waffles, but you don't like to eat too many for fear of getting fat and no longer being desirable. However, that would never be the case. You listen to country music as a guilty pleasure, tap your pen when you're thinking hard, prefer to use blue over black, and like your loose jeans and hoodies best. Sunshine, I can tell you what flavor your favorite ice cream is and your routine when you're getting ready for bed. I know everything about you."

Her mouth was hanging open, and I could see the shock in her eyes. "Yet, you continue to be a naughty girl and lie to me, but really you're only lying to yourself." Stepping away from her body, I backed out of the shower and leaned against the sink with my arms crossed.

"What?" Kirby turned around and stared at me, her eyes going to the outline of my cock behind my wet jeans. She licked her lips, and as sexy as that was, it wasn't enough for me to give her what she wanted.

"I told you to tell me what you wanted. That meant to tell me the truth, Sunshine. Bad girls don't get to come. Now wash up, and no playing with yourself. I'm staying right here to make sure of it."

"Are you kidding me?"

"Does it look like I'm kidding?" Her lips pressed into a firm line as her hands clenched into tight fists. "You're going to learn that I don't like liars, and have more control than anyone you've ever met." She sucked in a deep breath and wiggled her legs together, and I knew the pressure inside of her had built to the point that she was now uncomfortable. "And you know what else you're going to learn?"

She crossed her arms over her chest and glared. "What's that?"

"That you were made for me. Once you let go and finally allow yourself the freedom to break the chains of conformity you've wrapped around yourself...." I stepped forward, spread my arms to span the length of the shower, and leaned in toward Kirby. "I'm going to fuck you the way you've only ever dreamed about, and no one will ever be what you need but me. I'm the part of you that's been missing."

Her brow cocked up, and so did the length between my legs with that single look of challenge. "You're pretty confident."

"No, I'm very confident, Sunshine...." Reaching out, I snatched her chin in my hand, forcing her to step closer. "You'll see."

I stared at her full lips and wanted to take another taste, but I needed to wait. She needed to say the words first. The moment the words left her mouth was the moment she took the final steps toward accepting who she really was.

Stepping back, I released her chin. "Now be a good girl and hurry up and get clean. I really want to get out of these wet jeans."

CHAPTER 28

KIRBY

I'd never wanted to strangle a man so much in my life and that said a lot considering who I'd been dating. The ache between my legs was still messing with my mind and was only enhanced when said male decided to strip fully in front of me. He took his time wandering around his work area. As hard as I tried, I found myself staring at his hard body and the toned lines of his legs, ass, and abs. He had an assortment of intricate tattoos, and then there would be this odd one like the angel and devil fucking on his ass cheek that didn't seem to fit with his personality. This struck me as strange, and not Cain-like. Either way, they were sexy and made him look even more dangerous, if that was possible. When he walked toward me, he was talking about something I couldn't comprehend because his hard cock bounced in front of him. I knew what he was doing, yet I still couldn't peel my eyes away. Hello hormones, goodbye logical thought.

Cain finally put on track pants that he pulled out of some cupboard in the wall, but it didn't help. The constant swaying of his cock was still apparent even with the stupid pants on, and the situation only managed to play with my brain. As a final bit of torture, he laid down behind me.

Are you fucking kidding me?

How was it you could concurrently want nothing to do with someone and want them to promise you the world and never leave you? My mind was a mess, my body was in worse shape, and I didn't even dare look at the thing I called a heart, because it flat-out scared me.

No matter how much I tried, I couldn't fall asleep. Cain's taller frame was wrapped around me with his arm around my waist, and he was currently holding my hand. Of course, my ass was snuggly pressed up against the full length of his cock while he continuously hummed soft songs that vibrated down my neck and out to the tips of my fingers and toes.

Could one human possess another? It felt like Cain was slowly taking over my thoughts, actions, and emotions. The problem was I didn't want to fight it. Somewhere along the line, I'd given up the fight and realized he was right. I didn't want to live the nine-to-five and be normal. I didn't mind things that others found disturbing. As chained up and contained as I was, I felt freer than I ever had. This was just another conundrum that was Cain Buchanan.

"Cain?"

"Hmm?"

"Can I ask you something?" I kept my tone purposefully soft.

"I'm tempted to tell you no, for lying to me before, but what would you like to know?"

"How many people have you killed?"

My body tensed up, and Cain pulled his hand from mine to rub it up and down my hip. It took a minute, but I slowly relaxed again.

"That's not the question you want to ask me," he said, and his voice was quiet and soothing like he was massaging me with his voice.

"Yeah, I do."

"Stop lying, Sunshine. Be honest with yourself and ask me what you really want to know."

"Can someone like you love?" I swallowed hard.

Not even sure where the question came from, I froze. He stopped humming and pushed himself up, so he was staring down at me. It was the most suitable position I'd seen him in so far. He was the monster under the bed, the thing that mothers warned their children about, and as those blue eyes penetrated mine, I could barely draw a breath.

"Is that what you want...for me to love you?"

I looked away from his unnerving stare and focused on the metal table legs that had been my only view for days. My mind flashed to the woman that had been there not long ago and waited for the fear or guilt to hit, but it didn't.

Using his finger, he forced me to look at him, and I regretted asking the question. I hated when he did this. I couldn't stand that he was able to reach inside my mind and pull out all the things I didn't want to see. It wasn't fair that he had that ability over me because I felt powerless. "Is that what you want," he asked again.

"I don't know," I said honestly.

I'd never been more confused and torn in my life. I felt like I'd been split into two separate personalities.

Cain tilted his head and inspected my face. I knew what he was thinking. He got this overly serious expression when he was deep in thought. It was subtle, but I noticed it. I saw it as I saw the glimmer of something sadder. His range of emotion may not have been the same, and his urges may have been deemed sick, but under it all, he was still just a man looking for the same things the rest of us were—a place where he belonged and someone to share it with.

"I wouldn't know what love is, but I can say that from the first moment I saw you, I knew you were different and that feeling has only grown into something more persistent."

"So you never loved anyone? Not your parents or a girlfriend or even your brother," I asked, genuinely curious.

"Not my parents. I watched my father die and let it happen. That only brought me joy." My eyebrows shot up as I sucked in a deep breath. I couldn't picture killing my father, even with the separation, him moving away, and us growing apart. "Don't look so shocked. My urges started young, and although I've harnessed them into what you see now, I wasn't always as contained. As for loving my mother, I didn't love her either."

"Did you kill her?"

"No, Abel did, but if you want me to be honest with you, I was planning on killing her at some point. There was no motherly attachment between us." He said and moved a piece of hair away from my face. He was always a contradiction.

"This got dark fast." Cain smirked, and I wasn't sure what was funny, but I found myself smirking along with him.

"That's good, Sunshine. Let it out. Let the world see the real you.

If you want to laugh, then laugh. If you want to cry, then cry, but don't be fake anymore. Not with me." His eyes were so penetrating that I couldn't help but wiggle under his stare. "I've never had a girl-friend, and as far as my brother goes...I guess I do love him. I mean, I only want to kill him when he gets on my nerves, but that is fleeting, and I've always felt protective of him."

The chain rattled, reminding me I was still tied up as I moved my arm toward Cain's face. I looked at my wrist and sighed, letting my arm drop before I touched him, but he grabbed my hand and laid it on his cheek. The gesture was so simple, such a little thing, but maybe because of who and what he was, it felt like it held more weight. Could the monster really learn to love? Could he be more than what he'd been for years?

"What does it feel like when you look at me," I asked, unsure where I was getting the nerve to ask these questions, or why I even wanted to know.

"I see sunshine on a cloudy day," he said, and I rolled my eyes at the song lyric and tried to pull my hand away, but he held it firm. "You make me feel warm in what is an otherwise very cold shell." He didn't move as I pushed myself up, so our noses were touching. "You should be afraid of me," he said softly. "When I first saw you, all I wanted was your fear and your eyes."

My body shook, thinking of how close I'd come to becoming his prey. I was still chained but in a different way. He'd somehow claimed my heart, and that terrified me.

"I am scared. Everything about you scares me, and yet...I want more of the days we had when you brought me coffee and we created art together."

Cain rubbed the side of his cheek against mine. "Then why do you want me," he asked, voicing what I'd been avoiding earlier. "If I scare you so much, why do you look at me with hunger in your eyes?"

"I don't know," I said, closed my eyes, and tried to capture his mouth with my own.

"Yes, you do. Don't overthink it, just say what comes to you. There is no one here to judge you." Lifting his head out of my reach, he forced me to stare into his eyes, which looked like twin pools of cerulean blue. "I will never judge you, Sunshine. You are free to be who you were really meant to be with me, but you need to let go. Stop thinking about what the outside world would think about you. Now tell me, why do you want me?"

"Because you make me feel alive."

That statement was an oxymoron, yet it was the truth. The killer, the man that took lives, made me feel alive in a way that affected the fabric of my being.

Cain's lips crashed against mine, and the world spun on its axis. The kiss was like a burning inferno that had just erupted as he ravaged my mouth. It was as if we couldn't get close enough. Our tongues lashed together as the heat that had been there from the moment I'd seen him at the side of the road reached a boiling point.

There was too much space separating us, and I wrapped my arms around his neck and pulled him down on top of me. God help me. It felt so right. If I'd wanted to, I could choke him out right now, it would've been easy to wrap the chains around his throat, but I didn't. I didn't want to, even though I should.

Everything about him felt exactly as it should. He was no longer Cain, the serial killer that the FBI wanted. He was no longer the man who kidnapped me and could slit my throat in my sleep. Right now, he was simply the man I was falling for whether I wanted to or not. If

I'd been walking on a tightrope, then I'd just fallen off and was plummeting toward an unpredictable finale. I could land on my feet or break every bone on impact.

"Tell me you want me," Cain said as he broke the kiss and pushed my head to the side so he could nip at the area.

There was no hesitation this time. "I want you."

"Do you give yourself over wholly and completely?"

I paused. "Can we work up to that?"

The smile he gave me would've stopped the Devil in his tracks.

"Oh, my sweet Sunshine, you're already there. You just need to say the words." His biceps and shoulders flexed as he pushed himself up to hover over me. "I can't fuck you unless you say the words." Leaning on one hand, he slowly wrapped his fingers around my throat, and it reminded me of a boa constrictor getting into position to crush its prey. "Say you give yourself over. Say you want to stay. Say you want to be here with me."

The thread I'd been hanging from finally broke in my mind. My heart had wanted this almost from the moment we met, but my mind had kept the door slammed closed because he wore a monster's face. But it hadn't mattered because he had been leaning against it as he relentlessly tapped from the other side for days. My mind was tired of fighting, and I licked my lips as my mouth opened and the words he wanted to hear came tumbling out.

"I give myself over to you, and I want to stay."

His blue eyes seemed to grow dark and more intense. A small noise came from him that sent a shiver up my spine and had my back arching off the ground. Cain ripped open the front of the nightshirt, the seams easily giving way with the brute force.

There was no stopping the scream that ripped from my mouth as he dropped his head and sucked one of my nipples into the heat of his mouth, and swirled it around with his tongue. They were still sensitive from the earlier teasing, and his mouth was demanding as he sucked, drawing them into hard peaks.

"I need you to know I won't always be this nice to your body. I have certain needs that have to be tamed." His eyes were feral as he lifted his head. I was beyond turned on, like a powerline hit by lightning.

"Do what you need to," I said, shocking myself further when I realized I meant it.

A growl left his lips, and I would've sworn he was part animal for a moment. I lifted my ass into the air as he grabbed for the waistband of the latest sleep set I was wearing. He pulled them off, tossing them to the side a moment before his hands pressed into my thighs, forcing them to spread apart as far as they could go with the cuffs around my ankles.

"Oh fuck, yes," I cried out as he sank between my spread legs.

The mad and fevered version of this man was even more tantalizing than the equally dangerous and controlled one. His mouth was incredibly hot, and his tongue lashed at my pussy like he was punishing it with hard flicks and deep licks.

I cried out again as he let out another growl, with his face buried between my legs. His hands painfully dug into my ass and jerked me closer to him. Grabbing my calves, he pushed my legs up and then out to the side, which brought my pussy up off the ground. I was getting a front-row seat to exactly what he was doing.

The pleasure of his tongue swirling circles around my bundle of nerves was only surpassed by the visual of him doing it as his eyes stared into mine.

"Cain, oh fuck, yes, yes, right there, ahh," my back arched off the thick foam bed as the climax stormed up and ripped through me. My hands went to his hair as he continued to lick and drive the climax into waves of pleasure that didn't want to end. My body felt frozen as he pushed me to new limits.

When he finally stopped and slowly pulled away from my grip, I wanted to yell and tell him no. I should've been wiped out from what he'd just done, but instead, I wanted him to rip those pants off and take me again and again until I blacked out.

My mouth watered as he pushed himself to his feet, and as he stood towering over the top of me, I shivered, but this time not out of fear. The jogging pants that he'd put on were not doing anything to hide what was underneath them.

I couldn't peel my eyes away as he hooked his thumbs in the material and pushed the band down over his cock, which was as intimidating as the man himself. A flash, a memory of him pushing himself inside me the night of the corporate party, came racing back, and my body quaked with the thought of him inside me again. I didn't want this time to be a fleeting memory or something that faded between reality and a dream state. I wanted to feel every inch of him sliding into me and every one of his muscles flexing as he came.

"You claimed me that night, didn't you? The night of the party," I said as realization finally hit. The idea was so sexy, as insane as that sounded.

"Yes, now get on your knees," he ordered, his voice so rough it was like he'd just gargled with whiskey.

It took me a moment to make my body respond, especially as I watched his hand stroke the cock that was standing tall between his legs. Flipping over, I did as he said.

"Grab the rail," he pointed to the rail my ankles were tied to and reached out. I grabbed the rail and then yelled as his hand fisted my hair. He yanked my head back to just where it became painful and stopped.

"I'm going to fuck you hard, and you'll scream and come harder than you ever have. You've submitted to me, Sunshine, so this body of yours is mine." I felt like I should say something, but when I opened my mouth, all that came out was a moaning, "yes."

"I'm also going to choke you, Sunshine, and it will feel like I'm going to kill you. I know you'll panic at some point, but you need to trust me. Do you trust me," he asked as his other hand slowly snaked around my throat.

"Yes," I said, and I did. I knew him well enough to know if he wanted to kill me, this was not how he'd do it, and if anyone was going to know the fine line between life and death, it was Cain.

"You're such a good girl, Sunshine."

That praise shot through me and had me whimpering with anticipation. Without any further warning, Cain slammed his cock into me so hard and fast in a single stroke that it drove the air out of my lungs. I would've screamed if it wasn't for the hand securely wrapped around my throat. His fingers pressed into the soft skin, and my air supply was significantly reduced to mere little gasps.

My body shivered uncontrollably as he leaned forward and growled in my ear like an animal. He was everything primal that had been bred out of society. His instincts were that of an apex predator, and something about that called to me. He'd managed to reach in, and even though I was chained up, he'd found a way to begin to unchain my mind. I'd always wanted to be more frivolous, to do what I wanted and say what I wanted when and how I saw fit. But morals, ethics, what was right and wrong, and what was expected of me all stood in the way and held me back like a thousand hands pulling in the opposite direction I'd wanted to go.

His pace started out slow, letting me get used to how he filled me, but that didn't last very long. I could feel his patience slipping even though I couldn't see his face, and I knew before the strokes got longer and stronger that he was on the edge of letting go. The fear of what that would feel like was quashed by my need to have him use me the way he wanted.

"Fuck Sunshine, you test me."

He didn't waste any more time, and it felt like he was trying to fuck right through my body. Each thrust was on the precipice of pain, yet it was so sweet and delicious as he filled me like no one else ever had.

"Such. A. Good. Girl," he groaned out each word, and I wanted to hear him say that to me forever.

Cain's hand tightened just a little more, but as he predicted, the panic set in, and everything in me screamed to grab his hand to stop him before it was too late. He released my throat and let me take a gulp of air, and I managed to let out a small scream as he changed positions just enough that he pushed deeper into my body. Each glorious thrust pushed me toward a climax that I knew would be the first of many my body would crave forever. He was becoming a bad addiction.

His hand pulled back on my neck and cut off the air as he whispered words that no longer made sense in my ear. My brain had entered this fog, and it felt like I was floating above the ground. My mouth hung open as I tried to suck in more air. But then my body decided it didn't need any as long as he never stopped fucking me. It was a potent combination of agony and carnal need.

Spots dotted my eyes, and I let go of the last thread of fear I was clinging to and gave myself over to whatever he wanted to do. At that moment, I knew if he wanted to kill me, I'd let him. He released my throat once more, and the room's cool air rushed in, making me gasp just as the orgasm hit my body with a force so strong that the air stopped moving in my chest all over again. My body felt suspended as the climax tore itself from the depths of my body and then crashed into me like a wave.

"Yes, Sunshine. Come for me, come all over me. You feel fucking incredible."

Grabbing my shoulder and pulling harder on the handful of hair, he didn't ease up. The orgasm that had only marginally begun to subside started up again.

"I...can't...," I cried out as all the emotions and sensations blurred into something that felt like it was too much and not enough.

"You can. Let go of the rail," Cain said, and as soon as my hands loosened, he pulled me into him, and I cried out as he filled me further.

His teeth sunk into the skin at the base of my neck. The pain was like a sharp stab right to my pussy and pushed me over the edge again. I screamed this time like I was trying to scream the house down. Cain groaned loudly, his teeth pressing a little deeper as his pace picked up to an impossible speed. The sound of skin slapping equaled the groans and yells we were making.

"Oh fuck, Cain, please come. I can't take any more," I yelled out.

He let go of my shoulder, and a release of endorphins coursed through my system as he freed my neck and hair to grip my hips. His fingers dug in, and it should've worried me that this was his 'nice side,' but I wanted more. I wanted all he could give me and then some because I was being a greedy bitch. He was mine.

"Yes, yes, yes," I yelled as our bodies came together.

"Fuck Sunshine!" Cain yelled, and it was the most beautiful thing I'd ever heard as his body tensed behind me.

I could feel him releasing and climaxing inside me, and I pushed back into his body, wanting everything he had. With a final thrust, he relaxed and let my body fall forward, but he went with me and blanketed my body with his own.

My heartbeat was loud in my ears, and our bodies were sweaty and spent. I was sore in places I didn't know you could be, and I was going to be bruised all over tomorrow, and I'd never felt more satisfied and complete.

Cain stretched his hands out and gripped my hands to link our fingers together as we lay still joined.

"I've never been with anyone else without a condom, only you," he whispered in my ear. It felt like he'd just sung a love ballad. My heart swelled with joy as my brain processed that piece of information. "You're mine now, Sunshine. You were from the second I saw you, but now you're really mine, and you know what I am, but I promise you that I'll never lie to you, and I'll never hurt you the way others have."

"So, does this mean you're not going to kill me?" I turned my head enough to see the expression on his face.

"Only if you become a threat. Otherwise, I'd kill anyone and anything for you. All you need to do is ask." My body shuddered under his. "I brought you something else from your mother's house," he said, and I could feel him smirk into my neck.

Cain lifted himself up, and I sucked in a sharp breath, feeling empty with him no longer filling me. Turning on my side, I watched him walk across the room to a cupboard and open the door to pull out a canvas bag. He could walk around naked all day, and I'd never grow bored of those wide-muscled shoulders, cut arms, and drool-worthy abs.

He sat down beside me and opened the bag. He first pulled out my teddy bear. Smiling, I took the gift my father had given me as part of my high school graduation gifts. I held it to my chest and rubbed the soft fur on my face. Cain then pulled out the picture that sat with the bear, and tears pricked my eyes as I stared at my father's smiling face.

"I also grabbed this."

He pulled out my old diary, and my eyes went wide, but I didn't try to snatch it from his hand. Cain didn't feel bad about invading personal space. Why would he? He stalked, captured, and killed his victims, so taking a diary was low on the list of things he'd even think were wrong.

"Why did you take that," I asked.

He shrugged, his wide shoulders lifting and falling, which reminded me of something he'd done as a child. "It allowed me to try and understand you better."

"You wanted to understand me?"

"Yes, I like to understand everything."

That comment explained a lot about Cain.

"Why do you say you don't know your father," he asked and held up the diary to show the pages that told the truth. I swallowed the lump in my throat before looking down at the picture in my hands.

"This is not my father, he's my dad, but my mom says she doesn't know who my biological father is. She cheated on my dad, and they split when I found out by accident." It was my turn to shrug. "It doesn't matter now, I guess."

"Do you want to know?"

"Yeah. Just to know where I came from, you know?"

"Not really."

I looked up into his eyes, and it was hard to comprehend that, for someone so intelligent, how emotionally limited he was. He watched his father die and didn't care. He walked in on his mother being murdered and helped clean it up. He killed with ease, but the concept of wanting to know who my real dad was, seemed to be lost on him.

"But, I'll find out for you." His stare never wavered. Shocked, I watched him stand and then hold out his hand. "Let's go shower and then I'll make dinner and bring it down before I fuck you again. I plan on having you many times tonight. Then tomorrow, I'll find the answers you want."

Placing my still shackled hand in his, it seemed more like a piece of jewelry now. I wasn't sure if I'd run if he took it off, and as I stood and he drew me into his body and kissed me, the idea of running was pushed back in my mind, the image becoming an out-of-focus picture.

Hello
Sunshine

CHAPTER 29

CAIN

I wasn't sure why I offered to do this, but the idea of doing something to please my Sunshine was important to me. Very little outside of my needs and everything that protected those needs interested me at all.

I hopped the fence into the backyard of Margaret Lawson for the second time with no fear of her suddenly showing up like last time. She was being a very naughty woman and was at a particular man's condo, and I now wished I had a camera in Peter's place. I was pretty sure their relationship had been going on before Kirby left for what they thought was a vacation, and I was pretty sure that Peter hoped she'd never come back.

I slipped Kirby's key from my pocket and let myself in the back door. I'd already shut off the alarm and cameras, and even though I'd only been in here once, I knew the home. It always astounded me that people were so blasé with their information. My Sunshine hadn't been the exception to the rule regarding this particular pandemic in society. I'd break her of the habit, just like I was starting to break through her mind and unlock the door that held her dark desires. The ones she pushed down and tried to hide. The fantasies had her downloading images of murder scenes. On the surface, her actions seemed innocent enough considering her schooling, but I knew better.

She'd cowered and looked away when I killed Barbara in front of her, but I caught her more than once watching, her eyes glazing over and a passion I recognized beginning to form. She understood the beauty of my work, and I now understood why I was drawn to her from the very beginning. Yes, her eyes were the most stunning amethyst orbs in the world, but it was deeper than that. The recognition and acceptance of my world she understood on a cellular level.

The memory of what we'd done all last night was enough to make my body shudder. She'd asked me if I could love. I honestly didn't know. It was like saying I would cry when I'd never shed a tear. Yet, the idea of having her in my life until my end warmed me in a new way, and I liked it.

The cotton booties I'd slipped on my feet made a soft swishing noise on the carpeted floor as I slipped up the stairs to the room I was after. Kirby had another code she said was for a safe in her mother's house, but she'd never been in it. The number was in case something ever happened to her mother. My mother didn't have a safe, and she didn't have a backup plan in case she died. My mother didn't worry about things like that. No, she preferred to place all her items in a shoebox and stash it away in the closet like that was a place a criminal wouldn't first look. I often wondered how two people of such meager intelligence ended up having me.

Reaching the office door, I pulled out the lock-pick tools from my back pocket. This was one of the greatest inventions I'd ever come across. The liquid plastic would squeeze out of the end of the device on a thin piece of metal and fill the shape of the keyhole. It took sixty seconds for the product to harden once it came into contact with air, and just like that, you had a key for any door.

Grabbing the handle, I pushed the door slowly inward. The office was exactly how I pictured it would be—perfectly even lines on the shelves and nothing out of place anywhere on the desk. The walls were such a deep burgundy color that it looked like red wine had been used instead of paint. Crisp white trim circled the room. It was even around the window and door, but the framed accolades were what stood out.

The shelves and surfaces were full of them but free of any kind of family photos. There was nothing personal that told a story about who Margret was outside of work. Not a single picture of Kirby could be found. I circled the desk to be sure, and there was a picture of Margaret shaking the President's hand sitting in a frame on the desk, but other than that, the room was barren of any emotional ties. I was starting to wonder if Kirby got her inner demons from Margaret. Maybe she was made more like the killers she chased than she liked to admit.

Running my hands over every surface and corner, I found the holy grail behind a set of filing cabinets. With a quick flick of my finger, the lock released, and I was able to swing the filing cabinet away from the wall. I wasn't sure what exactly I was after, but the thing was that Kirby's unusual eyes were more than just rare. They were such an exotic color that legends and myths about eyes like hers were made. Purple eyes were only possible if, somewhere in her genetic makeup, at least one person had a bit of albinism, which was almost as rare as her eyes.

Someone not obsessed with eyes may not know that particular fact, but that was the thing about a collector. We learned all there was to know about what was collected. Kirby mentioned that her mother got pregnant on a mission and that she had a moment of weakness with some random guy. I called bullshit. Margaret was many things, but fucking a random guy type, she was not.

This meant one of two things. Either Margaret was raped and didn't want to admit it, or Margaret knew who Kirby's father was and had kept it a secret her entire life. I was betting on the second. I didn't have any reason to believe that was the case, but I'd studied Agent Lawson almost as much as I had her daughter, so it was a gut feeling.

So that left one question. Why would she lie?

I punched in the numbers from Kirby's phone and knew if this didn't work, I was going to have to run for the exit. "Moment of truth."

With the press of the last number and a quick twist of the handle, the door gave a soft clunk and pop sound as it released. Flicking on the phone's light, I rummaged around inside the safe and found an assortment of expensive items. The fancy watch and diamond jewelry set would've been enticing if I'd been a typical robber, but I wasn't. Zeroing in on the files, I pulled them out one at a time. I thumbed through the boring documents, not seeing anything out of place until I reached the thick investment portfolio.

"What do we have here, Margaret? You're quite the devious woman, after all. I'm impressed."

I took pictures of everything that would be useful and then some. The folder looked innocent enough at first glance, but the very last page had a name on it that was well-known in these parts. Looking closely at the paperwork, it seemed like a business agreement, but it didn't read properly, at least not for any normal business.

With a smirk, I put everything back in just the way it had been and locked the doors on my way out. Walking out the back door, I hid among the bushes and was just about to jump over the fence when I could hear a couple talking as they walked down the street. There was the distinct jingle of a collar.

As soon as the dog reached the other side of the wood fence, it stopped and pushed part of its nose through the slat. I held perfectly still as it began to growl and then bark, making my jaw clench together.

"Come on, Daisy, stop it," the woman said.

Yeah, Daisy, stop it.

"It's probably a cat or something," the man commented.

Or something would be correct.

As soon as they were out of sight, I made my move and hopped over the fence and cut across the street to the park, where I took off the booties, gloves, and mask I was wearing. My mind whirred as the information traveled around in my brain. A smirk crossed my lips as I watched a car pull away from the shoulder. There were moments in life you had to let go, and this was going to be one of those moments with my Sunshine.

Sometimes people needed a gentle shove to have them embrace their true selves, but I was prepared to throw my Sunshine off the cliff and see if she could grow wings.

MARGARET

"Oh fuck yes," I screamed and dug my nails into the young ass that was feeding me his cock. I'd gone far too long without sex, and it was like I'd been starving for it.

"Mrs. L, you feel so fucking good," Peter groaned as he picked up the pace.

He wasn't able to last very long, but he could get it up multiple times. I'd taken the night off to come over and talk to Peter about ending things before Kirby got back from her trip, but as soon as he opened the door and offered to open a bottle of wine, the idea went out the window. Besides, my daughter had clarified her intentions with Peter, so why not take him up on his offer?

I gripped his ass hard and arched off the bed as I came.

"Yes, dig your nails in. I love that," Peter said and picked up the pace. A few thrusts later and he froze in place as he came and then laid down on top of me, panting. "You're amazing, Mrs. L. I don't want this to end," he said, rolling off me and flopping on the bed.

"Kirby's trip is going to be over soon, and she will be back. Are you prepared for the blowback if we keep this up and she finds out?"

"Yeah, about that. I don't think she's going to want to see me again," Peter said and sat up.

"Why? I thought you wanted to marry her?"

Peter rubbed the back of his neck, and it was easy to tell that he didn't want to talk about it, but I needed to know what had happened. "Tell me, what's going on, Peter?"

"We had this stupid fight, and I was a bit of an ass. We were fighting in the car, and I pulled over. We fought some more, and it got a little physical, she was hitting me, and I had a hold of her hair. Completely in self-defense, of course. Anyway, she got out of the car, and I left her on the side of the road."

"You left her at the side of the road? Do you even know if she got home okay? You know there is a serial killer in the area, right?"

Fuming, I stood and began to pace as I thought. I would never win any mother of the year awards, but I didn't want to end up at a murder scene and have my daughter's face staring back at me.

"Yeah, she was fine," he said but looked down.

"Are you sure? I haven't heard from her, and I've left her a ton of messages."

"She used the ticket, didn't she," Peter asked, but I wasn't sure.

"I think so. I don't know." I pulled out my phone from my suit jacket to find out, but the phone rang, and Kirby's name came up. "It's like she knew we were talking about her."

I showed the screen to Peter, and he nodded as I answered.

"Hey, finally. It's nice of you to call me back."

"I've been busy. I plan on staying another two weeks, so I need you to make sure that it happens and that I can still come back to classes," Kirby said, and my mouth fell open.

"Hi, mom, how are you? Would've been a kinder hello." I mocked my daughter. "I'm not doing that, especially for you to gallivant around Europe. No, you come home in a couple of days like you planned, or you're out of the FBI program." I paced as my anger flared. My gaze flicked over to Peter. "And what is this I hear about you having another fight with Peter over something stupid. When are you going to stop acting like such a child and grow up? Peter wants to marry you, and you should be focusing on school and him."

"First of all, Peter is nothing more than a narcissistic, self-centered, fucking asshole. Marrying him is never going to happen. Second, you will make sure that I have two more weeks off, or I'm going to make it known to everyone you try to impress that you only got your job by sucking cock."

"What?" I yelled and stopped pacing long enough to stare at the phone. I wasn't sure I heard my daughter correctly. "What the hell are you talking about?"

"Don't play me. I know all your little secrets, including the bank account you don't want anyone to know about. Make it happen, or the rest of the FBI and anyone else I can find to listen will also know. I'm sure that a tabloid or two would pay for the story."

The phone went dead in my ear, and I stared at the thing in a panic. How had Kirby found out? Ugh...actually, that didn't matter right now. All that mattered was that I ensured no one else uncovered that information.

Grabbing my clothes off the floor, I began to get dressed.

"What did she say?" Peter said as he stood and came over, but I wasn't in the mood to be consoled.

"She said that she was going to be away longer and that the two of you are finished." I tucked in my blouse. "I guess that means we can keep fucking after all, screw her. I'm sick of her attitude."

"Fuck yes, that is what I wanted to hear," Peter said, wrapping his arms around my waist.

"I have to go. There are a couple of things I need to take care of."

Peter pulled me into a hug. "Come back when you're all done. I want a celebration round with you."

I kissed him on the cheek and marched for the door. Kirby was playing dirty, and I needed to do some damage control before this became a problem.

CHAPTER 30

K IRBY

I was in the middle of painting my latest image of Cain when I heard the door unlock. I stood up with a smile until I saw who it was. Cain's brother Abel stuck his head in and looked around before his eyes landed on me. They may be the same color as his brother's, but his stare made ice flow through my veins. The way he moved reminded me of a snake. He was coy and sneaky with his movements as he came in and closed the door.

"My brother's not here," he asked, and the hair stood up on the back of my neck.

Keeping my voice even, I gave him my best-relaxed look and lifted my shoulder in a shrug. "Not right now. He was running a quick errand. I don't have a clock, but based on when he left, he shouldn't be long."

Abel stepped forward, and it took all my strength not to let him know he scared the fucking shit out of me. I had no reason other than a sixth sense that this man would eat me alive. I'd thought Cain would, and maybe at one point he would have, but Abel looked at me like I was a T.V. dinner he wanted to eat or maybe crush my bones. It was hard to tell, but neither was good.

There was no spark or connection. All I felt was cold as I stared at the man who liked to cut people into pieces and mangle their bodies almost beyond recognition. He was the wild card in the deck, the joker you never saw coming.

"What is it about you?" Abel said as he stopped, just shy of my sleeping foam.

His head twisted a little from side to side like a bird would, which only added to my creeped-out meter.

"I'm not sure what you mean."

"What is it about you that has changed my brother? What are you doing to him? Do you have a magic pussy? Are you a witch? That's it, isn't it? You're a witch with a magical pussy that has turned my brother into someone I don't recognize."

"You think I'm a witch, like a real witch with spells?" I couldn't help but smile, which didn't seem to help my cause as Abel's eyes narrowed into a glare. "Does it look like I have magical powers? I mean, if I did, I wouldn't worry about turning your brother into whatever, and I'd undo the chains and unlock the door instead."

Abel tapped his chin, the chains around his neck jingling as he did. His moment of confusion gave me a chance to look him over. The brothers were very identical, but there were subtle differences. Cain had a freckle near his left nipple. It was a small thing, but Abel didn't have one. Abel's voice was just a fraction higher than Cain's. It was so close to being the same that anyone who hadn't spent a lot of time with them wouldn't notice, but the clothes, on the other hand...

Cain wouldn't be caught dead in a brightly colored Hawaiian shirt or ripped jeans with stains on them. Even the shoes on Abel's feet were nothing like what Cain would wear. Cain liked clean and crisp items, and he wore mostly black. His shirts were fitted to his sexy chest and abs.

"If you're not a witch, then it means that you're simply dangerous to Cain and not to me," he said, and the soft smile on my face fell. His hand reached behind his back. I didn't need to see to know he had a knife and planned to use it.

I took a step back and bumped up against the wall.

"Don't you think you'll upset your brother if you hurt me?" I was grasping at straws, but I needed to stall for more time.

"I think he'll learn to forgive me. After all, we have a bond that can withstand anything," he said as his arm slowly began to pull his weapon out when we both heard the outer door unlock.

Abel took a step back and fixed his shirt to hide whatever weapon he had as the metal door clicked shut. Cain stepped into the room and froze as his eyes traveled between myself and Abel.

"What are you doing in here, brother," Cain asked, his tone accusatory.

I sagged with relief at hearing the anger and protective manner of his voice. Strangely, he'd become my protector, not my killer. It was an insane thought to feel safer with him than with the rest of the world, but I did. There was not a single doubt in my mind that he would kill anyone that tried to hurt me, and by the look in his eyes, that also included his brother.

"I came here looking for you," Abel answered.

"That doesn't explain what you're still doing here when you realized I wasn't. It also doesn't explain why you're that close to Kirby after our conversation," Cain said.

Everything about how he was slowly making his way across the room told me that he was going to snap and there would be a brawl. I'd seen enough bar fights to recognize the tension, but the look in his eyes screamed murder.

"I told him he could wait for you in here. I didn't think you'd mind," I said, and both men turned their heads to look at me, but their expressions were completely different. While confusion was on Abel's face, skepticism was what I got from Cain. "Do you mind? I just thought that with him being your brother and the two of you so close, you'd want him to wait," I said.

Cain came to stand in front of me, and his look said he didn't believe a single word I was saying. I swallowed hard. He held out a coffee from Mode that I hadn't noticed him carrying. "Jorge says, Hi, and he looks forward to seeing you when you get back."

I took a sip of the coffee and couldn't stop the moan. "Thank you."

Cain turned his body to face his brother, and I wasn't sure if he was going to push more or let the lie stand. "Okay, brother, why did you want to see me?"

"Um...I wanted to know if you could build me a box?"

"A box," Cain asked, and I slowly stepped away from the two

men to let them speak and sat down to continue my painting and sip on my delicious coffee.

"Yes, a box. Here I'll show you what I want. I drew it on this napkin," Abel said, and I smiled, sensing Cain wanting to groan at the napkin. I tuned the two brothers out, their voices becoming background noise.

"Why did you do that," Cain asked, making me jump as he knelt in front of me. I blinked as I looked up from my work and stared into his serious expression and intense blue eyes. "Why did you stick up for my brother? I know you were lying, and I want to know why."

"Are you going to kill me if I don't tell you?" His eyes narrowed, his jaw twitched, and I knew I was pushing his buttons and enjoying it way more than I should've been. For a reason I couldn't explain, I dipped my finger into the green paint and wiped it on his nose.

I yelped as he grabbed me and hauled me to my feet by the front of the shirt I was wearing. My back banged against the wall, and my heart jumped into my throat. His eyes searched my face, and I wasn't sure what he was looking for until he spoke. "Do you want him? Do you want my brother?"

My eyes went wide, and my mouth curled up at the corner. "Is that jealousy I hear in your voice," I teased, pushing my limits.

A growl left his mouth, and he pushed me harder against the wall. I could see the needy beast inside of him. The thing that made him a serial killer was staring back at me, and god help me, I wanted to poke at the beast, push its limits.

Wrapping my arms around his neck, I leaned into him, and he loosened his grip so I could hold him.

"No, I don't want your brother," I whispered in his ear and then kissed the side of his neck right on his clown tattoo.

"Then why," he asked, his voice breathy.

I leaned back enough so I could see his eyes. "Because he is the one you've truly cared about your whole life, and I could tell that you were getting ready to hurt him, which may have ended your relationship with him." I kissed the corner of his mouth. "He's the only family you've ever loved. I didn't want to come between that."

Cain smoothed back my hair and searched my face. "You do know that he would've killed you, right?"

"Yeah, I know," I said and loved that he hadn't wiped off the paint.

"You could've let us kill one another, and you would've been free."

"But would I really be free?" I said.

His face shifted to a dark desire so fast that I wasn't prepared for the breath-stealing kiss. I was gasping when Cain broke away and laid his forehead against mine. My lips were swollen from the assault. Cain's thumb touched his nose, and he showed the paint on it before wiping it across my cheek, and my heart swelled.

Stepping back, he wandered to the drawer I'd seen him in once before, but instead of fear, all I felt was excitement as he pulled out the ball gag. I'd secretly fantasized about it since he first put it on me.

"Do you know what I'm going to do to you?" I shook my head no. "Do you want to know?"

I nodded and licked my lips as he stepped forward. Reaching out, he hit a small button I'd never noticed by the cupboards, and I screamed as my arms and legs were suddenly pulled tight against the wall in a spread-eagle position. I stared in confusion at the chains that seemed to pull me by an invisible force.

"What's going on?"

Cain stepped up close to me, leaned in, and inhaled deeply on the side of my neck. Goosebumps rose all over my body as I responded to the adrenaline surge that made me want to run away and fuck him hard at the same time.

"It's magnetic," he whispered and ran his tongue up the side of my neck. "Pull on an arm." I did as he said, and sure enough, I could move my arm forward, but as soon as I relaxed, the strength of the magnet pulled my arm wide again. "Are you going to be a good girl and let me put this on without forcing you to open up?"

"Yes," I whimpered as his teeth nipped the soft skin on my neck. "I'll open up."

Cain's hand slipped into my hair, pulling my head to the side. The image of a vampire came to mind as he moaned and then laid his teeth along my vein like he intended to bite me."Mmm, Sunshine, I bet you taste good. Now lean your head forward and open up."

Once more, I did as he asked. As he fit the ball into my mouth, my body shuddered as my pussy clenched with anticipation. My nostrils flared as he stepped back and looked at me.

"I've wanted to do this to you since I first saw you," he said and undid the belt on his jeans.

He'd barely touched me, and my body was singing for whatever he had planned. As he popped the top button on his pants and peeled the black T-shirt off, it was good that the chains kept me upright, or I would've fallen down at his feet.

Making his way to another drawer, he pulled out his leather case that I knew held all his knives and then laid it out on the table.

"I warned you, Sunshine, that I wouldn't always be kind to your body, and you agreed." His eyes flicked up to mine as he pulled a long sharp blade from the case. Terror mingled with desire, and it was going to my head. All I could do was nod, so that was what I did. "Do you still agree?"

Cain held up the knife like he was testing me, and I nodded again, a smile spreading across his face.

"Oh, Sunshine, you're such a good girl."

His fist wrapped around the front of my shirt, and with a quick slice, the fabric fell open and exposed my breasts to the air. My nipples were already tingling as they hardened and ached to be touched.

He could've easily removed them with the Velcro on the sides, but this was a trust test. I knew it without him having to say the words. He wanted full control over my body, and the consent to do what he wanted was maybe more important than the act of fucking me. With a few more perfectly placed cuts, the material was pulled free. I sucked in a sharp breath and shivered as my back was pulled up against the cold wall.

He worked quickly, and my eyes followed his every action as he sat the blade down and ran his finger across his other tools. I was no longer the wary animal in his grip. I was an eager participant in whatever he decided to do.

There was a distinct thump in my ears as my heart pounded hard. I didn't know what he was going to do, and that was part of the thrill. Cain turned around and had the same tool in his hand that he'd used to carve Barbara up.

My eyes went wide, but I didn't struggle as he watched me. I stared into his eyes, those of a hardened killer, and accepted that this might be it. A peace washed over me. It would seem to anyone else a strange time to be the most relaxed and accepting of oneself, but that was the mystical power that Cain had over me. I could fight it, or I could accept it.

"You look concerned but not quite scared," he said as he stepped forward. "Are you scared of what I plan on doing?" I shook my head no. "Are you sure?" As soon as I nodded, he smiled. "I may not know if I can fall in love, but I can tell you that my life, whatever that looks like, is not complete without you in it."

He was always hard to read, but his eyes were kind in this quiet moment between us. I felt like I was getting to peer under the surface of the man who could be cruel to others but could be so much more. My heart fluttered as my stomach did backflips. Tears pricked my eyes, and the last thread that tied me to my past life dissolved into nothingness.

He held up the sharp tool with what looked like a scalpel with a sewing foot on the bottom for me to see. Cain adjusted the tool and pulled the blade up so that only a tiny tip was seen below the foot.

"I'm going to cut you, but it won't scar. Do you trust me?"

Our eyes locked as I mumbled, "yes," through the ball gag. The look he gave me was penetrating right down to my soul. Nothing else in the world existed but this man.

"It's important that you don't move," he whispered.

I shuddered with anticipation as the blade touched my chest. I closed my eyes and let him create. There was an intoxicating sting to the feel of the blade slipping down my body and over my stomach. The sunshine song played softly in the background, and Cain began to hum along as he drew the blade across my skin. There was a sharp sting but no real pain, and the more he did it, the more my body enjoyed the sensation.

Opening my eyes, I looked down at him kneeling before me, and he was so focused on his task, on his art. He was a true perfectionist. If he'd been a billionaire, maybe he would've simply been called 'exotic with unusual tastes.' I couldn't tell what he was creating as his hands glided smoothly over my skin. It didn't seem to matter what he did, though. He effortlessly kept me on this precipice between sharp pain and pleasure. He made it so strong that the world blurred. They were no longer separate entities to me. They were one and the same.

It could've been a minute or an hour when Cain stopped and stepped back from my body. My eyes felt heavy as they fluttered open.

"You are as beautiful as any work of art," he said as he walked away and came back with a handheld mirror.

Holding it up so I could see his work, I whimpered as my eyes took in the two figures kissing. The image was of the two of us, and the background was filled with intricate lines that made flowers and what looked like raindrops. The image was only accentuated by the trickling of blood that was making its way down my body. Cain laid the mirror down and surprised me as he undid the gag in my mouth. My jaw ached from being forced open for so long, but as he kissed me, the pain faded away.

He dropped to his knees and stared up at me, his eyes shrouded by his lashes, but I could feel the heat of his stare. I watched in fascination as he swirled his tongue around my skin and slowly licked his way to my core, which was already wet and ready for him.

My voice sounded rough as I cried out when his teeth latched onto my sensitive clit. "Oh fuck, Cain," I said, my head pressing into the wall as my back arched. "Oh fuck, yes."

Those were the only words that formed as he sucked hard, drawing the sensitive little ball of nerves into his mouth with voracity.

Cain already had me standing on the edge looking down, just waiting to be pushed over, and now he'd become the gale-force wind doing just that.

"Ahhhhhh," I screamed as I came.

The force of my orgasm could've rivaled a volcano. My head was light, the room spinning as intense pleasure flooded my system and filled the far reaches of my limbs. Not a single spot wasn't filled with the tingling response of the climax.

Cain gave the area a final swirl of his tongue before he began to travel up my body, lapping up the droplets of blood as he stood. Another time in my life, that would've horrified me and grossed me out, but now seeing him swallowing another part of me down only made me feel more connected to him.

I'd officially lost my mind, my heart running along beside it as they played tag in the darkness because of this man, and all I could think was give me more.

His tongue drew a wet line all the way up my skin, and he held his mouth open, showing me the few speckles of blood a moment before he dropped his mouth to mine. The metallic taste wasn't as strong as I'd imagined, but there was something so erotic about the taste of my blood mingling with his tongue as it explored my mouth.

"I'm going to fuck you now, Sunshine," he growled against my lips.

The sound of his zipper lowering was loud in my ears like it had been amplified to let me know he was coming for me.

"Yes," I whispered back.

"You're mine and only mine."

"Yes."

The guttural sound that Cain made had every muscle in my body quaking. He drew his tongue along my skin once more, and this time he gripped my hair hard and crushed his mouth to mine. The need that had already been burning bright took on a life of its own. Cain released my hair to grab my ass and pulled my legs around his waist as he thrust himself inside me. He swallowed my scream down as thoroughly as he had my blood. Releasing my head, he reached up and gripped my hands, and my nails dug into the back of his hands as he fucked me hard.

Every inch of his cock demanded that I come again. Even without the words, the order was there, and I could feel the rise in my body once more as he thrust into me with no abandon. Teeth gripped my lower lip and drew it into his mouth as Cain made primal groans of pleasure every time he slammed home.

"Cain, fuck me harder," I screamed as that sweet and blissful peak of carnal need and pain streaked toward me like a head-on train.

The loud panting turned into mewling cries of incoherent words as he pushed me over the ledge. I came so hard that I didn't even know it was possible to experience this level of ecstasy. The screams continued to fall from my mouth as Cain's pace quickened like he was rutting me into the wall.

"Fuck, Sunshine, fuck me," he yelled and squeezed my hands hard as he came.

I could feel every release and jerk his body made, his face twisted into a mask of agony. He slumped against my body, his head falling to my shoulder as we caught our breaths. Laying my lips over the pulse in his neck, I loved the feel of it pounding hard for me. I did this to him. The man that had little to no emotion lost himself with me. There was no greater compliment. There was no greater 'I love you' he could ever say.

I was one hundred percent his now. I would do whatever I needed to protect this. To protect what was mine. If anyone else thought they could touch him...then they would find out what kind of monster I could be.

He was still hard inside of me, and my muscles clamped down on his cock as he went to move away. Desperation to keep him close came over me.

"Do it again," I said, my throat horse.

Lifting his head, Cain looked me in the eyes and placed a gentle kiss on my lips. "I think it's time I showed you a little trust."

Stepping away from me, he dropped my legs to the floor. A moment later, I landed on my knees, and my arms were released with the touch of a button. He ripped his jeans fully off, and they landed on the floor in a heap. Those intense eyes found mine as Cain stepped in close and stared down at me. His cock was right in front of my face, and I was still wet from our multiple orgasms.

Grabbing my hair, he yanked my head back.

"Open," he ordered. My jaw dropped, but he gripped my chin in his other hand and forced my mouth wider. "There, now clean it."

I glanced at his cock, the tingling excitement building steadily in my system all over again. Just as I was about to slip the head of his dick in my mouth, he stopped me with a hard jerk on my hair.

"If you bite me...." He lifted a brow, not needing to finish the threat. I knew it would be the last thing I ever did, but I had no intention of biting him. I wanted more of him, all of him. He released my chin, and I moaned as he slid into my mouth. It seemed so naughty to be tasting both our climaxes on my tongue. He was opening doors to new desires with each passing second, and I wanted to experience every single one with him.

Grabbing the back of his claves, I pulled, wanting him closer, and was surprised when he stepped forward. Slipping my hands up his legs, I loved that he shuddered under my touch. Wrapping my hands around his still-hard shaft, I looked up into his eyes and took him as deep as I could. Swirling my tongue around, I moaned as I licked every amazing inch of him.

Cain groaned, the sound once again closer to a growl as I worked at taking him deeper. "You like that," he asked, pulling my head back off his cock. I nodded, my mouth hanging open. "You want more?"

"Yes," I managed before he stuffed my mouth full once more.

Pulling out all the way, he repeated the process a number of times until I was a drooling mess. Instinctively, I tried to wipe my face.

"No, leave it. I want to see you drool for me. You're a naughty girl, Sunshine. You're making me want to fuck your mouth hard. Slam my cock down your throat until you choke on it."

My body flushed, and as impossible as it should seem by this point, I wanted him to fuck me again. The human body shouldn't be able to feel like this after everything we'd already done, but now that he'd turned on the tap, it had become a floodgate of need coursing through my body.

"Yes, please," I begged.

The corner of Cain's mouth pulled up, his eyes glinting in the light, and the trickle of fear he created only added to my wanton desire.

"You got it, Sunshine."

Gripping my hair with both of his hands, he allowed me to guide him back to my mouth, but after that, I was completely out of control. Tears streamed down my face as he slammed his hard shaft down my throat over and over again. Like everything he did to me, he seemed to know exactly how much to push so I wouldn't pass the point of pleasure and pain. Then he'd back off and then start again.

My hands gripped his muscular legs and savored the feel of him as they flexed with the powerful onslaught.

"Fuck, Sunshine, you have a hot mouth," he growled as he picked up the pace. My nose hit his stomach with each powerful thrust. "Yeah, that's it, Sunshine, take it, take my cock."

Looking up at him, I'd never seen a sexier sight as he rocked back and forth with his head tilted back. The pleasure was evident on his face as the muscles in his neck strained. I was going to be sore. My throat had never taken a beating like this, I'd never been used so roughly, but I never wanted it to end.

"Are you ready for me, Sunshine," he groaned, his head tilting forward to look down at me. I couldn't answer with him plunging in and out of my mouth so fast and hard, but I willed him to see the answer in my eyes. "So good, Sunshine, so fucking good. Here I come."

His fists gripped my hair painfully as he drove forward and held still as he came down my throat. I could feel the hot liquid traveling down, making my body shiver with a carnal need. As soon as he released my hair, I slowly pulled him out of my mouth and was assaulted by his lips. He kissed me and licked at the mess dribbling down my chin.

"You wet for me again, Sunshine," Cain asked, breaking the kiss but not giving me time to answer before ravaging my mouth again. His hand went between my thighs, and I whimpered as his fingers slipped inside me.

"You are a slut, Sunshine," he said, pushing my shoulders until I lay down. "But you're my slut, my Sunshine, mine. Every last inch of you is forever mine. If that means that I love you, then I guess I do."

"Yes," I barely managed to get out through my sore throat and swollen lips. "I love you."

He smiled as he pushed my knees apart. "Good girl, Sunshine, very good girl."

Hello
Sunshine

CHAPTER 31

CAIN

As soon as I could move, I pushed myself up and off Sunshine. My arms and legs were shaking with the extreme workout, and I flopped over on my back to catch my breath. The chains rattled, and I looked over as she slowly rolled into me. It was strange to have her cuddle into me like this. I wasn't the type to want the physical connection she was seeking, yet my arm wrapped around her and held her close.

We lay there quietly for a few minutes before Sunshine lifted her head to look at me. Her magnificent eyes were glazed over with the lasting effects of what we'd just done.

"You want to go clean up, don't you," she asked, her voice soft. My lip twitched. "I can see it on your face. It's bothering you that your tools are dirty and sitting out and that we are a mess." She smiled at me. Raising up, she kissed my chest and then pushed herself up into a sitting position. "Go for it. You're not going to relax until you do."

My brow cocked at her. Did she just give me permission to do something? And why did it feel completely normal for her to know me that well? Moreover, why was I okay with it?

She yawned and grabbed the blanket pulling it around her as she pushed herself up against the wall. She stared at me calmly, waiting for me to move.

Getting on my knees, I leaned forward and kissed her lips. There was no hesitation as she opened herself up to me and cupped my cheek.

"You like ordering me around," I asked, as I nipped at her bottom lip. How could I still be tempted to take her again?

"Maybe a little," she said softly as she stared at me from under her thick lashes.

"Hmm," I said, and she smiled.

I forced myself away before I tried to fuck her again and pushed myself up to stand. She was right. I was edgy, wanting to get everything cleaned up. I walked to where my knives were displayed on the counter, and with quick efficiency, I cleaned my tools and the gag. Putting them away, I turned to lean against the table and stared at my Sunshine.

"I called your mother earlier," I said, and Kirby's big eyes slowly lifted to my face. She blinked like she was trying to comprehend what I was saying.

"My mother, why?"

"Well, thanks to my app, she thought it was you." I shrugged.

Grabbing the key to unlock her wrists, I returned to Kirby and knelt down in front of her. Catching her eyes, I said, "I called her to get you more time off before you need to return to the academy. Don't worry. I've received high praise from your teachers for the work I'm handing in on your behalf. They seem to think that I have a unique and in-depth perspective into the mind of a serial killer." I smirked.

She rubbed her eyes, and I thought she was going to be angry at first until she burst out laughing. She waved her hand at me and covered her mouth like that would stop her hysterical giggling. Tears flowed from her eyes as she continued to laugh, and I had no idea what I said to cause this kind of reaction.

"I'm sorry, I just love how all the FBI and my mother are talking to the murderer they're chasing and have no fucking clue." She slumped against the wall, a smile on her face. "Serves them right for being so fucking arrogant."

My brow lifted as I mulled over what she said. "So, you're not angry?"

"No, I'm not."

She crossed her legs, and the blanket opened like a magic veil. I loved seeing her sitting like that. Naked with my artwork on her body and her pussy well used from us having sex. Yes, I wanted more of this, a lot more.

Sighing, I reached out and cupped Kirby's chin, forcing her to look at me. In response, she nipped playfully at my hand, her teeth gripping my finger gently before she turned it into a kiss.

"Do you want something to eat?"

"Yes, I'm starved," she replied, and her cheeks pinkened to a deep shade of red. "You made me work up quite an appetite.

"Does your jaw hurt?" I stared at the bruise from where I'd gripped a little too hard.

She shook her head no. "Little stiff, not sore."

I smiled. "Well, I plan for you to become famished, Sunshine."

The statement was meant to be matter-of-fact, but Sunshine's eyes flared, and she moaned as she bit her lip seductively. Yes, there was a lot more I wanted to do to her tonight, but first, we needed to take the next step, so I held up the key. Her eyes widened as she stared at the strangely shaped key I'd made specifically for the custom cuffs.

"Is that what I think it is," she asked.

"Yes," I said and slid the key into the lock on her ankle.

It had to be turned three times to the right and then a half-turn back to the left to unlock the cuff. The leather broke apart, and her foot was free. She licked her lips, and as much as I was sure she wouldn't run, there was always the possibility that she'd try and kill me for her freedom. But it was time to take the risk.

I unlocked her second ankle. Before I freed her wrists, I grabbed the care cream I'd given her, squirted some into my hands, and methodically massaged it into the red mark on each ankle.

"Thanks, that feels a lot better," she said, her voice barely a whisper.

Looking up, I realized her eyes were closed, and her head was leaning against the wall. Pleasuring someone before had never felt like this. The person I fucked or worked on may or may not have gotten off, which never mattered. However, with her, it did. My Sunshine had lit a spark in me, and I felt freer than I ever have in my life. New sensations invaded my senses almost daily from having her around. Did that mean I suddenly gave a fuck if I killed the next fifty people who unwittingly walked up my driveway? No.

Unlocking her wrists, I put the key in my pocket and kept an eye on her as I squirted more lotion into my hands to take care of the marks. There were some light cuts at the edges of her skin from her pulling or moving, so as the last of the cream was rubbed in, I lifted her wrist to my lips and laid them across the marks.

Standing, I held out my hand to help her to her feet. "There are clothes upstairs for you to put on. Are you ready?"

She looked down at the foam mat and then at her sketchbook. I knew what that meant. She'd created a new piece of artwork for me. There was something unbelievably satisfying to know that she wanted to paint my likeness as much as I wanted to paint her. She bent and grabbed the pad, her teddy bear, and the picture she'd set up like a small bedroom and clutched the items to her chest.

"Now I'm ready."

I tapped in the code for the door lock. With a loud click, I let go and pulled the door inward. For the first time, Kirby got to step out into the lower basement. The area was outfitted with everything I might need. She paused and stared at the television screens and the large chair in front of them.

"You were watching me?"

"Yes, I never left you alone, even when you felt alone." I looked down at the top of her head as she stared at the now-empty workspace.

"How long have I been here?"

"Three weeks tomorrow."

Her eyes went wide, and she looked up at me. "Three weeks? Wow, time flies."

"Is that a good thing," I asked, unsure how to judge her reaction.

"It's a baffling thing. Everything just kind of blends together," she said as I guided her across the large space to the stairs that went up to the farmhouse.

From outside or even upstairs, you'd never know this large space existed, which was what I loved about it. I unlocked the thick metal door and stepped into the hall to let Kirby emerge. It was dark because of the time of day, but she looked around and blinked like the sun was shining through the windows.

"I grabbed some more of your things and bought you some stuff I thought you'd like," I said and led her down the hallway and up the stairs to my bedroom.

She was quiet and looked around in a way that worried me she was going to try and bolt. We entered the bedroom that was now twice the size it used to be when I was a kid. I'd decided to knock out the wall between it and the sewing room that had been on the other side. Kirby's reaction fascinated me. She wandered the space, still clutching the few items that had been on the floor and still as naked as the day she was born.

I tried to see the room through her eyes. The paintings I'd completed of her were hanging on the soft grey walls. The first one I did, hung as the centerpiece of my collection. If my brother ever came up here, he would've thought I'd gone mad, but luckily he never made it further than the door to the basement.

The comforter was grey and white, but I'd added some purple pillows to help it feel more like it was her space too. The dresser held her jewelry box and a number of other small things I'd been able to take when I was at her mother's home. I'd also slipped into the campus and taken all her clothes, books, and computer equipment when her roommate was in class. I would've liked to have seen the look on the girl's face when she returned to a half-empty room.

She paused as she reached one of the paintings I'd just finished of her. It was of her lying down on soft green grass with a sunny glow shining down on her back, and her lips were curved up in a small smile.

"These are exceptional, Cain," she reached out and touched the canvas painting. "You really are talented."

"Does that mean you like them?"

"Love them."

"You asked me how I see you. I'm not good at forming words to express emotion, but all these images and the many more I want to paint tell you how I see you."

She turned to look at me, and I wanted to toss her down on the bed and take her again right there, but instead, I gently took the items she'd brought upstairs from her hands and set them in prominent places around the room.

"I'm not much for decorating, so if you want to change something, go ahead. Did you want to shower?"

"Yes, please."

Walking over to the bathroom door, I opened it and pointed inside. "Everything you could want is in there, and your clothes are hanging in half of the closet. All your underwear and socks are in here." I tapped the top of the dresser.

Walking back over to where she stood in the center of the room, I couldn't help but admire her beauty and the artwork I'd created on her stomach and chest. It would be healed in a couple of days, and I already knew the next masterpiece I wanted to create using her as my ultimate canvas. I knew I needed to control how much I played with her, but the thrill it brought was well worth the wait.

"I'll go make dinner. Come down whenever you're ready."

"No chain or rope, or will you sit and stare at me?" Her small smile spoke volumes.

"Not anymore." Leaving her in the room alone, I jogged down the stairs and began cutting the vegetables for the stew I'd planned on making. As soon as I could hear Sunshine in the shower, I jumped in the one on the main level and quickly rinsed off. Everything was simmering by the time the water turned off upstairs, and my Sunshine wandered down.

"It smells good down here," she said.

I watched her out of the corner of my eye as she spotted the large knife on the counter. I knew she'd go for it. She snatched it off the counter and pointed it at me.

I slowly turned to face her and wiped my hands on the dish towel as I analyzed her face. She looked very uncertain about what she wanted to do. This was the moment that she needed to decide who she would be once and for all. While the cuffs were on it was easy for someone to think they knew what they wanted, but what would they do once set free of the shackles? Sunshine had expressed that she loved me. I believed her. I'd looked into her eyes and saw what she was thinking and feeling, and the same emotions danced in her eyes now.

"Stay back. I will kill you," she said as I stepped forward. "I said stop," she said, and her hand shook.

I knew she wasn't scared. She was tougher than that. She had a war going on inside her, and it was just a matter of who would win out—the old Kirby or the new Kirby ready to emerge.

"Is this what you want, Sunshine? You want to kill me?" Reaching out, I put two fingers on her wrist and lifted her arm so the blade sat against my throat. "If you're going to kill me, then slit my throat, make sure it's deep enough and a clean slice, or I'll just be angry."

Her lower lip trembled as I moved my hand away from hers and kept my hands out to the sides. "I don't know...."

"You don't know what, Sunshine? You don't know if you want to kill me? You should want to. Isn't that what society teaches you? Isn't that what your school is training you to do? To kill those that threaten the rest? Wouldn't it make the world safer with one less murdering psychopath destroyed?" Her hand trembled harder, and she backed away from me, tears trailing down her cheeks. I watched her take one step at a time until she reached the front door and fumbled with the lock behind her.

I didn't move. I didn't try to stop her. As soon as the door was open, she spun around like she was going to run and then stopped. Her whole body was shaking so hard that I could see her physically fighting off the reaction.

"Are you going to chase me, kill me, find me again," she asked and looked over her shoulder at me.

"No, Sunshine, I'm not." I didn't know if I meant it forever, but I meant it at that moment. I needed her to pick me. I needed to know I was her choice. It was the only way to truly trust what we had. It was the last move on the chess board.

"You need to choose what life you want to live. You may not have come to me willingly, but I've shown you who I am, what I am, and I've never lied to you. With me, there are certain things that you need to accept, but I'll always be here for you, and I'll always treat you as the rare piece of art that you are. If you go back, you're choosing to live a lie and hide who you really are and possibly the ability to feel like you do with me ever again, but it is your choice to make."

"I don't understand," she said and turned around to face me, the knife pointing down to the ground. "You stalked me, practically raped me, and then kidnapped me all for what? Just to make me fall in love with you and then let me go."

"You truly love me," I asked, and the same possessiveness I always felt about her flared brighter in my chest with her second declaration of her feelings

A blood-curdling scream ripped through the house as she stomped her feet and slammed the door closed. She looked wild, her hair a mess and her hand shaking with the knife still in it. She looked like she just stepped out of a slasher film, and it was fucking hot. I wanted to sit her on the counter and fuck her until she was screaming my name.

"Yes, of course, I love you. Do you really think anyone else would stay? What have you done to me? I can't go back, but to stay is crazy."

Checkmate.

I slowly walked forward and held out my hand, and she looked at it for a long time before finally placing the knife into my palm. With predatory precision, I grabbed the front of her shirt and slammed her up against the wall, the knife now to her throat. Her eyes were wide, and her chest was heaving under my hand. "One day, I'm going to fuck you with a knife to your throat. You look so fucking sexy, all worked up."

Removing the knife from her tender skin, I dropped my head and kissed her. For a brief moment, she was stiff under my lips, but then like she was made of butter, she melted and wrapped her arms around my neck.

"Do you want to kill me, Kirby?"

"No, never. But we need some ground rules if this is going to work."

"I love rules that I make," I said, the corner of my mouth lifting as she glared at me. "We can talk about all the rules you want later," I said, picking her up so her legs could wrap around my waist. Walking back to the kitchen, I laid the knife down and then laid her out on the table like she was my meal. "Say it again. Tell me how you feel."

"I love you," she whispered and pulled gently on my hair.

"I wish I could feel what you feel," I replied and ran my thumb over her lower lip.

"Tell me what you do feel."

"I feel like I don't want to go another day without you in it."

A smile spread across her cheeks as her eyes glittered under the kitchen light. "That is love, Cain. I don't want to go a day without you in it either."

I smirked down at her. "Then, I love you too."

CHAPTER 32

KIRBY

I didn't think life could get any better than this, it was the most fucked up of scenarios getting to this point, but I'd never been happier. Cain and I had found a rhythm to our day that felt so right that my body sang with joy. He was a demanding and aggressive lover, but for someone that didn't have the range of emotions others did, he was also the most thoughtful and considerate person I'd ever met. I was all in on him and trusted him with my life. There was a strange high in knowing that he was as wild as a tiger and could rip me apart at any moment.

It took a great deal of arguing, but I finally convinced him that I could only be with him if he stopped killing random people and only went after specific targets we chose together. I'd settled on targets that the FBI was hunting already. I'd decided it was best to return to school and be our eyes and ears inside the organization. This way, I could assess if the targets were a real threat based on their crimes and have an entire file to hand over to Cain.

That had been the hardest sell-job of my life, but I couldn't handle another Barbara asking me to help her. I still had limits, even if he didn't.

In a few days, I would return to school and resume my school-work as if all was normal and I'd completed my trip as planned. This was all his idea, almost like he'd been planning on having me turn into his partner. Had I been manipulated? Were my decisions my own? I'd asked myself these two questions a million times and kept coming back to the same answer. It didn't matter. It didn't matter how we got here. The point was I didn't want to leave.

The days he was out on the road towing vehicles was when the boredom would set in, like today. He was up and gone by six-thirty, and I was left with very little to do. The vacuum roared as I moved into the living room to continue cleaning. We both hated a mess and disorganization, and now we had a schedule to take turns cleaning the entire house. The vacuum was the best part, or it was until it stopped working. I turned around to see if I'd pulled it out of the wall and sucked in a deep breath as my eyes locked onto Abel.

It was easy to tell that he'd been drinking even though it wasn't close to lunchtime. I could smell it wafting off of him, but his eyes were bloodshot, and his words were slightly slurred when he spoke. I caught the glint of a blade in his hand, and I swallowed hard. He was dangerous at the best of times, but right now, the look in his eyes had a cold sweat trickling down my back. I hadn't worked out in weeks and flexed my muscles, readying myself for the fight I knew was coming.

"What are you doing here, Abel," I asked, my eyes looking around for the best possible weapon as I ran through all my training.

This was a different scenario than the mad dash through the woods with Cain chasing me down, but it was no less lethal. He was already holding a weapon, and like Cain, he was a foot taller with at least seventy pounds on me.

He smiled like a cat that had just killed the canary, and there was no guessing with him. I was the next bird on the menu. He brought a massive knife up and rubbed his forehead on the back of his arm. Abel saw me as a threat to the relationship he had with Cain. I understood that during our last confrontation, but I hadn't seen him. Cain hadn't mentioned him, so I thought they'd sorted their shit out, but apparently not.

"Well, isn't this cozy? You're a regular little Susie-Homemaker. So are you Cain's maid now?"

He laughed at the joke, but I didn't crack a smile at the rude comment. There was a statue sitting on the coffee table, a lamp behind me, and a tall decorative vase in the far corner. Cain was a minimalist, and there weren't many choices unless I could get to the kitchen, but that was a long run from this spot.

"I'll ask you again, Abel, what are you doing here?"

"Ahhhhhhh," he screamed and grabbed at his hair, allowing me to take a large step toward the coffee table and my best potential weapon. "Don't fucking do that! Don't sound like him. You're not him. You're not my brother."

"I'm not trying to sound like Cain, but considering you wanted to kill me the last time you visited, and you're holding a knife, it seems like a pretty fair question," I said.

Abel took a step forward.

"Even that..." He pointed the knife at me. "Even those fucking words sound like him. He hasn't killed or fucked someone with me since he got serious about stalking your ass. He's my brother. Mine! And somehow, you've fucked up our relationship." He took another threatening step, and I moved until my legs hit the coffee table.

"I'm sorry, Abel. Maybe it's just that I'm the new shiny toy at the moment," I said and knew it wasn't true, but I was hoping to reach him before this got a lot worse. "You know what it's like when you get a new plaything, something that interests you and holds your attention for a while."

"You know..." He tapped the side of his head with the sharp point of the knife. "I thought about that. I've spent days in my house thinking those exact words, but here is the thing...." Abel took another step, and I grabbed the statue off the table and took a step away from him. "My brother has never kept anyone longer than seventy-two hours, and he's had them strapped to the table the whole time. With you, he never put you on the table. Instead, he feeds you and fucks you, and now here you are, wandering his home free as a bird. Naw gurrl, you're the fox in the hen house."

I wasn't sure I'd ever classify Cain as a hen, but I got the analogy. "Why don't you come back for dinner? I'm making ribs, homemade fries, and corn, and we can discuss this. Abel, you must know if you hurt me, Cain will not just be angry. He won't forgive you."

Those red-rimmed eyes held so much anger and hate as he stared at me.

"No, I don't want dinner. I want him to find you unbreathing and for him to realize who he still is. You've fucked with his head. You've warped him into this...." He waved the knife around. "Domesticated thing, this lap dog that you control."

Abel spat on the floor, and my eyes went wide. Cain would kill him for spitting on the floor, let alone insinuating he was being controlled. Add in killing me, and Abel was digging his own grave, but Abel was so angry and hurt that he wasn't seeing straight. Then again, with a personality like his, did he ever really see straight?

I managed to move to the blank space between the living room and the dining room and waited. My self-defense training was coming back to me, but it was always a harder fight when someone was drunk.

"I'm going to kill you like I killed our mother. It will be a reunion for us, a good old go-back-to-the-beginning reset. He forgave me for killing her, and he'll do the same now."

"You're fooling yourself, Abel. Cain planned on killing your mother, but you took that from him and made a mess he had to clean up, but at least he already wanted her dead. He doesn't want me dead."

"Fuck you! Don't tell me what my brother wanted." He took a large step forward, and even drunk, he held the knife steady. My fear wanted to take over, but I forced the feeling down. I knew how to fight, and I would fight with my last breath. "You don't know my brother the way I do. Y-you don't know what we've been through to get here...or how we think and do our shit. That's our shit—for us only," he slurred.

"Did he tell you our mother was still alive when I ripped her intestines out with my bare hands and played in her blood? I'm going to do the same to you." His muscles flexed, and his face darkened into a rage-filled mask as he came at me. I held my ground. "You better run." His tone reminded me of a low-growling animal.

"Not a chance," I said, then jumped out of the way of his charge. He ran into the dining room table and sent the closest chair flying across the floor.

"You fucking purple-eyed bitch," he snarled.

I wanted to hold up my hand and ask him what the fuck that was supposed to mean.

Abel swung his arm in a wide sweeping arc with little to no real skill for fighting, unlike his brother. However, the blade was as long as my forearm making it extremely dangerous, so I backed out of the way. He came at me again, with the blade slashing through the air like his hand was connected to a rubber band. With each strike, I avoided it and found my opening. Using his momentum, I hit his hand with the statue.

"Ahh, you fuckin donkey shit biscuit," he growled out.

I would've laughed if this wasn't a life-or-death moment. The statue became a shield, and I felt like I was in an old swashbuckling movie as he took a swing. I blocked it with the solid marble figure. Sweat was running down my body, and my hands were getting slick on the smooth statue's texture.

"You need to die, just fucking die!"

I brought the statue up to block the next blow, but the damn thing sailed out of my hands and crashed into the wall, knocking a framed picture to the ground. Shards of glass scattered everywhere as it smashed on the floor.

Catching Abel off guard as he stared at the damaged painting, I jumped in the air and landed a roundhouse kick to his face. He grabbed the side of his cheek, and I didn't wait for him to recover before landing a hard blow to his side and jumped into the air to bring my fist down onto his jaw. I caught the angle wrong and felt my hand crack on impact.

"Fuck," I swore, and shook my hand out.

Abel stumbled back from the blow, and not wasting a second, I came at him again, but he blocked the shot and shoved me hard. His hand felt like I was being hit by a small bus, driving the air from my lungs. My hands wrapped around his wrist with the knife as he drove me backward into the wall, and I screamed as the shards of glass sliced through my socked feet.

I saw the fist coming and moved my head out of the way so that he only grazed my jaw before slamming his fist into the wall with a loud cracking noise.

"Bitch, fucking bitch."

Abel pulled the hand with the knife forward and brought me with him, and I screamed again as the glass dug deeper into my feet. I needed to pull myself together and force myself to focus. He slammed me against the wall again, but this time when he pulled forward, I used it as an opportunity to drive my knee up into his dick.

His eyes bugged out, and his upper body went slack. I drove my knee up a second time and caught him in the side before giving him a hard shove. Abel stumbled back and fell over the ottoman. His hand with the knife smacked into one of the two television screens, cracking the screen because the knife speared into it.

Abel moaned, his head falling to the side as I limped toward the kitchen. Each step was excruciating, but I needed my phone to call Cain, and I needed another weapon. I reached the knife block first and pulled out the longest knife I could before looking for my phone. I realized I'd left it upstairs.

"Ahhhhh," I yelled as I was tackled from behind and driven to the ground. Again, the air was pushed out of my lungs on impact, and the knife flew out of my hand, sliding under the oven. I drove my elbows back, hitting any part of his body I could, and landed a few solid blows against his ribs.

"Fuck! Fuck you bitch," he snarled as he fisted my hair and smacked my face off the floor. White spots exploded in front of my eyes, and I went limp in his hold.

"I was just going to kill you, but not anymore. Now you're going to experience the full Abel treatment."

His weight lifted, and I immediately rolled onto my back and began kicking at him even though the glass hurt me with every blow. "You're like a back-alley cat, but I've slit their scratching throats too," he said as he started to walk, dragging me by the hair.

Screaming, I tried to get on my knees, but he'd jerk hard as soon as I tried, and I was thrown off balance again, my ass finding the floor. I heard the lock for the basement door and began to struggle harder as terror shot down to my toes, giving me a boost of adrenaline.

"Stop fucking fighting, would you," Abel roared and slammed my face off the closest wall.

I lunged for his leg like a rabid dog and bit as hard as possible until I tasted blood. His yell of pain gave me a burst of gratification until his fist found the side of my face, and stars lit up my sight again. My limbs went weak, and my brain couldn't seem to remember why I was struggling in the first place.

Small whimpers left my mouth with each painful bounce as Abel drug me down the stairs like I was nothing more than a bag of garbage. Fear lanced my heart, but I still couldn't make my limbs work properly and ended up moving like a wiggling worm on the end of a hook.

"Don't do this, Abel," I mumbled as he tossed me on the metal table. "Cain loves you...don't ruin that."

"He'll love me more for this," he said and went to tie my hand down.

"No, let go," I yanked my hand away, caught Abel in the chest with my foot, and then screamed loud as the glass bit into the arch, sending sharp shooting pain up my leg.

"Ow, you cunt, you cut me," Abel snarled, and I took the opportunity to roll off the table but landed hard on the cold floor.

"Cain," I screamed, begging him to hear me wherever he was as Abel walked around the table. My body shook as I pushed myself back along the floor, leaving red streaks from my bleeding feet.

"He won't want you anymore without your pretty eyes. I'm going to pluck them first."

Tears flowed down my cheeks in steady streams as the song "You Are My Sunshine" began to play in my head.

CAIN

It was a slow day. I'd been moving around from one road to another and listening to the scanner for any possible jobs, but it seemed like no one was out today. Two cars still needed tires, and the oil changed back at the shop. It didn't pay as much, but I'd be able to get in a mid-day fuck session with my Sunshine, which made it worth heading home early.

She hadn't wanted me to go to work today, and she'd been very fucking tempting as she stood in just a T-shirt when she handed me my coffee. The schedule I kept as regular as clockwork almost went out the window after I kissed her lips.

I pulled up to the gates, punched in the code, and then rubbed my eyes as I waited for them to open. Abel was next on my list of things to do. Abel needed to feel wanted, or he would slip off the imaginary choker chain I had around his neck.

Pulling up to the front of the house, I expected Sunshine to come out and greet me like she'd done all week, but the door stayed quiet, and nervous energy settled in my body. Jogging up the steps, I noticed only the screen door was shut, but the house was quiet. Too quiet.

Had she taken off? Did she decide she didn't want this life with me after all?

The screen door slammed as I whipped it open and ran inside. I skidded to a stop in front of the living room and stared at the damage. I zeroed in on Abel's knife sticking out of the television screen.

I should've killed him, was all I could think as I ran through the hall and spotted the small pool of blood by the door leading to the basement. I was going to kill him if he'd hurt her. Abel would end up tasting my blade. A feeling I'd never experienced settled in my stomach as I ran down the stairs and across the basement to the closed door of my work area.

I punched in the code, but the door wouldn't budge. Son of a bitch, he changed it. Luckily, I'd been prepared for a time this might happen. Not that I thought it would be Abel that I'd have to use the override code for, but in hindsight, he'd always been the ultimate threat. My fingers held down the four buttons that would release the door and override the system.

As soon as the lock clicked open, I was bombarded with Abel's annoying one-hit-wonder music and an ear-piercing scream. Fear was an emotion I'd never felt, but I felt it now. It felt like an ice bath had been dumped over my head as rage boiled in my gut.

"Cain," she screamed. "Cain, help," Sunshine yelled for me even though she didn't know I was there. "No, get away from me."

The part of me that I'd locked up tight when I was a child, the part that was a wild and savage creature wanting to rip the hearts from its prey, stormed to the surface as I shoved the heavy door, slamming it open, shaking the thick wall.

Gone was the methodical man with control. He'd been pushed aside and replaced with the raging bull that ran across the floor as my brother lifted a knife over Kirby's face. All I could see was that knife piercing her skin. A roar that could have rivaled any beast ripped from my chest as I leaped over the table at my brother. Abel had been so focused that he didn't see or hear me coming, and his eyes went wide as I tackled him to the ground. He hit hard as I rode him to the ground, and the knife skidded away from his hand.

"I asked you...." My fist found his face, the blow so hard that I heard his nose break over the sound of the music.

"I ordered you...." My other fist found his face. Blood flew, and a tooth flew out of his mouth, but I still didn't care.

"And I warned you to stay away from her. You never listen. You never fucking listen."

I hit him three more times before standing, my hands shaking and covered in blood. Abel groaned, his eyes rolling back in his head. I stood and walked over to the knife he'd dropped. Bending over, I grabbed the knife, a knife from my set, something else he was never supposed to touch, and waited for him to stumble to his feet.

He was a mess. Blood coated his face, smeared his hair, and ran down his chin in a steady line. Abel's nose was broken and off-center, so I waited for the old protective sensation to surface, that thing that would stop me from killing him like all the other times. But it didn't rise. There was simply nothing as I stared at my brother's battered face.

His hand slowly reached for the table I didn't dare look at because Kirby had been quiet since I came storming in, and I wasn't ready to confirm if she was indeed dead. She was a glimmer and spark of life inside of me. Sunshine had become the one thing that made me feel like more than just a killer. I'd always have that, I would be a legend, but I'd been looking for her and didn't know it. I couldn't picture my life without her and if Abel took that....

"I was doing this for us," Abel said as he pulled himself to his knees and slowly stood.

"No, you did this for yourself. If you really wanted to do something for me, you'd have done what I asked to begin with."

"You don't see it, but I do...." Abel coughed out blood and spat it on the floor. I snarled at him as my body shook with the fury that narrowed in the world, so only he existed. "She's changed you. She made you a weak pussy. You're pussy whipped, and it's going to get you caught."

I laughed, the sound bitter as I took a step closer, and Abel stumbled back.

"Is that a joke? Have you ever looked in the mirror to see the fuck up you are? The thing I have to control so that you don't get us caught every time you walk out the door?"

I took another step, and he rounded the table to stand at Sunshine's head. Even though I didn't want to, I looked at her face. Her eyes were swollen, black bruises already forming from where she'd been hit. A red handprint was around her throat, but her chest was rising and falling, and other than her feet, which seemed to have taken a lot of damage and dyed her socks red with blood, she seemed unharmed. A tightness in my chest released as I realized she was alive and going to be okay.

"For years, I've looked after you, made excuses for you, cleaned up one disaster after another, and ensured that we remained safe while you did everything you could to fuck with that. Do you want to know what Kirby has done to me, brother? She has given me the gift of not having to fucking worry every second about what I'll come home to. I'm tired of you and your shit and your out-of-control killing."

I took another step, and he moved around the table, his eyes watching my every move, but it didn't matter. Abel loved to kill, but I was the beast in the darkness, and I wanted his blood.

"But it's always been us, the two amigos, the unshakable bond, Frick and Frack. I am the Ren to your Stimpy."

"Stop it, stop quoting that bullshit to me." My muscles coiled, and with a single jump, I landed on the table like I was doing a box jump and straddled Kirby's body protectively as my brother stumbled away and fell on his ass. This was the primal side of me, the part of me that was wilder than man. This part of me that longed for death, I could taste it on my tongue. "She is mine, not yours, mine. The only thing that had been holding us together was my tolerance of your crap, but not anymore."

I spun the blade I knew so well in my hand and prepared to jump off the table. I could picture the feel of the blade piercing my brother's heart and what it would look like to watch him die.

"Don't do it," Sunshine said softly, the only voice that could cut through the visions of murder dancing before my eyes. "Don't kill him. Kick him out, stop speaking to him, lock him up, but don't kill him."

"What?" we both said at the same time.

Her lips were swollen, and she licked them before continuing. "He's your brother."

"I don't care. He knew that you were special to me, and he was going to take that from me. Does that sound like a real brother to you?"

My hand flexed and relaxed on the blade as my mind screamed to kill him. But Kirby lifted her hand and laid it on my knee, and it was just enough to calm my mind to listen to her.

"No, he's a fucking prick, but you can't kill him because of me. Maybe not today or a month from now, but at some point, you'll miss him and resent that you killed him for me." My hands worked at the bindings that held her hands as she spoke while my eyes stayed trained on Abel. I shook my head. "Cain, don't let him become the thing that comes between us."

I stared down at her beaten face with her eye swollen closed. My Sunshine's beautiful face that my brother tried to destroy. I screamed bloody murder as I pushed the killer down, that was begging to be set free. It felt wrong to let Abel go. I knew he'd continue to be a threat, but Sunshine was right about one thing—I'd miss him at some point. I stared into his eyes as he continued to hold perfectly still. It was the only smart thing he'd ever done. If he'd run, I would've gone after him.

"Well, you heard her. You're going to get a free pass against my better judgment. Now get out of my home," I ordered, my voice rough with the anger still burning throughout my body.

I could still picture slitting his throat, and I needed him to get away from me before I changed my mind. When he didn't move fast enough, I hopped off the table and advanced on my brother. He jerked to his feet but limped as quickly as he could for the door.

"Abel," I called out as he stopped to look at me. "You're dead to me. Whether this knife pierces your heart is inconsequential, your actions have had the same effect. Stay on your half of the property, and if you cross the line to my side, or hunt down Kirby again, I will end you as swiftly as you've ended our relationship as brothers." My voice dropped to a raspy growl. "I never want to see you again."

Pain filled his eyes, but I remained unfazed and made sure he was gone and out of the house before I returned to my Sunshine's side.

I laid my lips on her forehead and just took a moment to appreciate that she was still alive. I didn't like being on this side of the hunter, prey equation, and it solidified for me why my Sunshine had asked me to change my hunting patterns. This feeling was one I never wanted again. I didn't dare think about what I would've come home to if I'd put in a full day of work on the road. My body shivered with the thought.

"Are you okay?"

"My feet are all cut up," she said, pushing herself up onto her elbows. "I tried to stop him. I tried to reason with him. I'm sorry that it came to this," she said as fat tears filled her eyes and trickled down her cheeks.

"Don't apologize for my brother. I've done enough of that over the years for fifty lifetimes. He knew what he was doing when he chose to come here, and he knew the consequences. If it weren't for your request, he would be dead right now, so as far as I'm concerned, he owes you his life."

Gripping her face softly, I laid my lips against hers. "Let's get you to a hospital."

"No."

"No?"

"Hospital means records, and I don't want this on record. Pull the glass out yourself, you have great hands, and I trust you. I'm going to need antibiotics though."

I stared into her amethyst eyes and knew I'd chosen well. She was the other half of my soul. She was the flame that lit the way in the darkness.

"I love you," I whispered, and then stood to get a sedative and my tools.

CHAPTER 33

KIRBY

It was already midnight when we left the house for town. He told me that there were things I needed to know, and he would ensure I had all the facts and answers before returning to school. I wasn't sure what he meant, but I trusted him, which was all that mattered.

I could just make out my reflection in the glass and see my right cheek was still swollen from the abuse it had taken. It had only been two days, yet it felt like it had just happened. Cain would hold me and softly sing as I fell asleep, but there was always a point when I'd wake up with a start, and then fear would slice through me when the same face greeted me as Abel's. I couldn't tell Cain that. I knew what it would do to him if I did. Cain seemed to be so in tune with my body that the moment I'd wake up, so would he, and he would hold me tight until I fell back to sleep.

Cain was still tempted to kill his brother, but I knew it would change and ruin us even if he couldn't see it. Many would've said I was crazy, but considering all my choices over the last few weeks, I think letting Abel live was low on the list. Cain gave my hand a squeeze and looked over at me.

"Where are we going," I asked as we pulled onto the main street that led toward the downtown core.

"Peter's condo," Cain said, but his face gave nothing away.

"Peter's? I don't want to see that asshole again."

"I know, but you need to see him one more time, there is something you need to know, but I promise not to kill him unless you ask me to." He gave me a small smile. "And he will never hurt you again. I can promise you that."

I did feel safe whenever I was with him, but it was more than that. I didn't want to see his arrogant, abusive face again. He was in my past, and that was where I wanted to leave him.

"Okay," I said as we pulled into the underground parking area of Peter's condo. "Is this safe? I mean, what if someone sees us?"

"Then they see us, but they won't."

I looked over at Cain as he smoothly steered the truck around the multiple levels until he came to one fairly quiet level and parked in a spot for employees. I raised my brows at him.

"I told you I always have my ways," he answered before I could pose the question. "Pull the hood up on your hoodie, but don't look like you're trying to hide your face, just that you're cold."

I gingerly slipped out of the truck. I sucked in a sharp breath as my feet touched the ground. The cuts on my feet were a painful reminder of what almost happened and were going to take more time than my face to heal. I slowly wandered around to the same side Cain was on as he grabbed the large black bag from the back seat. We made our way to the employee elevator and waited. Cain took his phone out of his pocket, and I watched him closely. It was fascinating to watch him work. He pulled up an app and then held the phone down at his side. As soon as the elevator doors opened, he tapped the button, and we stepped inside, the doors closing silently behind us.

I wanted to ask a million questions, but I figured I'd ask later and wrapped my arms around myself and rubbed like I was cold. The doors opened to the floor I'd been to many times before, and my stomach churned. It made me feel sick to think about the last time I'd seen Peter. He was a douche, and I should've left him long ago, but then I may not have found Cain. Even though anyone else would say, 'that would've been for the best,' to me, it wasn't. I'd hated my life and had been floundering, trying to find myself, but not anymore, not with him. I had found a purpose I loved, a partner I connected with on every level, who saw the light and dark in me and accepted me as I accepted him.

"I'm going to unlock the door. I want you to stay behind me and remain quiet."

I nodded as he pulled a key card out of his pocket and slipped it into the door. He pushed it open, and I slipped through on high alert, looking for where Peter might be. At least now I knew how Cain had so efficiently snuck in here.

Cain paused long enough to pull something out that looked similar to a gun from inside his jacket. We made our way quietly down the hall toward the bedrooms, and I could hear him moaning and looked up to Cain for confirmation that Peter was, in fact, having sex.

Cain held up his hand, and I stopped walking. He held a finger over his lips and motioned for me to stay where I was. I'd never known any of Cain's victims to be shot to death, so I doubted that was what he was up to, but I prepared myself for a bang anyway.

Did I care if he killed Peter? I searched inside myself and found the answer to be no. I didn't give a fuck what he did to the man. I also stopped needing a reason for what I felt. It was tiring, and Cain accepted my decisions and didn't want me to justify myself. It was freeing and terrifying to feel so unsanctioned.

There was a distinct yell from two voices, one Peter's and the other one...was that my mother? No, it couldn't be. I'd joked about it and wondered if Peter had the hots for my mother, but even she wouldn't stoop so low. Would she? The fact that I even had to ask myself that question said a lot about how our relationship had been.

A few minutes later, Cain came out into the hall and waved me over. For some stupid reason, I was scared to turn the corner and see if I'd been wrong about her all this time and if she really would do something like this to me. Broken up or not, if she was in there, she didn't care about my feelings at all.

Stepping into the room that only had one small light on, I spotted Peter first. He was tied up with some bright red rope with a red ball gag in his mouth and was strung up to look like a puppet on strings.

"Did you do that, or was he like that," I asked, my tone quiet.

"I did it just now." He cocked his eyebrow at me. "It's not like I've never tied someone up and put a ball gag in their mouth before."

"Good point, but your skill still baffles me," I said as my eyes went from Peter's slack face to the bed and the woman that was also tied up in a precarious position.

My mother looked like a cow that had been hogtied. Even though I thought I'd heard her voice, I didn't believe it could be true until now. My eyes roamed over my mother's face and her naked body, and I had to cover my mouth as bile traveled up my throat. Who did this to their daughter?

"What did you do to them?"

"Drugged them," he said and held up the thing that looked like a handgun. "It's a mild tranq."

He was always so calm and matter-of-fact. He knelt and began lifting one item at a time out of his bag.

"This is what you wanted to show me? My ex and my mother are having an affair," I asked and couldn't stop the hurt and feeling of betrayal in my chest. My heart hurt as I realized she was never going to love me. Maybe my mother was more of a psychopath than Cain?

"Yes, but there's more. I'm going to go take care of a few things to ensure we are not discovered, but they will wake up soon, and you'll have the answers you've been looking for."

"Are you leaving me here?" I said as a soft moan left my mother's lips.

Cain's mouth curled up at the corner. "No, I'm never leaving you."

I watched him walk out of the room like what he said wasn't profound, and I couldn't help but smile. I didn't know which answers he was referring to, but I sat down in a chair and stared at the fucked up tableau.

My mother came around first. She mumbled random words that

made no sense before she groaned and tried to move, only to realize that she was stuck.

"What the hell is going on," she asked, her eyes searching the room before they finally landed on me. "Kirby? What are you doing here? What have you done to me?"

My mother tried looking over her shoulder to see how she was tied up, but it wasn't going to do her any good. Cain was an expert when it came to knots and different ways to tie people up. Again just another fact that at one point would've terrified me.

"I'm kind of wondering the same question. What the hell are you doing here," I asked and watched her face closely.

"I...this isn't what it looks like...we—this was a mistake, an accident," she stumbled through her words, and I knew she was lying. My mother was rarely ever shaken, but when she was, she always stammered.

"I call bullshit," I said and stood from the chair.

"Kirby Lawson, untie me right now," she ordered, and all I could do was laugh. Even now tied up with her hand caught in the cookie jar, she refused to treat me like a daughter and instead tried to order me around like one of her subordinates.

"No, not yet. How long has this been going on? I want the truth."

I crossed my arms over my chest and walked closer to the bed. She was still a beautiful woman. All the boyfriends I'd ever had would comment that she was hot MILF material. Now I had to wonder if my mother was a real Mrs. Robinson.

"I told you it just happened. We were commiserating over you being gone so long, and we both missed you, and it just sort of happened." She wouldn't look me in the eyes, and I shook my head.

"Oh, fuck Peter, yes, just like that. Kirby is such an idiot to let you go."

I whipped my head around and stared at Cain as he stood in the doorway with a phone on showing a video. He stepped forward as the scene played out, and even though I didn't want to see this, I couldn't look away.

"I still don't like having sex in her room, Mrs. L. I get what you said about this being a 'fuck you' to her, but it feels weird like she's watching us."

"Turn that off right now," my mother ordered from the bed. I looked between her and the video. She was scared.

"No, I think I'll let this play out. What else did you say, Mother?"

"Don't be silly, Peter. No one is watching, and besides, my daughter is a selfish train wreck that would be going nowhere without me. She was lucky to have you and couldn't even manage to hang on to the one good thing in her life."

Cain hit pause, and I covered my mouth.

"There is a lot more, but you get the idea," he said, and my mother tried to look around me to see who was talking.

"What is this? Did you hire a P.I.?"

"You would think that," I said.

That question made me laugh. Peter began to moan and blink, and the look on his face was one that I wanted to photograph and frame.

He tried to speak through the ball gag in his mouth, and I caught the word 'sorry' in his jumbled mumble. I held up my hand, stopping him.

"Save it. I'm not interested in hearing what you have to say."

"So, you've been caught in your lie," I said to my mother. "What else should I know?" I directed the question over my shoulder to Cain.

"Ask her about your father," he said, and my eyebrows shot up.

Turning back to my mother, I cocked my head as she licked her lips. "What about my father?"

"I don't know what he's talking about. I told you before I don't know who he is. Your father and I were going through a tough time, and I made a mistake. Why are you stirring up these old wounds? Are you purposely trying to upset my daughter and drive a wedge between us?"

"Don't get pissy with him. He's the only one in this room that has been honest with me from the day we met." Walking forward, I leaned over my mother and grabbed her chin as Cain had once done to me. "What should I know about my father?"

"I told you. Nothing," she said and tried to yank her head away, but I held it firm.

"She's lying," Cain said. He was my calm, my steady as the turmoil of emotion began to brew.

"Shut up," my mother snarled at Cain. Not a smart move, but she didn't know that yet.

"Tell me," I said to her, and she clamped her mouth shut. "Unbelievable. Even now, you can't be straight with me. Fine, have it your way." I glanced back at Cain, who was still hovering in the shadows. "What should I know?"

"Do you want to know all of it?"

"Yes."

"Your father that you call Dad didn't simply drift apart from you. When he and your mother got a divorce, he was a stay-at-home father and would've taken your mother for half of everything. She didn't like that, so she told him she'd press charges against him for abuse. She said that she'd use the full power of her position to make his life miserable and ruin him if he didn't leave you behind, and she wasn't giving him a cent."

My mouth fell open, and I looked back at my mother. "You were blackmailing Dad with fake charges? What kind of demon mother are you? You first cheat on him, rip apart our family, and then proceed to threaten him?"

"I'd worked my entire life to get where I was. I had to fight tooth and nail and claw over anyone that got in my way to reach the top of my game, and I wasn't letting your father drag me down into a heated battle in court over money that was mine. If he'd been a better husband in the first place, I wouldn't have stepped out."

I stumbled back from the bed. "What the fuck? Do you even hear yourself? I spent years agonizing over why Dad didn't want anything to do with me, I blamed myself for him leaving, and this whole time you knew why and kept your mouth shut?"

"Don't be so soft and naive, Kirby. I'm a woman working in a man's world. You do what you have to do to stay ahead. That means in your professional and personal life. Besides, you were hanging around him too much. Your head was always in the clouds like his, wanting to flit from thing to thing with no purpose. He supported you to do whatever you wanted, even when it was a stupid idea. Not that separating you two did any good. You're still a waif of a personality. So embarrassing."

I bit my lip but refused to cry. This woman wasn't getting any more of my tears. "Arrogant, always so fucking arrogant. What else should I know?"

"That's it, now you know everything, so can you untie me now?"

"That's not all," Cain chimed in. His voice was soft and yet as lethal as a blade.

"Tell me," I said and knew that he would.

"She knows who your real father is," he said, and my heart jumped in my chest.

My mother's eyes went wide, and she was terrified for the first time ever. "That's not true, I don't know what this guy thinks he knows, but I don't have a clue. I told you it was a one-night stand."

"So, you keep saying, but since you haven't exactly been honest about anything else, you'll have to forgive me if I don't believe you." I looked over my shoulder, and my eyes locked with Cain's. "Do you know who it is?" He nodded. "Tell me."

"Don't you dare." My head whipped around to look at my mother.

"I'm pretty sure you're in no position to order anyone around."

"Your father is none other than Director Kyle Mulligan." My mother gasped and squeezed her eyes tight. That was all the confirmation I needed. I turned to look at Cain and felt a little faint.

"My father is the head of the FBI, like thee head of the FBI?"

"Yes, and not only that but...." Cain flicked through his phone and handed over the images of an account with more zeros than I could count. "This account is a blackmail account. Your mother has been blackmailing him since she got pregnant and funneling the money away into an offshore account. On top of that, she's managed to use the information to get promotions even when she didn't have as much experience as the other candidates."

My brain fritzed out. It was like I just comprehend how evil and conniving my mother was. I'd always known her to be a cold-hearted bitch, but this was way beyond that. How often had she said that she and Mulligan didn't get along because he was a chauvinistic jerk who didn't want to see her succeed? How many times had I cried on her shoulder that I missed my dad, and she said, 'obviously, I wasn't special enough for him to keep in touch?' It was all lies. Everything she'd ever told me was a lie.

"Don't listen to him. He has no proof."

Cain took a step forward and placed a hand on my shoulder, giving me a reassuring squeeze. Turning to face my mother, Cain stepped into the dim light so she could see his face clearly, and her face was screwed up. I could see the wheels of confusion spinning as she looked him over. She really had no idea who he was, and there was something so poetic about that to me.

"You hired a mechanic as your P.I., and you think you should believe him?" My mother laughed, but my face stayed serious. "You can't be serious? You're seriously going to believe the ramblings of this random guy over your own mother?"

"Yeah, I am."

My mother shook her head back and forth, and I could see the disgust in her eyes. She'd never loved me, not really. I'd been nothing more than a pawn in a much larger chessboard in her life, and I was disposable if she needed to move her Queen.

"I'm sorry I had to be the one to tell you all this, but I thought you needed to know," Cain said, and I looked between my mother and Peter and thought about how perfect they were for one another.

I took a deep breath, wrapped my arm around Cain's waist, and looked up at him. He lowered his head and gave my lips a soft kiss.

"Ah, well, this explains it all. A money-grabbing mechanic seems about right for your taste. So how much money do you want?"

"No, not quite," Cain said. "I took the liberty of cleaning out your account, so Kirby has all your money now. Never trust a hacker near a computer. Luckily for me, I have a few that owe me and like money." He smiled, and I stifled a laugh. "The money you stole from her father as you clawed your way to the top is all gone. I felt it was only fitting that it would go to her since it should've been hers in the first place." Cain shrugged.

"You what?" My mother screamed, her face turning tomato red. "I'll fucking have you thrown in jail for this, you thief. That money is mine."

"I think it's time I formally introduced the two of you," I said.

"I don't want to meet this guy formally, I want you to untie me right now, and I'm having him arrested."

A smile curled up at the corner of my mouth as all the emotions washed away and left me feeling empty and used.

"Well, I'm going to introduce you anyway, and I have to tell you this is going to be fucking ironic for you, and it brings so much fucking joy to my soul." My mother's face twisted into confusion, but I continued before she could spout off any more of her bullshit. "Mother, this is Cain Buchanan. You know him as the mechanic you interviewed, but you already know him. More specifically, you know his work. I want to introduce you to The Chameleon."

My mother laughed and then stopped as she looked between our serious expressions, and hers slowly fell. Cain stepped forward, and the cold mask of the killer was pulled into place.

"It's finally nice to meet you as the real me, Mrs. Lawson. I've enjoyed watching you very much as you chased your tail to find me."

The way he spoke sent a chill down my spine, and it wasn't even me he was directing it at—I watched my mother swallow hard as her eyes grew wide. Cain knelt down so he was at eye level with her.

"Your theory about there being two killers was correct. I thought you might like to know that and wanted to congratulate you on your persistence. I happen to have a twin with peculiar tastes, but we've worked together since children to perfect out teamwork. It's too bad all that information will be destroyed soon. All your hard work going up in smoke...figuratively speaking of course. Right now, as we speak, your computers are sadly experiencing difficulties as a virus makes its way through your system and destroys all your precious files."

"This can't be real."

"I'd like to thank you for your daughter. She is...." Cain looked up at me, and my heart warmed. "She is exceptional, even if you don't see it, and I'm going to enjoy spending the rest of my life with her."

"No, this can't be happening," my mother said.

"Sunshine, what would you like me to do?" I looked at my mother, who was now sweating so much that her face had a sheen to it. Then she looked at Peter, who was trying hard to play the part of possum, but I remembered every shitty, abusive thing he'd ever said or done, including when he attacked me in his car. Walking forward, I looked down at my mother and then knelt beside Cain so I could stare into her eyes.

"Maybe you should've loved me over your image or ambition just a little bit more. Maybe I wouldn't have fallen in love with a man that's going to happily kill you and display you for all of your agent friends to find."

"Kirby, don't you dare do this. I'm still your mother," she said, and her tone was begging, but all I saw was her condescending face spilling her lies.

"You're callous, mother—callus, cold and self-serving. I'm not sure how I ended up being birthed by you, and I'm happy that Dad was in my life, even if you think he was a bad influence. He accepted me, he loved me, and he was around. Do you know I don't have one birthday picture with you, and you weren't at my high school graduation or cheer championships? I want you to think about all those mistakes you've made while all you concerned yourself with was getting to the top."

I winced, and Cain helped me stand up straight. I looked at Cain as the anger that had been boiling a moment ago began to twist into something much worse for her. I no longer cared at all. I was numb. I was empty. She'd abused my heart so much that it no longer beat for her.

"How good are you at framing someone?"

"Do you even need to ask?" he said and smiled. I shook my head no and gave him a little smirk.

"Kirby, please. I'm asking you not to do whatever it is you're thinking," my mother said, and for the first time, there was no bravado or arrogance. She was just a woman, but it was also too little too late.

I looked into my mother's eyes. "I want you to know that whatever happens from this moment on, you caused it. Your decisions have sealed your fate," I said, my voice as calm as if I were ordering a drink from a menu.

Linking my finger with Cain's hand, I brought it to my lips to kiss and made sure my mother could see me. I felt his reassurance, I felt his acceptance, and I felt his love. He was part of me now as I was part of him.

"Kirby, please don't do this," my mother said, but I ignored her.

"Kill her, frame him, but...." I snarled, my hand clenching into a fist. "I don't want him ever to be found."

"I love it when you talk dirty to me," Cain said. He wrapped his arm around my waist and kissed me until my head felt light. Opening my hand, he placed the truck keys into my palm.

"You're not going to want to see this. Why don't you get us coffees and muffins from *Mode* and meet me back here in a couple of hours?"

"But, he's not open."

Cain leaned in close to my ear. "It's amazing what you can accomplish with a little extra money." He kissed my cheek and smiled. "Jorge is excited to see you."

I wrapped my arms around his neck and kissed him hard. The mumbling screams coming from the two captives were nothing more than background music.

"You'll never know, dear, how much I love you," Cain softly sang against my lips.

"Until you take my sunshine away," I finished for him and then turned and walked out, making sure to close the door behind me.

"Kirby, please don't do this! Kirby!" I heard my mother scream before the door clicked closed. My mother was my past, Cain was my future, and I no longer cared what happened to her, but I was going to see Dad as soon as possible. We had some catching up to do, and I wanted Dad to walk me down the aisle.

Who was I now?

That still remained to be seen, but what I wasn't was the girl that let life dictate how I should live, what was right and wrong, and who I should love. Cain was mine. I was his, and I'd die to protect that. I'd die to protect him and what we have, and I knew he would do the same.

EPILOGUE

KIRBY

As I walked the long corridor to the main office area, my heels clicked. I had a newfound power inside of me. I found myself more confident, and people sensed it. As I strode through the hall, the mass of people seemed to be moved by a magical hand. It felt like I owned them. My dark navy coat fluttered out behind me, and I knew I belonged. I'd found my calling, and just needed to put the final pieces in place.

I was in the midst of planning our wedding, which Cain found amusing and unneeded but agreed to do for me. Holding out my hand, I smiled as I stared at the stunning diamond and amethyst engagement ring. It amazed me that the man that could easily take a life could also be so thoughtful and sweet. The house was always filled with purple flowers, he knew exactly how I liked my bath, brought me a muffin and coffee a day from Mode, and he never missed a dinner. I was starting to think that everyone needed a Cain in their life.

Cain was encouraging me to take the bull by the horns. Today that was exactly what I was going to do. It was time the FBI promoted me, and I was no longer ashamed or worried about what anyone thought. It was time that I formally introduced myself to my father.

Our conversation about my idea crossed my mind as I marched along the hallways.

"I don't understand why you want me to kill these guys," Cain said as he looked through the folder I'd given him.

"Because these guys are the kind of guys I'm fine with you killing." He lifted a single brow at me, and I instantly wanted to kiss the look off his face.

"What is this? You want to turn me into Dexter?"

I smiled and then laughed. "Yes, I like that. Cain, you're the apex predator. Why not prove it? Random people are easy and mundane," I'd said, and his eyes flared at the challenge. "These guys are a challenge, more worth your time and exceptional skill. Besides, they are the type to think they are better than you, and wouldn't it be entertaining to prove that they're not?"

"You're sweet talking me, but it's working," he said.

"Alright then, who do you want to start with first," I asked and sat down on his lap.

He pushed the folder away, laid me on the table, and kissed the dip between my breasts. "I want to start with you."

Hanson had taken the lead on my mother's murder which I expected since he'd been her partner when she died. He was also still the lead on, The Chameleon Killer investigation, so when he offered to keep me in the loop, I thanked him profusely. I also managed to cry like I was supposed to beside her grave. I'd stared around at the agents and stifled a laugh as I watched Cain pretend to be a janitor in the distance. If they only knew. I deserved an award for that performance.

Did I have guilt now that she was gone? No. She was a threat, as Cain would say, and threats needed to be eliminated.

Did I miss her? No. I missed what I thought we could have. I missed the fantasies of a mother-and-daughter relationship filled with love and respect. Those were things she'd never given me, things she never planned on giving me. Cain had released the beast that had always lived inside my mind. The one I never wanted to acknowledge made me different from everyone else. Cain would tell me that I was his spark, his sunshine, and he was the thing in the darkness. But to me, I felt as if we lived somewhere between the sunshine and the darkness, like a delicate and dangerous ballet.

I'd managed to talk Cain into traveling to England to meet my dad. The only way he'd agree to go was if we bought our own yacht and sailed there. Apparently, he's really not into airports or planes. He said he doesn't like people enough to sit in a sardine can for hours. I'd never been on a yacht before and was looking forward to the upcoming trip and alone time with him. I prayed that my dad liked him and got Cain to promise to be on his best behavior, but there was always a hint of worry when it came to Cain.

Cain and Abel were still not speaking. I had to admit that I was shocked and thought that the feud would only last a few days. As the days stretched into weeks, I secretly worried about what not having Cain in Abel's life would lead Abel to do. Now part of my day was spent monitoring him and ensuring the if he slipped and made a mess, I was there to cover it up.

If Cain knew, he would be livid, but I wasn't doing it just for Cain's sake. I was doing this for all of our sake. Abel was a loose cannon and was acting like a toddler in the midst of a tantrum because his favorite toy had been taken away. His behavior was dangerous, he was dangerous, and it was by my request that Abel was still breathing. I felt like I owed it to Cain to ensure that Abel didn't create a mess that we couldn't clean up.

I'm not sure anyone would understand our dynamic or why I loved him so fiercely. I did, though, and I'd lay my life down to protect his secret and knew that Cain would kill anyone that came for me. We were a team. The butterfly and the spider had merged to become one.

Mulligan's secretary jumped from her seat as I marched past her desk. "You can't go in there without an appointment. Mr. Mulligan is a very busy man."

"I'm sure he is," I mumbled but pushed his door open.

I stepped into his office and didn't care that he was on the phone and simply closed the door in his secretary's face.

"I'm sorry, I have to go, but I'll call you right back," Mulligan said and hung up his call.

"Excuse me, who the hell do you think you are?"

"Hello, Father. I think it's time we talked. There are a few things we need to get straight," I said, smiling at the terrified look on his face.

Yes, things were going to work out just fine.

Click here to read book 2 by T.L. Hodel: Twisted Abel

Thank You

For reading Unhinged Cain, book 1 of The Buchanan Brother's Duet

Please consider leaving a review for this book. Reviews are the best way to show your love and are always appreciated. It is because of readers and reviews like you that allow indie authors like myself to continue writing.

If you would like to be among the first to know about new releases then I invite you to join my Facebook Group: Crossfire - A Brooklyn Cross Reader Group or follow me on BookBub or Goodreads. My links can be found at the end of the book.

BROOKLYN

If you like it dark and edgy then look no further. Brooklyn Cross has always had a deep passion for writing that stemmed from a wild imagination. When she is not busy typing away about the next character you will fall in love with, you can find her walking with her dogs on the farm and sipping a hot cup of coffee.

In addition to getting her degree in business she was highly competitive in the equestrian sport of dressage, with aspirations of an Olympic dream. She is an entrepreneur at heart and has coached and trained many of a riding enthusiast or their wonderful mounts, but always found herself drawn to writing full-time.

"Writing is what I love. I just want to be authentic with my characters. To tell a story that others can immerse themselves in and enjoy, but also relate too. If I can make you smile, laugh, cry, or your heart pound then I have done my job. To drop people into my worlds and for a short time have you live alongside my characters, is what I have always wanted."

CROSS

Below are the links that you can use to find me if you'd like to follow me on my social media platforms.

Book Bub: Brooklyn Cross Books - BookBub
Goodreads: Brooklyn Cross (Author of Dark Side of the Cloth) | Goodreads
TikTok: Author Brooklyn Cross (@authorbrooklyncross) TikTok | Watch Author Brooklyn Cross's Newest TikTok Videos
IG: Brooklyn Cross (@author_brooklyncross) • Instagram photos and videos
FB Group: Crossfire - A Brooklyn Cross Reader Group | Facebook